Miss Pretty Please

by P. E. Fischetti

This book is a work of fiction. Names, characters, and events are the product of the author's imagination. Any fictional characters that resemble actual persons living or dead, are purely coincidental. The high schools and universities mentioned in the book are real places and are all great institutions. Events in the book are not based on anything real that has taken place there.

Dorrance Publishing Co
585 Alpha Drive
Pittsburgh, PA 15238
Visit our website at *www.dorrancebookstore.com*

ISBN: 978-1-6461-0681-3
eISBN: 978-1-6461-0992-0

Author's Note

Except for a scene in the opening chapter and some history about the characters, the core of this story takes place in the year 2029 and beyond. This era was chosen to explore the characters in the next generation of the Finelli and Santucci families. I have made several guesses about the end of the 2020s and the state of progress in society to orient the reader to the characters and their future. Otherwise, things are mainly timeless.

Also by P. E. Fischetti:
Big Train's Backyard
The Safety

For my wife Linda

~1~

At age twenty-five, Russell Santucci was in many ways struggling with a midlife crisis, twenty years too early, while trapped in the middle of a cold winter in an uneventful January 2028. Only when he played the piano did his life seem to have significance. Hitting the keys would beat back his hesitations of worth—a majority of the time.

While majoring in music at Georgetown University, he performed compositions from the greatest European classical composers with ease, but his heart knew he would never be the best or a star, even though he had talent. *It's impossible*, he thought, *the greats are just not beings of this planet*. And he knew greatness because it was expected in his family. His current great achievement was learning which piano bars in DC would let him work off his food and bar tab by playing background jazz and modern melodies for hours. To survive this mediocre, mastery of monotony, he would always eat a marijuana brownie before a performance, drink whiskey or scotch while playing the piano, and down a cup of coffee between sets of unexceptional accomplishment. That combination gave him a middling amount of happiness, but also the freedom and unending energy to play flawlessly without interruption. At moments, he would see the light in the middle of his darkness, a way to be great, an angle that could showcase his talent, *if I could only stay focused long enough*.

His family consisted of a half-dozen successful medical doctors, including his departed Grandfather, Gene Santucci (who he never saw but adored), his father Kenneth (who he saw but was distant), and four uncles (who were very busy).

Alex Santucci, his stepuncle, was a Washington baseball hero who had achieved true greatness. Twice an MVP, Alex was a slugger that led Washington to a baseball title in 2012 and almost in 2013. With his wife Sally Keegan at his side, he had captivated DC for three magical years when Russell was ten years old. Alex was adopted by Gene and Laura Santucci (Russell's grandparents) at birth and was always considered a Santucci, even though his real father was Phillip Finelli.

The Santucci-Finelli families were forever intermixed due to a friendship started in the 1960s between Grandfathers (Gene and Guy I) and continued with the Alex adoption. Alex's half-brother Guy Finelli had reached football immortality by 2020 in DC with three straight championships when Russell was in high school. Russell himself was a quarter Italian (his Grandfather Gene), a quarter Swedish (his Grandmother Laura), and half Danish (his mother Jill).

Russell's choices after graduation were at the very least; became a successful, nationally known medical doctor, or a universally loved, professional athlete. Neither of those choices seemed realistic or fit his artistically rich talent of performing music. For Russell, this hall of success and greatness that ran through the Santucci households led him to unfair comparisons in his head. The thoughts of having to accept a life of just-above mediocrity had become an obsession he worried about incessantly. Forcing him to calm his fears with alcohol or creative uses of pot. He knew the consumption of pharmaceuticals were around a dark and dingy corner if things did not improve, now almost three years after college.

He was not alone. In the late 2020s, DC was bursting with a population nearing a million people with a flood of millennials and zero-gens like himself. With pot legalization now maturing after a dozen years, hundreds of bars had basements brewing beer, roof gardens growing pot, and levels in-between selling both. Working in the getting-high industry or the almost getting-there social scene was a career industry for many in the city.

Before his junior year in 2023, he found a house to rent off Tunlaw Avenue, just north of the Georgetown campus and his bar connections. He easily found three friends to be his roommates, and two outstanding years of partying began. In the years since graduation, the parties had become more like the final part of *The Great Gatsby* – sad and pointless.

He had a depressing piano (by his own standards) located in the dining room, a Hardman-Peck, not because of the fine brand, but because it was an upright. He was holding out for an affordable, used Steinway grand piano, in his dreams the ultimate instrument for performing. He fantasized about the purchase, when located, that would be financed by his famously rich, stepuncle Alex Santucci, for many tens of thousands. And Russell would send him twenty dollars a month, hoping to pay it off by his thirtieth birthday. But Russell was never good with counting numbers, just playing notes and feeling the beat.

On this night, January 18, 2028, he discovered his fantasy: A magnificent instrument at a fundraising event to combat the disease of Parkinson's. It was also a birthday party for Anthony Finelli, who at 84 was finishing his second decade of living with the insidious disease and somehow surviving the battle. He was the older brother of Phillip Finelli and uncle to the famous Guy Finelli and half-uncle to Alex Santucci.

Russell ended up at Anthony and Flo Finelli's Parkwood residence because he was instructed to escort his eighty-eight-year-old Grandmother Laura Santucci to the event by his uncle Alex. Russell did not mind being an escort for his Grandmother, who was his close confidant; besides, he was interested in meeting Guy Finelli, the football hero, through his uncle Alex. There was security up and down Brookfield Drive, just three blocks from the Parkwood Enclave, to keep the press and crowds out of range.

After entering the front door and working his way through a semi-crowded living room, he was accosted by Sally Keegan, the wife of his uncle Alex and technically his aunt. She was now in her late forties, and still had the regal look of a princess with her perfectly cut, dark-black hair, blue eyes and impeccably dressed fashion appearance. She was famous in her own right as a talking-head on all the political shows during the last fifteen years as a professor in public policy at Georgetown University. She was loved by audiences on all waves of the political spectrum for speaking in moderate and non-political tones. Some thought she had a political future in running for public office. "My dear Russell, what a wonderful surprise to see you here." Sally put down her empty glass of champagne on a floating drone tray and wrapped her arms tightly around Russell's waist. She was petite, barely cracking the hundred-pound mark as she snuggled into Russell's mid-section. "Do you have time for one dance with your aunt… You're such a handsome Santucci."

Russell could tell the champagne had slightly unglued the usually unflappable Sally Keegan as he felt her micro-thin silky dress and tiny body press against his pelvis. For a minute, that seemed to last forever; he slow danced with his favorite aunt, a woman who he always had a crush on as a boy growing up in the Santucci family.

She seemed to find her bearings and slowly pulled away. Standing on her toes, she reached up and kissed him on his neck. "Thank you for the dance, Russell… I still have some schmoozing to do with this crowd. Enjoy yourself, my dear." Sally twirled away from Russell holding his hand just under her unencumbered breasts, giving him a hint of her sexiness. She smiled at him as she merged into the throng, leaving Russell feeling lonely in a crowded room.

As the excitement of the dance fused into his memory, he headed to the back of the house and down two steps into a grand family room with large windows, a vaulted ceiling, and a huge fireplace. It was packed with over a hundred people and many streams of conversations dominating the air. At the bar, he grabbed a scotch and downed it quickly, as he felt some stirring in his pants from his encounter with Sally.

In the far corner, he could see and hear a beautiful grand piano, *certainly a Steinway*, he thought, being played quietly by a young, teenage girl with red hair and classic shoulders. The mop of flaming hair dominated her face as she played Beethoven's "Moonlight Sonata" with a soft touch but rigid pace. She held back her strength at times, not wanting to be noticed, but playing the melody competently and on time.

Russell wanted to hear the notes of the perfectly crafted piano from a closer spot. He plotted a course to move around the mass of humanity to get in position. As he reached the blistering fireplace, ten feet to the right of the piano, he finally caught a full view of the red-headed teenager. She was eyeing her finger placement, like a chiropractor making perfect adjustments on a spine of keys. Her face was an astonishing combination of freckles and beauty, fully engaged with the keyboard. A quiet smile of self-pleasure was clearly in view. Russell tried to listen intently but instead was distracted by her sexuality that started with her smile and her mop of hair, to her already developed chest and athletic stance over the piano. Her green satin blouse was a bit small for her and clung to her perfect posture and arched chest. Eyeliner under her green eyes and red lipstick advanced her girlish look and gave her a future appearance as a young woman.

Russell was perplexed and nervous. He touched the piano and felt an immediate love for the instrument. At the same time, the tool he played between his legs grew, as his body felt an attraction to another confusing situation. He had never thought of himself as a pervert, *but I do appreciate beauty and of course the piano*, so he decided that was the excuse for the continued stirring in his pants. Or was it the remnants of his dance with Sally? *Besides, I'm just standing in front of the roaring fireplace, leaning against the stone, enjoying the party, and Jesus… nobody is perfect!*

It had been a month since his last sexual hook up. Just before the Christmas holidays, an on-and-off again girlfriend, who was now officially almost done. *Getting stoned before picking up Grandmother is making me horny*, he figured, but that was never his intention during this party. He had been concerned about being straight and facing a party of unknown Finelli people, most of them twice his age. He tried to settle himself down by grabbing a glass of champagne from a drone-tray roaming in the air above the crowd and downing it as he turned around towards the fireplace to reposition his member. After an awkward adjustment, he turned back towards the piano, hoping his now upright erection, was unseen and hidden by his sweater hanging below his belt. He looked around for another drone-tray to place his empty glass of champagne.

Pretty, young Annie Finelli finished her performance without notice from the noisy room. She felt refreshed and self-satisfied as she looked up through her hair to scan the room to the center and right of her to confirm that no one was watching. Relieved, she enjoyed the adrenaline abating in her body and sat back to evaluate her performance. She had watched her great-uncle Anthony Finelli play that piece many times. The sound and melody touched her in a way she could not explain, other than sensually. She had approached her great-uncle about how to play it, and he welcomed her interest and enjoyed every second teaching her on his magnificent piano. Anthony's playing was becoming more sporadic, but he was still capable at times. He became thrilled at the opportunity to engage with Annie. She was unusually womanly and patient for her age when she listened to him play. He was happy to endure the torture of hearing broken parts of the concerto, over and over. *At least it's not me playing erratically*, he thought, and cheered on how she improved with each lesson. Starting from scratch, Annie took twelve sessions to learn how to play the notes without fail, and then another twelve sessions to master it. A month before the party, she would run almost every day down the three blocks from the Parkwood Enclave to Brookfield Drive to practice her performance.

As she sat up to reset her perfect posture, a bigger smile came to her face as she remembered the experience of learning from her great-uncle Anthony, a hero in her life.

"Nice job… I liked your intensity on that piece." The vocals came from her left and took her by surprise. "Do you take lessons?" Russell moved in close enough to see the surprise in her eyes.

Her facial muscles went to a protected non-smile, as she tracked his face, looking for clues about the handsome intruder. Quickly, she noticed the intensity of his hands feeling the Steinway. "I did… but no, I do not… and who are you?" She was astonished at her unprepared response.

"I'm Russell Santucci. I majored in music at Georgetown University."

"Santucci? I live with Alex Santucci and Sally Keegan, and their twins."

"Yes… well I'm a grandson of Gene Santucci, he was Alex's adopted father."

"Of course," she relaxed as she processed the information of the odd meeting, "there are quite of few of you, yes?"

"Catholic family… what can I say!"

Annie was pleased with her the progress of her bantering and showed a half-smile, "I was a big fan of Pope Francis, but not quite sure about the new Pope."

"Too much of a good thing I guess; Catholics believe in suffering on Earth you know… But listen, you didn't answer my question."

"Yes, I did Russell, but not completely, I am afraid, you are correct." Not happy with being called out for an answer, Annie explained further, "I did for this piece. It is the only thing I know how to play. But really, I do not have time for more lessons in my life now."

Russell hesitated for a moment. He had never had a conversation with a teenager that lasted this long and was not sure of his next move. Her eyes were green and magnificent. He noticed her half-smile releasing her beauty. It made every thought of his go away. "Well you should," he said as he finally found words. "You're quite good. Maybe I can help you sometime in the future? I have played and taught piano for too many years."

Her smile grew larger. "That is a very nice offer, but I play basketball at home a lot and run track right now at school, which takes up most of my free time." She stopped for a moment and let herself think about the future with Russell being her piano mentor; she felt a stirring in her stomach as her nervous system was shooting adrenaline like a gun fight in the wild, wild west. It was a disturbing, yet overall pleasing experience. "Of course, it would have to be with this piano!"

"Yes of course this piano. It is…" he laid his fingers on the keys, almost fondling the texture, "quite something… Well, maybe I'll see you again when you are graduating or something, or when your schedule slows down a bit before that. Nice to meet you. I have to find my Grandmother and make sure she is okay."

Annie stood and adjusted her blouse and skirt, now sporting a full, wide smile with a twinkle in her eyes, and extended her large, thin hands to shake with Russell. She loved feeling the fingers of a piano master run up her arm. It gave her a warm tingle that she wanted to feel again.

Russell was happy to escape the dark hole of her young beauty. He turned around quickly and moved into the crowd for a chance to adjust his pants again and find another drink. His member had grown even larger, feeling like Mount Everest, but acting more like Vesuvius, as it was literally pushing out his sweater. He ordered two double scotches at the bar in the kitchen as he hunched over trying to hide his situation. He gulped down one scotch leaning on the counter and took the other with him as he meandered through the living room to find a bathroom.

Luckily, the door was open, and his embarrassment was close to the end as he locked the door. He put down the second scotch on the sink and found his belt and zipper. He let down his pants and underwear and carefully rolled up his sweater, opening the air around the tall structure protruding from his pelvis. It granted him some immediate relief as his member seemed to be in the stratosphere. *What is wrong with me?*, he screamed in his head, a*m I now officially a pervert?*, as he looked up the definition on his phone. He scanned it feeling horrified, "a person whose sexual behavior is regarded as abnormal and unacceptable," his mind was yelling out loudly, *What have I become!* Silly suicide options filled his mind, as he stared at himself in the mirror and downed the second scotch. After he finished, he looked down at his "Vesuvius" and was overwhelmed with his hardness, realizing the only solution. He turned off the light and prayed for two more minutes of privacy as he closed his eyes and put his head back. Quickly, he found his warm and thick member, and the pleasure of his touch was extreme ecstasy. He thought of her, *a freckled face, with deep penetrating green eyes, a growing smile and an arching chest growing through her tight blouse, she is whispering to me, "I felt something too!"* He entered a dimension of pure pleasure as he reached the apex of his fantasy.

Gasping several times during his climax, he tried to regain his normal breathing quickly. He reached for a mountain of tissue to contain the volume of his volcanic eruption. He looked in the mirror and was shocked to see his flushed face in a drunken stupor and his clothes in disarray. He ran water over his face several times, picked up his pants, and flushed away the evidence, waiting for the spinning water in the toilet to disappear without clogging the house plumbing. His surfer-hair look reappeared with some adjusting, as he looked one last time to hide possible leakage to his pants. He hoped to look like a normal person and not a monumental pervert when he reentered the party. *Maybe it was just seeing and hearing the Steinway while feeling buzzed*, he tried to convince himself that seeing the young beauty play the Steinway was a minor detail.

"Whew... time to find Grandmother and get away from these Finellis," he said to himself in the mirror.

He quietly opened the bathroom door, hoping for a clean getaway, but he saw two large humans blocking the hallway, dueling in loud conversation.

"Hey, there he is...what happen to you—throwing up already?" Alex looked sternly at his nephew.

Big Joe Finelli, son of Anthony, bellowed with a laugh as he started to pass him to get into the bathroom, hollering, "Hey loser, I got a fire hose to unload. Get the fuck out of the way. Christ, we thought you were sleeping in there." Big Joe roared as he grabbed Russell by the shoulders and moved him like a shower curtain to the side. Big Joe was now head football coach at Maryland and treated his players with the same love, loudness, and physicality.

Feeling folded, Russell turned to Alex in terror and muttered, "No... no... just had to really piss."

"Wow, you young guys... I guess driving drunk after the party doesn't affect you much. Try not to smash my Acura. I love that car!" Alex implored.

"Yeah... oh no no, I just had some champagne and a little wine... I'm okay really. I just was going to look for Grandmother... to see..."

"Cool it, cowboy, I'm just dicking with you!" Alex noticing the scotch glass. "I know you're cool, right? With taking care of my mother, got it?" He smiled warmly. "Come on Russell, I want you to meet my brother Guy. He was asking about you when you were talking with his daughter at the piano." Alex Santucci grabbed his nephew by the arm and pushed him through the living room crowd. "He's over to your right with all the women, of course." Alex slapped Russell on the back and pulled him into his six-foot, four-inch frame for a big side hug.

Russell's terror eased for a moment, but then another strain of panic started when he saw the six-foot, six-inch, not quite thirty-four year-old, two-hundred-forty-two-pound athlete, who left football at age twenty-five and shocked a nation. He felt some wetness leaking into his underwear and quickly checked his pants and shirt for any evidence of his crime. Luckily, no seepage to his pants. The clean-up had been a success. Just some uncomfortableness as his member receded to sea level.

Suddenly, he thought, *O Christ what did Alex see? Was it obvious?*

Guy Finelli extended his hand like a right hook and overwhelmed Russell's talented but delicate right hand. Russell recovered enough of his manhood to perform a strong handshake.

"Hey Russell, I've heard about you for years, but we've never met. Apparently, you are quite a pianist, according to Alex."

"Yes, that was my major at Georgetown, and I play a lot at night, but I'm not an accomplished pianist or anything like that..."

"Russell, you have to learn to become cocky about your talent," Alex shouted and then turned to his brother. "He's unbelievable, Guy. You should listen to him some time. It will blow you away, no bullshit," Alex added with another slap on Russell's shoulder.

"I would love that. I know Annie would enjoy seeing that. She seemed taken by you over in the corner. It's unusual for her to talk to a stranger."

Russell's panic level rose again as he looked at Guy's eyes. He was a big man with dark hair and great skin. His shoulders were perfect and wide. *Guy could kill me in a second if he tried to tackle me right now!* Russell recovered to the present and blurted out, "She seems to be very talented... and busy!"

Guy hooted hard as he looked at Russell and then Alex. With a thunderous laugh, he extended his arms like a lightning bolt, a move he had done a thousand times to running backs, and in a flash landed his shoulder into Russell's mid-section, lifting him off the ground for a moment. Russell felt the air leaving his chest, imaging Guy doing that at full speed to someone. As his feet hit the ground he felt terrified while listening to Alex and Guy laughing in unison at his expense.

"We should get together. I would love to hear you play. Maybe Annie can take some lessons?" Guy implored with great enthusiasm.

Barely clearing his voice after regaining some air, Russell sneaked out, "Would love to... sure that would be great!"

Like leaving another running back on the field, Guy Finelli vanished from his sight, swept up by a crowd of admirers, like everybody at the party, who were dying for a moment of his time.

Alex gave Russell a hug, "Best of luck with the job search Russell. Let me know if I can help or if you need money. We'll get together soon, maybe I can get you that Steinway huh?" Russell beamed a warm smile. "Hey, my mother is in the great room over there, take good care of her for me. Love you man."

"No problem Alex," Russell took a deep breath and felt lucky to escape. *Maybe things will change for me now*, he tried to reassure himself. *I can't act like this anymore*, he pleaded, *I need to get serious about life.*

After he found his composure, he readjusted his sweater and turned towards the great room feeling isolated in a still crowded living room. He seemed to be in an endless episode of *The Twilight Zone*, when his Grandmother appeared in front of him.

"There you are Russell. I am definitely ready to go… a bit of a mad house here, but really a lovely party." Russell was more than eager to exit this bad dream he was in, but his Grandmother turned around and presented someone behind her. "Annie, I want you to meet Russell, my grandson, the pianist?"

Annie Finelli stepped forward, appearing magically next to his Grandmother. "Yes, Mrs. Santucci, Russell and I met at the Steinway. He seemed to like the instrument quite a bit, like it was his own," she smiled. "He was fondling it while I was playing Beethoven." She delivered the remark in a serious face and stared at him with her stunning green eyes.

"Russell, isn't she something?" Laura laughed with a rare exuberance.

"Quite something, Grandmother, but she is right, I do like the Steinway. It does have a great feel." He extended his arm into Laura's arm to escort her to the front door.

"Well, that explains that, doesn't it, Annie? My grandson is quite a concert pianist, and he does know a beautiful instrument like that Steinway."

"Well maybe my father can arrange a private concert sometime for just us, and my cousins, of course," she continued her stare, aiming for a checkmate on Russell being uncomfortable.

"Anything for Guy Finelli and his children, I suppose." Russell did well to protect himself from Annie's onslaught as he paused and returned her stare gracefully. "Very nice to meet you, Miss Finelli."

Annie nodded with respect at the move and smiled as her eyes finally beamed with excitement, "You as well, Mr. Santucci."

Russell, feeling another growing awkwardness in his pants, turned and led his Grandmother out the door. He was trying hard not to faint.

"A real miracle, just to be alive, that Annie Finelli. Or Miss Pretty Please as her Grandmom Carol calls her. Now she is something special, I think."

"You may be right Grandmother. She could be a real killer of guys in the future, if you know what I mean?"

"Yes, indeed I do Russell, but the right one for her must be special. Like you, maybe? I just hope I'm still alive to see it someday." Laura Santucci laughed with joy as she squeezed her grandson's arm.

"Grandmother, a couple glasses of champagne, and you say the craziest things."

~2~

Annie Finelli had a near photographic memory that turned out to be her best friend. But as she grew up, this gift led to a low-level of anxiety and sometimes a minute of insane fear that she was a product of artificial intelligence—part cyborg and part human.

Her bloody birth from a murdered mother seemed a convenient story; while having an undercover, football MVP, and superhero Guy Finelli as her father. His spectacular athletic talent came partially from being an unusual physical specimen. As far as she guessed, *it could all be a CIA plot that put her parents together*; Anna, her mother and FBI agent, was pregnant with her near full-term and then murdered, *just maybe to keep her quiet*. Of course, Annie theorized that her bright red hair came from human genes, but her outstanding, growing athleticism was mainly cyborg, *even though athletic greatness seemed to permeate her family*, she speculated. Either way, she seemed to be smarter than anybody else.

Since the championship years ended in 2020 when she was almost six-years-old, Annie learned to stream information and history from the Cloud directly, to protect her mind from irrational fear and to control what she learned. *Fake information was everywhere*, she feared. This insecurity led her to have scarce interest in kids her age, except her twin cousins. Annie always wondered if any real humans had the closeness between them in grade school like her cousins. For eight years of school together, it was a beautiful thing to witness. She tried to remember behaviors that led her to good feelings, but it was hard work. She had no natural talent in feeling emotions, *because of the cyborg thing*—she imagined. But now as a junior at Walter Johnson High School, there were millions of situations to keep track of and hundreds of humans growing out of puberty around her, to care too much about the real reason for their closeness.

The twins, Phillip II and Philomena II, were a year older, but also juniors, and attending Georgetown Prep and the Academy of the Holy Cross respectively. Their campuses sat in their fortresses across Rockville Pike from each other as the best of the upper crest, Catholics schools, that the affluent east coast had to offer.

All of this was less than two miles from their multi-home Parkwood Enclave, where half brothers Guy Finelli and Alex Santucci lived with their father and Guy's mother and all related children. The twins went by Hill and Lil now, or sometimes Lilly, because Annie had renamed them when she first learned to talk, quite late for her age. When she finally found language just months before her third birthday, she realized it was more efficient to give the twins monosyllabic nicknames.

The first word she uttered with consistent meaning was, "Please." She formulated the importance of that word after months of observation of other brattish behavior. In the rare events that she put up with play groups without the twins, Annie, as a two-year-old, would listen and watch intently what attention these kids received from their parents. Most of the time, it mattered not what words they uttered, barely understandable or mostly garbled, it was the magic word of *please* attached to it that made transactions come their way.

Annie decided to wait on unveiling her mastery of the English language—a few more months and she relied on pointing with the word *please* attached—to highlight the needed necessity. She received attention quickly from the adults in her life, especially from her grandparents Phillip and Carol Finelli. They became helpless at trying to be fair in showing equal affection to their grandchildren, because Annie clearly became their favorite. She had something, an indescribable distance scraping the boundary of real connection; and yet, her personality acted like a magnet for her grandparents. She was like a comet that sped through the solar system daily to make a circadian link with them. They were magically held hostage to see Annie every day of her life. It was a demand, a ransom that they willingly paid, with affection and attention for these years since she first uttered *please*.

When Annie turned six, Carol designed and sewed a green satin blouse that lit up Annie's red hair and green eyes. It was quite big for Annie, but she was pleased knowing it would be her special blouse for years to come. She had no concerns about how big it was, and just rolled up the sleeves to her elbows and tied the front into a knot that showed her tummy. She exuded prettiness as she modeled it at her birthday party. Carol had sewed into the label on the back collar, *Miss Pretty Please*. Annie's eyes opened with unusual emotion when she first read it, and then quickly put in on, whispering, "Am I Miss Pretty Please, Grandmom?"

Phillip and Carol restrained their joy as they nodded, hoping for a hug from Annie. It came in like a flush of hearts. Their private nickname for Annie, Miss Pretty Please, would become her special calling card in the future.

The grandparents did not travel overnight without Annie unless a Cloud Presence (a 3-D hologram of a phone call), the latest fad for over-involved parents and grandparents, was set up in their family room for at least a half hour a day for them to converse after school. It was little Annie's time to talk and listen intently to her grandparents. There was a lot of information to absorb about the family and of course herself. By her calculations, her Grandpa Phillip, who was in his late sixties and on six different heart medications, had a growing percentage of not being around at some point.

She would constantly remark, "Are Lil and Hill aware of all this information?"

Phillip and Carol assured Miss Pretty Please that, "Everybody has a lot to learn about themselves."

Her Grandpa figured out that his answers needed to be succinct. His telling her about family history had to be chronological in order, starting with how her mother, Anna the FBI Special Agent, was shot and bled to death. After which Annie was snatched from Anna's womb by her father, Guy Finelli, who became the world's greatest defensive football player and helped bring down the Baltimore drug lord, The Turk. Explaining just that scene took many weeks.

Carol was more of a storyteller, which would cause anxiety for Annie. She would drop her head when the story would go off the tracks. Eventually, her Grandmom became trained by Annie to tell her stories more directly, and at times, Carol used her executive skills by summoning the Cloud to create holographic, power-point slides to help Annie follow a story. At a very young age, Miss Pretty Please learned to direct her grandparent time like a CEO running a tight thirty minute meeting with their board of directors. These sessions helped her abate her irrational fear of feeling part cyborg and assisted her confidence in gaining her humanness.

~3~

Russell sought out a different church than the priests at Georgetown to confess his self-perceived sins of perversion. He waited the rest of the winter, during which he increased his drinking and stoning, to find St. Dominic's, a Catholic Church just south of the National Mall and over-looking the Southwest Waterfront in DC as a safe haven to confess. Alex and Sally had grown an affection for Father Higgins and that church community after getting married at President's Park during the magical 2012 season.

Russell thought a good old-fashioned Catholic Confession would work to solve his guilt, but once he knelt in the confessional, he panicked, because bringing it up was too embarrassing. So instead, he sought a long-term counseling relationship with a lay Deacon on staff, Vincent Robey. During an initial interview, Russell felt he could trust the Deacon while he talked about his general lack of ambition and current mediocrity. The second time they met, Russell could not wait any longer, so he blurted out, "Deacon Robey, I think I may be a pervert!"

"Russell, please call me Vince. Now tell me, what causes you to feel this way?"

"I got turned on by a thirteen-year-old at a party with hundreds of people watching and had to masturbate in a bathroom for Christ' sake to feel some sanity," Russell muttered as he ran his fingers through his overgrown locks of blondish hair.

"I see… has this happened before or since?"

"Fuck no, are you kidding me?" Russell tried to compose himself, "Sorry for the cussing, Deacon."

"It seems very helpful right now, Russell. Tell me a little bit about your interaction with her."

"She was playing this amazing Steinway. It was gorgeous and sounded so pure. When she stopped, she looked at me, and we had a conversation. Not long, but her eyes and her presence just… well."

"So, she seemed older than her age?"

"Yes, but she looked right through me, Deacon. Her eyes seemed to see my soul."

"You felt love for her?"

"I was pretty high to be honest, but I guess maybe. She shocked me with her ability to interact. We were at the same level."

"And your body reacted?"

"Unbelievably… I've never had that happen to me before. And now it's the only thing that gets me super excited."

"Have you been with anyone since?"

"Well of course, Deacon, I'm not celibate!"

"I see… Russell, tell me about the rest of your life right now."

For the next twelve weeks, they met every Wednesday and discussed everything in his life except Annie Finelli. During their last session, just before their goodbyes, Russell asked Vince about his initial concern, "So Vince, do you think I'm a pervert or just generally fucked up about life?"

"My son, you are a healthy young man who felt a connection with a young soul that affected you greatly. She sounds like a very strong young lady. Now that you understand what happened, you probably will avoid that reaction again and just talk with her like a gentleman if you ever see her and without getting a hard-on." They laughed together, "But to answer your questions, hell no and maybe just a little. You might think about getting stoned or drunk less often, but you are a great talent. God will help you find your path, if you talk with Him. Now don't be a stranger and remember you can always call me."

Russell felt strong as he thanked Vince for his help. His conscience was relieved when he finally realized he was probably in love with the Steinway and not the girl. His feelings were confirmed when the piano was delivered to his rented house on Tunlaw before the end of the counseling sessions with Vince.

But the mystery of the power of Annie Finelli over him was not entirely answered.

~4~

After spending most of her first five years with just family members and avoiding the notoriety of being the love child of the world's most famous football player, Annie met the outside world in the fall of 2019. She started kindergarten in the local public school, Parkwood Elementary. The kindergarten experiment lasted until October when she was pushed ahead to join her cousins in first grade. She completed her assignments in record time, answered the teacher when necessary, but never said a word to the other kids in her class or on the playground. The principal, guidance counselor, and school psychologist decided that Annie was brilliant, and needed the comfort and familiarity of her twin cousins, away from all the busy-bodies and noisemakers of same-age playmates. All of her elders agreed.

Some observers might have thought she was autistic or possessed a narcissistic personality, and just maybe had dissociative or borderline tendencies; but in reality, she was a bit hyperactive, which she hid very well and with great discipline. In the old days, her great-Grandmom Rose Finelli would have said that she liked to "stay busy."

Luckily her father, Guy Finelli, and her aunt, Sally Keegan (the twins' mother and Annie's custodial mother), did not listen to the labels; they knew her to be focused and without time for distraction. Her fun with humans, since she could walk, involved activity that she could control. If she watched television, it had to have a point, a story preferably without commercials. As a toddler, Annie loved to watch Aesop fables, a Cloud-streamed series from Carol, portrayed with animated characters playing out proverbs with morals for life.

It provided a sketch or an outline of how to deal with people. She watched with her cousins in their comfortable den on a mountain of pillows. There, Annie experienced physical closeness that was safe and led her to learn feelings of love for the first time as a human being.

Besides her grandparents, only her Aunt Sally, and sometimes her stepmother, Patty O'Neil, could invade her personal space and give affection that was comfortable to her. Guy and his half-brother Alex (Sally's husband) were tolerated when they invaded her personal space, because she had learned from Sally that they were trustful and important. Eventually, she did learn to have feelings of love for her dad and uncle, mostly when watching them as they played ball with her in the Parkwood Enclave. Seeing their magnificent athleticism in person, or from career Cloud highlights, gave her a sense of unadulterated joy. It helped to be thrown in the air occasionally by such giant men creating a sense of weightlessness that she learned was thrilling.

Annie had no instinctual feelings, except those from physical manifestations. Even those had to be named from watching the Cloud or from Aunt Sally. The learning curve had started with her cousins as a child and seemed to be stagnant at the beginning of grade school. Then, her cousin Hill found a Cloud-series on "Pistol Pete" Maravich at the age of six and fell in love with basketball. Annie experienced the Maravich magic one day as she sat atop pillows in the den with her cousin and became mesmerized. Soon, Annie realized that she wanted to learn everything that "Pistol Pete" could do with a basketball. Included in her fascination was a need to grow her vibrant red hair into a "Pistol Pete" flop. Looking like a fifth *Beatle*, the flop of hair danced around her dark-skinned, but freckled, twenty-five percent Italian face every time she did a crossover dribble. She practiced every basketball drill from the Cloud that she could find about "Pistol Pete" for hours, handling the basketball like a play doll every spare minute for the next five years with her unusually large yet skinny hands.

Only Hill would be allowed to play basketball with her because he understood the greatness of "Pistol Pete". Otherwise, Annie had no interest in playing actual basketball games against opponents. She was too busy learning to replicate Pete's famous shoot-out with Dan Issel and the *Kentucky Wildcats* when he scored sixty-four points and Issel the Epistle had fifty-two points—without a three-point line. By the summer of 2024, at the age of ten, Annie had mastered every basketball ball-handling skill imaginable, and was getting strong enough to shoot the basketball flawlessly from fifteen feet and in. She would fall asleep at night recalling every stat of "Pistol Pete", but she could never understand how a human being could average 44.2 points per game in a NCAA basketball career. Just before falling asleep, she would whisper, "and all without the three-pointer!"

~5~

She took up watching a Cloud-series on volleyball during the summer of 2024, before the Olympics started in DC. At age ten, her summer that year was taken up by the local swim team and gymnastic camp activities; but for a week, she stayed with her cousin Melissa at her mansion in Howard county with Hill, Lil, and her little half-brother Anthony II, who was almost four. Her father Guy, stepmother Patty, Uncle Alex, Aunt Sally, and grandparents Phillip and Carol would join for an evening or two. They all played volleyball on the lawn looking down upon Route 97 from high on the hill, while the sun nestled down in the western sky. *It was as close to heaven as I could imagine*, she thought. From one of her heroes, Pope Francis I, she learned with certainty that it was a place her slain mother looked down on her. For the first time, she labeled that special feeling as delicious because it left a good taste in her mouth and filled her soul with joy.

At the end of summer 2029, when her junior year was about to start at the age of fifteen, she would finally play a team sport in high school, where she would have to interact with other people and depend on them for her success. After two years on the gymnastic, swimming, and track teams, she chose the girls volleyball team.

WJ varsity volleyball Coach Janet Melendez knew that two generations of Finellis had starred on WJ girl volleyball championship teams in 1984 and 2014, and clearly, she knew about the greatness of her father in football and her uncle in baseball. She had watched Annie on the track team for two years, as a volunteer assistant, and helped her become the best girl's high-jumper and long jumper in the county as a sophomore. It was her suggestion to Annie—after the track season was over in May—to join the volleyball team, and as with most conversations with Annie Finelli, it was quick and to the point.

"Annie, can we sit and talk for a few minutes?" Janet picked up her gait to stay with Annie.

"Can we do it while I finish my cool down around the track?" Annie stated while looking forward.

"Of course, Annie… that makes sense."

"It will take me about three and a half minutes to walk around the track or I can walk slower if we need five minutes."

"Actually, one lap should work Annie. Listen, I was thinking, you should try out for the volleyball team this summer." Janet tried to get Annie's eye contact.

Annie turned her head to focus her brilliant green eyes on her coach and brushed back her orange-red floppy locks behind her head ban, without slowing her cool-down lap gait. She focused totally on Janet's dark eyes for the first time and noticed that her hair was jet black like her Aunt Sally's. The dark skin and youthful smile from her face, added a genteel tingle to Annie's tummy area. "Coach Melendez, how did you know I was thinking about that idea?"

"I've been watching and coaching you in track for two years and saw you in the gym embarrass the boys in a coed volleyball workout. You blocked the boy's best hitter on an eight-foot net and spiked a couple passed them as well."

"Yes, Coach, that is correct," she paused as she reviewed the memory in her mind, "Actually, Coach… both of their hitters tried to get it passed me while I was rotating through the front row." She beamed an unusually big smile recalling the memory and seeing their faces wither with embarrassment. "But to be fair, Coach… I did hit a couple out of bounds." Annie caught herself off assignment and slowed down her breathing again. "I really do not like playing near the net. It seems too close and gets in the way of slamming."

Janet tried to stay up with Annie, even in her slowed-down pace, and with only a half a lap to close the deal. "Well, you might like the libero position in the six-two formation… you know, setting sometimes and playing defense in the back row."

"Except I believe that would keep me from slamming from the back row."

Janet could see the finish line ahead and was growing confident a deal could be made. "Well, I think there could be an adjustment made for that."

A puzzled look fell upon Annie's face but, at these times, she knew to trust Coach Melendez. "I am not fully versed on the volleyball libero position, but

I would like the challenge of playing defense and serving from the back row; and of course, slamming from behind the ten-foot line."

A faint but restricted smile came over Janet's face as she crossed the finish line with Annie. She swallowed hard as she realized the best high school, female athlete she had ever witnessed was going to be on her volleyball team. It took her a few long seconds to regain her composure and catch her breath; she looked at Annie, the girl they called *Miss Pretty Please*, who was quietly holding herself at full attention, an unusual moment in the universe as the trajectory of her personal orbit was about to make real contact with another human being.

Janet felt a deep, uncharted, maternal emotion as she gazed at this young lady, full of pure energy. She finally answered, "Yes, Annie, that's right. And slamming, of course!"

~6~

Russell was pondering the phone message from his Grandmother, who had just turned ninety and decided that he could not possibly disappoint her. He was now settled for the first time in his life at the age of twenty-six in his position at Georgetown Prep, a very private Jesuit High School, as the Director of Music Education. Thinking about his first full academic year at Prep near the end of May 2029, he walked around his one-bedroom suite on the fourth floor of Boland Hall, which had been refurbished during the early twenties. The ninety-three-acre campus once included a full nine-hole golf course around the school before the expansion of buildings at the beginning of the century. Almost forty percent of the school's population were minorities and received grants to pay for most of their education but did not live on campus. Now, less than one hundred of the five hundred attendees lived on campus from all over the United States and the world. These were the really, really, rich families that paid over one-hundred-thousand dollars a year to have a child live on campus and get a worldly education. His fourth floor featured several problem teenagers, like the son of owner Burton Parker of the Washington Potomacs football franchise. Hall Prefects still lived on each floor to monitor the evening study halls and curfew. And each floor had an apartment like Russell's for department heads willing to live on campus. The elevator at the end of the hall in front of his door was off limits to kids, but most of these educators had an open-door policy to interact with the students after class and into the evening.

His front expansive window looked out over the valley of hills that contained the remaining three golf holes, bordering the bustle of Rockville Pike.

On the other side of the Pike, nestled in a hillside valley heading towards Rock Creek, was the Academy of the Holy Cross. But now the Metro with apartment buildings on top, the Swarthmore Music Hall and the Georgetown-like townhome village all destroyed the once pristine and picturesque country-side between the Prep and the Academy. It made him furious.

So, he sat down at his prized possession of a piano and played a couple of notes, then laughed at a memory about the travels of the Steinway from Anthony Finelli's house, to his rented house on Tunlaw, to his Grandmother's house on Johnson Avenue for a year, and finally to Georgetown Prep to be carried up four floors; and every move made without a scratch of his prize possession.

Now, after the phone message, he realized taking his Grandmother Laura to Annie Finelli's fifteenth birthday party at the Parkwood Enclave was his only option and not a big deal. It had been seventeen months since he had lost himself over her, but through counseling and maturity, he was over it. Besides, he had a girlfriend for the past year, but he had to admit the relationship was in constant turmoil. Ironically, she had found this job for him, but he had grown distant from her because of his interest in it. *She is sometimes just too much trouble and way too dramatic*, he complained to himself at times. As for his alcohol and drug intake, he was mostly sober these days, but when he did get high; it was to deal with the drama from the relationship.

"Call Laura Santucci," he ordered the Cloud. "Grandmother, I would love to take you to the party. I will pick you up at four p.m., okay? I won't be late."

His confidence was in high gear as he looked forward to seeing the Enclave from the inside for the first time. And he was positive the embarrassment would not happen again.

~7~

It was always on Annie's birthday, May 26, that her family remembered her mother, Anna Cobb, because it was the day that she was murdered. Now, on her fifteenth birthday in 2029, Annie believed that they were making an extra big deal about it. She always wondered why people wanted to know how she felt about it—the Memorial Day Massacre, that is…being born into a bloody mess at the hands of her famous father Guy Finelli. He had found the knife, always hidden by Anna in her boot, after they had been ambushed by "The Turk's" gang of six and cut into her protruding belly to give life to their daughter. This was after trying to revive her when her heart stopped from a gunshot blast that blew out her femoral artery in her right leg. To be honest with herself, Annie did really appreciate her father's quick thinking and surgical skills.

"I wish I could have known her," Annie would repeat every year even though it seemed silly to say. "It was a very sad time for my father," Annie added. She had worked through her irrational fear of being part-cyborg, and almost putting it behind her, but there were times of great stress that it filtered through her consciousness. From all the research, she learned through the Cloud, it was probably a sign of mental illness. She was at peace with that possibility because she was confident of her brain's ability to out-think it. Anyway, she liked to think of it as her alter-ego.

Now that she turned fifteen, she loved being almost legal to be with boys and was enjoying life. She could figure out the best outcomes of any situation and focus on that. At a birthday party, it was about eating the cake and opening presents. She could not wait to say, "Now can we blow out the candles and eat the cake?" But patiently, she would open her gorgeous eyes and painfully listen, empathetically, to another relative tell her a story about Anna. For Annie, most stories about her mom seemed disconnected from her, like a well-thought-out fairy tale, all ending with being saved by her father's heroism. It seemed to have nothing to do with her, but she appreciated everybody's effort, and each year, she was willing to give some attention to it even though it seemed to slow down her birthday cake eating. She wanted it to be up-tempo, like the way "Pistol Pete" played basketball.

Anna's parents, originally from Ohio, had stopped visiting with their grandchild after the 2020 Championship GAF (Global American Football) Contest, having been relocated to Arizona by Guy following the arrest of "The Turk" and the take down of his organization. Someday, Annie wanted to visit them, but not now, as she was trying to keep up the tempo and get through high school, maybe by her sixteenth birthday.

Annie had one exception to feeling disconnected to stories about her mother. She liked it when her father talked about Anna. Now at thirty-four, her father, Guy Finelli, was still a famous person, an ex-great football player, a philanthropist, a movie star and producer, and to some a superhero. To Annie, the sound of his voice resonated throughout her body, it was a tone-smooth baritone, like her Grandpa Phillip. It also did not hurt that he was very good looking. He was a giant to her at six foot, six inches with big shoulders and massive hands. She was within a foot of him at five foot seven or almost eight, she would say.

They had a pleasant relationship. While both were a bit distant at times, which was okay with Annie for now, she knew that her dad would be there if she needed him. Besides, she had Aunt Sally, who was still her favorite person.

"Well… blow out the candles, you silly!" exclaimed Lilly.

"Annie, are you awake? Let's eat the cake already!" implored Hill.

"Give her a moment, you animals, she's making a wish!" Sally corralled her almost sixteen-year-old twins and gave Annie her most precious commodity – space.

A wish… what a silly idea, Annie thought. She was concentrating on a picture of her mother that would always chill her spine. It was from a descriptive story by her father of the first time they met. Her father would become misty-eyed when he told it. Anna Cobb was an FBI agent poising as a teenager at a summer swim meet before Guy became a senior in high school. She was in a bathing suit with shorts, while her naturally curly red hair covered her freckled face. Suddenly, while she talked on her cell phone, she looked up at Guy Finelli as he approached, whispered something into the phone, and said, "Good luck. Guy Finelli." The story always caused a *tingler*, a term made up by Annie to define the extra dopamine ordered by her brain, delivered through her nervous system to "chill her spine." In other words, an emotional reaction.

"Thanks Aunt Sally. I got it!" They locked eyes for a moment as she felt the tingler leave her body. Annie stood erect with her chest arched out, showing off her amazing athletic figure that was getting ready to perform. She recoiled and slowly took in a deep breath, rising her chest to a rare sight of full exposure, and suddenly shook the fire out of the candles.

As the lights came on, he was in her sights, looking so handsome and gentlemanly. She felt his eyes on her body. And a giant tingler rushed down her spine into her fingers and toes. A rush of blood was shaking her chest. She crossed her arms in front to keep her body from exploding. It felt like a roller coaster and weightlessness. She knew it was right. *Why is everyone else here?*

~8~

"Russell, you know your Grandmother does not like to be late. At twenty-six, I thought you had learned to be punctual. What happened to you?"

"You won't believe it, Grandmother, I ran out of gas. I was fifty yards from the station, and the Acura just stopped… right on Old Georgetown in front of WJ. It was embarrassing."

"I see… but with these new cars, how can you run out of gas?! They seem to start beeping at a quarter tank, if I remember correctly. Besides, don't you have an electric car yet?"

"No, I'm driving an old 2009 Acura TL, a real gas guzzler all the way."

"Not Alex's old car?"

"Exactly, I love this car. It's particularly attractive to the girls, and it is extremely fast."

"Well, I approve of the first, but not the second. Besides, women should be climbing all over you without the car. A Santucci, handsome, a Georgetown graduate, a concert pianist! What else are girls looking for these days? Now what happened to this girlfriend… is that on or off?"

"Still on, at the moment, but it may be in a downward spiral."

"Well, that is good news. She is a kind of a flake, in my opinion. Too much drama, my dear."

"You may turn out to be right, Grandmother. How did you know?"

"That's my job as a Grandmother, my dear Russell, to know if a girl is right for my grandson or not. But she is very pretty, which can throw one off, I guess. 'You have to feel it in your gut,' my husband would always say."

Russell was making the turn onto Parkwood Drive and heading up the last block to the Enclave, forty minutes late to the birthday party. "Thank you for the advice, Grandmother. We're finally here."

"Yes, just in time for the cake cutting, I suppose. Oh, by the way dear, how much is a gallon of gas at the Wildwood station these days? That has to be the most expensive gas in the area!"

"Actually, not that bad, just under seven dollars a gallon."

"Wow, you could make a car payment with that tank of gas. I can see the three-dollar carbon tax is not working on you."

"I don't really drive much these days with living and working at Prep. And I Metro a lot or Cloud-Cab sometimes."

"That is comforting to know with the partying that you do. Now let us go in quietly without causing a stir. Maybe no one will notice we are so late. You know Rose Finelli would be horrified, this was her house you know, much smaller, but beautiful. There was a party on a Saturday night in June of 1986 I believe, before the wedding of Phillip and Carol, mainly outside. All of this stuff was not here." She pointed to her right as they walked through the gate of the Parkwood Enclave entrance. "It was all slate and stone with a water fountain, twenty tables set up, it was a beautiful party. A hundred bottles of champagne that the older Guy Finelli had bought. Phillip was launching corks all night. That was forty-three years ago… my goodness, it was quite a party and now it is their house."

Intrigued by the history, Russell tried to clarify, "You mean Carol and Phillip, right? So, you were best friends with Phillip's parents, Guy I and Rose?"

"Yes, Gene and Guy were inseparable for twenty years. As a couple, we had so many good times, Rose was an angel and could put on an Italian meal like no other hostess—her meatballs and manicotti were legendary!"

Suddenly, Russell's mouth was watering, his hands were sweating, and his stomach was growling as he walked through the door. He was officially hungry.

In the middle of the family room, Laura released her grandson's arm from her elbow and kissed him on the cheek as she whispered, "Thanks for getting me here but be careful." She moved to the right quietly and started some *hellos* as the candles were about to be blown out by the birthday girl.

Russell had moved up closer to the dining room table because everyone had gathered around Annie on the other side, cheering her on as she readied to blow out the candles. In meticulous fashion, her posture arched her chest forward in a balanced stance with her hands on the table for maximum push off and air release. She coiled back for a moment to gather oxygen. Her eyes closed, the left side of her red hair and her braided right side hung down over her face for a moment. Russell felt locked into her. He could not wait to see her eyes and face again.

Annie arched forward, releasing her air on the candles. Her force traveled across the table. Russell felt a swirl of air past his ears. He saw her eyes lock on to him and a smile beaming with joy. Her chest was in full view, matured to an eye-popping level by male standards. He stepped back a moment to take it all in. And in just a moment, it all made sense – he knew she was the one.

~9~

The summer vacation of 2029 started in June with volumes of volleyball at the Parkwood Enclave for Annie with her Grandpa Phillip, cousins Hill and Lil, brother Anthony, and stepmother Patty all standing in to help when needed. July involved two intensive, week-long clinics with a week to recover in between. August started team training and practices leading up to her first season as a volleyball player at WJ. Annie decided to give up team swimming in the Fall, but she still wanted to compete on the outdoor track team in the Winter and Spring.

Most of the team practices were very confusing for Annie because she was trying to decipher between the memories of all her responsibilities on the court and five other teammates in the way. As a gymnast, high-jumper or swimmer, she had rehearsed her roles to improve upon and make perfect. Every time she learned her role in volleyball, it was complicated by a teammate doing something too fast or too slow. Methodically, she was gaining some traction by focusing on the defensive, middle-back position. There was very little traffic back there, and it helped her see the whole game ahead of her. She was also a natural server but refused to show her jump serve in team practice until she had perfected it.

At times, during practice, she had to wait a few minutes for her turn to be on the court. Most of the girls would get water or socialize with the boys watching the practice. But Annie never left the side of the court, always watching the routes of hitters and the defensive positioning. But presently in this moment, she was thinking about her birthday party and seeing Russell again. A dynamic daydream, recalling their conversation at her party as though it was still happening. For a moment, she took her sight off the volleyball court and shut her eyes.

Ten feet away, across the table, all by himself, she could see him gazing at her sudden stare, and then their eyes fit like a soft glove providing comfort with their warmth. Without awareness, she handed the knife to Sally Keegan to cut the rest of the cake, and never left his sight as she moved around the table ignoring congratulations. Finally, she worked her way to the middle of the room and found him. She wanted to touch him all over but stood in an appropriate pose with hands clasped in front of her. "I had no idea you were coming to my party. How many years has it been?"

"Maybe one or two… you have grown up into a beautiful lady, congratulations!" he opened his arms towards her without thinking and, in a second, they were hugging.

Annie could feel every morsel of the touching, every scent of his smell, every sound of his heartbeat as her right ear nestled into his chest for a moment or two. Then, some awkward tension she had never experienced before, followed by a wonderful conversation with Russell, and interrupted by eating cake and more congratulations. And she watched his eyes the whole time. "You brought your Grandmother quite late, she must not be happy with that maneuver," she finished with a smile.

"You're right about that, but I ran out of gas right in front of your high school coming down Old Georgetown Road."

"I believe that is very difficult to do these days with cars, especially with all the warnings from the dashboard and such."

"Yeah, I know, I just heard that… but honestly it is not the first time."

"Oh, do not worry, you are in good company with my Grandpa Phillip Finelli."

Russell was relieved and became curious at Annie's attempt to make him comfortable about his bad habit. "Wow, to be in same company with your grandpa. How so?"

"Apparently, before the twenty-first century cars, he ran out of gas twenty-one times. My Grandmom Carol says it matches the number of women he had sex with, in his life." Annie smiled, pleased with her storytelling. "What are you doing these days other than running out of gas and driving your Grandmother around? Oh yes, and giving piano lessons?"

"You have quite a memory… actually very well. I'm living and working at Georgetown Prep as the head of Music Education."

"Thank you, I do have quite a memory. Sometimes too good, especially when I am around a lot of people, but yes that sounds great, congratulations. My cousin Phillip, or as I call him Hill, goes to Prep. You may have seen him play basketball for the JV. He averaged 17.8 points, 6.4 assists and 6.2 rebounds a game. He will be a starter next year on the Varsity. At six-feet, five-inches and still growing, he is quite good; a bulls-eye shooter and a great passer as a shooting guard." Annie spoke about her cousin with authority, hoping to impress Russell with statistics. Then, she thought of a joke in case she was being too technical about her cousin, "but he still cannot cover me one on one."

Russell loved watching her break into a smile and crack a joke. *She is really developing a personality*, he thought. "I'd like to see that match-up." They shared a laugh. "You know, now that you mention it, I have seen the name, but I haven't run into him yet. I'll make sure to meet him."

"Well, actually, he is right over there talking to your Grandmother…in reality his Grandmother too…but I forget that sometimes because I think of him as my brother. You know how the Finellis and Santuccis are intertwined!"

Wow, she is shooting off some good ones, Russell thought, impressed by her wit. "Yes, I do Annie." Russell realized he was overstepping his time with the birthday girl and others might notice. He started to say good-bye. "Listen, Annie…"

She stepped towards him to engage him further. "Russell, my Grandpa lived at Georgetown for a year from the Fall of 1982 through the summer of 1983. He was a Hall Prefect in Boland Hall on the fourth floor and apparently would sneak my Grandmom up to his room during the summer of '83."

Annie whispered the last part, getting on her toes and touching his shoulder to reach his ear. Russell tried to stay calm as he felt the warmth of her fingers. "Is this legend or from a good source?"

She leaned back and stood poised again on her feet, very happy with her interaction with Russell. "My Grandpa and I talk almost every day. He is quite a storyteller."

"Yes, he is and quite a writer too. I have read all three of his books. *The Tackler* is my favorite, based on your great-Grandpa Guy Finelli I, I believe."

"And you are correct," She pointed directly at him and smiled. "He is pretty special and probably a better overall athlete than his sons. Only in the last few years have I beat him in one-on-one." Annie felt empowered talking about her family. She was floating on air speaking to Russell. She wanted to savor every moment and then she thought of one more story. "You know, running out of gas can sometimes save your life!"

Russell was amused and felt calmer as he took her personality into his soul and enjoyed every detail, "Are you trying to make me feel better or making fun of me?"

"I am not very good at joke making, though I am improving my skills in storytelling, which I understand can lead to joke telling." She smiled and stepped a little closer. "My Grandpa, one night, was returning to Georgetown Prep about two a.m. after partying in a DC bar during the summer. His 1973 Pinto was ten years old and on its last legs. His gas tank was below the empty line and he knew he was close to running out, but he was a light away on the Pike before making the left into Prep." Annie intently tried to focus on the storytelling as she felt her spine tingle and her hands warm. "Well, apparently, the NTSB had come out with a recall for his Pinto in 1978 to fix the gas tank from exploding on rear impact. For various reasons, like being a cab driver for two years and a bike rider, he never brought the Pinto in to get fixed. So, he felt the less gas in the tank, the less chance of blowing up, but of course that strategy led to running out of gas often." Her body was feeling a full reaction to her unfulfilled sexual needs. Normally, masturbation would take care of her needs, but this was something different. She needed touch and actual physical closeness with a human being. *Was this what Sally Keegan would call love?*

"So, then the light turns green, he hits the gas pedal. Apparently, it had a clutch pedal and a gear shift. Amazing manual labor, huh?" She smiled, *he is listening intently but is a little fidgety,* she thought. "Anyway… BOOM! He gets smashed from behind and gets pushed as the other car bounces off a little, and then BOOM! again, causing skidding until both cars finally stop. He has a seat belt on, but his neck snaps back, causing him a lifetime cervical pain. He then bolts out of the car in the middle of Rockville Pike with no traffic coming anywhere and finds a spot fifty yards away waiting for the explosion. So, after five minutes of assessing his neck and body for injury and no explosion, he starts to walk back to the car. In the meantime, no cars have come by either way. Finally, as he gets to the accident scene, the drunkest person he has ever seen gets out of a 1965 Bonneville, which apparently was a big and long car, and stumbles past him to lay on the grass of the medium strip. Finally, the police arrive, I guess someone called from the Grosvenor Apartments because they did not have cell phones. So, my Grandpa talks to the police, who are looking through the Bonneville and count twenty-three cans of Bud on the passenger side floor." She paused to catch her breath, realizing she had never talked so much to someone she really did not know, but she was feeling endorphins like she had run ten miles. "You see, the empty gas tank strategy worked. No explosion!"

"Wow that is quite a story! Thank you… but I do have one question." He reached and took her hands in his and got closer. "What is the NTSB?"

Annie exploded in laughter and playfully put her hands on his chest to fake pushing him away, "Well, if you must know the National Transportation Safety Board."

"Ahhh… now that does make me feel better!" He hugged her again and said goodbye, proud that his pants were not stretched by his member, but afraid that his heart and soul were being scorched by the firestorm of Annie Finelli. A scary sign of love. He was sure of it.

Coach Melendez called on Annie as she was not taking her place in the next drill. A rarity of focus. "Annie… Annie." She walked over to her quietly and touched her shoulder. Annie woke up from the daydream and smiled. "Are you okay, Annie?" Janet asked.

"Yes, Coach, just dazed a little bit… sorry."

"No problem, rotate in when you're ready."

Annie labored through the matrix of bodies and finished the drills. Coach Melendez could see that too many teammates on the front line with the net was not her best spot. Quickly, she decided to keep her only in the back-row rotation where she could focus on defense. "Annie, I think the best thing for the team is to have you play the back row defensively and improve on your serve."

Annie agreed with her coach's assessment on the backrow positioning but was unsure about improving her serve. "Coach, I think my underhand serve is perfect. I will get that in play one-hundred-percent of the time. My overhand serve seems to be hovering around ninety to ninety-five percent, losing a point one out of ten or twenty times, therefore my over-hand serve seems not to be worth the risk." She had failed to mention that her jump serve was hovering around fifty percent, which was an embarrassment to her.

Janet Melendez was happy that she decided to have these conversations in her office. She knew these expressions of logic and mathematical formulas for the success of a volleyball serve would not go over well with her teammates. "I see, Annie. Of course you should do what makes you comfortable, but I will point out that nearly fifty percent of your overhand serves are unreturnable, which I believe offsets the five to ten percent of those not put in play."

Annie listened intently and then she reviewed her memory of every underhand serve in practice games and whether it led to a point gained versus her overhand serve totals gained. The coach was right, if she served eighty percent or better overhanded, her team scored more points than when she served underhanded. She had missed it but was glad that Coach Melendez was doing her job. Annie felt a tingler realizing that trusting her coach was a good decision. "Thank you, Coach. I will make sure my overhand serves are at least eighty percent or better."

"Annie, remember this is just practice, so just keep slamming those serves without feeling any pressure."

Annie smiled and left Janet's office and thought to herself, *Pressure? What pressure is she talking about? This is just a game. Pressure is what my father did: Changing lives and fighting violence in Baltimore. Now that's pressure!*

~10~

The school year started the Tuesday after the Federal Career Day Holiday in September 2029. Career Day had replaced Labor Day after the 2024 election when the new congress, after four terms of a democratic president, voted to replace Labor Day because it represented a socialist element in the country. It was not a popular decision in the Finelli Parkwood Enclave of houses.

Phillip had rebuilt his parents' house on the corner of Parkwood and Everett in 2012. By 2017, Alex and Guy bought out the eight lots surrounding their parents' house. Guy and Patty first built on the two lots next to his parents on Parkwood, while Alex and Sally built on the two lots above on Oldfield. Two other lots facing Everett were left over as guest houses. Guy's sister Grace, and husband with their two children Laura and Walter, lived in one of the two guest houses. They were considering building on one of the extra lots in the Enclave.

The nine lots had a ten-foot high security wall from the rest of the block and a ten-foot black iron fence surrounding the lots on top of a five-foot stone wall holding in the hill from the sidewalk. It was over a third of the block, with each house sitting up high above on the natural hills of granite rock below the topsoil.

When the extra daylight appeared in early March, Security would open the two ten-foot high gates in the middle of the block from dawn to an hour after dusk providing for an open highway of running from one end of the block to the other, better known as Annie's Sprint, or for a game of Block Tag.

Annie demanded this change when she was two months shy of age seven in the Spring 2021. The Santucci mansion had been finished and overlooked all the lots. She was finding that catching her twin cousins in the game of tag or sprinting from lot to lot was getting too easy inside the Enclave, and that having more kids from the neighborhood participate would make the game more exciting. Then, one night, her case for opening the wall became clear, because nothing could hold her back. An hour after dusk, Annie realized she had to make a mad dash. Starting atop the Everett side of the outer stone wall, with her back laying against the black-iron fence on her grandparents' lot, she became *Flash Girl* blasting through her grandparents' backyard with guests looking on and then darted up the next three lots like a climbing bullet until she reached the wall and scaled it with a right, left, right, left, right, then atop the spires of the wall, flipped herself over, and cascaded down the wall like a determined pole vaulter. She sprinted with glee from her escape down the middle of the block gliding and sifting through eight more back yards most with three-foot high fences, which she hopped over easily, and finally reaching the sidewalk at Saul Road. After this stealth-like run landed her in new territory, Annie walked back around the block answering the stares of neighbors with a polite smile, as they pondered whether a swarm of fireflies had lit up their backyards or was it *Flash Girl.*

~11~

Being a student in 2029 in the on-going social experiment called Montgomery County, meant there were no books to carry or lunches to remember or money to pay. Each student had a thin acrylic pad (TAP) that had a smooth surface on one side for writing or typing and a large smart phone on the other, which connected them to the Cloud then folded and fit in their pocket or purse. All learning was done through the TAP when they were at school. At home, each student had a workstation to plug in the TAP with a keypad and larger screen. By eight p.m., each school night, parents would start to receive half-hour updated information on their child's progress on each assignment. This usually happened once for most families, because ninety-eight percent of students completed their individually adjusted assignments with help from the Cloud, if necessary, by eight p.m.

Each student had a scheduled day at home per week, doing a day of assignments and housework. It was a way to keep the in-school population down and school construction costs low. Montgomery County schools had been the first in the country to employ the system. It was meant to help students learn life skills like cooking, banking, vacuuming, laundry, general chores, and landscaping. All seniors had half-day internships for the year.

On the school campus, everything was on camera, and every student was on GPS. In school, there was no violence, no drugs in the hallways, and no bullying in the lunchrooms or bathrooms. Food was accessed each day and custom delivered in the lunchroom based on each student's caloric needs. Exercise was expected at the end of each class for ten minutes as the daily lesson for each class was reviewed. About a third of the students learned from full-time homeschooling, accessing classes through the Cloud, but most students enjoyed the social interaction and the athletic competition available by being in school. At the start of a second national term of conservative leadership in the country, Montgomery County continued its successful socialist approach to running government and their school system.

Annie looked forward to volleyball practice every day after school. Her adjustment to high school was going well. By her junior year, she had learned every social ritual possible, even making out with a boy once at a school-sponsored, DJ techno-dance party. She had considered going farther, even to sexual intercourse at the age of fifteen, but the current pleasures of masturbation made that idea irrelevant. She was open to exploring heavy petting, which she discovered on the Cloud as a confusing term for the action involved; but the boy she made out with seemed not to be interested. Annie was surprised considering her breasts were more than average size for her height and weight, and certainly soft enough in her opinion. Her interest in the boy did not last past the thirty minutes of kissing.

She projected, somewhere between the ages of sixteen and twenty-one, sexual intercourse would be added, and therefore lessen her need for masturbation. Part of her formula included anecdotal information from her trusted Aunt Sally, who relayed her experiences of waiting until later in college to deal with the emotional action of intercourse. This made little sense to Annie, but Sally Keegan was very smart and looked like royalty, so she took the anecdotal information very seriously.

In fact, Sally Keegan had prepared Annie fabulously for the teen to woman experience with the correct make-up, hair-style, and of course, clothes. As a fashion icon, Sally helped Annie look stylish at school but not stick out. Annie's twin cousins, Hill and Lil, were fashioned in the elite-school look, wearing uniforms during the day, and both being the most popular kids and the best looking at their schools. Annie had no interest in that confining look but understood the process. Sally Keegan and Alex Santucci were still the most famous couple in the DC area, and the twins had a role to play. Annie had watched many shows on Prince William and Princess Kate before he became King. She thought, *they seemed perfect as they played the most famous couple in the world, and Hill and Lilly were almost the same but just not married to each other.*

What Aunt Sally's training did not include was preparing Annie for all the social interaction among girls, in and around team sports. Annie described it as *girl stuff*, especially a team sport like volleyball. On her other sports teams—swimming, track, and gymnastics—she could avoid most of the team or girl stuff. In volleyball, half of the activity was giving high fives or meeting in endless huddles after every point. Annie found it exhausting. What she hated most was getting congratulations for hitting a serve out. She would seek out Coach Melendez almost daily with the same concern. "Coach, why is it that we reinforce mistakes with congratulations? It seems to make very little sense, and it makes me forget my next assignment."

"Annie, we are supporting each other in good times and bad times. It is meant as a good thing for a teammate."

"I see, Coach… but clearly the fist bumps are less intense when you make a mistake, so to me it is just distracting. I already know that people support me. How about if we save some energy and just congratulate a winning point or serve?"

Janet listened intently and tried not to burst into laughter. She was a single mother with two boys, ages eight and ten, so having teenage girls in her life, especially someone so special and complex like Annie, was a delight. At times, she thought that Annie was just plain odd, but most of the time she was struck by her brilliance, putting her thinking ahead of most of her teenage companions. It was exciting to get Annie's attention because it gave her an excuse to really gaze at her. She had grown into a dazzling looker. Her beaming red hair this month, had several corn rows on her right side that helped pull it back. Annie had asked Sally to incorporate it into her fashion look. It showed one side of her luscious freckled face that Janet wanted to pinch because it was so cute. Her shoulders were wide, holding up her statuesque neck. She had legs like a running back and an ass most girls would die for and boys would like to grab hold. On most days, her breasts were a mystery because she seldom wore anything but a sports bra. Like most female athletes, her well-proportioned figure showed better in a regular outfit. During a summer volleyball picnic, she wore a bikini under her t-shirt and shorts. When she stood to go swimming and unveiled the bikini, the turned heads of the few boys hanging out were noticed by all the girls on the team. The girls had seen Annie in her underwear, but never in a bikini. Most of them were either turned on or giggling from watching the boys stretch their necks. After a dive in the pool and two laps of a perfect freestyle stroke, including a flip turn, she emerged up the pool ladder with her breasts 'at attention' ready to explode from her top. It was exactly like her mother's sensual athletic figure.

Janet finally focused back to the current issue with Annie, "Maybe we should talk about that idea at the end of practice, Annie."

"But Coach that is your decision to make. I'm just giving you the logic of it. Besides, nobody would understand it coming from me."

"That's a good point Annie. I'll think about it and let you know."

Annie decided to dress up on the first game day, listening to her aunt's recommendation, choosing a push-up bra to expose an appropriate amount of cleavage in a v-neck sweater along with a stylish skirt. Her bangs would be clipped to the side with her hair curled to hang away from her face. Wearing some heavy eye make-up for the first time, her green eyes looked like lasers. As the opening game approached on a Thursday during the second week of school, it was the talk of the attendees and filled the gym with boys from every grade.

The WJ Girls Volleyball team was a group with little height. They had won the county championship in 2028 for the fourth time in Janet Melendez's seven years of coaching, but she had lost four seniors of six feet, two inches or more to Division I Colleges. This team had no seniors among her best eight players. She had one junior, Beverly Broomfield, who was a great hitter, setter, defensive stopper, and her best overall player, but barely hit the six-foot mark with her shoes on. Another player, Serena Saurez, a great center blocker but not much of a hitter at five-feet, ten-inches. She played power forward on the basketball team and with a wide base, she had a knack at getting her fingers on the volleyball. The front line was completed by Maria Tallchief, a freshmen sensation still growing at five-feet, eleven-inches. She was raw but had a wingspan of a six-foot, five-inch person, and a calmness unusual for a freshwoman. She was from upstate New York and had been a ballerina until a growth spurt three years ago helped her decide to shed her tutu for a volleyball jersey. She was elegant and looked like an Osage princess.

On the back line with Annie were two sophomores, Karen Jennings and Corrine Jefferson, who played much like Annie. They were older than Annie by a few months and knew her from gymnastics and track, but never had become friends with her, because... well... Annie did not have friends. They both thought of themselves as lesbians but not openly and were not attracted to each other. Each of them had a crush on Annie, but Karen was really in love with her. So, they decided to dive into volleyball like Annie did during the summer. They quickly became magicians defensively, and with Annie, they protected the back row like the Korean DMZ. Rarely would a ball ever hit the floor unless it was on the line. They listened to everything that Annie would tell them and performed their roles flawlessly. Annie started to appreciate their work because they could position themselves perfectly and run the same routes for every play. It gave Annie a sense of space she needed to succeed.

The main problem for Coach Melendez was rotating Karen, Annie, and Corrine to the front line. Karen and Corrine were not jumpers, and Annie hated the net. She had two decent substitutes, Whitney Warfield and Taylor Summers, who could power the ball if it was perfectly set and block it if it was straight in front of them but did little else athletically, and in the back row, they were useless, unless they were serving.

Both Karen and Corrine were amazing setters for being so inexperienced. Annie could set, but she hated it. Coach Melendez had sleepless nights going into the season with such inexperienced setters. She knew she would have to use Beverly Broomfield to set from the back line. To be honest with herself, Coach Melendez thought, *this season could be a nightmare*.

Student athletes paraded during Thursday's last period for the fall season's opening rally for the boy's football and soccer, and girl's hockey and volleyball teams. The only consistent winning teams were soccer and volleyball. The gym was packed with testosterone-laden boys and estrogen-filled girls hoping to visualize their favorite sexually fantasized athlete walk across the gym floor. Each team chose a song to walk out and stand in some order in front of the crowd. The boys teams were not organized but were good at preening for the girls. The girls hockey team attempted dancing together, doing a weave with their hockey clubs to the most recent techno-pop dance hit as they filed in, but their hearts were not into it.

The defending county champion girls volleyball team were the last to be introduced, and they were ready to set the world on fire. The standing room only crowd had all seen or heard about Annie Finelli's sweater look but were not ready for what happened next. Two weekends before, Karen had hosted a team party to plan their entrance and decide on the music for their routine. Each team player was encouraged to bring their favorite tunes.

~12~

In 2025, the Maryland State Legislature passed a law that increased the "Romeo and Juliet" exception to the Statutory Rape laws to include any age of older person of any gender for those women sixteen and older. It was a wave of young feminism that pushed the Maryland Legislature to pass it and re-election money raised for the governor to sign it. A legal affidavit was required, witnessed by a notary public, and a parent's or legal guardian's permission for those ages sixteen and seventeen prior to any sexual act, defined by genital contact or penetration. This controversial exception was brought up by Deacon Vincent Robey when he resumed counseling Russell during the summer of 2029. He had no idea of the laws involving a fifteen-year-old and a twenty-six-year-old. He assumed it was a bad idea legally.

In the resuming session of counseling, Russell reported his feelings in detail about seeing Annie at her fifteenth birthday party and her behavior towards him. Deacon Robey was in shock but worked hard not to show it. He thought Russell was done with this obsession and became worried about his mental state, especially teaching at a school. Albeit an all-boys school. Vince settled down when he heard Russell describe more of his actions. He knew he was not a saint, but not a pervert either. Then, Vince took a deep breath when Russell said that he would prove his love for Annie was real to himself by making a list. A Plan of things to do over the next three years. And when it was done, he would marry Annie Finelli. This information did little to calm Deacon Robey, but he was willing to listen intently.

First on his list was to see his girlfriend, Abbey, and patch up the relationship for two reasons: to make sure he would have access to regular sex (at least once a month would get him by), and as a cover to keep people from setting him up or a new woman coming after him that he could rebuff with "I'm in a relationship." And maybe to keep down any rumors that he was gay (because he lived at Prep), or that he was interested in a fifteen-year-old woman. Vince was not thrilled with this as the first step but understood the practicality of it.

Second was to start counseling again in the summer. He needed to be sure that his feelings were on course. Seeing Deacon Robey would force him to be truthful about his intentions and not because he was a potential pervert. Russell called it becoming spiritual because he felt good enough about his relationship with God that if he invested time in that relationship, his proclaimed love for Annie would be real. Vince liked this one very much.

Third was to figure out a way to see Annie without causing alarm. He knew she would be willing. He needed to get her Cloud connection at the least. Texting was still the last bastion of privacy in 2029, when deleted. Maybe piano lessons would be the solution, he concluded. Vince knew this idea was big trouble. He suggested to work on the first two before considering the third step.

Fourth was to get to know Hill and Lil, her cousins. As a teacher at Prep, it would be easy to gain access to Hill, he surmised. They had met at the party and Hill seemed thrilled to find out that Russell was a teacher who had a suite and piano at Prep. Russell also met Lil or Philomena II, at the party. She was clearly a party girl, he decided, with luscious blonde locks from her dad, Alex Santucci, and royal features from her mom, Sally Keegan; and a flirty way of interaction when smiling, but a stay-away-from-me-bitch look when she was not. Luckily, she was all smiles so far, the two times they had met. In his experience, Russell assumed that young women with her statuesque looks and a killer petite body had that stare built into their personality as a defense against, well… dick-headed males. In his knowledge of being at Prep for an entire school year, her personality was typical of the dozen or so elite hierarchy of young women at the Academy of the Holy Cross.

Vince liked this idea but realized he was falling into the quicksand that Russell was jumping into and how deep it could become for him as a counselor. If he continued this journey with Russell, it would become an undercover operation for at least three years. He would be screwed if something went wrong. After the first session, he studied his notes on Russell that started a year and a half ago; he realized he was past explanation to any investigation in the future; he was in deep, but he realized he was IN.

As Russell pondered the possible fourth part of his plan, he became concerned that if he moved too quickly to get to know Hill and Lil, it would seem a little much and lot too late. Technically, they were his cousins through adoption as well, because Alex was his uncle, but the adoption thing and the age difference were not an excuse for his indifference, non-interest, or whatever he called it for not knowing them so far. His concern was only about himself growing up, and it might backfire on him. Suddenly, he felt small for being a self-indulging asshole most of his life. Another issue to talk with Deacon Robey about. He made a note.

Russell had met one teacher that taught music at the Academy, at a mixer they both chaperoned, Sandy O'Malley, who went to Stone Ridge High School in Bethesda, and then Fordham University in the Bronx, New York. She could help. Sandy was fun and playful, but Catholic all the way and therefore married her first love. Her talents included a beautiful singing voice that could boom from her lovely chest.

They were friends, otherwise he would have loved to have her sexually. When they talked, he would crudely focus on playing with her chest in his mind. Then, he got his chance when he spent an evening with her while playing his Steinway. She chimed in singing some blues. After three beers and several shots of *Jack Daniel's*, she put down the lid of the piano and crawled on it to face him with her chest taking over the keys and the cleavage within striking distance, singing a jazzy version of the *Rolling Stones* "Satisfaction."

Russell was one verse away from climbing on the piano after her and giving her some satisfaction but knew it would be a mistake. Instead, he stopped playing, went around the piano, turned her over, climbed aboard and gave her one long, passionate kiss while feeling some of her hanging fruit. He then backed off and pulled her up and said, "Let me get you home." He picked her up, carried her down the elevator to her car and drove her to her apartment; which was across the Pike overlooking the Metro. He parked her car, walked her upstairs and handed her off to her husband. Delighted with his self-defined act of chivalry, he ran the mile and a half back to Prep. The exercise helped him deal with his extended hard-on.

A few days passed, then she called to thank him for the rescue.

"Sorry about getting so drunk the other night. I guess I needed to let go for an evening. Thanks for the rescue and getting me home."

"Anytime, Sandy. We'll do it again sometime," he said quizzically.

"Why not... it's not getting any better over here," she said with a sigh, but she quickly broke the silence with a lurid question, "So Russell, how did they feel?"

He laughed over the phone, "Well Sandy, they were quite a pair. I appreciate the pleasure. It was something. I could spend hours with those beauties."

"Oh Russell... it was the least I could do, as the Stones said, 'you can't always get want you want, but sometimes you get what you need.'"

Over the next week, Sandy and her husband came down to watch him play at a jazz bar in DC. She got enough drinks in her to join him and sing a couple of tunes. It was a blast, he remembered. The husband seemed amused and harmless. Sandy and Russell both agreed to try and hang out together in the future, *maybe they could stay a little more sober next time*.

Russell thought it could be a perfect friendship or maybe he was just desperate to talk to someone about his feelings for Annie that was not a deacon. In the next piano session at his suite, he spilled his plan to Sandy. She was astonished and playfully suggested that she leave her husband to take care of his temporary insanity. He eventually won her over with tears of emotion as he spoke of his embarrassing feelings of affection for Annie. Even though she thought it was lunacy, Sandy knew Russell was not a pervert. And after hearing his complete plan, including the counseling with Deacon Robey, she realized how much he really needed a friend to get through this without fucking up his life and, more importantly, the young woman. Besides, she thought, *the Finellis and Santuccis were super famous families, not to mention rich as hell.* They would appreciate her effort in avoiding a scandal. She quickly warmed up to the adventure and realized the sudden advantages to the friendship. The memory of the kiss was also an advantage she thought, *a nice distraction for both of us maybe*. At the end of the conversation, Sandy mentioned that her father knew Guy Finelli.

"How?" asked Russell.

"Well, my father is Brooks O'Malley and was an Assistant FBI Director before he became Director," answered Sandy matter-of-factly.

"What?!" Russell said with panic in his voice.

"You know the Baltimore gang that Guy Finelli brought down?" she answered with excitement.

"Holy Shit!" Russell was feeling more anxiety.

"Don't worry Russell, my dear boy, your little secret is just our thing. We're here to help each other, right?" She finished her drink and gave him a kiss. They stared at each other for a moment, he wanted more but waited. She kissed him longer this time as they descended on his couch together. She put her hand on his crotch as he grew in status. He reached under her sweater and quickly found pay dirt. His pants were unzipped, and then she took off her sweater and the containment. She was clearly in charge. He lost himself in her breasts, swimming in as she leaned over him. She started playing with him intently, alternating strokes with fondling his lower package. They kissed the whole two minutes before his explosion. She rolled off him and found her sweater, happy the evidence missed her clothes. In the bathroom, she laughed at the sight of her dishevelment in the mirror. *This could be fun if I can stay sober and avoid fucking him*, she thought.

He cleaned up and made another scotch to calm down his nerves.

She came out and hugged him. They kissed again. She said, "You owe me one Russell, or shit maybe we're even I guess for getting me home last time." She laughed, "We called that the Mary Magdalene," as she made sure his pants were zipped up and he was settled.

"Oh, that is crude Sandy!" Russell cried out.

"Crude but true, Russell. Jesus was human, you know, she was a saint and that was the compromise," Sandy said, loving her metaphor.

"So, you're saying he paid her back somehow?" Russell asked.

"I would say she did most of the consoling, but I'm sure he performed a miracle or two."

"Oh, is that what you call it? A miracle?! I can see I have my work cut out for me to get us even."

"See you soon, I hope. Don't worry dear, this could be fun." She pledged to be there for him and would get him to a Holy Cross event or two in the fall to increase his chances of bonding with Lil.

Both Hill and Lil, he learned, were very, very protective of their sister Annie (as they affectionately called their cousin). *I will have to win them over*, he figured, to have any chance to be with Annie in three years' time. But more importantly, he thought, *what would happen during that time before her legal adult status. Yes, at age sixteen, she could sign something and get permission for whatever; but that would never work for her or me*, he thought.

He was getting frustrated with himself and wondered if getting Sandy's breasts in front of his face was just screwing up his head. *How did all that just happen?* Russell pondered, *it could be a mess with Sandy, but I need her, and I like the Magdalene thing*. Surveying his options, he decided to get back to part one of the Plan and patch up things with Abbey, before Sandy's chest became the end of his Plan.

~13~

Since Annie moved to the Parkwood Enclave almost nine years ago with the Santuccis, she became enamored with her grandparents' (Phillip and Carol) house. She loved the smells of the kitchen and the fireplace and was spellbound by the real physical books in their library, but in the past year, she had spent most of her time in the grand house listening to her Grandpa's music albums—real vinyl records with covers. Her Aunt Grace was the unofficial curator of the collection and spent hours with Annie listening and discussing some of the music, going over the rules of handling the albums, and using the turntable. Annie was the only teenager in the world allowed to touch the collection. Grace started her with the A's and wished her good luck in her discoveries.

After a fast start, Annie got bogged down in the B's for months, (Bad Company, Badfinger, The Band, The Beach Boys, The Beatles, Boston, Jeff Beck and David Bowie, etc.). Finally, after her birthday in May, she reached the C's and spent many hours stuck on *The Cars*. When she listened to *The Cars* second album, "Candy-O", her heart jumped out of her chest. Their sound and lyrics made her feel alive and sexy.

An infatuation for bassist-singer Benjamin Orr developed as she looked up pictures of him and became enthralled by his voice. It was a pleasant surprise. Even though the material was written by Ric Ocasek, a line in the first song "Let's Go," sung by Orr, made her feel understood by someone who might fall in love with her personality. She was captured by the line, "She's a Frozen Fire, She's my One Desire." A romance was created in her mind about the woman character, *Candy-O*, and Benjamin. The next songs, "Since I Held

You" and "It's All I Can Do," seemed to continue the torrid affair, but his feelings seemed to crumble with the cheating, fast-car drama of "Double Life." Even though in reality it was *Candy-O* doing the cheating, Annie saw it differently and more trouble would follow. She hearkened the darkness of the short-techno-rock song, "Shoo Be Doo," which made Annie realized that *Candy-O* could not trust her love with Benjamin. And finally, the song "Candy-O" gave Annie feelings of power over her emotions with men because she displayed her domination. All of this she interpreted in less than nineteen minutes of music.

When Annie learned that Benjamin Orr died of pancreatic cancer in 1990, she felt like a *Frozen Fire* that lost her *One Desire*. In his honor, on June 12, 2029, she gathered all the relatives in the Parkwood Enclave as well as Uncle Anthony, Aunt Flo, and Cousin Joe from down the street; to show off a cake she made to celebrate the fiftieth anniversary of the release of *The Cars* second album,"Candy-O". Of course, she made everyone listen to it, eat cake, and dance.

It was the first time Annie dressed up as *Candy-O*, from the famous album cover, modeling the work of the great artist Alberto Vargas—known for his sketch work of pin-ups in Esquire and Playboy in the 1950s and 1960s. He was coaxed out of retirement by *The Cars* to do the "Candy-O" album cover. She discussed the model named Candy Moore, who posed for the cover, voted as one of the sexiest album-cover in rock history, and that *The Cars* drummer David Robinson was responsible for the idea.

The family was so enchanted by Annie's energy and imagination for the event that they had little reason to protest seeing her in a sexy leotard with full-length arms, like the red head on the album cover. The Enclave was rocking, with the cousins dancing and eating cake. Even Phillip could not resist dancing with Annie as *Candy-O*.

There was little doubt that the song would be used for the pep rally when Annie revealed her black leotard look at the volleyball party as she played *Candy-O* for her teammates. None of them had heard of the song, much less *The Cars*, but immediately fell in love with it, and of course the album cover. They sketched a car on a white sheet that resembled the album. Then used Karen's bed mattress along with a bounty of pillows, and built, on the dining room table, a great looking hood of a car for Annie to lay on. As she slowly practiced getting into the perfect position on the hood, they all agreed it was wonderful.

The team worked harder on the musical choreography for their routine than volleyball practice in the week leading up to the rally. Coach Melendez was supportive, knowing that the team chemistry would pay off in the long run. But even better, she loved watching Annie Finelli come out of her shell. As a complex teenager, she was mesmerizing and worth the season of coaching. She knew the routine would blow away the school.

~14~

Teenage giggling sent a high-pitch sound wave throughout the dark gym as they waited for the excitement to begin. The girls on the volleyball team were the final group to do their routine. They watched silently, bounded together in a corner with a collective energy, as their prop was brought out to the middle of the basketball floor. Four boys volunteered to carry out a long ten-foot table borrowed from the wood shop class covered with a clever tarp, drawn to look like a *Ferrari* sports car from the 1960s. Annie Finelli led her teammates onto the gym floor to take their places. She was wearing a black, partially see-through, skin-tight leotard, with black-stiletto high-heels and bright-red lipstick with long red-hair extensions that matched her curled red-hair perfectly. It flowed gently over her chest, shoulders, and back.

Annie took a spot leaning on the side of the pseudo-looking *Ferrari* about five feet from the first row of bleachers that was jammed with ninth and tenth grade boys, who had come early to earn their spots. The Cloud had given them instructions on their phones to witness Annie in her leotard up close. They were now unofficially the first members of Annie's Army. Girls and other genders found spots in the succeeding rows. In this era of the pansexual teenager, all types of fans would find attraction to Annie.

A spotlight caught her in a pose with her arms folded over her chest as the music started. A gasp came over the boys for a moment before a collective wow and then a few whistles. Suddenly, the boys stood, one after another, clapping and cheering as the intro from *The Cars* started to play the short techno-intro to "Candy-O" and "Shoo Be Doo." Her teammates all dressed in white leotards like cats, came to surround Annie—or now the luscious target of love, a character named *Candy-O*. They tugged at her arms and her legs as the song "Candy-O" started. Her teammate, Beverly Broomfield, lip synced the words to the boys in the front row especially:

"Candy-O, I need you so."

Annie sprung open her arms with fingers spread and shed her teammates, all falling to the ground. She escaped her captors and jumped into the crowd, kissed a boy, and then twirled to leap away quickly. She ran to the car and crawled on the hood. The boys who got a touch or a feel shrieked like rejected lovers.

"Candy-O, I need you so."

Now all members of the young crowd were energized, especially those boys with hard-ons from catching her body. They all stood and pleaded.

"Candy-O, I need you so"

Beverly and her teammates surrounded the car as Annie turned on her back and slowly into the pose from the album cover. The team fell away, and there she was:

Candy-O!
Her right hand is on her forehead with eyes closed,
flowing locks of red hair spread around the fender,
her stomach flat against the sleeping engine,
supporting her chest proudly pointing towards the sky,
red fingernails from her left hand ready to scratch the headlight,
dug in at the edge of the hood her right stiletto heel sprouts a knee,
muscular left thigh folded across her pelvis,
as her left toe feels for the road below.

Now the whole gym continued the chant.

"Candy-O, I need you so."

And after the spotlight went black and the music stopped.

"Candy-O, I need you so..."

Quickly, Annie and her teammates gathered in the dark to a corner of the gym and put on their volleyball uniform covers and stood fourteen strong.

"Candy-O, I need you so..."

The gym lights came back on as the prop of the car was being removed. Coach and acting athletic director Janet Melendez took the microphone and tried to give her speech about supporting the Fall sports at WJ, but it was hopeless.

"*Candy-O, I need you so…*"

The odor of teen sexuality was sweating through the gym.

Annie, the WJ Icon was born!

~15~

Seeing Abbey was like planning a trip to Florida, Russell believed. Even with a non-stop flight, unchecked luggage, and a no-line rent-a-car pick-up, there was uncertainty to be prepared for, like getting sunburned. Russell knew every moment of a potential evening together was like applying suntan lotion to the back of his neck—don't forget a vulnerable spot even if you cannot see it.

Laura Santucci often described Abbey as flakey, which usually means someone that leaves things in their life unattended and falling apart. Russell thought she was the opposite. Abbey always found herself intertwined with solving too many problems, but not for the lack of energy or effort. She was always having trouble with something (add *her* to each of the following): job, car, money, roommate, family, food, exercise, clothes, or cat. Otherwise, she was (add *very*) smart, conversational, current, fashionable, caring, affectionate, athletic, active, and sexy.

Russell always was surprised by the first hour of their interaction. Their initial hug was great and always lasted at least thirty seconds, ending with a long kiss, and sometimes a grind that would get his member going. If he could control himself, they would have a conversation next. She would listen well, seemingly using her beautiful blue eyes to feel the intent of his words. If a movie theatre was the next immediate activity, Russell would be in love by the end—after the cuddling and heavy petting for two hours. If one of their places was available within a ten-minute car ride, a beautiful and quick love making would follow. The best nights after love making would proceed wonderfully with a delivery of sushi and orange chicken, quickly, to accompany them sitting to watch an hour or two of television at ten p.m. usually about King William and Queen Kate and then old episodes of *The Crown* possibly. With Abbey usually asleep by the end, Russell would carry her to bed and tuck her in. He would seal it with a kiss; and of course, leave a thoughtfully written goodbye note before he drove home to wake up early for work the next morning. This would end an evening perfect for both.

Russell realized the "greatest hits" package with Abbey would be ideal, as an every-other-week-activity to keep the Plan viable. After several conversations on the phone with Abbey, they agreed on a date schedule starting after Independence Day. The schedule and the tightly arranged activities were overwhelmingly successful through early November. These wonderful nights—eight to be exact—boosted the good feelings about their relationship for the first four months. With sex almost a certainty every other week, Russell felt like he got his rhythm and groove back, which helped him replace his masturbation fantasies about Annie.

Abbey liked to be on the bottom and for Russell to be in charge. She rarely had an orgasm, but loved when he kissed her nipples to erection, fondled her breasts flawlessly, kissed her neck and face endlessly and her lips passionately. The affection Russell gave her all night made her feel wanted.

The last two dates ended up in Russell's suite. After sex, as they waited for the food delivery together at the Steinway, Russell felt inspired and thrusted into a Beethoven concerto, that sent a chill down her spine and inside her vagina. She held him tight, feeling on the edge of paradise waiting for him to finish the job. Finally, the delivery man came and interrupted his performance. Abbey grabbed the order at the door and downed a few pieces of sushi for energy. She then grabbed Russell before he could hit the orange chicken and guided him to the couch with him awkwardly on the bottom. She grinded him hard with her pelvis, while her breasts flailed over his face. In minutes, she orgasmed as he reached hardness. She dug her face in his to keep her screams of joy from echoing down the fourth-floor hallway. As she seemed to finally pause, Russell flipped positions with her and rammed his new hardness into her. She was in a new territory of heaven and held on for the ride.

Russell reached his peak in minutes, rolled off Abbey, closed his robe, and immediately sought out the orange chicken. The delaying of dinner and television watching seemed to be a nice detour to the evening. They both agreed it was worth trying to replicate in two weeks, as they started November riding sky high with good feelings.

Their communication during the next two weeks was merely texting and a weekly Friday night talk on the phone. Russell's idea was to keep the Plan working with limited interaction. He tolerated the phone calls because it usually made the every-other-week Saturday night date flow better.

Abbey used most of the time to vent. At times she was obsessive-compulsive about certain things, but just not very good at it. It led to many unnecessary complications in her life. Russell was showing unusual patience with the phone calls, and Abbey appreciated the effort. The Plan was working well.

But then, three events in November helped bring the feelings about their relationship down into critical condition and maybe even into relationship intensive care. When the month was over, Russell had his work cut out for him to stabilize their relationship and decide whether to strengthen it again – or maybe just pull the plug on the Plan.

~16~

The final game of the volleyball regular season was on November 15, just a week before Thanksgiving and two days before a nine-day break from school. Coach Melendez had slowly brought her young team to the brink of another county championship. They had started the season with two losses for the first time in her coaching career. The mistakes were so plentiful in those games that she stopped keeping track. Finally, in the second match, they managed a late rally to win the third game, mainly because she begged Annie Finelli to break out her jump serve, trailing 23–13 and down 2–0 in the match. She hit six winners and managed twelve straight points. The team impressively put together some offense from the free balls the opponents barely managed to return off her service. The team played well in the fourth game, but fell short 25–22, making Coach Melendez happy with the progress.

Annie played solidly in those matches, rarely making a mistake. Coach Melendez realized that she could not substitute for her when she rotated to the front row. She was becoming too valuable, and the rest of the team knew it. She agreed to rotate through the front line, and only hit from the left side, helping her to stay away from the net play when she was slamming. The problem was that Annie did not like blocking at the net. Janet assured her that Beverly Broomfield and Serena Saurez would slide over to block all left side hits. Coach would substitute Whitney Warfield and Taylor Summers as Annie rotated to the right for smaller, non-blocking Karen and Corrine. They managed to win four matches in a row with this strategy.

The Magruder High School coach had scouted them during this winning streak and noticed a window of opportunity during these rotations. The subs were not as athletic as Beverly and Serena, and without Annie blocking, it was hard to stop good slamming. Magruder won the first two games of the match easily. But before the third game, Annie decided to take on her fears of the net and to start blocking. She told the coach, "I need to play my position if I am going to rotate through the front line, Coach, nothing else makes sense. Call a timeout if I hit the net or fall into it. This is unlikely, but I will need a minute to recover if I do."

Coach Melendez realized the strength it took for Annie to expose herself to everyone about her fears and then decide to play through those fears for the team. They knew she was different, but a special different, with a mountain of talent. The *Candy-O* experience had made the team come together like no other unit they had been on before, and Annie was the reason. She had become their leader without leading, but by producing. By performing as *Candy-O*, Annie went outside of herself to make the team unique and exciting, and now she would defend through the front line because it was best for the team. She was quietly becoming their leader and the best player in the county. It was now time for the team to play their individual roles without questions and give total effort.

In game three, Annie started serving with two winners and five more great serves for a 7–0 lead. In the next rotation, Karen Jennings set her three times behind the 10-foot line, and she slammed three winners. Beverly Broomfield warmed up from left front with four slams. Magruder called timeout down 14–1. The Magruder Coach looked at his shocked team and assured them that their game plan was still solid. "Let's get her to the front line and win this thing."

They haven't seen nothing yet, Coach Melendez confidently thought. After two rotations, Beverly, Serena, and Annie were on the front line. Karen and Maria Tallchief were returning everything defensively, passing to Corrine Jefferson to set her front line. In one hellacious exchange, Beverly and Serena were blocked by Magruder's front line of monsters. Maria even sent two slams over from the back line, but they were both blocked. Somehow, Annie kept those balls alive and saved them to Karen, who sent them over deep in Magruder's court. Finally, after receiving the last save of a slam from Karen, Corrine sent a beautiful set to Annie on the far left. Time was aplenty for a Magruder's triple block to become a great wall. Annie worked her approach, remembering in detail how she broke the six-foot mark in high jumping last spring. She felt that same easy spring in her knees as she rose and floated, almost three feet above the net, and uncoiled on the ball with a new intensity that seeped out from her soul. Her mind was not in charge for this moment; just an emotion of pure will, as she slammed the ball over the three pairs of hands below her and on to the wood floor.

Karen kept up the serve and Corrine kept feeding Annie. She slammed three more to get to 20–3, causing a Magruder timeout and a very quiet home gym. A slight volume of whispers started up in the stands that seemed to be looking for words describing the performance. The coach spoke about adjusting their blocks, one player answered, "Coach, I just can't get that high!"

Karen served out the game to win 25–3. The fourth game was another offensive explosion by the potent WJ front line for a 25–5 win. Finally, in the fifth game, Magruder found their defense and kept Annie in the back row for a commanding 8–3 lead, needing only fifteen points for a win, Magruder tried to exchange points, but Annie would not have it. After a timeout, Coach Melendez had her patrol the net like a hawk and block every slam, while Beverly took over the left side slamming. Quickly, they landed back in front with ten straight points and a 13–8 lead. Annie rotated to server and went to an underhand knuckler that landed just over the net untouched. Then, she quickly served an overhand knuckler without jumping, which was returned as a free ball. Beverly got under it and set Annie from the back row. She sky-ed without effort and landed a cut fastball slam on the backline. And the match was done.

Annie accepted hugs from her teammates and crossed under the net for handshakes with her opponents, but she was a mess. After the match, it took a long conversation with Coach Melendez to talk her down.

"Annie, you were fantastic out there!"

"The net seemed inside of me and all of over me. It was hard to see the ball. I caused many fouls for myself and teammates."

"No Annie, that didn't happen. It was just uncomfortable for you, but you showed great courage to work through it for the team. You were very brave out there."

Annie could relate to braveness and courage, it was a Finelli trait, but the term made her uncomfortable, "I do not think my playing rose to bravery, this is just a game Coach." She paused for a moment as Janet stayed quiet. "I will need to practice and see the ball better, I missed so many."

Janet knew that was not true but decided to agree with her, "Practice is always a good idea. What you're trying to do is very hard for somebody five-feet, six-inches."

Annie looked up and gave a green-eyed stare to Coach Melendez, "I am almost five-eight with my shoes on, Coach."

Practice became fierce for the next month as Annie learned to change the image of the net in her mind from an adversary to a trusted protector. She had rarely thought about the players on the other side of the net. Other than the usual handshaking ritual with opponents before and after each game—which she thought was meaningless and not a proper way to meet people. Annie decided to only worry about her teammates on her side of the court.

Volleyball was a unique team sport, she analyzed back in the spring; it was the only team sport, other than doubles in tennis and badminton—to keep the only physical interaction of the two teams above or at the net. And that was only with the ball or the net always between them.

Slowly, she trained her mind to see the net as a protective barrier to keep the opponents of giant girls from causing interruption in her performance on the front line. This would help her focus on improving her slamming, which she had broken down into four parts: the approach, the leap, the spike, and the landing. Her spike contact with the ball was already exceptional because of her improved jump serve at ninety-five percent efficiency. She could slam from behind the ten-foot line with great contact and force to place it deep in the opponent's court. Annie had learned the physics to make exact contact with the volleyball, like some of her perfect skills with the basketball: Spinning it on her fingers, circling it around her body, dribbling behind her back, between her legs, and catching it behind her to name a few.

Now, she had to incorporate the power of her body into her hit. Watching her undersized cousins slam the ball with great power, she realized how much torque it took with their backs to increase velocity of the volleyball and create a downward spin as it came over the net. This technique made it almost impossible to block.

The advantage that Annie possessed over any girl that played in the state, was her jumping ability. Most coaches in the league had never seen her play and certainly not on the front line, where she was showing a combination of skills rare in an athlete. Even if they had scouted WJ, Annie had just started to dominate games, and she was just starting to develop her torque while adding high altitude. Winning the county long jump and high jump as a sophomore was not covered anywhere in the DC media, only in the track subculture. Coach Melendez was the only county volleyball coach to have coached both sports. She enjoyed the post-game chats with the losing coaches, especially the men, being dazzled and confused by the talent of Annie Finelli. Once they realized who her father was, they would usually answer with, "I see."

It was an amazing thing that the student population was just awakening to the phenomena of Annie Finelli as an athlete. Becoming *Candy-O* started the buzz, now with eleven wins in a row, a star was known throughout the school.

The school newspaper, *The Station*, was finally on the story. The staff was trying to be hipper by changing the name last year, getting away from the baseball theme with *The Pitch*. With "The Big Train" as the school mascot, they thought more students would relate to *The Station* as the place to be. They knew most of the students did not know about Walter Johnson being the greatest pitcher in baseball history and thought it was good to keep them in the dark. Annie tried her hardest to understand what they were trying to do, but thought it was a mistake and disrespectful of seventy years of publishing. Besides, she thought *The Pitch* name was clever.

She never got angry at things; she would proceed with a guarded reaction to the stimulus that her brain processed, sometimes it would pass down her brain stem and into her soul, but this was usually about positive things like seeing Russell at her party. Negative stimulus would get re-routed through her incredible memory many times for an answer. Sometimes, backing away was her response. Occasionally, a thought or a stimulus would reoccur. She assumed this to be a feeling. This happened in this newspaper case, so she took further action and refused to be interviewed by a student reporter after winning the track titles as a sophomore, until they changed the name back. Then, she thought her family should be involved. She insisted that her father and Uncle Alex stop donations to the school last year. Now, shut out of a *Candy-O* interview and a possible volleyball title interview, she was certain *The Station* would change back to *The Pitch* after they won the county championship.

In the last week of practice, she started to really show off her jumping ability as she streamlined her approach to becoming "The Slammer." It was a nickname she received from Beverly Broomfield, herself quite a slammer, for her dominance since the Magruder match. In that game, she used her sky jump, as she called it, only a couple of times, with an unrefined approach. Annie spent hours and hours developing her approach to the long jump and high jump in track, finally getting the exact number of steps and speed together. It was the high jump approach that helped her the most for her volleyball slamming approach. After a month of practice, she had perfected it and pulled it out before the last match for the county championship. None of the practice watchers, now in the hundreds, had seen her jump in the Magruder match or since, because in the last six wins, they won without her heroics. Everybody, especially Beverly Broomfield and Serena Saurez, were playing like stars. The flow and the positioning on the team was exceptional. Annie did her part, but nothing flashier because the matches were not close.

When it first happened in practice, silence overcame the room. Annie herself had to retrieve the volleyball slammed into the floor, like a race car passing the checkered flag. The boy team managers, now numbering a dozen, stood like statues trying to comprehend her ability. On blocks, during the practice, against Beverly, Maria, and Serena, she would effortlessly reach the exact apex needed and hang in the air like a helicopter. She felt like a well-oiled machine now on the front line and at the net. The word was quickly in the Cloud about her jumping ability. Tickets to the final match were not going to be easy to obtain.

~17~

Annie decided to speak up. Her story telling skills were improving and she had one that was weighing heavily on her mind because winning the championship would mean so much to her and the group of girls on the team. She knew the current eleven-game winning streak would mean nothing once they took the floor against Whitman. They were 11–2 as well. Most kids her age never planned for adversity, but she knew they were facing it. Their high expectations from the streak might end up costing them the championship.

Annie sat in front of her locker, sweating from the practice. She had a towel with an ice pack on her forehead trying to cool down. Next to her were two more towels, one wet but not dripping and the other very warm and dry. She lifted her head, sat up, and put the ice pack down. She stood up and turned to her teammates and started to talk forcefully while they were not attentive, "My Grandpa is a really good story-teller about things in his life and our family, and I really like to listen to him. This story, I think, might help us out tomorrow."

By the end of those words, all thirteen of her teammates had gathered around her as she stood at her locker. Karen Jennings and Corrine Jefferson were sitting the closest. They loved Annie and were always within shouting distance of her. As Annie sensed she had her teammates attention, she took off her sweaty practice jersey. "This story taught me a lot about expectations, because it was a day that meant so much to the whole Washington DC area on January 14, 1973."

Coach Melendez noticed the inactivity and the quietness in the locker room and came out of her office. She could hear a calm voice speaking strongly and recognized it as Annie. She stood in the next row of lockers and stayed quiet.

"It was called Super Sunday, because Washington was in their first Super Bowl against the undefeated Miami Dolphins that started at three p.m., and Maryland, ranked second in the country in college basketball was having a showdown with undefeated and third ranked NC State at ten a.m."

Annie removed the rest of her garments and stood naked in front of her teammates. Most noticed the beauty of her body, but everyone appreciated her willingness to be uncovered and vulnerable in front of them. It was a giant sign of trust.

She picked up the wet towel and washed herself from her toes to her ears. After, she held the towel hanging over her breasts and pelvis. Some of her teammates felt their hearts racing at the significance of the moment and the loveliness of her body. Others were turned on sexually and tried not to giggle. Karen hugged Corrine as she tried to control herself.

Annie continued without a beat, "My Grandpa was nineteen and went to the Maryland game at the iconic Cole Field House, thinking this would be the greatest day in his life, watching his two favorite teams in the world defeat two undefeated teams and win a Super Bowl Championship for DC." She dropped her wet towel, grabbed the other one, and dried off her C-sized breasts, between her legs, and around her back. This was a routine Annie did after every game and practice because she never took a shower at school, which was normal for a lot of girls in high school. This dry shower routine was quite efficient and well-organized, but a bit eccentric. Usually, nobody noticed because they were yelling or having fun in the showers. "At ten a.m. on a Sunday morning, he stood with the other fifteen-thousand fans to watch the tip-off. He had never seen in person, the NC State superstar named David Thompson, a six-foot, four-inch guard, who could jump like a *serval cat* that captured its prey with a ten-foot high leaping ability." She smiled at her added information and color imagery to the story. "Legend was that he could take a nickel off the top of the backboard." Karen and Corrine felt some relief at being able to giggle.

Annie turned to the locker and showed her tightly impressive buttocks and her well-defined hamstring muscles, which most of them had never noticed. She stepped into her panties first, shimmied her ass as she pulled them up, then slipped her bra on without help and grabbed her blouse as she turned back to her audience. "My Grandpa stopped whistling when he noticed that State's seven foot, four-inch center Tommy Burleson was not in the jump circle. *Holy Shit*, he thought, *that's David Thompson jumping against Maryland's six-foot, eleven-inch, All-American Tom McMillen!*" They all laughed now enthralled with her storytelling. "Apparently, it was no contest, Thompson with ease seemed to stop in midair and flip the ball back to his little five-foot, four-inch, point guard Monte Towe for a fast break layup."

Annie buttoned her blouse slowly, leaving the top three open showing some sexy cleavage from her recently purchased push-up bra. Finally, she stepped into her skirt and backed her butt into Karen Jennings to zip up her skirt, who happily complied and added an affectionate pat with a smile. Annie responded with a quiet, "Thank you, Karen." She lifted her eyes back to the group and continued her storytelling, "The game was spectacular and very close, fast breaks back and forth with lots of scoring, and lead changes. As the game clock ran down to under thirty seconds, Maryland's Tom McMillen made a corner jumper to tie the game 85–85 with seconds to go. State called time out." Annie put on her shoes, grabbed her bookbag, and bent over to fluff out her hair. She had the group intrigued and in tight, "Monte Towe had fouled out and David Thompson, who had scored thrty-five points was doubled-teamed at the top of the circle. They had to throw it in to the tall Tommy Burleson standing twenty-five feet from the basket. Everyone was screaming around my Grandpa, as the clock counted under five seconds left. Burleson panicked and fired up an unusually long shot for himself and it hit the back of the rim. The crowd exploded expecting overtime, but my Grandpa could see David Thompson outside the top of the key, now unguarded, staring down his prey, like that *serval cat*." Annie was happy to return to her added imagery. "He took off, darting towards his target and lifted off just before the free throw line to fly high above the mortal players below. With his right hand, he snagged the basketball surging skyward as the clock showed a tick left." She paused, took a breath, and leaned over with her hands on her hips and asked, "Do you know what happened next?" Annie stood up and held her right hand up high like she had the basketball and waited for some guesses.

"He slammed it… no, he missed it… but he got fouled… he dunked it." Her teammates answered.

Annie waited for quiet and finally said, "Nope. He could not dunk it or slam it, because it was illegal in college basketball at the time."

"No, that's impossible… No dunking in basketball, that's insane… Well, what happened, Annie?" the teammates yearned for clarity.

"My Grandpa said it was outlawed because of Lew Alcindor in the 1960s."

"Who?" Several teammates asked meekishly.

"After he turned Muslim, he changed his named to Kareem Abdul Jabbar!" Annie clarified with a grin on her face, enjoying the attention of the group.

"Oh, yeah…we heard of him… Why didn't you say so?...Yes, a Muslim like Muhammad Ali!" The crowd responded but implored for the answer. "What happened Annie?"

"My Grandpa had never seen it before or since, David Thompson stopped in midair, put the ball in both hands, and dropped it in the basket, like a quarter into a collection plate, without touching the rim."

"Oh, my god they lost… That's horrible Annie… Well, what happened in the Super Bowl… they won, right?" The teammates got closer to Annie with curiosity.

"Hold on, listen… Cole Field House just buzzed with disappointment, as State celebrated. The fans all knew they had seen something special, but they were bummed, and it was noon on Sunday and no bars were open." Annie continued.

"Very funny… could they drink at nineteen?... No, that's illegal!" Giggles emanated from Karen and Corrine.

"Actually, at that time it was not in Maryland or DC. But everyone was too bummed to party. Besides, they had Super Bowl parties to go to." Annie added some hope.

"Not a bad consolation… yes, a double header party day…that is sweet!" the crowd agreed.

"You know what happened to NC State that year?" Annie tested her teammates with another question.

"They went undefeated…won the NCAA…didn't make the tournament." The front line of Serena, Beverly and Maria answered.

"Very good, but only two out of three of you are right!"

Serena and Beverly high-fived with their "undefeated" and "won the NCAA" guesses, and jointly laughed at Maria's "didn't make the tournament" guess.

"Sorry, Beverly, but Serena and Maria are right." Annie clarified the winners.

"That's right Beverly, we got you!" Maria coming back with a victory, playfully joined up with Serena to harass Beverly.

Beverly protested, "How did they go undefeated and not win the tournament?"

"They were ineligible because of NCAA probation in recruiting of David Thompson. He was bigger than Michael Jordan at the time. Anyway, they won the NCAA tournament championship the next season."

"Wow, that's some crazy shit Annie!" Beverly complained with a smile.

"You can never be certain about anything Beverly." Annie smiled and continued, "so my Grandpa went to a big party at his brother's house and by three p.m. everybody was buzzed enough to forget about the morning and expected a win by Washington."

"Oh good… was there beer?...yea, pizza too… how big was their TV?" the teammates were in on the party scene.

"I think beer, hot dogs, hamburgers, that kind of thing. The TV was like twenty-four inches or something and no cable, internet, cell phones."

"That's silly Annie… now we know you're making this up!" Her backcourt mates Karen and Corrine giggled again while protesting.

"It is all true...," Annie smiled with her green eyes shimmering at her biggest admirers. "Anyway, the game starts in Los Angeles with Washington favored to win after crushing the defending champion Dallas Cowboys in the NFC title game 26–3. But they proceeded to play their worst game of the year, by missing two short field goals and two sure touchdowns; one that hits the crossbar on the goal post, and another when the Charley Taylor, my Grandpa's favorite player of all time, slips on the Coliseum loose turf and cannot hold on to the football. It was a nightmare all day for DC fans. And It should have been a runaway for Miami, but Washington was only losing by 14–0 with less than three minutes in the game after Washington's defense intercepted a pass in the end zone."

"Wait Annie, how does a football hit the crossbar on a sure TD." Beverly asked.

"Good question Beverly." Annie was so happy to see Beverly engaged with the story. "Apparently, they would place the goalposts on the goal-line, hence the name." Annie added with gusto.

"What?...wouldn't someone run into them…or throw the ball into it?...whoops I get it now." The teammates laughed in unison.

"Yes, they moved them to the back of the end zone a year later." Annie was having fun at the banter and her ability to handle the interruptions. "So… Washington is down two touchdowns and Miami is driving again, running the ball and using the clock; but Washington finally stops them with two minutes to go. Miami lines up for a short field goal attempt to ice the game, everybody on the Miami bench is celebrating, their fans are yelling 17–0 for an undefeated season and the final score of the game. The announcers are about to crown them champs, but amazingly Washington blocks the Field Goal try."

"No way… Miami sucks… yes but they're down two TD's… what happened, Annie?" the front-line was closing in on her.

"The kicker was from Cyprus, Garo Yepremian, a soccer player who was not very good with his hands. He picks up the football and starts running away from these giant men with burgundy helmets and decides to get rid of the football because he might get killed. So, he attempts to throw a pass."

"That's crazy… What for… Why would he do that?" Whitney, Taylor and the other bench players inched up closer to Annie.

"And worse, it slips off his hand and is just about to fall to the ground, but he bats it up in the air and a Washington player, Mike Bass grabs it and runs seventy yards for a Touchdown!"

"Holy Shit… That's impossible… This can't be true… There's one TD… I knew they'd come back!" The teammates erupted with excitement.

Annie waits patiently for her teammates to calm down a bit, "Anyway, Washington gets the ball back and the offense tries to move it quickly downfield. Miami fans are peeing in their pants." Annie was enjoying enhancing the story.

"Did your Grandpa say that… that's funny… come on finish the story I gotta pee too!" the front line shouted.

"Billy Kilmer the Quarterback is looking downfield for Charley Taylor, who is wide open, a second too long and gets sacked. And Washington finally loses 14–7." Her teammates collectively let out a big sigh and end up closer to Annie. With her eyes glistening, Annie relates, "My Grandpa said it was his worst sports day ever!"

Her teammates circle her with hugs and giggles; at first it feels good, but Annie panics a little bit and ducks out and starts to walk away, but her teammates call her to come back.

She stops and turns with tears in her eyes and pleads uncharacteristically, "I do not want Thursday night to be the worst sports day ever!" Annie drops her head and lets her teammates surround her with support.

Coach Melendez was around the corner shedding tears of joy in private when she heard Annie's teammates answer as a unit, "No way Annie that's not going to happen. We'll be ready, Annie!"

Annie gave the thumbs up sign and walked away.

It was midnight, and Karen Jennings could not sleep. All she could think of was Annie's nakedness while telling her story. She started to touch herself for some comfort and found wetness already. After a couple of minutes of probing, all she could imagine was Annie close to her. She was well on her way to total pleasure when her phone buzzed; it was Corrine.

"Are you sleeping?"

"I'm too horny Corrine, she's all I can think about!"

"Me too Karen… Tell me what you're thinking!"

"I can see her breasts, they're so perfect. She's cleaning herself. It's just me and her. Now I have her towel, and I'm drying her back and then I drop the towel… Now have my hands on her ass, and I get closer and reach around to feel her breasts."

"That's intense Karen… keep going… keep going," she says softly.

"I come around her front and lick her nipples, they're so strong. Oh my god, Corrine. I can't talk anymore…" Her breathing rushed hard for the next minute, finally reaching her nirvana. She took some time to catch her breath and finally spoke. "I'm still pulsating, Corrine…thanks for listening."

Corrine was feeling herself ready to explode, "Anytime Karen… I'm gonna go."

"Oh my god… I think I'm going to come again… bye Corrine."

~18~

For the first time, Russell was ecstatic to drive his Grandmother somewhere. He was dying to see Annie and watching her from the bleachers at the volleyball championship game would be perfect. He was there way early to pick up his Grandmother because he wanted a good seat, right behind their bench if possible and see her warm-up. He had contacts at WJ, to get in early with his Grandmother, though being Alex Santucci's mother, it was not hard to convince the athletic director.

After they were settled in the bleachers, he worked hard to hide his intrigue from Laura about Annie. They watched parents hovering around the players stretching, but Annie could not be found. She was in a spot under the opposite bleaches doing her stretching on a yoga mat away from the growing crowd. Laura slowly started with some questions to find out Russell's interest. "Now my dear, isn't it nice to get here early and get good seats?"

"Yes, Grandmother, I'm trying to get more responsible in my old age. I teach at a school now you know, so I have to be on time."

"Luckily you don't have to drive to work, my dear. I'm sure that helps."

"That definitely helps. But getting up early in the morning, exercising, less drinking also, helps me see the big picture of responsibility better." Russell tried to emphasize his maturity.

"You seem happier, Russell, and maybe there is someone special in your life."

"Abbey and I have been spending some special time together. I think she might be somebody that I could…"

"Sorry to interrupt my dear, but we have talked about her before, and at length I believe!"

"It's hard to slip anything past you, Grandmother."

"I was referring to someone else and maybe that was incentive for you to come early today?"

He refused to answer and changed the subject by pointing to the banners, hanging from the ceiling in the gym of the county baseball titles in 1993 and 1994. "I have never seen Alex's baseball banners, Grandmother. Wow that is something, isn't it? How sad it was that my Grandfather didn't get to see those banners." Russell looked towards his Grandmother who was misting up at the thought of losing her husband so quickly, some thirty-eight years ago. He was happy about the diversion working, but not about the sadness it caused. Purposely, he changed the subject. "Hey, there is the county and state football title that Guy Finelli won in 2011. Those are really cool banners, especially the state one!"

"Those boys were something extraordinary, this school should be really proud of them… and I hope Annie can bring some attention to them, if they win today." Laura had recovered nicely from being misty eyed and let her grandson know she was on to him. "I'm sure you'll be happy to see Annie perform. I think you are quite a fan of hers. She is something special, my dear boy."

Despite his attempts, she had brought the subject back, and all he could do was plead his case. "Grandmother, she is only fifteen-and-a-half years old, but yes, I am fond of her, so I'm glad you approve, but you know my interest can only be for the long-term, like almost three years from now. I have a Plan that needs to be kept on the down-low, like a CIA operation without leakage to the press."

"I'm pretty good about keeping things on the down-low, I had a little period of love-making during Alex's championship season before he was traded to Washington in 2012. The gentleman was the owner of the Kansas City Crowns."

Russell was smiling to hide his shock at hearing the story; he was aware of the tragic airplane crash of the Kansas City owner, Mr. Garcon, just before the trading deadline, that led to the trade of Alex to DC. "What can I say, that must have been bittersweet. Does everybody know?"

"Not really. I never talked about it, except to Alex and Sally, but a lot of good came out of it for our family and, of course, the city."

"You are quite a trooper, Grandmother, I'm sad for you, but happy that you had that experience of love."

"That's well said, dear, you can always talk to me about your long-term Plan and thank you." She kissed him on the cheek, "Now where is that young lady we came to see?"

Annie was still on the mat, now meditating. She was in her own world.

Suddenly, Russell felt a light slap to his left ear and then a set of soft hands to his face and a kiss. He looked up and saw two couples. Alex, the slapper, moved passed him to hug his mother, followed by the kisser, Sally Keegan, then from nowhere Guy Finelli stepped up and shook hands with Russell, and introduced his parents Phillip and Carol, "Russell, I believe… right? These are my parents," he said, guiding them in front of Russell as he stepped to the side. "Mom, Russell is the pianist I was telling you about. He commandeered the Steinway from Uncle Anthony and has it at Prep with him. He would be perfect for Annie."

Phillip interrupted with his handshake to Russell, "Your Grandfather Gene would be very proud of you, a concert pianist, wow! You know, Gene, was always the life of the party. I hear you're quite the party animal, yourself."

"Oh Phillip, really," Carol interrupted her husband, "You have to forgive my husband. He likes to tell stories. You know writers like all the attention!" Russell smiled at the sweet-looking woman, who at sixty-four had her girlish looks and figure. Working out every day, she had retired from an executive position in the health IT world a couple of years ago, although she still served on a couple of boards, taught at Maryland two weeks out of the year, and gave presentations about once a month. She was still in high demand as an expert in her field. Otherwise, she loved to travel, mainly with her daughter, Grace, for weeks to Europe, and hang out in Cape Canaveral quite a bit from October to April with her husband and sometimes the grandchildren. "It is so nice to meet you. Annie and her cousins seemed to dominate you at the party, and I entirely missed you at Anthony's party a couple of years ago."

Russell was certainly not happy about hearing the subject of the party fiasco again. He was praying she would drop the subject. "Annie talked a lot about you after her party. You made a real impression. She told me you would be quite a catch for those stylish Georgetown women in DC." Carol paused for a moment and took in Russell's soft looks and handsome hair, "You know, Russell, she rarely talks about anybody. I think she remembers you from the Anthony party in 2028 more than her birthday party…"

"Carol, please, do you think Russell cares about that?" Phillip interjected, rescuing Russell from a terrifying subject again.

Russell was horrified at the overwhelming attention by the Finelli crew. Did they know about his Plan? He wondered as he jumped in the conversation, "That is perfectly fine Mr. Finelli. My Grandmother has talked a lot about you." Hoping to redirect this conversation barrage away from the subject of Annie and the past parties.

"Please, it's Phillip, I'm seventy-six and feeling old already," Russell was relieved with being able to laugh and release some nervousness. Then, another direct hit, "You know, after the volleyball season, Annie would like to start piano lessons, on the Steinway of course. She says you would be perfect!"

Russell was relieved that part two of his Plan might have a chance to come together, but he still did not want to sound too interested. "Well… maybe we could work something out. Do you have a piano at Parkwood? Sorry, but you know at Prep, they might have a problem with Annie being in my suite. I would have…"

"I'm afraid that Annie has her mind set on lessons with the Steinway, Russell. There's no way around that. Unless you want me to get my son to move it over to his house?" More laughter from Phillip infected the conversation. "Now that would be funny dear…" he said, turning to Carol with his laughter.

"My husband is a real comedian, Russell. I agree though, Annie is very headstrong. We could easily get Sally to call the headmaster at Prep and…"

"No, no… don't worry about calling, really Mrs. Finelli. I'm sure I can work it out… maybe we can start after Thanksgiving?" A quick recovery by Russell to avoid the disaster of the Prep Headmaster being alerted about a fifteen-year-old girl being in his suite. He could handle it on a level lower than the headmaster to get permission, he hoped.

"Oh, my goodness, your manners have been well taught, Russell, but it's Carol… only sixty-four here, and that sounds lovely. Thank you for taking care of this. It is very important to Annie. We can text each other the details." She moved on after a quick hug.

"Yes, of course," he said as he watched them both take seats, on the other side of Alex, Sally, and Laura. He took off his jacket, sweating from the pressure of the conversation, and wondered if he would survive the current onslaught by Annie's elders.

"She seems ready." The giant Guy Finelli appeared again sitting next to Russell after climbing up the three rows of bleachers with one long hurdle. He stretched across him to complete his thought to Sally Keegan, just to the right of Laura. "I talked to her a minute, she didn't say anything or look at me.

She's totally zoned out." Guy sat back, turned to Russell, "This will be fun, hanging with you!" Russell nodded and wiped his brow full of sweat. He was stuck in the middle for the moment, and heat of the gym was totally upon him.

"I hope she's okay, Guy. Did she have her eyes down the whole time?" Sally leaned across Laura and laid herself on Russell, who could smell her gorgeous black hair and feel her chest across his forearm. He had fantasized about her since the slow dance at Anthony's party; *it's unavoidable considering she's a certified beauty*, he figured.

"No, she was looking at her teammates, assessing their readiness I'm guessing."

"Okay, that's much better than the stare-down; Russell, this is going to be intense! I'm so glad you're here." Sally squeezed his leg and winked at him as she pulled back. The attention caused an unexpected stirring in his pants.

After a couple seconds, Guy leaned back across Russell again to reach Sally and whispered. "To be honest Sally, I feel sorry for the Whitman volleyball team!"

~19~

The crowd was watching every move of the warm-up drills by both teams. For the first time, all season, there was media watching. In 2029, that could mean anybody, but usually it meant individuals that wanted to see an event and felt an imperative to write a story about it. That story might go to a publication, now staffed with just editors and opinion writers, which sometimes were the same people. Actual reporting of most sporting events was done by independent contractors; sometimes real reporters with sources from real grass root connections—the people or anybody that wrote for a blog. This way, publishers could avoid the deadly costs of employing the writing talent. Reporting fake news from other websites was out for traditional publications. They tapped the revolution of college-age kids, discovering news in most urban areas, from a large base of university talent. It was the *in* thing to do—the watching of events. Like Uber or Lyft in the taxi industry, independent reporting kept the costs down. It helped in the sporting world that almost every event was filmed and sent to the Cloud immediately. Editors could check the Cloud if necessary, to verify the outcome of the reporting. The score of the event was in the Cloud, but the story of the score came from the event before. This was the Era of Reporting Darwinism.

For this game, MCU (Montgomery County University) had two reporters at the game. Ironically, retired Hall-of-Fame reporter Ron Roswell was on the Whitman side watching his granddaughter play. He was well aware of the talent on the WJ side of the net. He had followed the brothers, Alex and Guy capture DC, and wrote about it, seizing numerous awards for himself and the

Washington Daily. Now seventy-nine, he still wrote once or twice a week for his self-published blog and could not be happier. Occasionally, the *Daily* picked up an article by him.

His granddaughter Rhonda Clarke was a senior, already signed to go to the volleyball powerhouse, Penn State. Her father was Jamaican and was a college basketball player at Georgia. She was six feet, four inches, and by far, in his opinion, the best player on the court. She let WJ beat her last year for the championship and was back for revenge. Ron had not witnessed the Annie Finelli phenomena in person but watched her on a highlight package against Magruder. She was impressive, but raw, and seemed a bit distant from her teammates. The program listed her at five feet, eight inches. In person, she seemed shorter, but on film, she could jump unlike any female he had ever seen. Confidently, he cheered Rhonda as she slammed a few during warm-ups, but he nervously eyed the Finelli girl leap with grace and slam with ease during warm-ups. *She was a Finelli*, he remembered, and in his experience, *that was not a good thing for the opponent*.

Coach Janet Melendez had been here before and won, she was not as concerned about the outcome as she was about Annie's mental health. This was quite a leap in six months to be so successful in a team sport after having never played a team sport. She decided to take her starters on the court and away from the stands to give them final instructions.

The bleachers included a mixed chorus of at least twenty guys and gals, each dressed in black leotard looking like Annie's, *Candy-O* character, repeating the cheer, "Candy-O, I need you so… Annie, Annie we need to know… lead us now and show us how… you're the finest gal around!" *It was silly*, Janet thought, but that was why she loved high school kids so much.

Beverly Broomfield and Serena Saurez had been here last year and won the title. They were the only veterans on the team. Karen and Corrine were feeling nauseous before the game, and their late-night phone escapade had cost them a good night's sleep. Maria and Whitney seemed unaware of the pressure on them, grooving to their Cloud music. They had played a lot of sports and seemed ready for what was coming. Annie Finelli was in another world; she participated in the hitting and serving drills but had not spoken to anyone since she arrived at school in the morning. No one knew what she was thinking.

Coach Melendez started to remind the team about their opening strategy. Annie would start serving with good defensive blocking as their first focus. If they could muster some offense by setting up Maria Tallchief that would be even better. She said a streak would come either early with Annie's service or with the Annie, Serena, and Beverly rotation up front. With those three hitting, they would be hard to stop. The team broke and took their places.

Annie stood still for a moment, curious about the crowd in the stands. It just dawned on her that the gym was packed and hearing the *Candy-O* crowd especially made her smile. As she continued to look past her coach, who was returning to the bench, she finally noticed the combined Finelli-Santucci group behind the WJ bench. Her green eyes connected with Russell, who was focused on her, and felt a chill that gave her a tingler. She was very pleased that Laura needed such a handsome driver.

Her dad and Sally were smiling and giving her the thumbs up. *My Grandmom looks worried, but my grandpa is probably saying something reassuring*, she thought. She looked up at the hanging banners and hoped to add to those descendants from her grandpa, but more importantly, she wanted this to be his best sports day ever.

She was ready to perform now. After all the emotions were recognized and processed, it was now clear in her head; she could remember every detail that would be needed to perform. It was showtime!

She slammed the ball with two hands between her legs, front to back, back to front, and repeating it for several steps as she crossed the service line. Then, she started a dribbling show with her posterior to the crowd; around her back, through her legs back and forth, on one knee and then on the other, finally flipping the ball to inside her elbow and rolling it up and down on each arm, then to each shoulder and settling it behind her head for a moment, popping it over her head and on to a finger, spinning the ball on three different fingers on each hand, and then spinning it through her legs and behind her back. Finally, she bounced the ball up fifteen feet or so as she settled her hair into perfect position and let the ball land into her left hand.

Some of the crowd were distracted by cheers or the pre-game handshakes, which Annie was avoiding, and did not witness the fabulous "Pistol Pete" show. Her family and Ron Roswell could not take their eyes off her. The referee blew the whistle, and Annie approached the first serve, rolling the ball around herself several times and flawlessly into the toss. She hit a non-jump, medium-fast serve with severe a drop. It hit the Whitman floor before the back-row defenders could step forward. Her teammates knew not to congratulate her and returned the ball to her in a jiffy. Her second serve, started with her back against the wall of the gym, then stepping forward, dribbling between her legs into a high toss and rising into a modified jump serve that nailed a back-corner line. On her third serve, she spun the ball on a finger, popped it over her head, and landed it on her horizontal back, rolled it to her neck, and over her bowed head to the floor in front of her, where she picked it up after one bonce, then took two steps into a little-higher jump-serve that was unreturnable. For the next four serves, she dribbled into a variety of serves at different speeds and locations for a 7–0 lead and a Whitman timeout.

Ron Roswell turned to his wife and asked, "Honey, did you see that?"

"Yes dear… Rhonda hasn't got a set yet, what are the other kids doing?"

"Looks like they're trying avoid the serve!" Ron lamented.

Janet gathered her team near the service line with Annie a few feet away holding the ball. "Okay, we got our first streak… let's be ready to play defense and set up our line when we get our best rotation up front. Remember to defend the net, first Maria alone, then Beverly and Maria together, then Serena and Beverly next. Then our next streak will come with Annie, Serena and Beverly up front." She looked at Karen and Corrine, who both looked a little lost and said, "You two… do your job and defend, then nothing fancy on your serve—get them in, please!" She sent them out of the huddle, and paused to look at Annie, who had the ball on her right hip, staring at her, emotionless, and then eased a small smile and winked at her, like saying, *I got this coach.*

Annie backed up, waited for the whistle, and ran up into a ferocious jump serve, at warp speed, but the missile somehow came softly off Rhonda's strong forearms and was a perfect pass to the server, who returned a set to her for Rhonda's first spike. It was Whitman's first point, and the game was on.

Karen and Corrine each missed a chance to pass correctly to Beverly to set Maria. Another was hit into the net. Finally, Annie took over the middle-back and passed properly to Beverly to set up Maria for a point. The two teams exchanged services, and Coach Melendez had her best front-line rotation and a 10–4 lead. Maria took over the setting from the back line with great passing from Karen and Corrine, who both appeared to be settling down. A streak of five slams in a row followed, and suddenly it was 15–4, causing another Whitman timeout.

Annie spoke her first words of the day as she finally joined in on the huddle, "Coach spoke the truth about the streaks, they will lead to beating Whitman." Everybody was quiet as a small smile emanated from Coach Melendez.

Beverly answered, "Let's keeping up the good passing. Karen and Corrine lead us to victory on defense. Let's nail down this game." Coach Melendez looked at Annie and her teammates and realized it was time to be quiet and put out her hand. Everyone including Annie put their hand on top as they broke with, "Let's go Big Train!"

WJ won the first game 25–10, and the second game 25–12. Both games were no contest. It was a team effort so far with Beverly Broomfield dominating the front line and limiting Rhonda Clarke on offense. The third game started with a big offensive effort by Rhonda Clarke, followed by a back and forth defensive effort by both teams. Whitman led 20–17 at a timeout. Annie stood outside the team circle as Coach Melendez pleaded with her team to improve their passing. "There are too many free balls happening. Our offense has shut down."

Annie was watching her opponents for the first time in the Whitman huddle. She did not usually like to focus on them, but she leaned in the huddle and spoke, "Coach, they look exhausted, it is really hot in here. I like it, but they tend to be accustomed to perfect air-conditioned conditions. It is almost winter, but it is unseasonably warm today compared to the normal temperature for this date."

"Annie what's your point?" Beverly stopped her.

"My point Beverly is..." Annie looked at her trying to understand her interruption, "let us change the tempo. We have been going to you a very high percentage. Instead, set me up in the back line on a few times and then go back to Beverly. Then when I get up front, I can set her instead of always hitting."

Beverly amused, "Annie, you don't like to set."

"That is true, Beverly, but that does not mean I am not good at it!"

Coach Melendez gave final instructions and put her hand in the middle, but Beverly and Annie were already on the court done with the huddle thing. The next service came over, Karen passed to the middle of the court, Serena faked a set, and Annie came flying behind the 10-foot line and slammed the volleyball into the Whitman floor side. Maria Talchief hit her best serve of the game, and it flew back over the net off a defender. Annie saw an opening and again leaped from behind the line, hit a medium pace slam, and it landed deep behind the Whitman players for another point. Maria hit another strong serve that was set up to Rhonda Clarke, but Beverly was a bit pissed, ran across the front line, and blocked it with one hand. They exchanged serves for the next four points with Annie now in the front line with Serena and Beverly and the score knotted at 22 each. Corrine decided to serve underhand nervously, and the ball barely made it over the net. Whitman players dove into each other and hit it out of bounds. At the normal high-five routine after each play, which Annie hated, she took Corrine by the shoulders, "Corrine, you have a great serve, hit it hard this time." Corrine giggled at the attention and followed orders.

Her serve was powerful and surprised Whitman. It returned as a free ball, which Karen passed beautifully to Annie, who set across to Beverly. It was like avoiding the posse, with three blockers stuck in front of Annie, Beverly slammed it home to make it 24–22.

Whitman took their final timeout as the crowd started to roar, followed by the mixed chorus screaming their cheer for *Candy-O* to come home. Everybody stood hoping to witness the county championship. The team stayed on the floor as Coach Melendez sat in her chair, dripping with perspiration, watching Annie ready to make some magic. The serve by Corrine was short left, it was quickly set in the middle to Rhonda Clarke. Annie and Beverly both got hands on the viscous slam, but it still spun back over the net. Falling backwards from the block, Annie popped it up with one fist for a perfect set to Beverly. She recovered nicely and started her approach to the slam that would win her second championship, but she stopped and somehow flew a set back across to Annie, who had sprung to her feet and instinctively leapt from a standing position, two feet over the net, and pounded it straight down over the net to the floor for her first championship win.

Annie hopped into Serena's arms, and they both fell into Beverly coming from the other side. She gladly caught them as the three of them playfully fell to the ground, followed by Maria, Karen, and Corrine jumping on top. Coach Melendez and the rest of the squad joined the scrum of happiness. Annie felt a spontaneity of feelings she had never experienced, as she laughed facing upwards with pounds of teammates celebrating on top of her. Joyously, she escaped out of the pile of fun and ran up the bleachers, diving into Sally's arms and then grabbing her father with Russell innocently in the middle and showered them with kisses. Unofficially, Russell and Annie had their first kiss. It looked accidental and innocent, but she was well-aware of bonding her lips with his for a long second or two.

~20~

Russell watched the celebration on the court as the two teams finally shook hands and congratulated each other. The bleachers had cleared out with most of the fans milling on the court around the players. He was waiting for a clear path to guide his Grandmother to the car and home. He was feeling a buzz, similar to several bong hits. Feeling her body so close to his and kissing her lips was something he had only fantasized about. Luckily, he had twenty-four hours to get ready to see Abbey. It would not be an easy adjustment.

Annie enjoyed for the first time mingling with the other team, she sought out Rhonda Clarke and was amazed at her height. *This is why I never focus on my opponents*, she thought. Rhonda was very sad, but smiled when Annie said, "I will follow your career at Penn State, you will win a championship much bigger than this one." Suddenly, Guy Finelli appeared with a friend, "Annie this is Rhonda's Grandfather, the great sportswriter, Ron Roswell." Ron hugged Rhonda and shook Annie's hand. "Very nice to watch you play Annie, like your dad, you are something special, best of luck!"

Annie was speechless, all she could say was, "Thank you… thank you." She wanted to say, *I know all about you.*

Russell had escaped to the car with Laura and hoped it would be an uneventful ride. But Laura could not stop talking about Annie, "That girl was amazing. Do girls really jump like that Russell, and how did she learn all that dribbling and spinning the ball on her fingers like that? She should play basketball."

"It was fun to watch, Grandmother, thanks for asking me. We're on for Thanksgiving, right?"

"Of course, my dear…you're bringing that girlfriend of yours, Abbey, right?"

Russell was happy the conversation was not about Annie, "Yes, I believe she's looking forward to it. I hope the family goes easy on her."

"That's usually not the problem, if I remember correctly, I think she likes the spotlight. She's a bit of a drama queen…don't you agree my dear?"

"She's improved, Grandmother…not as much drama lately."

"Well, try not to be late, surely that's who you learned it from. Anyway, my dear grandson, it should be fun. And I hope nobody brings up kissing Annie after the volleyball game!" she kissed him and left the car quickly, laughing the whole time. Russell suddenly was horrified.

That night he received two phone calls that would make the weekend more palatable. Abbey called sounding distracted at work. She informed Russell that she would have to cancel their date Friday night, *though she had been looking forward to it*, because the group at her part-time job (sending personal Cloud notices to the elderly about purchasing driverless car time), demanded that she attend their holiday party (oddly before Thanksgiving). She reported being their favorite and just could not disappoint them.

Russell gladly acted slightly heartbroken, but warmly supported her decision to go and support her workmates. In reality, *Abbey is infatuated with the boss*, he thought, who ran the company. It was a phase, Russell figured, because Abbey usually did not sleep around, but this might work in his favor as a future "get out" of the relationship scenario. *I guess it might have to be part five of my Plan*, he considered.

At the dining hall in Boland Hall, Russell was sitting by himself enjoying the alone time, trying to settle down, and thinking about inhaling a large volume of scotch in his suite on the fourth floor. He was looking at his phone and checking all the updates flashing in his face. Suddenly, a motion of humanity came into his view and started hugging him. "I thought I might catch you here. You didn't answer my call… Anyway, I need you tomorrow night!"

"Sandy… Wow, it's a surprise to see you here! Are you here for a confession or just meeting one of the Jesuits for absolution?" Russell quickly recovered from his surprise.

"Russell, you wish I felt bad about our little episodes," she sat on the table in front of him and leaned towards him. "I really need you for tomorrow night!" She stood up and took the chair next to him. "The Thanksgiving dance is at the Academy on Friday Night, one of my chaperones flunked out on me. What a putz!"

"Why are you so certain that I'm free tomorrow night?"

"Oh, is it a 'fucking Abbey' night… literally! Sorry I couldn't resist, darling."

"Sandy, your jealousy is so heartening, it makes me feel wanted."

Sandy laughed. "Hey, I heard about the volleyball game. Hill said he saw you there. Really Russell, are you fucking kidding me? I thought this obsession was undercover?"

"I had to take my Grandmother, so I had cover, but I got ambushed by the Finellis. Jesus, it was a nightmare! Hill was there?"

"Do you think Hill and Lil would miss their cousin play in a championship match? They dressed up with the *Candy-O* chorus. They said it was a blast." Sandy reported.

"Holy shit!"

"Everything is cool Russell… they knew you were there because of your Grandmother. It's cool like the *Red Hot Chili Peppers* were cool, sweetie just chill!"

"Fuck me!" Russell dove his head into his hands.

"Maybe later, my dear… but I do need you around six p.m. tomorrow night, okay?"

Glad for the distraction, Russell relented, "I'll be there!"

~21~

The Academy had built Holy Cross Alumni Hall with a stage that tripled as their playhouse, social hall, and church sanctuary in 2027. It was designed like Alumni Hall, built for the Franciscan Monastery in northeast DC. It was a tan brick structure inside and out with six arched entrances on each side and a grand one leading in from the foyer after the main entrance. A hallway lined outside the arches without doors on three sides. The ceiling was made of arched wood that formed a peak in the middle. Several modern-looking, tinted glass windows let in sun or the night stars from the ceiling. Tonight, it was decked out for the Fall Thanksgiving Ball. Besides the home school Academy of the Holy Cross; the girls of Stone Ridge, and the boys of Georgetown Prep and Landon were invited. Only guests of the Academy were allowed besides students from the three other schools.

Russell decided to appear in black tie for the occasion. He had several options to choose from based on his career as a performer. He was looking forward to seeing Lil and Hill and to hang out with Sandy. Since it had been a torturous couple of days, he felt the need to get stoned with his favorite herb by consuming a chewy brownie. He thought it would be perfect for the tasks of the evening. Of course, one of his jobs would be to make sure no one was drinking or toking, but Russell never saw himself as a policeman, just a noisemaker to corral the herd inside the dance hall.

Sandy noticed him right away and took him to the side, "Oh my god, you are so handsome, I could go Mary Magdalene on you right now!" Sandy was full of excitement, dolled up for the event with a lot of make-up, and her hair curled in a Colonial style draped around the sides of her face and cascading over her large chest. *I think she looks adorable*, Russell thought

"I'm glad you approve of my attire. Why don't you show me around? This place is fabulous. It looks like it's been here forever even though it's fairly new."

"Yes, some big donors really stepped up. We finally have some business CEOs as alumni."

"How many kids do you expect tonight?"

"We stopped it at two-hundred tickets. A shit load of boys from Landon and Prep love to come to this dance. What can I say, my girls here and at Stone Ridge are awesome!"

"How come I didn't meet you in high school?" Russell asked while feeling turned on by Sandy.

"Thank god, you would have defiled me before I went to college. Don't worry, my father, Brooks O'Malley, had me watched!"

"Really… You must be shitting me?" Russell fell for the joke.

"Of course, I'm shitting you! Now don't be an idiot… Come on and follow me, let's meet some of the chaperones. Don't worry, they all know you have a girlfriend; right? Don Juan."

"Yes… Don't remind of that right now." Russell worried.

"Christ, you are a basket case Russell! Let's have some fun."

"Got it!" Russell agreed.

Sandy, feeling confident in her designer dress, tastefully highlighting her figure, slid her arm inside his, as she presented her handsome friend to her staff of chaperones. As a group, they were low key and young, but very eager to please Sandy. They seemed to have most of the jobs covered. Finally, they went outside for some air and walked around the grounds to view the stars. It was a lovely night as Sandy pulled out a flask and drank down a gulp or two. Then offered it to Russell. "No thanks, I got a little buzzed before I came over." He smiled like a chesire cat.

"You started without me Russell, how rude!" she gently kissed him. "Did you miss me at all these past few weeks?"

"Of course, I did…" Russell hesitated for the right words; he felt close to Sandy and did not want to screw it up. "You look lovely tonight, Sandy." He kissed her back, "It's getting a little chilly out here."

"You're right, the kids will be coming up the road soon. Maybe we can hang some after the dance?"

"That would be nice, thanks for asking me to come." Russell answered with sincerity.

On the way inside, Sandy told him to help at the door, checking names during the initial rush of kids, otherwise he would walk around the grounds every fifteen minutes or so to keep the kids inside whenever possible. She would check in with him every half hour or as much as possible.

The hall was dark except for the disco ball that replaced the usual Catholic Cross hanging from the ceiling, sending stars of light cascading in mesmerizing circles. It was 2029, but a dance was still a dance. The DJ was sending some slow instrumental rhythmic sounds, softly settling one's soul, until the teenage tension would transform the tunes into raucous recreation. The refreshments were staged beautifully to attract those nervous boys trying to keep their hands and mouths active. The excitement of the arriving crowds would escalate as the vacancy of the floor would become noticeable to those first peering around the archways to watch the parade of lights. The pulsating music would entice those brave enough to start dancing, and then it would be crammed quickly like a school of fish following their lead couple.

Russell stood in front of the check-in tables with the front doors open as the first few attendees showed up. Most of them traveled in packs of four or five, usually all boys or all girls. The nerdiest looking ones came early to sample the refreshments and check out the lighting. The cool crowd would be casually late. Any drinking or smoking would be done off campus. Cameras were everywhere at the Academy, like most schools, and warning of school suspension was on the tickets.

Unlike the prom or homecoming, the attendees did not bring dates. Even if you had a boyfriend or girlfriend, you came with your companions before meeting up with your significant other. It was an event to meet people and celebrate the holiday, to dance and hangout. The kids had most of the Fall to work out their dance styles and routines to the best Summer pop songs. You came to an event like this prepared; even the boys had a step or two that did not look awkward. This private school generation was serious about their dancing.

During a lull, Russell went inside to the bathroom and was caught by Sandy coming out.

"Everything okay?" she said slowly trying to catch his eye. She was on the prowl tonight, and Russell looked good in the role of being the prey.

"Slow at the door right now, just came into pee and warm up a second."

"I'm glad you're getting comfortable and warming up." She attached to his arm and snuggled in with her chest. "It will start really happening in ten to fifteen minutes." She dragged him down the hall and unlocked a door. "Hey, let me show you my office tonight." It led into a room with tables and couches, locking it behind her she announced. "This is the teacher's lounge. Pretty cool, huh?"

Russell walked ahead of her and turned around with a laugh, "not bad for a girl's school!"

Sandy rushed up and pushed him down on the coach and knelt over him, "You should be punished for being mean to your teacher." She kissed him passionately, as he quickly moved to get a hold of the treasure under her dress by unzipping it and pulling it down past her shoulders along with her bra. The lovely pair emerged, and he took his time to feel every part of them. "You sure know what you want, Russell. Are they as good as you remember?" She uttered between kisses.

"Can you blame me Sandy, these are my favorite toys... It's hard to stop playing with them."

After two minutes of serious petting, she jumped up and backed off him to rescue her dress that was down around her ankles and put her breasts away in a safe place. As she zipped up, she playfully reported, "That was a little preview of your reward, if you do your job well tonight!"

Russell was fully hard and wanted to complain, but he was enjoying the show and knew better. "You are a tough boss, Sandy, I'm just here to follow instructions."

On his way back to his post, Russell took another trip to the bathroom to make sure he looked presentable. It only took a few moments and then headed back to his post. He could see a large number of kids were coming up the hill from the parking lots as he stepped out the front door.

"They love to come together. Lots of them, kind of tailgate in their cars until they see enough cool people heading up the hill," reported Alan Cahill, a teacher at the Academy. "At least that's the way they've done it here for the last four years I've been chaperoning."

"Hi, I'm Russell Santucci, a friend of Sandy's. I teach at Prep."

"Alan Cahill. I teach here with Sandy, nice to meet you, she told me you were coming to chaperone. I think that makes her very happy to have a friend like you here tonight. I guess you know the famous brothers?"

"Well, kind of... Alex is my uncle, so we're close, but I've only met Guy a couple of times. Actually, I saw him yesterday at the volleyball match at WJ."

"I'm such a big fan. I have Philomena or Lil as you know her in my American History class. She's a pretty classy girl if you ask me. Quiet, but nice to everybody who isn't scared to talk to her."

"Really? That's nice to hear."

"Yep, hey thanks for coming." They shook hands. "By the way, I think she's bringing her cousin tonight, the Finelli girl."

Russell turned his head away from Alan and walked outside to grab some air and prepare for another possible shit storm. *I thought she hated social gatherings, suddenly she's Kim Kardashian*, he complained inside of his head. And before he could strategize the situation, there she was, walking up to the door with Hill and Lil on either side of her.

Annie was in a kelly-green, long v-neck sweater with multiple strands of silver chains laying on her somewhat open chest with a pure-white skirt and matching heels, the outfit was worth thousands of designer dollars thanks to Sally Keegan's guidance. The bangs of her red hair were pinned to the sides and the rest of her hair behind her delicate ears. With this style, you could see her pretty green eyes, just a shade darker than her sweater. *She carried the sophisticated, coed-casual look beautifully, while being in her school colors*, Russell assessed. Yesterday, he had witnessed and felt her sweating athletic body next to his for a moment. He loved both looks. *The girl had range*, he chuckled. He stayed quiet as the trio walked by, not noticing him standing to the side. But he decided to catch them at the sign-in table and have a conversation before the noise inside made that impossible. He caught Lil first after she signed in, "Lil, hi it's Russell Santucci." He said tentatively.

She looked up and giggled, maybe trying to hide some liquor intake, "Oh yes, Russell, how nice to see you. You know my little cousin, Annie, and my big brother, Hill, of course." He had fifteen minutes of life before her as reported to him by their shared Grandmother.

"Yes... quite a trio of cousins. I'm sorry I missed you and Hill at the volleyball match. That was quite something." Russell answered with emotion.

"YES, IT WAS!" she added forcefully, "my little cousin tore up those Whitman snobs. I saw you though," adding a '*I know something about you*' giggle, "you got sandwiched by my parents and uncle. I hope Annie didn't hurt you as well."

Annie stepped up and stood next to Russell, "Do not be silly, Lil, I was just thanking him for coming to the match."

"My goodness, Annie, is that what you call it?! Come on you, my silly sweet sister, let's check in." She waved Annie to join her while turning. "Nice to see you Russell."

Annie was not ready to leave quite yet and reported, "Lil, you are a sweetheart, but I am going to hang out with Russell for a few minutes, I will catch up with you and Hill inside."

"Annie… Mom will kill us if we lose you tonight, you're our guest! You have to stay with us," Hill explained, who was approaching six feet, five inches and one-hundred eighty-five pounds from basketball training. He was overprotective of his cousin.

"Thank you, my dear Hill, I will just be a few minutes. I need to tell him some things from the match." Hill and Lil finally retreated and went inside. Annie turned her attention to Russell. "Well, this is quite a treat to see you two days in a row. Did you know I was coming?"

"Don't be silly… My friend Sandy asked me to chaperone."

"I am sorry about the kiss in the stands. It was not like me, but at the time, I felt close to you." She took his hand, "I know that is how you feel about me."

Russell lost his courage and wanted to hide. The cat was out of the bag. He had no response to this adult-like fifteen-year-old confronting him about his feelings. He tried to organize his thoughts in a heartbeat, "Annie this has to be part of a Plan, whatever we feel right now or for the next thirty months has to be at a distance from each other. You're in high school, you have to be a kid…and I will, of course, continue to be a struggling adult."

She smiled at his description. "I like the way you put it. Whatever this is, I want to be a part of the Plan." Her eyes were gentle and her posture statuesque in her answer, but then she morphed and became a teenage girl again, "Now give me your phone." She dialed in warp speed and handed it back. "Done, problem solved, now we can communicate to each other! Was that… maybe, step three of the Plan?"

"Actually, that's about right Annie." Russell confirmed as she waved to him and then squeezed his arm as she left. She turned before entering the door and touched her heart, suddenly he was paralyzed with fearful excitement by the "frozen fire" growing in his.

~22~

Russell spent most of his time chaperoning by roaming the outside campus. The darkened sky, protected in a small valley of rare undeveloped acres in the suburban countryside; and the fresh, but soon to be freezing, night air, helped him collect his thoughts. The impending coldness was keeping most of the kids inside and warm. Those that came outside, cooled off for a few minutes, and then headed back in quickly when the night air chilled their excitement.

Sandy finally found him and urged him to watch the dance with her for a while. "The kids are starting to get into dancing, and you have to come and see." She loved to grab his arm and get her chest into him. It was intoxicating to feel his warmth. She felt like a teenager herself, when she was around him. Overall, she knew it was a fling, just some fun while he worked through his obsession, but she liked the benefits of being along for the ride.

They walked together inside and stood in one of the arches on the side. The music was pulsating. A 2029 marriage of the 1980's techno-music revolution and the twenty-first century version of swing dancing. It could be as simple as a two-step with a partner with an occasional twirl or varying acrobatic versions of performance; they called it techno-swing. Some liked dirty or flirting dancing to it, especially popular with the Landon boys, but laughed at by most of the Catholic school kids. Russell and Sandy watched the energy flow from one song to another. He caught sight of Hill and Annie dancing together and then Lil and Hill twirling and then Lil and Annie executing a rehearsed routine.

This is incredible, Russell thought, *to watch two designer-dressed girls act uninhibited like they were in pajamas at a sleepover.* The three cousins were simply having fun at a high school dance like they did for years growing up together at the Enclave. Finally, a Prep kid stepped in after they finished and started swing dancing with Annie. She seemed up for the challenge. After a few minutes, Russell could see his face, it was Burton Parker, Jr., the son of the owner of the Washington Potomacs, DC's professional football team.

He went by Junior Parker and lived at Prep on Russell's floor at Boland Hall. Russell had limited interaction with him, but he seemed like a nice, respectful kid. He acted like he had a lot of confidence, probably a real lady's man. Most of staff at Prep did not like him. They told stories of him being drunk in the dorm and being a real spoiled brat, and asshole to some of the foreign kids. He led the dorm kids with demerits, according to the Prefect on the fourth floor that Russell knew very well. Junior had avoided suspension several times because of the donations coming into Prep from his father.

He played on the basketball team with Hill. In fact, according to Alex Santucci, he was a point guard that liked to score, sometimes a lethal combination. At times, he had all the weapons, a great outside shot, an ability to penetrate and score or pass, and a good eye for steals on defense. Other times, he was just a ball-hog. Hill and Junior were sort-of-friends as teammates, but Hill was more interested in getting Junior to pass the ball to him, since Hill was the one who could really shoot. Russell and Hill's father had watched a practice one day. Russell could see that Hill was the upcoming star on the team, and the coach kept yelling for Junior to pass off the ball before getting another charging call in practice.

Finally, the dance was ending, and the lights rose slightly. The staff of chaperones ran around like crazy for a half hour, shuttling the kids to the parking lot and making sure they all had rides. Russell walked Hill, Lil, and Annie out to their car. Lil was the first to give him a hug, "Thanks for chaperoning, it was fun to see you. I understand we'll see you for Thanksgiving… How exciting! Will you play the piano for us?"

Russell seemed surprised by the hug as he looked at the prettiest girl at the dance, "That sounds great, Lil!"

Hill did a man-hug, "Hey, I expect to see you at most of my games this year. Maybe you can bring Grandmother to one. See you at Thanksgiving!"

"Sounds great, Hill, best with the season!"

Annie gave the longest hug with a slight kiss on his neck and then turned quickly to catch up with her cousins at the car, she yelled back, "I will see you at Thanksgiving!"

Russell stood and felt a biting chill roll down his spine. He imagined another disaster coming in a week. This was taxing his heart, he feared having a coronary at the young age of twenty-six.

The clean-up was easy with everybody chipping in. Sandy herded the group together at the end to thank them and wish all a happy Thanksgiving. She hugged most of them as one from the group announced they were going to *Hank Dietle's Tavern* up the street on the Pike, a walk from Prep, and invited Sandy and Russell. It was the only dive bar left in the high-income city of Bethesda, which made it especially cool to those from the area, but more importantly it had a great pool table.

Sandy said, "I'm in for a couple beers…but it will be in a half hour or so." She explained that she had to close up, and Russell was her ride. They assured her they would be there until closing.

As soon as the lights were off, and the front door was locked, Sandy took Russell to her "office," the teacher's lounge. She had a brownie to share with him that was baked with herb. Russell was relieved. He was not sure he could be with her straight while thinking about Thanksgiving.

They cuddled for a few minutes while the brownie kicked in and then clothes started to fly. She had him naked while she kept her panties on. She turned him on quickly when her breasts came out. He was surprised but pleased at their appearance and, for a few minutes, he forgot the mess he had created with his obsession.

Russell decided to delay his gratification and make sure Sandy was rocking. He convinced her that he could do a deep-sea dive on her without wanting to plunge in her later. She was pretty wasted and laughed a great deal when he started. She was a natural girl without trimming. He found the untamed bush a pleasure to get lost in. He took his time and calmed her down, so she could concentrate and enjoy the pleasuring. Pretty soon, she was lost in joy and sat there misty-eyed for a minute. Afterwards, Russell sat there holding her hand and comforting her. She sat up and started to kiss him again and felt for his member. Russell protested at first, but her delicate hands perfectly brought him back to hardness. "You know I want you badly, but this is the best I can do, my dear. Sit back and enjoy!"

He followed orders and let her take over. She sat beside him, so her breasts were within reach. She bent over and took him inside her mouth; after five minutes; she finally tasted his joy. It was as close as they could get to intercourse. Her marriage vows were being bent, but not broken, she figured. Most of the time she could act happy, except when she really thought about it, like right now being with Russell. They dressed and hugged for a minute. She could not get enough of their physical closeness.

Without talking, they walked to the car, holding hands and looking at the stars. Russell warmed up the car and turned on some music, as he waited a few minutes while she put her head on his shoulder. Finally, he put the Acura in gear and rolled down the hill for the less-than-a-mile ride to *Dietle's*. The twenty-year-old Acura entered the long exit lane on to Rockville Pike from Strathmore Lane with no cars were coming. He dropped the shifter into low gear, spun some rubber, and hit eighty mph in under four seconds. Just in time to make a quick left into *Dietle's* with two wheels reaching for the road and spun into an almost empty parking lot. He stopped, put it in reverse, and peeled into a space.

"Now we're ready for a clean get away!" Russell announced energized by the ride.

"Wow… That was some little ride and parking job Russell," Sandy reported, feeling the wetness still between her legs.

"I think it felt just right, Sandy," he said, amazed at his satisfaction.

"Agreed, my dear, but I still have something stuck in my throat, I really could use a beer or two to wash it down!"

~23~

On Thanksgiving, it was expected to be at least in the fifties or sixties temperature-wise in DC on a regular basis. Indian summer was extending to late November, and nobody complained too much, especially the golfers, boaters, and other outdoors folks enjoying exercise. No major hurricanes had ripped through the Eastern shore in the last dozen years. Otherwise major rain and windstorms, somewhat hurricane-like, seemed to be the mainstream. Derechos and tornadoes were on the increase, causing major destruction mostly inland and away from metropolitan areas. After years of legislation and regulation to reduce carbon dioxide and store methane in the oceans from the previous two administrations, the present administration, just starting their second term, had reduced this approach. Since the idea was to slow down climate change before they could change the direction, people could not see the improvement, and a majority became convinced it was not an imminent problem. Except for the summers becoming unbearably hot, most people in Maryland liked the warmer weather especially in the winter. NYC was the new DMV, the DMV was becoming the Carolinas, which were becoming the new Florida or weatherwise the North was becoming the South and the South the tropics.

The morning Turkey Bowl game had become a regular match between the Finellis and the Santuccis. Each brother would lead their families into battle. Russell had been banned by his parents from playing any kind of contact sport since his was seven, when his playing of the piano was becoming a serious craft. After a few years of missing it, he enjoyed sleeping in onThanksgiving morning; but this year, he was excited to show up, assuming Annie was a regular performer on the Finelli team. Hill and Lil split up and played on each side for half the game. Otherwise, the game had some competitive moments, but it was mostly six seconds of activity at a time followed by a minute of laughter, hugs, and polite trash talking about who did what wrong on the last play.

Annie and Russell enjoyed seeing each other, but generally kept their distance, except when Annie made a point of covering him for several plays, playing a bump and run-into-him technique. This allowed for some moments of physical contact when no one was watching. When he was on defense, he made no attempt to cover Annie; instead, he played a lot of deep safety and watched her athletic talent across the field. She was super quick, with great hands, and pulled off some great leaping catches. He was in love with her whole being.

Being outside and enjoying the camaraderie with the two families, Russell felt hope that the Santucci dinner would go as well. Luckily Abbey had no interest in rising early on Thanksgiving morning to play football, and Russell was very supportive of her decision.

His parents came to watch, but of course they did not play. They were not football-type folks and were still worried about Russell injuring his fingers playing such a rough sport; but they seemed to enjoy watching their boy run around the field. Dr. Kenneth and Jill Santucci were both fifty-nine and very healthy. They played tennis, golf, and bridge for their competitive sporting. Otherwise, they kept fit with daily use of their home elliptical and bike machines, each spending fifteen minutes on both, while reading the *New York Times* and *Washington Daily* newspapers on the Cloud. They had met at *Harvard* and were married before Kenneth started medical school. They had a son, Raymond, immediately and were supported by their parents and student loans for five years. Once they moved to NYC for Kenneth's residency at *Columbia*, they enrolled Raymond in school and Jill worked managing a medical practice. Eventually, they moved back to Bethesda, where Jill helped Kenneth start his practice and had Russell five years later. They did everything together: work, exercise, tennis, golf, biking, eating, sex, and sleeping.

Their first son Raymond, twelve years older than Russell, was now a research M.D. working overseas for the CDC (Center for Disease Control). He graduated high school at age sixteen and left for Harvard when Russell was four. Raymond and Russell were not close as brothers, but liked each other when around, but Russell had not seen him in three years.

In some ways, Russell was their second, only-child, and they loved him dearly. His parents thought he was a prodigy on the piano at age five but realized after seven years of constant lessons and practice, he had the talent, but not the will to be great. When he went to Georgetown, they stopped hovering over his life. Instead, they remodeled their home in Bethesda, traveled to Europe, and joined a Country Club. Their house was a perfect home for them and was only a bike ride away from Laura's house on Johnson Avenue.

They arrived at Laura's house at noon to help with Thanksgiving. Alex and Sally arrived soon after. Two other brothers and their wives would arrive around two p.m. They were planning on sixteen at the massive dining room table.

Russell was waiting for Abbey at her apartment. She was late, of course, parading around in her robe and still wanting to take a shower, making Russell late for Thanksgiving dinner. He complained for the first few minutes, as she still was having trouble finding the right outfit to see his family. She turned to him with sad eyes, "I just want to look good for your family, Russell. I had to work late. I'm so sorry I overslept." Somehow, her robe fell open, and Russell felt his resistance fall away. "Sweetie, I just need a body shower, come in with me for a minute or two."

It turned out that Russell needed a shower as well after the football game, so he took up the invitation. He wondered if she was with her boss last night. They had been past the use of *trojans*, and with the discovery of an anti-venereal disease vaccine, including AIDS, multi-partner sex was back in for a larger part of the younger crowd. As he entered the shower, he did not care; she was naked and looking like glass with the water gliding down her skin. He slid in behind her, as she put two hands on the shower wall away from the water flow and bent over slightly. Slowly, he eased in her and forgot the tension of the day. Worrying about being late went away. His anxiety about Abbey at the dinner was diminished. The warm water rolled down his back as he relaxed and lost himself in the rhythm of intercourse. He was not worried about her reaction, but he liked that her grunts were in perfect sync to his thrusting. Russell's hands were on her diaphragm, just below her breasts, feeling her air coming in and out of her body. His hands moved to her breasts, cradling their soft and wet skin barely filling his palms, but feeling perfect. Her chest was heaving, her sounds getting louder. He was leaving his body and soul as he emptied into her but did not stop his thrusting until she pleaded for him to stop. She was done, and he felt empty.

Russell toweled off, dressed, and waited patiently for Abbey as he read the *Washington Daily* on his phone. Abbey took her time toweling, doing her hair, and picking the right outfit. Russell turned to the sports section and looked up the football schedule for today: Pittsburgh at Dallas at four p.m., Washington at Cleveland at eight p.m. He was excited about watching football and the Washington game with Alex and his other uncles. Then, he saw a guest column by Ron Roswell that was titled, "Annie Finelli Appears." It started, "Fifteen years after the murder of her FBI agent mother Anna, Guy Finelli's daughter appeared in the Montgomery county girls' volleyball championship match for Walter Johnson High School."

Oh boy, he thought, *this is just what I needed… to be in love with the fifteen-year-old daughter of the most famous football player in recent DC history and in the middle of the football season! And now she's on page one of the sports section read by millions in the DC area and the fucking country.* He had trouble not reading the article even though his anxiety was gaining by the second, "Annie Finelli led WJ to their second consecutive girls' volleyball title. Normally, that would not be a story on page one of the *Daily*, but in this case, what I witnessed was something special."

Abbey appeared in front of him, jolting him from reading his phone. He hid it quickly like it was pornography. She had her hair done nicely and make-up completed conservatively; but wearing only her panties and holding up two dresses, she asked, "Which one works the best, Russell?"

He recovered enough to point at the darker one, "very nice Abbey everyone will love it."

"Not too formal?"

"Perfect with your tallest heels."

"You know how much I hate heels, Russell… but you're right. Okay, thanks for being patient." She broke into a wide smile and bent over to kiss him, separating the dresses that were covering her breasts. She whispered in his ear, "You were a tiger in the shower, I never felt so dominated, I think I could come again!"

Russell was trying to resist but had his hands on her ribs under her breast and felt her warmth. He kissed her again and moved his hands all over her breasts. She sat on him and wanted more. He picked her up, dropped her on the couch, and dove into her freshly cleaned clitoris. He ate her up while listening to her screams of joy.

She sat back and tried to gain her breath after reaching her pinnacle. After a minute, she sat up, pulled up her panties, found the darker dress on the floor, and said, "So I guess I'll wear the darker one and the high heels." Russell had found his seat again and nodded while wiping his face. "I'll be just a minute and then we can go." she smiled feeling satisfied.

The ride to Laura's house was quiet. He had cleaned up before he left, but otherwise was trying to forget the crazy passion he had just experienced with Abbey. *Hopefully*, he thought, *the wine or scotch will be ready to drink*.

Abbey started talking about the party Friday night with her part-time job friends and her suspected romantic boss interest. Her energy level was almost frenetic during her description. Russell knew there was something going on but was almost relieved. He was concerned about managing this part of the Plan, especially the next three hours at Thanksgiving dinner.

"Listen Abbey, try to blend in with everybody. You're being a little hyper."

"You didn't seem to mind me being hyper just a few minutes ago," she shot back, but then recovered quickly, "You're right... your Grandmother and Sally are so sweet, but the rest are like vultures, with all their questions, especially your parents."

"Vultures? That's a little strong, don't you think? Listen, Jill and Kenneth are nice people, they're just elitists, sort of... kinda in a nice way." He tried to be comforting, "You have to realize the dining room will be full of smart people that listen well, so if you don't want the attention, then..."

"Got it, I'll try to stay in background. I just hope they like my outfit and the heels." She sat back and took a deep breath. "Jesus I am really hungry. I hope some appetizers will be served."

The house on Johnson Avenue was perfectly decorated for the beginning of the holiday season. Laura met them at the front door wearing an apron, even though she had a full-time, live-in houseworker that did most of the preparation in the kitchen. She was in her glory greeting her newly-favorite grandson and his problem girlfriend, "So nice to see you Abbey. What a pleasure to have you join us. I know you must be starved, here are some crab melts just out of the oven and some wine for you, Russell." Somehow, she knew what they needed as they walked in. "My grandson is always running late these days; he can't help it."

Abbey vacuumed down several crab melts and tried to respond with a full mouth, "Oh no Mrs. Santucci it was all my fault, really..."

Laura ignored her mouthful-of-food gibberish and sent them down the hallway.

"Everyone's dying to see you two."

Russell sucked down the glass of Pinot Noir and was looking for a quick refill, when Alex and Sally caught them before heading into the family room. Alex had a bottle in his hand and filled Russell's glass. Sally hugged Abbey and offered her some deviled eggs.

"Abbey, you look stunning in that outfit! Just love the shoes my dear, it certainly goes with that sexy body!"

Abbey giggled as she nailed down a whole deviled egg.

"Thank you so much. I wasn't sure if it was too dressy."

"Perfect… it would be nice to be young again." She turned to her husband, "Alex, can you get Abbey a glass of wine?"

He was up to the challenge and handed Abbey a full glass in seconds.

"So nice to see you Abbey." He dominated her with a hug. "Russell is such a lucky man!"

Abbey finally was feeling less famished and gulped down the wine, which Alex noticed and refilled quickly.

"Thank you so much Alex, you are so kind."

Russell finished his second glass and was starting to feel calmer. Next was his parents to meet. He knew they were not the glad handlers that Laura, Alex, and Sally were. He was not sure Abbey would be ready, but he was hopeful. They entered the family room and found his parents sitting comfortably in the corner chatting with his two uncles Peter and John and their wives. He knew they would barely acknowledge him and Abbey until they stood in front of them. He grabbed Abbey's hand and motioned her to put down her glass with his. Finally, the meeting he feared the most.

Kenneth and Jill finally rose to their feet and formally greeted Abbey with handshakes from Kenneth and cheek kisses from Jill without hugs. Russell was used to their rigidness, but he knew it might throw Abbey off of her game.

"I was worried you had taken a nap after this morning and forget to come," Jill smiled. "Abbey, it is nice to have you here. Hopefully you will straighten Russell out before he hits thirty." She laughed quietly. "Have you met Russell's uncles, Peter and John?"

Russell was happy for the distraction of seeing his uncles, aunts, and four first cousins, all in high school or college. His father sat back down quickly to watch the game on television that he did not care about. "Russell, this Detroit team covers the receivers like you did this morning trying to follow that teenage Finelli girl. What's her name, Russell?"

"Annie Finelli, Father. She's Guy Finelli's daughter. You know, the football player." He tried to placate his interest and stop the questions.

"Of course, I remember now, she must be around fifteen or so. Tragic situation, but she seemed very athletic and friendly to you."

"Well… we've met a couple times and they have asked me to start giving her piano lessons." He realized that the wine was allowing this flammable flow of evidence to be heard by Abbey, but he was hopeful she was out of hearing range.

"That's nice, son, maybe you can pay off that piano to Alex before you turn fifty."

Reinforcements came just in time.

"Russell and Abbey, where are your glasses?" Alex questioned.

Kenneth spoke to his younger adopted brother with a smile, "Russell has a client for piano lessons, Alex. Hopefully you'll see some money for that piano."

"Aren't you drinking yet, Kenneth?" Six-foot, four-inch Alex hovered over him, "I'm very proud of Russell. I told him that the piano was a graduation gift, but he insists on sending me money for it, which I am saving for him as part of his wedding gift in the future." He big-hand-slapped Russell on the shoulder, "Are we clear about that?"

Kenneth took on a look of dismay and stood up to get a wine glass.

Russell and Abbey finally retreated from the corner and found refuge in the distant living room. "Wow, that was something. I hope you survived my mother and the others…"

"I'm fine Russell. What was that all about with the Finelli girl. You played football this morning?"

"I decided for myself to play in the Turkey Bowl. It was fun and perfect weather outside. My uncle has been riding me to show up for years."

She looked at him suspiciously, knowing that this behavior was way out of character for him. "Tell me about the Finelli daughter, she's something of a mystery girl if I remember correctly."

"She grew up with Alex and Sally, and her twin cousins Lil and Hill. Now they all live in the Parkwood Enclave. You should see it. It's quite a set up."

"When did you go there?'

"I brought my Grandmother to her birthday party in May."

"Was that the first time you met her?"

"Actually, I met her at Anthony Finelli's birthday bash in early 2028."

"I assume escorting your Grandmother?"

"That's right. She's a close family friend to the Finelli's… Why, is there a problem with me going to a couple of birthday parties?"

"I don't know… It seems a little out of character for you to be seeing this fifteen-year-old girl in so many situations. Pretty soon you'll be taking your Grandmother to see her play soccer or something."

"Actually, we did go to see the county volleyball girl's championship last Thursday at WJ. She is a remarkable athlete."

"Oh my god, Russell, are you crazy? I suppose you're giving her piano lessons in your suite at Prep."

"That's starting next week. Are you jealous or something?"

"You are unbelievable!" She just stared at Russell, seething at his casual honesty. "You aren't even denying this."

"Denying what?" Russell was steadily playing his hand, ready to use his trump card if necessary.

Abbey sat back and finished her wine, "Can you fill this up for me?"

"Gladly, back in a second my dear." He knew he had her cornered because she was chasing her own obsession. He returned quickly with her wine and a couple more cheese melts.

"These are so good."

"Sorry… I guess I overreacted to what your father was saying and everything else. I think my blood sugar is low, thanks for the crab melts."

Russell was hoping the alcohol would kick in soon for Abbey. "No problem Abbey… we're cool. I want to hang out with my family."

"Oh sure, go ahead. Just give me a minute, I'll go into the kitchen and see how I can help."

Russell bent over, gave her a sweet kiss, and rubbed her face gently. Her objections had been overruled, and his Plan was still alive.

The dinner table was filled with all sixteen attendees, prayers were performed, and food flowed around the table flawlessly. The waiting was over for Russell, his favorite meal that happened once a year, now commenced. Silence dominated the next ten minutes as hungry appetites became satiated.

Abbey felt satisfied, calmed by alcohol; and now a plate of turkey, stuffing, mashed potatoes topped by gravy, cranberry sauce, corn pudding, and a bit of everything else, which she mostly inhaled. She had a weird sensation of leakage between her legs that reminded her of the ferocious sex earlier with Russell. She felt his warmth as she sat next to him. He seemed to be at his happiest listening to his uncles tell stories about his Grandmother and Grandfather, while exchanging quips with his cousins in response. Abbey eyed Russell's parents as they sat quietly across the table during the story telling, wondering what they were thinking of her.

At a lull in the conversation, Laura touched Abbey's arm and asked, "It's lovely to have you here, dear; what are your parents doing, if I may ask?

"My parents are divorced, my father's traveling in Europe on business, and my mom is in Maine. I told her it's too cold to come up there for the holidays. I grew up in Rhode Island, where my dad lives. That's cold enough, but Maine is brutal."

"Newport... Is that where you from?" Kenneth offered a hint of interest in a place they vacationed often.

"Actually, just north of there in Bristol, still a lot of water around."

"Jill and I love Newport. Do you get back there for the summers at all?"

"Yes, to see my dad. That's my favorite time of the year. Russell came up one summer for a few days in 2028."

"Russell, you never told us; you know how much we love Newport!"

"Yes, Russell and I had a grand time. My father is pretty progressive, he actually let us sleep together!"

The room was silent, except for the football game in the background. Russell grabbed Abbey's thigh under the table, it did not seem to help. "It was heaven, skinny dipping in the pool under the moonlight, and making it..."

"Abbey, can you pass me the mashed potatoes, please?" as he loudly interrupted Abbey's creative description. "I'm sure no one here wants to hear anymore."

"Russell... We do, go on Abbey!" two of his cousins chimed in.

Abbey covered her mouth as she passed the potatoes. "Sorry, Russell, I guess I was feeling the moment."

Russell whispered, "Well, the moment's over."

Another hour of conversation passed before most retreated to the family room to watch the end of the Dallas game. The table was cleared, and dessert was served before the start of the Washington game. Abbey helped in the kitchen for a few minutes and then went to the living room to sit for a minute. Suddenly, she felt wiped out. Within a minute, she was sleeping on the couch. Russell found her after fifteen minutes and covered her with a blanket. The Dallas game was finally over with the Washington game coming up soon at eight p.m. The smells of warm pecan, apple and cherry pies emanated from the dining room as the crowd, stuffed with turkey, were ready to sweeten their tummies.

Suddenly, there was a knock at the door, Abbey sprung up from the couch like she was late for work. The rest of the crowd was placating their sweet tooth in the dining room and making too much noise to notice. She sat up and fluffed her hair and fixed her dress. She went to the door, still in a slight trance, and opened it. For a second, she thought it was a handsome monster.

Guy Finelli towered over her in the doorway. "Hi, I'm Guy Finelli, and you must be?"

She awoke from her trance, "Abbey… I'm here with Russell."

He hugged her like a little running back caught in the backfield. Abbey felt her back crack as she got lost in his chest. "Well, Abbey, you are quite lovely! Where's the crowd?"

"I'm not sure… maybe in the family room watching the game."

"Well, I'm here for that. My family is right behind me."

Abbey held the door open as Patty O'Neil, his wife, said hello and passed through. Then a barrage of cousins: nine-year-old Anthony Finelli, and sixteen-year-olds Hill and Lil flew by with a nod in search of dessert. And then, there she was, carrying two pumpkin pies as orange as her hair. "Hi, I am Annie Finelli, you must be Abbey, Russell's girlfriend?"

She was stunned by her competition. "Yes… I'm Abbey… nice to meet you. Can I take one of those pies?" Annie volunteered one from her right hand and kept out her hand for a greeting. Abbey secured the pie and shook her hand. She felt dominated by the size and the strength of handshake. She quickly pivoted and guided her inside.

"I have never been here before. Is this your first time?"

"No, it isn't," Abbey answered feeling defensive already. "Just follow the hallway back to the dining room."

As Abbey trailed Annie down the hall, she took an appealing look at her tight fitting short black dress and heels that radiated sexuality and athleticism, as well as a presence of security and confidence. Abbey felt a darkness in her heart as though her time with Russell would now become limited.

She saw Annie deposit the pies in the dining room and receive hugs from Sally and Laura. Annie met Jill and Kenneth and, for a moment, was surrounded like a movie star in a crowd. She calmly answered some questions and backed away, clearly in search of someone. Abbey watched Annie enter the family room with all the men, led by her father Guy and Uncle Alex, leading cheers for Washington against Cleveland. Only one pair of eyes turned away from the noisy television and rabid fandom and saw her standing quietly. He stood up and walked towards her. She saw him and, without hesitation, gave him a hug. They separated and stood motionless with Annie saying something to him. He seemed to look joyful.

Abbey stepped forward to be noticed and directly looked at Russell. His eyes darted towards her. He put his hand on Annie's shoulder to turn her as he walked with her, "Abbey, have you met Annie Finelli? She wants me to taste the pumpkin pie she baked before it's gone."

"Yes, we met at the door." She watched as Russell and Annie entered the dining room together with Abbey left behind. She was waning in Russell's life and young Annie was gaining.

~24~

The ride home was solemn but polite. Abbey felt like a prize fighter that went twelve rounds without victory. As much as she wanted his affection, she pleaded tiredness as she went inside, leaving him with a long kiss and embrace. They made plans for the first Friday in December, knowing it would be delayed or cancelled perhaps. Maybe she would feel more hopeful tomorrow, but she could use a distraction over the weekend and catching up with her part-time work gang could be the tonic. She felt her boss closing in on her and maybe it was time to give in and see how it felt. Tonight, seemed like a heartbreaking situation, just when she thought it was getting better. *Were they getting closer or just spending more time apart?*, she wondered, *am I creating another life for myself with this part-time crowd or is it an excuse for a soft landing?* Abbey knew she could be fatalistic and sabotage herself. She was glad to finally get in bed. The wine had caught up with her.

Russell felt relief as he drove away, ready to be in his suite and at his piano. He was still jacked up from seeing Annie and the whole day of activities. Playing some piano and drinking scotch would settle him down. His life was now a whirlwind. It used to be morose and boring, except for the late nights at the bars he worked, drinking, smoking dope, and being with women. The last two years, he had become a real adult—teaching school, getting counseling, going out with Abbey. But since June, he realized he had fallen for Annie, made the Plan, and tried to follow it. It was getting complicated, seeing Abbey twice a month and enjoying it, while being with Sandy inappropriately. *The last week or so had thrown things into a tizzy*, he thought, *maybe I can right the ship and get on with the Plan.*

He would now get to see Annie once a week giving piano lessons. That was going to take some convincing the dorm rector, how special this student was and how much it would benefit Prep in the long run. The situation would have to be formal inside the suite. He was confident of that, having given lessons to all sorts of teenagers and having followed the appropriate procedures, including a door-open policy; it possibly will work. Word would get around quickly about the star quality of his student. Fortunately, they could walk the grounds after the lesson and get some time to talk. Everything about Annie fascinated him, especially conversation.

The first lesson was on Tuesday afternoon at three p.m. Fortunately, his floor was void of kids with mandatory afternoon activities for all students. She came straight from WJ, driven by Guy Finelli's bodyguard and assistant. Russell had agreed to drive her home, so he would not have to wait. Annie was wearing designer jeans, a turtleneck, and a WJ sweatshirt. The lesson was fun, lots of energy and nervous laughing. As the hour finished, she asked him to play something for her. She sat to the side of him and closed her eyes to listen. He lost himself in Chopin's "Concerto No. 1 in E- Minor" and played it magnificently. When he was done, Annie's eyes were misted and full of emotion. They clearly shared a love for the great composer of romantic solos for the piano. Looking at each other, they shared a quiet moment.

They grabbed their coats and headed outside for a walk. It was still remarkably in the upper fifties and pleasant. The campus was beautiful with leaves still hanging on some of the trees. They headed towards the soccer field past the chapel.

"We lost in the state tournament," Annie reported. "The team that beat us in the finals had all seniors. They were like a perfectly oiled machine. We put up a fight and lost in four games." She looked at him directly, "I am glad you did not come and see us lose. That would have made it harder to accept."

Russell was amazed at her openness. "I could have made myself invisible. You did win two matches to get to the finals and you made the All-State team. That's remarkable in your first year of volleyball. That has to be some kind of record."

"Thank you, I was awesome, and Beverly was unbelievable, everybody else tried their hardest. They were just physically better than us and did not make enough mistakes in the two closes games for us to beat them in the match."

"Did you enjoy Thanksgiving?" Russell inquired.

"Very much, especially bringing over the pumpkin pies and watching the game with everyone. To witness my father and uncle together watching a game, is pure entertainment."

"I know… your dad was calling half of the plays, and it was great to hear some stories at half-time."

"I thought Abbey was a little drunk, but I can see why you are attracted to her. She is very cute and sexy. I do not think she likes me." She stated without emotion.

"Well… It could have been worse, but we made it through dinner and the whole night without a major incident."

"So, Abbey being with your family can become dramatic."

"Exactly, I think that's her middle name."

"Abbey the Dramatic!" they broke out in laughter, continuing to come up with names describing Abbey. "I hope you do not mind me laughing about it. I am sure it is hard for her to be with your family."

"Don't worry about it. I think it's pretty funny."

"Are you chaperoning the Saturday Holiday Dance here?"

"Of course, it's Man-Da-Tor-Y!"

"Well I am coming with Junior Parker, Hill and his date, and Lil and her date. It should be fun. What do you think?"

Russell was caught off guard. "I'm sure it will be. They're having a DJ and a swing band apparently," as he tried to change the subject, *suddenly I'm feeling jealous about some kid that's a jerk*, he thought to himself. He stayed quiet for a second.

She noticed, "My cousins set me up with Junior, to get invited. I do not expect to have to be around him all night. That is for sure. I think he is kind of into himself, but he has been a gentleman to me. His problem is… he thinks he is better than Hill in basketball, which is not true by any metric you look at. To be honest, I think I could take him one on one." She smiled hoping to allay Russell's concerns.

"I'll keep an eye out for you guys."

"You do that Russell!" She gave him a jab in the ribs.

They made it to his car. He put the Acura in gear and rolled slowly out of the parking lot with his hand on the shifter in the center console. She gently placed her hand on his as they headed away from Prep. She gave him a smile, and he winked back at her. They stay connected for the two-mile ride back to the Parkwood Enclave and felt like a couple for the first time.

~25~

The dance started at seven pm on the ground floor of Boland Hall with refreshments available in the lounge area. No one was allowed in the dorms during the dance and all students were expected to be inside the dance from eight to eleven p.m. There would be a twenty-minute break shortly after nine p.m., when they would be allowed to go outside or get refreshments.

Russell was up in his suite playing for himself at the piano. It was a piece he had composed when he was fifteen but had ignored playing it until this past summer. He was now performing it with much more emotion, while expanding it with some new music. It had been years since he had enjoyed playing his own classical material.

His friend Sandy appeared at the open door to his suite. She was dressed in a strapless black gown that had a see-through black jacket over her chest and shoulders, buttoned up to her collar, giving the hint of covering her cleavage. Her blond hair was curled and laying on her shoulders and chest. Russell thought she looked lovely and very sexy. He quickly rose from the piano to hug her. She responded with a long kiss and tight hug, "I missed you the last two weeks. How was your Thanksgiving with the drama queen and the obsession?"

"As to be expected and very well."

"The word is that she's coming tonight with Junior. Will I have to hold you back from acting like a jealous maniac, or should I distract you in some other way?"

"I think you've made a good start with this appearance. I would feel bad taking this jacket and dress off of you."

"Oh, don't worry yourself... It's just a simple zipper in the back and not much else." She stepped away, closed his door, stepped back to him, and spun around. "This should distract you for a while."

Russell took the bait and zipped down her dress to her waist. Slowly, he slipped his hands around her ribs and under her breasts. She laid her neck back and waited for a kiss. Together, they made quiet sounds relishing their entanglement for another minute, before Sandy pulled away and said, "Time to put the girls away and zip me up. We will finish this later... I hope?"

As usual Russell was fully erect and wanted more, but he relented and followed instructions. Sandy played him like a patio umbrella – rolling him up and down to assure she was in control of the situation. "Why don't you perform that piece you were playing when I walked in. It sounds original, is it?"

Russell adjusted himself and went to the piano, happy to slide under it to hide his giant erection. He was adapting to acting normal with his member acting up, "yes, it is...something I composed as a teenager. It's kind of fun to visit it again as an adult." He started slowly with something new, a tune he had just thought of since his lesson with Annie yesterday; it was low on the piano keys and sounded dark. He had heard it before somewhere but could not place it.

Sandy stood behind him with her hands inside his shoulders, slowly massaging him. He moved into his old piece and played it with chords more vibrantly than before. She reached over his shoulders and down his chest, kissing him on the neck. He responded by playing with a stronger tempo. She moved in next to him and unzipped him quickly. He felt relief as his strong member reached the open air. Bending over she kissed it and gently stroked it as he kept playing powerfully. Her hair covered him and bounced lightly on his pelvis and she took him deeply, licking him as she lifted each time. He transitioned to a higher chord as he felt her stroking build up his euphoria. He played only with his left hand as he grabbed her hair trying to hold on. He knew it was coming, as he remembered the tune and the chorus of the song, at the volleyball game they were singing it, "*Candy-O, I need you so. Could you help me in? Candy-O, I need you so. Do you have to win?*"

Sandy rose up for air as he spilled down his member and over her hand. "Sorry, dear... there was too much to swallow. Just stay... I'll clean you up."

Russell kept his hands on the piano, lightly playing as Sandy cleaned up. "You are a monster at the piano. I just couldn't keep my hands away from you.

That new part had some real energy." She sat down on the bench facing him after she finished. Her hand brushed back his hair and ran down his pinkish cheeks. *It's a blast to be with him*, she thought, and she was fond of him; but in some ways, he was a play toy that kept her out of real trouble. They fulfilled needs for each other, and he was a good person. *Isn't that what friends are for?* She pondered.

"That was an out-of-body experience. I'm not sure I can put it into words. Honestly, it's a fantasy, I've never thought…well, maybe when I watched *Amadeus*, but that was Mozart not me. He was a rock star. I'm just a mediocre piano player."

"I protest, my dear, you are a special player, and I think you know that. Keep working on that piece, and it will bring the best out of you." Sandy kissed him softly on the cheek and patted him on the leg. "It's time to keep track of the teenagers at the dance and keep them from doing this kind of thing!" She stood and grabbed his hand to ascend from the piano bench together and then took both of his hands to rise on her heels to kiss him, "hopefully we can come back here after the dance and finish this up, if you know what I mean."

Officially Russell and Sandy were not on the list of chaperones, but both were expected to be there as extra eyes on the students. The dance would be smaller in scope than the Academy Thanksgiving dance. The Academy and Visitation of Georgetown, both girl's schools, were the only other schools officially invited, otherwise any high school student could be invited by someone from those schools.

Junior Parker had a family limousine at his disposal. He picked up Annie, Hill, and Lil at the Parkwood Enclave. Lil had a friend at the Academy named Malak who was crazy about Hill. Her brother Chahna went to Georgetown and came as Lil's date. She liked Chahna since he was a serious student and had manners that were impeccable. They were both attractive kids with jet black hair and dark skin. Their parents were engineers from India who worked for World Space, headquartered just north on the Pike in the re-built White Flint district of Bethesda. The six of them were cheek to cheek in the limousine as Junior poured each a glass of champagne that he had hidden away. It was a short ride to Prep, so they each had a quick glass. Junior then pulled out a fat joint and sucked the air out of it before passing it along. Annie was curious about it and took a quick hit, as did Lil. Hill passed thinking about the season starting. Chahna and Malak took quick tokes to show they were involved in partying. Both were new to the idea and already felt a buzz from the one glass of champagne. Junior had commanded the driver to station the limo in the

Dietle's parking lot until eight p.m. He continued the surprises with hot fudge sundaes that magically appeared from the limo's small refrigerator for everyone, decorated with cut-up strawberries and nuts. Junior was hyped-up from the alcohol-pot-sugar buzz and on his way to being wasted already, as he refilled the glasses of champagne.

"Let's celebrate! I want everyone to toast my beautiful date, for winning the county volleyball championship." They all raised their glasses for such a good cause. After sucking down his champagne, Junior turned to his date, "I'm sorry, Annie, that I didn't see it, but I read your performance was magnificent. Am I right, Hill?" as he reached to touch glasses.

"It was better than that, Junior, it was mega-tron magnificent! Here, here... Everybody toast to Annie!" the glasses and voices rose again in unison.

Junior was feeling infatuated with his date, "Annie, how did you learn to play volleyball so quickly and be so great?"

"Because she's my cousin silly!" Lil jumped forward and answered, as laughs exploded all around. "She's great at everything. And you know she could kick your ass in basketball, Junior!" feeling embolden by the champagne, Lil pointed at Junior emphatically.

"Oooooohhhhhs" and "Whoaaaaahhhs" broke out in the tight quarters of the limo.

Junior laughed at the suggestion, but Hill added, "Sorry, Bro, but my sister's right about Annie. She's got game," he added in a serious tone.

"Can she kick your ass, Hill?" Junior countered, feeling a little challenged.

"Usually...when we were younger, but I'm a lot taller than her now."

"Be honest Hill, she still kicks your ass!" Lil chimed up feeling on a roll.

"Okay, okay... let's ask the champion herself, Annie, my dearest Annie, please be honest. Can you really kick my ass in basketball?" Junior asked, trying to be his most charming.

Without hesitation Annie replied confidently, "Junior... of course I can... but to be fair, words are cheap. We need a challenge game to twenty-one by two or three-point shots."

"Now we're talking a challenge," Chahna chimed in, excited to be involved.

"I would pay to watch that," Malak added, holding on to Hill for reinforcement.

"Okay, Annie, if I win you come to my father's Christmas Party as my date."

Annie shot back, “And if I win, you will pass the ball enough to Hill to make sure he gets twenty points a game!”

“I don’t see how I lose either way, Annie. Deal!” Junior shook hands with Annie, while everyone was cheering. He opened the window to the driver and said, “Frank, after you drop us off, please go back to the Enclave and pick up Annie’s basketball stuff. Now off to Prep.” Junior commanded. He then turned back to the group and declared, “we can play during the break. I can get us into the gym.”

“Only the six of us in the gym.” Hill instructed, “No leaking this to the dance.”

“Got it, buddy!” Junior assured his teammate.

The six of them walked into the dance, fashionably late at eight p.m. The band was just taking over for the DJ, and the hall was packed with excited teenagers. Quickly, couples hit the floor dancing to the techno-swing sound. It was an exciting scene to be a part of, for these six especially. Junior and Annie were at full speed with great turns and swings to the music. Hill and Malak took things a little slower, staying with a conventional two-step. Lil was being adventurous, forcing Chahna into new moves and awkward misses. They were laughing at themselves and enjoyed being silly.

Sandy and Russell had spent most of their time in the lounge, but now entered the dance hall, following the stimulating sound of the band. They enjoyed the time they had talking, even with the passion they acted upon, it did not keep them from sharing with each other. Neither had any misconceptions about their relationships, it was a true friendship—always giving support to each other. Heeding each other’s needs was a big part of that support.

Russell wondered what normal was like for these kids. His teenage years were so structured that he adored chaos in college. Now, he was trying to get back to a real normal or even mediocrity, something he was more comfortable with, but it had to include fun and spontaneity. He remembered being at dances in high school and feeling total anxiety. His first real girlfriend was not until the summer after high school; since then, they overlapped one another until now at twenty-six. He was still overlapping relationships, hedging his bets on love and sex. A good buddy of his in high school, who had early and consistent experience with girls, told him, “Think of it like a roster of three, one coming, one steady, and one going. That way you always have the roster filled with talent, with an eye each on the horizon and the sunset.” In some ways, he was doing that now with Annie, Sandy, and Abbey. The relationship ride was a kid's carousel that always went in a circle. He was looking forward to grabbing the ring and settling down.

The break in the dance was coming up. The band had the hall jumping and fully engaged the students for over an hour. Now the kids went fleeing for the drinks, treats, and cool air outside. Russell had only seen Annie from a distance and had not crossed her path. Sandy grabbed their coats and his arm and headed outside. Sandy said, "I think something is going on at the gym." They walked to the back of the campus to the field house complex, a fifty million dollar structure built twenty years ago, it was a better facility than most small colleges built presently. Russell had a key, being a department head, and had been getting in the best shape of his life using the gym's resources. They found nobody around outside, but once they went in, the lights were on with four kids sitting in the stands: Hill, Malak, Lil, and Chahna. The gym was quiet as Russell and Sandy stayed in the entrance area with a wall of trophies.

"Let's go up to the suite level," Russell said. They quietly headed upstairs and finally heard two basketballs bouncing on the gym floor. They found a spot behind glass where they could not be seen.

"What the fuck are they doing?" Sandy seemed startled as she said quietly into Russell's ear.

"It looks like Junior and Annie are playing basketball with each other."

"Are they crazy? In the middle of the dance?" Suddenly, a loud banging on the doors echoed through the gym. Junior looked up and motioned it was cool to everyone as he let in a half-dozen kids, clearly his friends, as they slapped his back and laughed with him on the way in.

"I said it was supposed to be just us. We are going to get in some shit for this." Hill yelled out to Junior.

"It's just some friends of mine to even things out. I mean you guys aren't going to cheer for me, right? They're cool don't worry, Hill." Junior played his reassuring card.

Annie was warming up doing some dribbling drills and only shooting layups and runners in the lane. Junior flashed onto the court shooting three pointers and following up with a dunk or two. Hill walked on the court, "Okay, Annie and Junior, let's get this thing going. We got about ten minutes. You call it: heads or tail?" He flipped, and Junior got the ball first. "Playing winners, bring the ball back to the three-point line after change of possession. I'll call obvious fouls, otherwise try to play fair, especially you, Junior."

"No problem bro!"

Junior took the ball, checked it back to Annie, drove straight to basket, and ended with a dunk. His cheering section went nuts as he went by them with high fives. Annie stood stoically at the top of the key waiting.

"Junior, let's get back to the game… Enough with the celebration." Hill glared as Junior headed back to check the ball to Annie. Quickly he dribbled into the key and then launched a step-back jumper from beyond the arc for a three pointer.

Annie grabbed the ball, bounced it between her legs, returned it back to Junior and said, "Checked."

Junior went between his legs and headed left down the lane and fired an elbow jumper off the glass for two points. Quickly it was 7–0, but he was sweating profusely as he went back to check the ball. "Sorry, honey, just playing it straight, trying to win that bet!"

"Are you getting tired, Junior? All that sweating from the champagne, I guess." Annie retorted.

Junior took two dribbles to his right and drained another three-pointer. "10–0 sweetheart." He took the ball again and tried to crossover dribble, but Annie knocked it behind him and stole it. She dribbled in and out of the lane a couple times making Junior play defense. Suddenly, she spun to her right, went under the basket and worked it off the backboard for her first field goal. Lil roared from the sidelines with approval. The show was on!

Annie worked Junior all over the court and made eight layups in a row to go ahead 18–10. Junior was done, his hands pulling down on his shorts, as he tried unsuccessfully to catch his breath. Annie checked the ball with him. He jumped up on his toes trying to steal the ball, she dribbled through his legs and into the lane. Junior recovered and came from behind looking to block her potential layup. She went past the basket and back out to the corner, dribbling through her legs and around her back, waiting for him to get up. He rose from the floor and took a weak step towards her. She smiled and shook her head, then let go of her only jumper and nailed the three-pointer to win 21–10.

Hill, Malak, Lil, and Chayna roared from the sidelines. Junior's friends waved goodbye, yelling that they had to get back to the dance. Annie headed to the dressing room to get back into her dress and heels. The group wandered to head back to the dance. Junior sat with the two basketballs for a minute. He felt humiliated, and he knew it would be all over the dance when he went back. He slammed down the balls and went in to talk to Annie. *She set me up,* he thought, *all that dribbling stuff and taking advantage of me being drunk. No no…I felt sorry for her and let her get back into the game and I just got tired…so she tried to make me look bad.* He was in a tornado twister of thoughts and wanted to set her straight. He barged into the visitor's locker room and found her getting into her dress. She tried to cover herself as he came upon her, yelling accusations. He slammed her against the lockers. She tried to stay calm as her dress fell down around her hips. He tried to kiss her neck and feel her breasts as he felt aroused by her cleavage and bare shoulders. "Junior, stop… everything is okay, let me get dressed."

"That's what you think, you think you can humiliate me like that?"

"I got lucky, Junior, you had more to drink than I did."

"No doubt, sister, I felt sorry for you, and this is what I get in return?"

"Junior, let me get dressed. Remember your father's party, you need a date, right?"

He hesitated and backed off a second, "Yeah… You still want to go?"

"Of course, Junior, I am a big fan. My dad and my father, Guy Finelli… remember?"

He pulled back a couple of feet and looked away a second. Without hesitation, she slid out like *Flash Girl* scooping up her shoes and gym bag. He tried to grab her, but she was gone. She dashed through the gym and out the front door.

Hill first saw her half-dressed and screamed, "What the fuck happened?"

"I took care of it, Hill," she said in his face directly, "Lil zip me up and help me with my shoes."

"That mother-fucker!" and Hill took off. He ran like a bullet through the gym and found Junior in the locker room getting dressed. "What the fuck did you do to her, Junior?" Hill towered over him by five inches and forty pounds.

"Nothing, man, we were just talking that's all. She's coming to my party, dude... How cool is that?" Hill had enough and decked him with one punch and then started kicking him in the gut. Chayna flew in and tried to pull Hill off of him.

Sandy and Russell were ecstatic watching Annie mop the floor with Junior. They had left the booth and were taking their time coming down the stairs. When they reached the lobby, they heard some loud yelling from across the gym. Russell took off for the locker rooms, he busted in the home locker room and found Chayna trying to pull Hill off of Junior. "Hill, that's enough!"

Hill looked up and stopped. He got up and screamed, "That fucker assaulted Annie while she was getting dressed, she came running out half-dressed. He's a total piece of shit."

"Get out of here Hill and you, too, Chayna." They listened and retreated outside. Sandy had found Lil, Malak, and Annie, who maintained that everything was fine. She walked with them back to the dance. Russell got Junior to his feet and sat him down on a bench.

"Let me get you an ice bag for that cheek." He found the trainer room and came back with instant cold press.

"Thanks," Junior uttered, "That fucker cold-cocked me for doing nothing. Annie and I were just talking and making out after the game. She was cool and said she was still coming to my dad's party."

Russell felt like punching him on the other cheek but stayed cool. "We have to get you back to the dance," he said as he helped Junior to his feet.

"I'm turning that fucker in, man, he can't get away with that!"

"Junior..." Russell tried to keep his sanity and feel something but contempt for this brat of a kid. He grabbed his shoulders and finally made eye contact. It was not pleasant, but he knew it was important to get inside the jumbled head of this soon to be seventeen, over-active, testosterone-laden, growing male in front of him. Russell had been there not too long ago.

"Let's talk about that Junior... I don't think you want to do that."

~26~

The Christmas break at Georgetown Prep was two and a half weeks long starting in the middle of December. Ten days of exams followed the holiday dance on Saturday night. After the dance, Russell brokered a deal with the headmaster to keep the incident out of the news. He convinced Junior to keep his mouth shut and not press charges. He pointed out that if Hill transferred, he would have the scoring duties all to himself. He agreed grudgingly as he went upstairs to his room to heal his face and ribs—and to think about the mess he had made with Annie.

Hill was offered a chance to leave at the end of exams and transfer to WJ with a good recommendation. He knew playing with Junior was not an option anymore, and this way he could see Annie every day at school. Lil became immediately jealous at his chance for everyday contact with Annie, but then supported it with sisterly love.

When the WJ basketball coach heard a rumor concerning Hill's transfer, he fantasized about coaching a championship team. He quickly made plans to re-work his offense.

Russell and Sandy talked to Annie after the dance and she was more than happy to not press charges. She wanted none of the publicity and agreed with Russell's assessment that none of the adults in their families could know what happened, other than a fight between Hill and Junior. Hill, Lil, Malak, and Chahna agreed to keep the incident to themselves. The headmaster was sad to lose an athlete like Hill Santucci and his donor father Alex, but it was better than losing both donor families.

When Sandy and Russell went up for a drink in his suite after all the negotiations were over, they talked until three a.m. without laying a hand on each other. Sandy had called her husband to say that she would be very, very late and not to stay up. She would explain later. Eventually, they finished the scotch bottle and fell asleep on the couch together. At five a.m., Russell looked for water and took some Advil. He found a blanket and put it on Sandy. When he settled in bed, he heard Sandy come in, take off her clothes, and get under the covers. She snuggled up to him and was back asleep in seconds. At eight a.m., he woke up with a hard-on, but he turned away from Sandy and went to the bathroom. He thought for a minute about climbing on the naked presence in his bed but decided to let his hand work instead. He massaged himself quickly, hoping for relief, but failed. His stomach felt upset about the assault on Annie during the dance. It was also empty of food and was sexually frustrated. He got dressed and then whispered to Sandy to put on her clothes so they could go out to breakfast. She sat up, fully naked and rubbing her eyes. She stretched her arms over her head while arching her chest. Russell was intrigued but waited patiently for her to put her beautiful breasts away in safe keeping. Russell summoned the Acura to warm up before they headed down the elevator. Sandy gladly hopped into the warm passenger seat as Russell ripped the Acura out of the quiet parking lot. They made to the diner up on Rockville Pike through several, almost red lights in five minutes. Smelling the coffee, they settled into the same side of the booth and quickly ordered two black cups of the brew scenting the air.

They talked for two hours while ingesting eggs, sausage, gravy-covered biscuits, and corn beef hash. Sandy was the first to get emotional while talking about what happened to Annie. Russell had tried to block it out of his thinking, believing he would walk down the hall and choke Junior while he slept in his room. He had a master key to the fourth floor and knew he could get away with it. The anger turned to tears while seeing Sandy's eyes moisten. They sat in silence sipping their black brew while both gained their composure. Sandy wanted to comfort Russell, but realized his head was in another place when he ignored her nude body in bed two hours earlier. Finally, Russell dropped her off after ten a.m., unconcerned about her husband's reaction. He was confident that Sandy could handle it.

The following week was difficult for Russell as he felt a rage at every Junior sighting. Except for a couple of texts from Annie, he felt great anxiety waiting to see her at the next lesson. When Wednesday finally arrived, he was relieved she made it up the elevator without being noticed. Annie immediately fell into his arms and stayed there for a full minute. When she left his warm embrace, she quickly headed to the piano and started playing the homework she had practiced all week. Neither of them brought up the incident; instead, they focused on her lesson for the whole hour. She insisted he play for her again. Russell complied with his reworked piece. She was very pleased with it, recognizing the *Candy-O* influence.

On the way home, they held hands again as she finally spoke about the attack, "Thank you for saving Hill and me. The whole thing was my fault. I knew better than being with him alone."

"But he came after you in the dressing room, Annie, that wasn't your fault. You were just having a good time with your cousins. How would you know that Junior was a maniac?"

"I should have had Lil come in with me or have Hill stay at the door. My Grandmom and Sally would be very disappointed with my poor planning. I suspected that Junior might be aggressive physically, but since he knew Hill, I thought it would work out. You know it was just part of the Plan, right? I did not like him or anything. It was just a cover for being in high school."

"Did he hurt you?"

"He caught me with my dress down around my thighs. I had taken off my jersey and athletic bra and was just about to pull up my dress when he put his arms on me and started kissing me. I did not fight him and finished the kiss. He was fully engorged under his pants and started to go under my bra. I knew I was in trouble, so I kissed him again quickly and told him to give me a second. He backed off for a moment and was attending to his pants, that is when I saw an opening and darted out of there."

Russell was full of respect for Annie's escape and ability to think through the whole incident without tearing up, but again he wanted to harm Junior. He took a deep breath and thought of Saint Francis and his love of animals, *he would have handled Junior with patience.*

Russell never imagined himself as an imposing physical specimen, but in fact he was six feet, two inches and a fit one hundred and ninety pounds. Most juniors in high school were lanky and barely topped one hundred and sixty pounds. He was a good leaper in basketball, but was not a shooter, kind of like his Grandfather, Gene Santucci, who was exactly his size in college when he played for Fordham University in the Bronx and ended up in the top five all-time in school rebounding. Since he was never allowed to play contact sports as a kid, Russell only discovered his propensity to jump, block shots, grab rebounds in high school gym class, and then later in pick-up games at Georgetown. One year, he emerged from the smoke of partying and played on an intramural team for a season. He had a blast but turned his ankle near the end of the season and never rejoined the team again. Otherwise, he played tennis, mainly with his parents, and now worked out religiously. He was in the best shape of his life.

"It sounds like you thought quickly on your feet to get out of there." He looked at her for a moment, she had done her hair differently like at the dance at the Academy and had eye make-up on. *She looked lovely*, he thought as he squeezed her hand. "I understand, Annie, that you think you did something to deserve being treating like that, but in no way was it your fault, at all! Besides, you did kick his ass in one-on-one. We saw the whole thing."

"You were there? How did you know?" Annie sprung a huge smile.

"Sandy got a tip." Russell reported.

"Should I worry about you and Sandy?" she posed a playful frown.

Russell was shocked at the question but should have known about Annie's perceptive abilities. "We're just friends, and she's married."

"I see…" She smiled again and answered playfully, "I understand…I think!", and squeezed his hand to assure him they were okay.

~27~

The Christmas holiday could not have come at a better time. The week after the incident was tense, full of suspicion, and rumors on the Prep campus. Hill was not in school and of course not at basketball practice. He was reported to be sick and recovering from the flu at the Parkwood Enclave. The season would start with the Christmas Holiday Catholic League tournament. It was decided by the headmaster to delay the news of Hill leaving Prep until after the tournament started.

Annie stayed home from school as well and worked out with Hill at the Enclave on their basketball court that had a tennis-like bubble cover. Family friend Bonnie Bramlett, a former reporter and now a counselor/life-fitness coach, was brought in for the week to talk to both Annie and Hill by Sally Keegan. Grandparents Phillip and Carol were available as well.

Annie's father (Guy Finelli) and his half-brother (Alex Santucci) had ex-Assistant FBI Director Brooklyn O'Malley (Sandy's father) conduct a private informal investigation of the dance night events starting with interviews of Annie, Hill, Lil, Malak, Chahna, Russell, and Sandy. They wanted to document the details of the event for any future problem. The headmaster at Georgetown Prep allowed Brooks to interview Junior Parker and his six friends who witnessed the game prior to the incident. Junior, to his credit, did not lawyer up and answered all questions asked but denied any sexual assault (in accord with Annie's wishes), just a fight between himself and Hill about basketball. In Brooks O'Malley's confidential report, he agreed with the headmaster that no charges be brought in the case.

The Walter Johnson coach, Dennis DeBone, visited two of the Enclave sessions himself, assessing Hill's talent up close. What he was not prepared for was the athleticism of Annie Finelli. He had seen her run track, perform in the high and long jumps, and play volleyball; but he was taken aback by her "Pistol Pete" abilities handling the basketball.

The two of them together had a warm-up exercise that was like a globe-trotter exhibition with dribbling, passing, and lay-ups. They would practice rebounds off missed shots (provided by Grandpa Phillip Finelli from both sides of the key), that would turn into two-person fast breaks. Coach DeBone left both sessions with his head spinning. As good as Hill was, as a six-foot, five-inch, dead-on shooter and big rebounder, it was Annie who blew him away. She was a natural point guard, who was too fast and quick to be covered by one person. Up to this point, a high school girl had never made a boys' basketball team in Montgomery County as a valuable contributor. To most it seemed unthinkable.

On the Friday before Christmas break, Coach DeBone sought out Annie's volleyball coach, Janet Melendez for a conversation.

"Have you heard the rumor about the Santucci boy?"

"Who Hill, Annie Finelli's cousin? What rumor?"

"He's transferring to WJ from Prep. Apparently, there was an incident at a dance, a fight with Junior Parker after a one-on-one game with his date Annie Finelli."

"Holy crap! Dennis, that's crazy. My Annie on a date and playing basketball?"

"That's the story, Janet."

"The Potomacs owner's son…he's their star player, right?"

"I know…that's why I have to talk to you… Can you keep a secret?"

She stared at him for a minute, trying to process the story, she could only utter, "Depends..."

"Come on, Janet. I have to talk to you about this."

"Alright, settle down." She laughed trying to release some tension and then asked him, "Why don't you let me coach with you, Dennis? That science nerd you got is a loser."

"Are you kidding me? You don't have time for coaching basketball."

"I might!"

"Listen, this is important… I was at the Parkwood Enclave to see Hill and Annie workout on their court over there. That's quite a set up by the way."

"What... Are you making this shit up, Dennis?"

"No...really...Alex Santucci called me and asked me to come over to talk and watch his kid play. They have a covered court over there, that is pretty cool."

"Dennis, I have a meeting in ten minutes, let's speed this up."

"Okay, okay...but listen, that Hill kid is a stud! He's grown two inches and put on twenty pounds of muscle since last year. I think he would be the best 4A player in the county this year."

"And?"

"Well shit, you know I lost my best ball handling kid as a senior last year, and I have VERY below average talent at point guard this year, but this Finelli girl is better than any of them, RIGHT NOW!"

"Dennis, are you crazy? She has never played in a basketball game, forget it."

"What do you mean, never played on a team?"

"Never, never, never! No league, no pick-up game, no three-on-three. Just one-on-one games with her cousins, father, Grandpa and now apparently, this Junior Parker kid from Prep."

"That's impossible. Why would she be so skilled and never play on a team?"

"Because she doesn't like it. It's too confusing for her. She's done it for fun with her cousins since she was five or six years old."

"How did you get her to play volleyball?"

"I'm not sure, I think it was pure luck. I told her she could play in the back row and still slam it."

"You mean spike from the back row?'

"No, she used the word 'slamming,' not spiking. Listen, I must get to this meeting. Call me tonight."

Janet slapped Dennis on the shoulder and headed down the hall. She had nothing else to say and he was left speechless.

~28~

Russell did his best to walk down the fourth-floor hall of dorm residents on the last night before Christmas break with his stomach feeling a little upset. He was filling in for the Hall Prefect, who had asked for him to cover as he headed home to Texas for the semester break from graduate school. The duties were fairly simple, and the same for decades: Walk down the hall once or twice an hour during mandatory study hall from six to eight p.m.; make sure the doors to all rooms are open and each resident is sitting at his desk; no internet, radios, earphones, phone calls, game-playing, card-playing, sitting-on-beds, feet-on-the-desks, drinks, food, talking or singing to oneself were allowed during those two hours.

The current headmaster would surprise with walk-down-the-hallway visits, usually once every other week. If he caught someone in violation, it was an immediate one hundred demerits (two hundred and fifty was a one-day suspension). As usual, Junior Parker was the leader in demerits with three suspensions this year (overruled by the Appeals Board each time). Now that basketball practice had started, another suspension would be non-reviewable. After an earlier meeting in the week that included his father, the headmaster, the basketball coach and Russell, filling in for the missing Hall Prefect; Junior was told no more lucky breaks would be coming his way. Russell watched silently as Junior was near tears when his father Burton Parker, billionaire owner of the Washington Potomacs, caused a seismic crack in his backside with a verbal tirade about his behavior in front of everybody.

As he continued his walk down the lonely hall with thirty open doors, Russell remembered how he did everything possible not to get a huge smile on his face at the meeting. He reached the south end of the hall and turned to view the east facing dorm rooms and then back to his room. The first open door and corner room was Junior's, the farthest from the Prefect's room and the other side of the building from Russell's room. More importantly, it was bigger, had a regular sized refrigerator; supposedly always stocked with soft drinks, water, and snacks, and was next to the stairs on the south side of the building. It was a quick route to escape at night after the ten p.m. all-lights-out curfew. Russell stopped for a moment to view Junior sitting upright in his chair typing into his computer. Friday was the last day to turn in course work for the semester, and Junior seemed to be actually working. The Prefect was supposed to check the Prep-issued computer during study hall to make sure that only word processing was being used. Most kids found it too complicated to load the school computer with anything other than school-work, but Junior had all the means necessary if he wanted. Another automatic one hundred demerits could be assessed for each violation.

Russell took two steps towards Junior's room, then two more to walk inside and look around. One side had actually been painted blue and gray (Prep colors) with pictures of Junior in action on the basketball court. On the other side, the wall was painted burgundy and gold with pictures of Super Bowl LIII and LIV and GAF I championships by his father's football team. He was in every picture at ages five, six, and seven with his father holding him and the Lombardi Trophy twice and the Thorpe Trophy once. From all reports and from Russell's own eyes, Junior adored his father. His life ambition was to take over control of the Washington Potomacs Football empire by the age of thirty-five.

Junior turned his head to the side to notice Russell, "Mr. Santucci, sir, please come in. I hope you enjoy my room. Please help yourself to my fridge, anytime, sir." Russell was impressed to notice how perfect and clean the room was. Shelves had been attached to walls with mountains of historical biographies and novels. His clothes did not show a wrinkle, and his bed was made with accent pillows of blue, gray, burgundy and gold placed against the wall. Russell thought, *either Junior had a full-time maid, or he was obsessive-compulsive.* He opened the fridge and saw perfect rows of water, diet coke, mountain dew, and orange crush. He had deli meat, bread, cheese, fruit, and an impressive array of candy bars. It was obvious to Russell, how this kid could get away with murder. *His classmates must love him*, Russell thought as he closed the fridge, "No thanks, Junior." He walked up to his chair and looked at his computer.

"This AP English Lit course is killing me… I have one more review to write after this one to turn in. Have you read any of this Michener guy historical novel stuff? Brutal to get through."

Russell could see the report over Junior's shoulder. He was working on a review of the 1978 book *Chesapeake* by James Michener, one of Russell's favorite books. "Yeah, they are, but they're usually worth it."

"That's a good point. A lot of information in this one about Maryland. Kinda blows my mind. Almost done with this review. A thousand words for each book. Almost a back breaker!"

"Well, I won't interrupt you Junior. Just thought I would check in."

"No problem, Mr. Santucci. Listen sir, I appreciate you coming to my hearing and talking sense into me after the fight with Hill. I feel pretty bad about the whole thing. I thought we were pretty good friends… You know?"

Russell was taken aback by his politeness and openness. *He was either a great conman or manic-depressive instead of the previously observed obsessive-compulsive behavior,* Russell chuckled to himself. "Yes…very unfortunate but now you both have a chance to move on without facing charges."

Junior looked at him with a puzzled look, but then realized he believed that he assaulted Annie. He took a gulp and tried to think of some words that might placate Russell. "I see what you're saying, sir, I used poor judgement. I'm sure she hates me now." He turned away and became a young sixteen-year-old again, trying to be a man.

"I don't think she hates you, Junior, but it was a scary situation for her or for any girl in her situation." Russell felt unnerved as he wanted to grab Junior's neck but was starting to feel sorry for him instead.

"Of course, sir. Please, if you ever see her, tell her…" Junior started typing again as a tear fell down his face. He kept his poise and cleared his voice. "Tell her," for the first time he looked at Russell straight in the eyes and almost cracked. He turned back to his computer and wiped his eyes, "Tell her that I regret my behavior, and I am very, very sorry." He paused for a moment with his eyes closed. Tears were covering his face, but somehow his voice was not affected. "Sir… Something happened to me at the dance that I can't explain. She made me feel different, like life was worth living. She is a very special girl who acts beyond her years."

"Good night, Junior," Russell turned quickly, having heard enough, and made it to the threshold before, he heard his name again.

"Mr. Santucci," Junior stood up, at an even six feet he was a strong and handsome boy. "Thank you again, sir, and I hope you get a chance to, because I don't think she would ever talk to me again."

Russell composed himself before turning around. He tried to remember that he was the adult in this situation. Finally, he turned and locked his eyes on his foe. "Junior, I will do my best… Never is a long time." He paused for a moment trying not to blow this teachable moment. *After all, I am a teacher*, he thought. "I hope you have a good holiday and a good basketball season." He managed a smile.

"Yes, sir. You, too, Mr. Santucci. Thanks again."

Russell quickly escaped and walked rapidly down the stoically quiet hall. *That was enough checking for one night*, he thought. He got to his suite and took out the scotch.

~29~

Annie's personality was a dominate force at the Parkwood Enclave. She now had residences at three different houses available to her, each one stocked with clothes and amenities for up to a week. The Santucci house was her official space with Sally, Alex, Lil, and Hill. There was a nice bedroom with her own bathroom on the top floor, which looked out over the treetops of woods that covered the meandering Rock Creek that flowed below Parkwood Drive and the houses on the other side. The beautiful waterway and surrounding parklands drained most of the Montgomery county southern basin, and eventually worked its way through the middle of DC and emptied into the Potomac just east of Georgetown. The house was at the highest point of the block and looked bigger than it was with a huge deck off the back of the house and a twenty-meter heated swimming pool. Just below it was the basketball court with its winter bubble.

It was not until she started high school that she made a room for herself at her father's house, who lived with his wife Patty O'Neil and her younger, half-brother Anthony Finelli II. Their house was physically set below and over a lot from the Santucci house and faced Parkwood Drive on the two lots away from her grandparents on the corner. The residence was bigger in square footage than the Santucci residence but did not look as grand. There was a separate three-bedroom apartment over the garage that was for the twenty-four-hour security rotation and the head maintenance foreman. Guy Finelli had it built to make them feel part of his family. They were a loyal group of employees and well paid.

Annie had her choice of the three open bedrooms upstairs. Patty had always told her "whenever you're ready, we'll make one of these rooms special for you." Annie picked the bedroom next to her brother and shared a bathroom with him. Anthony was the only person that brought out her feelings of wanting to be maternal. It hit her soon after puberty at age nine. It took her a while to identify the change of how she thought of her little baby brother. Talking with Sally and Patty helped her define it. Once she learned everything she could about it, she wanted to become good at it. That meant spending more time with Anthony.

Feeling maternal had another side to it that blossomed after she met Russell two years ago. Having sexual feelings for an adult man, made her think about her mother in ways she never imagined. At age thirteen, suddenly she became interested in details of her mother's life. She methodically talked to Sally and Patty about Anna's life and how she acted while pregnant. Spending time with Anthony and falling in love during the past summer with Russell, made her finally realize that her mother really loved her. As heartbreaking as her death was, she was consoled to know that fact.

At nine years old and red hair to match her beautiful locks, she thought Anthony was the cutest boy she had ever seen. She started to read to him when he was barely two years old, at Patty's suggestion. At first, it was very uncomfortable having someone so physically close to her, but after a few times, she fell in love with him. In the summer before ninth grade, she decided to sleep there on the weekends, babysitting at times on Fridays or Saturdays for Guy and Patty. Anthony would always fall asleep in her bed around nine p.m. She would watch television late until Guy and Patty came home, at times staring at him breathing. It was hard for her to imagine that she was ever that endearing. *That was a great learning experience for me to become so close and learn to take care of another human*, she believed.

Recently over the past summer, after her fifteenth birthday, she took over the basement at her grandparent's house. Even though the house had been redone in 2011, the basement had stayed in the original form. A massive garage had been added under the family room with an elevator, which kept the privacy of the basement. The beautiful pine-wood paneling, now seventy-five years old, was built on a free-standing wall of two-by-four wood studs next to the concrete walls of the foundation. It added warmth and dryness to the room for a basement. She was given the job of oiling the walls every three months.

Her great-Grandpa Guy I Finelli built it in the mid-1950s. There was a large open area with a flagstone floor beautifully covered with handmade middle eastern rugs. A full bathroom in the corner, and two rooms on the opposite side; one housed a full kitchen and another a bedroom. She would spend hours in the kitchen reading or eating, imagining the meals prepared by her great-Grandmom Rose Finelli. If she focused hard enough, she could imagine smelling the garlic in the tomato sauce that simmered for hours on the stove after church on Sunday mornings. It was made over a thousand times according to her math for her great-Grandpa, Grandpa, and father and of course other members of the Finelli family. The meatballs delicately made and browned, then added to the sauce at just the right time. She could hear her great-Grandmom yelling, "Hey!" whenever someone came in to sample the sauce or pick on one of the meatballs. *It was an Italian thing to have a kitchen in the basement—it feels cozy and cool*, she thought.

At times, she would sit in the big room on one of the two wooden platforms, (with twin bed cushions) built into the walls, with drawers below and a solid oak desk between them – gazing at the grand basement. She imagined the steel beam splitting the middle and holding up the entire room with two two steel support columns, as well as the plumbing and lighting in the ceiling. All of the imagined substructure was encased and hidden in perfectly crafted pine paneling. The solid oak stairs from the main floor cascaded down ten steps onto a platform that turned you left into the room, *my father would have to duck*, and then down two, three-sided steps that reached the flagstone floor. Like the whole basement, it was an architectural gem that caused her to say out loud, "for goodness sake, this was a cold concrete basement that was turned into a special, warm family space for three generations and now a fourth... that is me I guess!"

This past year she had spent a lot of time with her Grandpa's vinyl record collection that was on display in the basement with a monster, old-school stereo set-up. Her grandparents never complained about the loudness of the speakers when she played music. Her Grandpa would talk about the difference between hearing vinyl versus digital and head or earphones versus speakers. After the hours she spent with his collection, she agreed that the vinyl sound was thicker and the music through speakers felt more real.

Her grandparents would move two floors up if they wanted quiet. Otherwise, they were thrilled at her continued interest. Since the *Candy-O* obsession with *The Cars*, she had progressed to the E's in her album listening, spending most of her time with *The Eagles*, *Elton John*, *Elvis*, and *Emerson, Lake and Palmer*. But her life changed again with *ELO*. At first, she could not understand the well-known obsession by her Grandpa, of *Jeff Lynne's ELO*. After delivering a critique to him saying "they were too busy musically and too simple lyrically," he asked one question, "How loud was it?"

She answered, "There is too much in the music to play it loud."

He disagreed and encouraged her to, "Play it at maximum volume, because each song is a full symphony," and assured her that, "the speakers and the house could handle it." He also gave her a specific playlist to focus on.

During the Christmas break, it was a nice diversion from the Prep experience to dive into the music. She had a rush of feelings from listening to the intensity of the music. The mixture of orchestral instruments and strong guitars rifts, heavy percussion, and soft interludes, had hypnotic effects on her in understanding her life. It seemed to develop exponentially when she thought of her mother's life every day that she listened. She could see it from Anna's perspective of being eight months pregnant, a view into the future of her daughter's life, and the hope she had for her baby. It was an out of body experience.

At the same time, she realized, the tragedy must have stunted her father's emotional development, being that he was four months short of becoming twenty. She made a note to herself to listen to this music with her father sometime.

Annie convinced Sally and Guy that having Russell come to her Grandpa's house for piano lessons in the near future was best for everyone. She did her practicing on her great-grandparents' Baldwin Acrosonic Piano since starting the lessons and was growing fond of it. Her Uncle Anthony had learned on it and it still had a lovely sound. Carol played occasionally, but not in front of anyone. At times, when she was hidden in the basement, she would hear her Grandmom play a piece or two. It felt comforting.

Russell came over the Wednesday before Christmas during the first week of break. She tried to control her excitement. They were alone in the house, while her grandparents took a long walk in the park. She played through her lesson with too much energy and made lots of mistakes. Normally this would bother her quite a bit, but she felt the music effectively and moved through the mistakes without losing focus. Near the end of the lesson, Russell would play a series of notes or chords for five to ten seconds and ask Annie to repeat it. He would alternate hands as he stood over her, playing to her right and then left. She could smell his closeness and see the strength of his playing.

When they finished with a flurry, they hugged naturally from a joy of accomplishment. Annie then turned and asked him to play something. She was feeling chills from their embrace as she stood over his shoulder. As he played another Chopin concerto, she let two of her fingers touch his right shoulder and closed her eyes, feeling his brilliance.

She heard the door gently close in the far-off family room. She gently lifted her hand as Russell kept playing. A pair of footsteps came softly into the living room, settling not to be noticed. Without interruption, Russell finished the concerto and played into his own piece that was improving with each effort. His confidence and energy were on full display. It was clear to Annie that he was a master pianist, coming out from his guarded personality.

The clapping broke the silence as Russell stood to greet Phillip and Carol.

"What a treat Russell, that was magnificent," Carol said enthusiastically.

Phillip's eyes were moist hearing the Acrosonic played with such intensity. "That was thrilling Russell," he expressed emotionally, as he shook his hand vigorously.

"He is a master… I really believe it, Grandpa and Grandmom... Simply a master!" Annie stated with authority and emotion.

Annie rode down the elevator with Russell to his car in his grandparents' driveway at the basement level. Before they walked out of the house, she stopped and turned towards Russell knowing they could not be seen by humans or security cameras. She embraced him, laying her head on his chest with her arms rubbing up and down his back. Russell held on lightly with his arms around her shoulders. She wanted to kiss him and keep that taste in her mouth for the next week, but she kept her discipline. He could feel her strong body pressed up against his member, quickly growing hard. She never wanted to let go and pressed herself closer to him. He wanted to let go but stopped. Finally, they ended the embrace and held each other at an arm's distance, looking at each other as they caught their breath. "When will I see you again over the holidays? At least at Christmas Eve…" she settled for.

"I look forward to it," he answered meekly.

"Yes, that would be nice. Thank you for the lesson and playing for me."

"It was a pleasure, Annie."

~30~

The Friday before Christmas was the last day of school for WJ. It was sparsely attended. Coach Dennis DeBone took that opportunity to escort his prize recruit into the administration office to officially enroll in class. Technically, Hill Santucci had finished his first semester at Prep, but to be eligible for the Montgomery County season, he would have to enroll before the county semester was over in mid-January. The team had started to practice in early December and would play in a tournament during the Christmas break, but the county season did not start until the new year.

WJ Principal Dean Resnick was there to greet the star pupil and his famous parents, Sally Keegan and Alex Santucci. They lit up the room and attracted all the personnel hardly working in the library, guidance offices, and stray teachers not in front of a class. Hill had his father's blond curls and physical makeup. He was now an inch taller as well. Sally, as usual, took the lead in greeting all the principal's staff and any hands that were extended. It had been seventeen years since the championship season, but she was still very much in the media as a political talking head and philanthropist. All the pictures taken were immediately in the Cloud generating excitement for the basketball season. A rush on season tickets during the week, based on rumors of Hill's recruitment, had sold out the county games except for students seats. Online sales of t-shirts and jerseys had generated thousands of dollars already.

Once in the principal's office, Coach Melendez and DeBone asked to speak with Sally and Alex. "We believe this year's team will be quite talented with the addition of Chamberlain Ebekwe from the South Sudan and now your son Hill. We will be dominant under the boards with Chamberlain and scoring with Hill. But we may have one problem, the point guard position. Coach Melendez would like to address this with you."

"Nice to see you, Coach, congratulations on another volleyball championship. We had so much fun at the Whitman game," Sally stated with enthusiasm. She liked Janet quite a bit and was thankful at all the attention she had given Annie over the past three years in track and volleyball. At this point, she was confused about her involvement in the meeting.

"Coach DeBone has asked me to become assistant coach this year with the basketball team. Basketball has been a passion of mine since playing in high school and college in Florida. I have never had a chance to coach, so I am pretty excited about the opportunity."

"I'm sure Dennis can use the help, since he will be spending a load of time finding tickets for parents. I remember the frenzy when Guy played here. It can get pretty crazy," Alex added, talking with great presence. Both coaches and Principal Resnick still could not believe the Hall-of-Fame baseball player was in their office. He still looked like he could play. Because of his support, the baseball program was still the best in the county.

"Thank you, Alex, I have certainly seen video of that season. It was something out of a movie. Of course, your three years of playing for DC was really a miracle. You and your brother have been a blessing to this school and the entire community."

Alex nodded and took Sally's hand as they sat back to listen.

"What Coach DeBone and I have come up with is pretty radical, but I think it will help all parties involved. We think Annie can play point guard for this team." She sat back to see their reaction and waited with her arguments.

"Our Annie?" Sally offered, "Janet, she's a girl… Am I right? And besides, she hasn't played with other people, much less boys twice her size." Sally rarely lost her cool but was on the edge of her seat at the moment.

"Actually, that would be pretty cool, Mom," Hill spoke up and tried to calm Sally.

"Was this your idea, Hill?"

"No no… This is the first I heard of it, but we've played together since we were five years old. And you know she's amazing, right?"

"So, Coach Melendez, are you saying of all the kids at WJ, little Annie Finelli would be the best point guard in the school?" asked Alex, softly holding back his wife with his left hand and tossing a tough question to the Coach.

"She may be the best point guard in the county right now. She just has to learn to do it with nine other kids on the court."

"Have you talked to Annie about this?" Sally said quietly, trying to regain her cool.

"No no, we have not. Coach DeBone watched her work out with Hill this past week, and I have seen her play in the past. She handles the ball like no one her age, boy or girl. She plays like Steve Nash, remember him? Besides, she can really, really jump!" Janet was excited about her presentation; she knew it was right after digesting the idea from Dennis earlier in the week. She was now totally on board.

"Mom and Dad, this might be perfect for Annie. After the Prep experience, she could really use something to focus on."

"Coach DeBone, how do you think the boys would handle it?" Alex inquired.

"Well first, she would have to compete and make the team and then become a starter. It would not be an easy task to be honest, but maybe by mid-season she could be ready."

"I see, so she could work her way in… I like that," Sally could see the picture now.

"Well, let's get her in here and she what she says." Coach DeBone suggested with authority. Sally and Alex sat in silence, not sure what to think of such a crazy idea. Neither could imagine Annie going for it. She was so busy with everything. Each of them felt stuck, hoping the other had something to say to put a hold on this madness.

Annie was called to the office. She was sitting in her literature class trying to care about a report given by a classmate. These days, it was all about students speaking in front of the class. Most leadership programs emphasized it from their research. Most teachers loved it. Everything was recorded, so they could sit in the back and do all their busy work and planning. Students gave feedback on every presentation, which was also graded for a minimum standard. Her teacher received a text message to send her and quietly tapped her on the shoulder. Annie had decided during the class that she would graduate high school in May 2030. She could take an extra English credit next semester and finish. It was time for some freedom when she turned sixteen in May.

She entered the principal's office with Hill, Sally, Alex, Coaches DeBone, and Melendez sitting facing each other. It felt ominous. Sally and Alex had a conference call with Guy Finelli to inform him of the plan. Sally had the final say but wanted Guy to be on board. He was all for it and immediately headed towards the school for the meeting. Annie sat next to Hill, who took her hand and looked right at her, "Annie, Coach DeBone and Melendez have come up with a great idea. I think it could be special."

Rarely was Annie clueless about a situation, but she looked at Hill and wondered if he was sick or something, "Are you okay, Hill?"

"I'm fine, you silly; just listen for a minute."

Just at that moment, her father walked in and pulled up a chair next to Annie, she whispered to him, "What are you doing here?"

"You'll see, sweetie."

Janet spoke first, "Annie, Coach DeBone had a great idea after watching Hill's workouts last week. First, he decided to hire me as assistant coach."

Annie was relieved but still a little confused, "Wow Coach Melendez, that is fantastic, you would be great coaching basketball. Have you always wanted to coach the boys' team?"

"Not exactly Annie, I just like coaching you. Coach DeBone wants you to play point guard for the WJ boys' team with Hill in the back court with you."

Annie felt her throat close up; she forgot to breathe for a few seconds. "Me," was all she could get her voice to say.

"Yes, you, Annie," Coach DeBone spoke up softly. "Coach Melendez and I believe we could win the county championship with you at point guard. You could be the most talented ball handler in the county. We want you to join the practices with Hill, and we will work you into the games, by midseason you should be ready."

Annie had so many feelings; she felt trapped for a moment. She looked at Hill, who held her hand tightly and at her father, who said to her, "you can do it Annie, I'll be at every practice if you want. It'll be a blast to mess with the boys. Just think of how cool it'll be."

Annie saw a confidence in his eyes that she never knew: It was the soul of a champion that believed in her. It was conveyed to him from his father and by his father's father—all champions. It was a connection they never had before and then he sealed it with this proclamation. "Your mom would love it! She was kind of a ball-buster, you know, with all the boys in the FBI."

Annie felt a tingler throughout her body and dove into her father's lap for a hug. She stayed encased in his giant torso with his strong arms for a minute, which felt like a loving eternity. *My Dad is right*, she thought, *it would be a blast*.

She had her answer. "Thank you Coach, but I need to take the weekend to think about it. I will call you Monday morning."

Everyone looked at each other at the meeting and watched Annie head back to class. "Well, I think that went well." Coach Melendez summed it up.

Annie had decided to play while curled up on her father's lap, but she wanted the weekend to be sure of her decision. The first practice was on Monday, Christmas Eve. She had until then to make up her mind. Friday night, she moved into her father's house for the Christmas break. She wanted to be near Anthony and share his excitement about everything Christmas.

~31~

Russell was having girl trouble. He was in love with a fifteen-year-old red head that he could not touch erotically – at least legally; was having great sex with his girlfriend – in a doomed relationship; and was involved with a married woman – trading great orgasms, but not intercourse.

At times, his triad of relationships seemed to make sense, but most of the time it was a nightmare to manage. His last encounter with Annie was on his mind a great deal. She had pushed things a bit too far. It provoked a situation that put him on the brink of a prison sentence. A very scary, but ecstatic feeling. He was unsure any of his confidants would understand or be willing to listen to him about his feelings on the subject. On the other hand, he was sure that she was the one. He felt special being in her presence, and certainly found her strikingly delicious.

For the holidays it was nice to be at Prep, by himself on the fourth floor. He left his door open to the hallway, enjoying the echo of the sound of his Steinway that he was playing flawlessly. Stress was leaving his body as he dove into Chopin concertos. It was a tonic for his tension. Somehow, the longer he played, the farther away his women trouble felt. He knew ultimately that he had to play out each scenario according to his Plan, otherwise nothing would work. The relationships were all interlocked. The strength of one supported the pain of another. The weakness of another made the pleasure of one magnificent. The first goal was getting to the end of the school year. Prison would be less likely when Annie turned sixteen.

They had a great conversation over the weekend about the invitation to play basketball on the boys' team and her decision to graduate in May. The first was an adventure that could make the semester go faster and the second was a step towards freedom for Annie. He was very happy about both. It might cut into their piano lessons, but he was willing to curtail that activity if necessary.

Suddenly, the elevator was rising. He kept playing wondering if it was maintenance or a cleaning crew coming through on a Saturday night. Unlikely, but possible with the holidays coming up. They were obsessive about keeping the dorm halls clean. Slowly, it opened. She stepped forward out of the elevator wearing a seasonal colored red dress buttoned up the middle and white four-inch heels. Sandy was ready to be taken out on a Saturday night. She walked into Russell's room and leaned over the piano keys as Russell played some slow jazz piece he had created. Her hair was laying over her chest, cutely hiding part of her face. She was ready to be entertained. "Are you free tonight? I could use a date."

Russell was surprised but not shocked. He kept Saturday night open, since Abbey was working, and he was staying out of bars lately. Occasionally, Sandy had called on a Saturday afternoon wondering if he would be free, but never had boldly shown up dressed to be fondled.

"I can see that... what did you have in mind, young lady?"

"I need to go dancing and maybe eat some food, but definitely a lot of alcohol. My husband decided to go home to his parents for the holidays. He said I was welcomed to join him, but he did not want to be around my family this Christmas. I guess that's not a good sign for our relationship, huh?"

"Depends, maybe it's about your cooking?"

"Don't be a wiseass, my dear. Are you going to be my friend tonight?"

"Anything for you, Sandy."

"Can you start with a drink?"

Russell rose from the piano bench, closed his door, and proceeded to make her a martini. She relocated on the couch. "How many olives?"

"Tons...and can you give me one of your famous back rubs before we go out?"

"At your service." Russell served her the martini with six olives, sat to her side, and got on his knees on the couch behind her. He unzipped her, took some cream from the table behind him, and rubbed it together on his hands. She was tight as a drum. He worked her neck muscles down to her shoulders and back up. After a couple of minutes, she was tearing up.

"Can I have another martini, but don't stop yet. This feels too good." After a few moments, she uttered, "I wonder if I fucked up my marriage Russell?"

He rose to make another drink, "Maybe...but it's more likely to be a joint venture by the two of you. Have you gone to counseling?"

"He wants to download a Cloud counselor in our living room."

"Well that's a start."

"If this marriage is going down, Russell, I don't think a hologram is going to fix it. How about that deacon you see?"

"That would be sweet if we could share deacons for counseling!"

"Is he good?"

"For me… I don't know about couples."

"Can you finish the massage?"

"Yes, my dear, first things first!"

Russell finished his mastery over her body without further clothes being discarded. He zipped her up and put on a shirt and jacket. They headed to a Bethesda Jazz club where they got some food as Sandy continued drinking. They danced for hours to a wonderful piano trio playing soul and jazz all night. Mostly slow dancing, they twirled leisurely at times only to embrace closer at the end. Sandy wanted Russell inside of her even on the dance floor. They made it back to his suite by midnight. She was feeling free of her marriage as she took off her dress and shoes. There was nothing underneath. They never made it off the couch as Russell pounded her with endless strokes. He was in another dimension with Sandy submitting to him. He made it last for close to an hour by stopping for minutes at a time to caress her endlessly. She chanted for him to explode in her over and over. It was all she wanted from him to survive the present pain of self-destruction.

She wanted to ruin her vows for certain, because she knew they already were in shambles. It would be the final straw for the crumbling marriage. If it was to be put back together, she needed to feel it completely torn down. She knew it was falling apart but was never committed to putting it back together. Now her family and his family would know. Maybe that would make a difference, because she still loved her husband.

Russell let go with a final thrust and wondered immediately about the consequences. He feared this would change everything between them. They spent the night trading an hour of napping for an hour of love making. By dawn, Sandy was satiated and fell asleep like a baby.

He walked around the suite naked and feeling empty, waiting for the sunrise over the hills of the Academy to the east. He knew the risk and how many years it would take to feel full again. He hoped it was all part of the Plan.

~32~

It was the first Christmas Eve and a special time for Russell to be at the Parkwood Enclave. An invitation was secured to bring his Grandmother and parents to the event, which started at Phillip and Carol's house for appetizers and champagne. The four of them had come by a car ordered by his uncle Alex. The dress code was black tie and long gowns.

Russell had been asked to play a piece on the Baldwin Acrosonic and planned a surprise short duo piece with his prized student, Annie Finelli. It followed a toast in the living room by Phillip with all thirty-two participants, "Since the 1950s, this has been a special night in this house. I can remember since I was about five, my mother, Grandmom, aunts, uncles, cousins, brothers, and neighborhood friends gathered in this place before we rebuilt this house and started hosting again. Tonight, we have some special new friends that are part of our extended family and we are thrilled to have them join us; Russell Santucci, his parents Jill and Kenneth, and Grandmother Laura." Phillip raised his glass, "Russell will play for us, so here is to him and his wonderful family, cheers and Merry Christmas!"

Russell chugged his champagne and settled on his bench. Annie stood to the right side of the piano away from the audience, wearing a black Chanel silk sleeveless evening gown with a plunging neckline, splitting her breasts. Very popular for even high schoolers this decade. Her hair had grown down to her shoulders, laying on her bare, freckled, well-sculpted shoulders. She tried to be a distraction and an inspiration while he played. And did not care which one. Russell was glad about both if he could gaze at her while he played.

The original piece that he was to play was created because of the emotion she caused in him.

The moving piece that he privately called "The Candy-O Concerto" lasted ten minutes, bringing silence and open mouths to the audience. Only a few of them had any idea of his talent. Annie sat down immediately, shoulder to shoulder to Russell for their short duet. He felt electricity from her bare arms that rubbed up against his black suit jacket. For the first time, he could see the bottom curvature of her substantial right breast. He thanked God for such a beautiful site. He smiled as he looked up at her eyes. She was excited about being checked out. She wished that she could show him more.

They jumped into the piece after a silent *one, two, three, four…*

After they were done, all glasses were put down and applause went on for a while as Russell and Annie became surrounded by everyone in the room. He hugged Annie and felt an extra pull by her as their bodies felt a fleeting friction of familiarity, that pleased him tremendously. It was an awakening as his body had been numb for days since being with Sandy.

Annie moved away and let Russell be the focus of the congratulations. She went to see her father, brother, and cousins. But wanted most to be with Anthony and share the rituals of the special night with him. Her cousin Lil was first to talk to her, "You are quite a little pianist, that was really cool. And that Russell is really something." She nestled up to her face and gave her a peck on her check. Lil was always affectionate with Annie even if it was rarely reciprocated. "Hey, are you really going to play basketball with Hill? Maybe I should really transfer to WJ."

"Yes, I am, and yes, you should transfer." They shared a hug and a laugh. "I would love to have you there every day, and I have also decided to graduate in May."

"Wow, that's a lot to manage. I was just kidding about transferring. I think Mom would go ballistic. Besides, I can be there after school every day for practice if you want."

"Awesome, you are the best cousin-sister ever!"

"Besides, I'm a queen at the Academy and would be just a serf at WJ."

"But the prettiest serf of the people!"

"Thank you for that, but I have my serfdom at AHC, besides you're the WJ queen."

"Not by choice, Lilly; it has all just seemed to happen."

At seven p.m., the thirty-two attendees were notified to brave the cold and head up the hill to the Santucci residence for dinner. One by one, they left the family room exit and headed on the flagstone trail through the back yard and up the lighted stairs behind the guest houses on the left to the Santucci residence on the hill. The night was clear and beautiful. The moon was three quarters full and shining brightly on the party. They entered the residence through the back deck above the heated outdoor pool. A large table had been set in the magnificent family room for thirty-two people. The feast of the seven fishes would be underway. The crab melts and oysters on the half-shelf appetizers had started off the night at the Finelli house. The entrees included Baklava, a cod salted for weeks served in olive oil with sliced peppers, salmon cooked on the grill topped with crab meat, pasta alfredo served with cherrystone clams and large shrimp, and white pizza, a pizza with no tomato sauce served with a mixture of Romano and Parmesan cheeses, with anchovies on the side.

Most of the attendees loved fish and waited a full year for this meal. Even those not endeared by seafood, learned to put their odd appetite to the side because the smell and taste was spectacular. Four different types of wine were served for each entrée. Annie had secured a seat next to Russell with Anthony on the other side across from Hill and Lil near the end of the table. They were near the window that had a great view of the eastern sky full of stars and the moon. Venus and Mars were following the moon across the horizon.

At nine p.m., the attendees were led with their wine glasses outside through the deck around the pool by the bubble over the basketball court and down the lighted stairs to the Finelli/O'Neil residence that faced Parkwood Drive. They entered through the patio and into another large family room with a wood fireplace blazing away. The desserts were set up around the room on various tables. A cannoli station would be the most popular, followed by the pecan and lemon meringue pies. The popular Italian pizzelles and strovelli were warm and freshly made, adding an unimaginable fragrance that would send the idea of calorie counting out the window.

Annie helped Anthony load up his plate with goodies as they sat in front of the fireplace and in view of the ten-foot Christmas tree in the corner of the room. He was too excited to worry about sleeping at his usual nine p.m. pass-out time. The sugar high from the dessert would keep him going to at least eleven p.m.

Russell spent most of the time escorting his parents around to meet Finelli cousins. Otherwise, he was interrupted several times by Guy Finelli with conversation.

He seemed very interested in his career as a musician and had some ideas about finding him places to play up and down the east coast. His connections in the entertainment business were endless and everyone wanted to do business with a superhero. The final conversation with Guy Finelli was a recruitment for playing basketball during Christmas break and beyond in the enclave bubble, "I hear you have some talent playing basketball, my brother tells me?'

Russell was surprised, "Well a little at Georgetown, my Grandfather was quite good at Fordham apparently."

"I need to organize players to play five-on-five with Annie besides high school practice. She needs to experience playing with men. I'm thinking myself, Alex, and my three buddies Cary Collins, Duran Hall, and Mark Pelligrini against Annie, Hill, Cousin Joe, Lilly, and you."

"So, let me get this straight: Five professional athletes, two in the Hall of Fame in their sports against two girls, an old man, one good high school kid, and me."

"Don't sell yourself short. Annie, Hill, and Lil can all shoot the eyes out of the basket. You and Cousin Joe can play defense and rebound."

"Still, it could be a little rough for us, but I'm in."

"It's supposed to be rough. We need her to play with some people in her face. Besides, we still have a little speed left." Guy roared with laughter as Russell wondered how he got himself in another crazy situation.

Guy stuffed a cannoli in his mouth that leaked chocolate pudding on one side and whipped cream on the other. With great athleticism he caught any leakage with his free hand, stuffed the overage in his mouth, and then slapped Russell on his back, installing fear into him that he would encounter on the basketball court. *A shoulder to my chest would send me to the emergency room*, Russell thought, but he knew it was worth the possible pain to be included in the family.

"So, glad you're in. It'll be fun!" Guy muttered through the whipped cream all over his chin. "Man, these things are awesome. Let me make you one Russell."

Within a minute, Russell was delicately biting on the best cannoli he ever had experienced as Annie saw him across the room. She shuffled across to him and took him by the hand, "Let me show you my room upstairs!" She proudly smiled and pushed him upstairs before anyone noticed. They made it to her room holding hands. "This is where I spent most weekends hanging out with Anthony. We share a bathroom and watch TV in here most nights. He always falls asleep on my bed around nine p.m., like clockwork. He is doing well tonight though."

"I'm glad you get to spend time with him and your dad, who just recruited me for basketball practice. I'm going to be on your team."

"Pretty neat idea, huh? I told him you could rebound and jump."

"I should've known. We're going to get killed you know?"

"It is only for practice, no one will keep score, but we could outscore them for sure."

"O your father will keep score but I'm glad you're confident." Russell loved her self-assurance and truth telling. He was sure that she had thought out the whole sequence of the game and the ten players involved. It was similar, he thought, to listening to all the keys in his head he would play for a concerto before a performance, but her task was a lot harder. *Too many unknown variables*, he surmised.

"I have a present for you," she pulled out a small box from a dresser drawer. They were cufflinks. "For your next performance." She put her arms around his neck and looked at him with her green eyes. Her lips got closer and closer. Russell was melting in her arms as he felt her chest against his. Their lips touched softly and sat together for a bit. She pulled away and took his hand to exit back to the party. Before they headed down the stairs, she turned to him, "I hope you like my gift and Merry Christmas, Russell!"

"Merry Christmas, Annie." He kissed her again and pulled back, but then she held him close and kissed him again. They savored the seconds but stopped in unison and looked at each other with joy in their eyes. "And a great New Year, I think it will be a great, great year Annie."

"It already has been a great night, Russell."

~33~

On Christmas Day, Abbey showed up, unexpectant, at his parents' house as dinner was finishing. She had a Bloomingdale's bag of presents for his parents and Grandmother. And something for Russell later in the evening, she hoped. She looked beautiful, wearing a short navy-blue dress that showed off her legs and chest. Diamond earrings and necklace surrounded her face, painted with heavier than usual eye make-up. Her brownish-blonde hair had been curled and hung beautifully around her neck and back. She looked ready for a Hollywood screen test.

They made it through the end of dinner and dessert without too many questions. His parents were being the perfect hosts. Even his Grandmother was behaving. Abbey dominated the conversation with some nervous storytelling about the ski trip that she went on and visiting her mother in Maine.

Russell was certain the ski trip included fucking her part-time weekend job boss. *She was feeling guilty about no communication with him for almost two weeks*, he thought, and the drop-in visit—looking like a movie star bearing gifts was more evidence to his point. Luckily, Russell felt very little jealously about it, only some concern for her feeling guilty about it. He was glad to see her happy as she showed some effort to keep the appearance up about the relationship because that worked for him. Looking like a knock-out and drinking some extra wine would make him happy to undress her later. He was already imagining her without the blue dress and just the diamonds on.

After dropping off his Grandmother, Abbey moved into the front seat and gave Russell a warm juicy kiss, "I'm so sorry I didn't call you, but I knew you would be disappointed in me."

Russell sat quiet for a minute, trying to extend her guilt feelings as long as possible until he would talk her down. "Abbey, I'm happy for you. You know I was very busy and can take care of myself. Sounds like a great time out west skiing. That crew must really be fun, right?" He could not help himself taking a long look at her eyes as she shifted to another lie.

"Yes… it was fun, but I really did miss you Russell. It killed me not to talk to you. I was so scared you would be furious."

"Have you ever seen me do furious? Abbey, you can always call me. I'm glad you got to see your mother." His artful response allowed her some cover by complaining about her mother for ten minutes. She just finished as he pulled into his parking place at Prep. A spot right next to the side door and a quick ride up the elevator got them inside with the door closed in a hurry. He pulled out a bottle of wine and poured two glasses as they sat on the couch.

"It's so quiet here right now…that must be nice," Abbey said quietly as she snuggled up next to him with her wine glass. "I hope you like my dress, I bought it for tonight because I wanted our time to be special." She turned her back towards him as she finished her glass of wine. "Do you mind unzipping me, dear?"

Russell followed instructions and saw nothing underneath. Abbey flipped off her shoes and let her dress fall. She fell towards him and started kissing him and unbuttoning his shirt as Russell worked to get his pants off. She hung over him as her breasts swayed in rhythm. Russell was turned on by her aggression. Her compact breasts felt perfect as their nipples extended downward. She found his member while kissing his lips and put it slowly inside, like trying on a new shoe. He felt some discomfort as she went up and down. She was so intent on her joy; Russell became just the means. Within minutes, she screamed out and collapsed on his chest finally leaving his lips. Russell removed himself and settled her down. Within minutes, she was asleep. Russell left the couch and covered her with a blanket. He was still hard.

Walking around the suite, he filled his glass with more wine and started to touch himself. It felt like freedom. He thought of his young flame and her beauty, the taste of her lips excited him more, as he stroked himself hard. Her breasts impressed on his chest; he could still feel as he got closer. Suddenly, he heard his name, "Russell… Please, please cum in me. I want you to finish."

Without hesitation, he ran back to her and saw her legs open, waiting for him. She was wet and stretched now; while he felt full and long, plunging in her smoothly. He closed his eyes, imagining his young love as he quickly reached orgasm and came calmly in her for quite a while. He retreated from the couch as Abbey turned to her side and pulled the blanket over herself. Russell went into the shower to clean himself. Annie was now in his head while he was with other women, making the Plan harder to follow.

~34~

Basketball practice was going smoothly at WJ. Coach DeBone was keeping it simple with lots of running, defensive drills, and three-on-three rotations. Coach put Hill and Chamberlain with Annie as his prime three. They would be the two players most likely to score, so he figured to let Annie get them the ball from the beginning. She led the running drills with her speed and worked hard on the defensive drills with her quickness but got pushed around by boys with at least thirty to fifty pounds on her. She scored at will in the three-on-three drills when not passing to her two scorers. In the four rotations, they won 5-0 each time. All the boys watched her intently and could not help themselves from accepting her talent. The first game was in a tournament over the weekend in Frederick County. Coach Melendez thought that it would be a mistake to start Annie until midseason. She could help from the bench, while getting used to big bodies around her. Coach DeBone disagreed after seeing her talent in practice and wanted to play her right from the start. "She has star quality, Janet, something really special."

"I know Dennis, but she has this thing about physical-ness with other humans. Take my word for it. It is a learning process. Something she will figure out. She is a genius you know."

Dennis was too excited, "I want to come out flying Janet and blow some folks away… Take charge!'

"Yes, I get it. Like a typical male, you can't control yourself. But let's get under the radar a bit. She will be getting too much attention as it is. We don't want to set her up to fail."

"You're right, god dammit...you're right!" Dennis turned away upset at his eagerness to showcase Annie's talents. "That young woman will change the world Janet I can feel it." Dennis turned back to see Janet's soft dark eyes.

"Maybe Dennis...but let's worry about starting the season first."

In the afternoon, practice at home would take place with games in the evening in the Enclave bubble. Patty O'Neil was running the kitchen feeding the ten participants. Most were in great shape, except for Cousin Joe. He walked through most of the drills and sat out half of the shooting time. Cousin Joe had creeped over three-hundred pounds again on his six-foot, four-inch frame and was saving his energy for the evening games. He was looking forward to swatting away some shots and knocking over some of his ex-ballplayers in the five-on-five competition.

Phillip and Carol had volunteered to do some officiating in a casual manner. Guy and Alex ran a two-man pick and roll for most of the first game with Duran and Mark at the three-point line taking open jumpers. Cary was having fun tipping out rebounds over Russell. Guy and Alex dunked at one point five times in a row in a game to twenty-one baskets. When it reached 19-3, Hill called timeout. "Okay, we got them we're want them, they're gassed! Let's push down on the accelerator."

Annie pressed the ball up quickly and drove to the basket for an easy bucket. Russell stole the inbound pass and fed Hill for a jumper. Annie robbed the basketball from Duran at midcourt and scored again quickly. Cousin Joe swatted away three floaters in the lane by Guy, Alex, and Cary for fast break layups to Lil, Hill, and Annie. Mark, Alex, and Duran all missed jumpers. Russell rebounded everything and fed Annie, who twirled up the court like a magician and assisted Hill for three more jumpers. Two more thefts by Annie led to easy layups for Lil, who was having the time of her life playing with the boys and her cousin. Alex called timeout at 19-14 with his hands on his hips, gasping for air. Hill was right: they were out of gas. The timeout did not help as the kids scored seven more baskets. The Pros lost 21-19.

After the scrimmage, the ten players, Patty, Sally, Phillip, and Carol all watched a replay of the game at Guy's house and ate together. It was a party with tons of food and beer. Everyone was an analyst, making comments about their playing. Cousin Joe and Guy dominated most of the joke-making and giving people a hard time. Hill, Annie, and Lil were off limits for the jokes, but received outstanding praise for their playing. Patty made sure there was enough ice packs for everyone but most of the guys headed outside to the ice and heated jacuzzies in Guy's backyard with lots of beer. The ice jacuzzi got plenty of use to dull the aches and pain, especially for Cousin Joe and Alex. Once the ice and beer took away the pain, the steaming hot jets of water in the jacuzzi took over.

Hill was happy to watch Annie on the replay again and again. She played in fast motion and mostly stayed away from contact with other human beings. He knew that would be different at the high school level, those little guards were just as quick and would get up in her face. She would have to face it and make the adjustments to that kind of defensive positioning, and *it was not going to be easy for her*, he thought. It was fun for him to play with his dad and uncle, sister, and cousin. He was getting to know Cousin Joe and Russell better. One was loud and funny; the other was quiet and calm. He also loved to be around Guy and his football buddies and especially the beer. He thanked each of them individually for coming at the jacuzzi over and over as he drank more beer. The football players hardly noticed because beer drinking was always a part of the celebration and comradery. Besides, Hill did not seem to be just sixteen.

Ever since the Prep incident, Hill had increased his drinking. He had been into alcohol since he was twelve. For a couple of years, it was on the rare occasion at an adult party or entertainment that was frequent at the Enclave. The three households led to more entertaining and more access to alcohol. He developed a taste for beer from the first sip. It was the sour taste that was pleasing. The buzz did not become exciting until he was fourteen. In high school, it was his artsy friends who had buzz parties with marijauna, klime-a-bored (a speed drug like ecstasy), and alcohol. The artsy kids did the first two and Hill stayed with beer as his drug. Drug testing had been declared unconstitutional without cause in the State of Maryland, but was still in the lower courts, and drug rehab was available at every medical corner. Pot never seemed to work for him, but alcohol was soothing.

Only recently had he tried *Absolut Vodka*, made in Sweden. It was clean, non-smelling, and worked quicker. He also liked the Swedish connection. The weekend after the Prep incident felt like a whole year in limbo. Finally, he went out to a small party on Sunday night with WJ friends, telling them he was transferring. They wanted to celebrate and brought out the *Absolut Vodka* drink. It soothed his anxiety and felt great to have the stress go away for the evening. He loved being accepted by a crowd of friends he would see every day.

His girlfriend Malak did not attend and was away for the weekend. She was not a drinker and was very serious about her academic career. His sister Lil could keep up with anyone partying but was also a health freak. At this point, no one would have guessed that a problem was building for Hill. He was a budding superstar high school basketball player, a son of a DC hero athlete and a Washington academic-media darling.

~35~

Junior Parker was back on top. He led Prep to capture the St. Francis tournament crown in central Pennsylvania. All the top Catholic school teams from Pittsburgh and Philadelphia were in attendance. It was three games in three days, and Junior scored 35 points a game in a blistering performance. He had found his stroke early and could not miss. His ball handling was fabulous, and his matador defense never hurt him, collecting dozens of snowbird layups after missed shots by his opponents. The rest of the Prep team were workman-like players that focused on defense, rebounded well, and passed the ball around, which were three things he was less versed in.

His father, Burton Parker, had made a special request to Guy Finelli and Alex Santucci and their families to join him at a private party for New Year's Eve at the World Space Stadium in DC. He wanted to heal the division between his son Junior Parker and Hill Santucci; and asked that Hill, Lil, and Annie—and dates—come and join his family for a special celebration.

Mr. Parker had contributed well over a hundred million dollars over the past decade to their Baltimore Foundation, *The Safety*, and was an initial investor in their first two movie ventures for another hundred million. He also asked Russell Santucci to perform something special for the evening and to bring a date, at Junior's request. A jazz trio was also providing music for most of the night.

When Alex and Guy brought together the cousins, as well as Sally and Patty to discuss the invitation, Annie was the first one to speak.

"I think we should all go. This is a chance to get all of this behind us. You will not have to worry about me. I can handle Junior." She smiled as she sat down.

Her cousins knew about the attack, but the adults did not. They only knew about the fight between Hill and Junior. Hill and Lil were relieved to hear her support for the evening. She also accepted a call from Junior, asking her to attend as a friend. It was short and courteous. Junior was on his best behavior, full of confidence from his weekend MVP tournament performance. She did ask if she could bring her brother Anthony. He said "of course," and added "it would be perfect because his sisters Brandy and Hannah would be there." They were nine and twelve.

Junior said that he would bring their nanny to make sure they were okay, especially when they fell asleep. Annie appreciated that and thanked Junior. She knew that Russell was performing for the evening and she would not miss it for anything. Putting up with Junior for a few hours was worth a chance to see Russell and listen to him play for the evening.

Arriving at the site of Guy Finelli's ultimate achievement in sports was thrilling for the group of twelve that came in two limousines. Russell came with a surprise friend, Sandy O'Malley. She was feeling alone, and Russell did not want to babysit Abbey again at another party. Lil was excited to have her favorite teacher to party with for the evening.

The World Space Stadium, built at the site of the old RFK stadium, was now ten years old. The sixteen-petaled ocular retractable roof, that opened like a camera lens, was in oculus position (open) to see the stars. The field was in beautiful condition because of the mild temperatures in the fifties during the night. There was still one game left in the Potomacs season and a semi-final for the college football season upcoming at the magnificent stadium in January of the new decade, as well as the NCAA College Basketball *Final Four* tournament in the Spring. They went down on the field to run around. Little Anthony and his new friend Brandy took full advantage.

Owner Burton Parker met them on the field and handed out autographed footballs to the cousins. Annie fired a couple of passes to her Dad and Uncle. Mr. Parker shook his head, seeing the grace of the spectacular athlete Guy Finelli and wondered how many more championships he would have won if he had not retired at age twenty-five, after only five professional seasons and three championships.

"He still has the skills and the body," Burton exclaimed as he stood next to Patty and Sally, two of his favorite women, "I know he did the right thing for the country, he is a true hero, but… " His eyes teared up as he tried to go on, "I just really miss him being part of our team."

Junior joined in with Annie, Anthony, Hill, and Lil running and throwing passes. They were in their glory, watching their fathers trying to cover each other. Guy still had sprinter's speed, and Alex had great agility to stay close enough with his younger brother of eighteen years.

Out of an elevator on the sidelines appeared a familiar face: Charlotte Roberts. She had married Burton Parker three years ago in a quiet ceremony in 2026. Junior's mother and Burton's first wife died of breast cancer in 2023. The sudden loss sent Burton into a long depression and seclusion. He missed the entire 2023 Potomacs season exploring in the Himalayas, Thailand, and New Zealand to find a new meaning in life. A year later, he started spending time with the agent for Alex and Guy, Charlotte Roberts. They had known each other since 2012 when she came into Alex's life by a seemingly once in a lifetime coincidence. It was later learned that her adopted parents had tried to make it happen for years.

During the summer of 2012, after Charlotte and Alex met in Houston on a road trip, they became great friends and in short order discovered that Alex's adopted father was Charlotte's birth father, Gene Santucci who had an affair in 1982, while in Cincinnati with Charlotte's birth mother. She was born on Alex's seventh birthday in 1983 and was adopted by a couple in St. Louis where she grew up. They figured out to be stepbrother and stepsister. Charlotte had a blood relationship with Russell Santucci as a half-aunt or something like that. The details were all very strange, but she became someone Alex could trust when he was being thrusted on a national scene in the summer of 2012. They had so much in common and felt an immediate trust. She never left his side during his famous streak until the Championship in November. Eventually, Alex financed her life while she went to law school and became the family lawyer and agent. She immediately took over all financial and public relations for Alex and then Guy Finelli. She hired Patty O'Neil to deal with the press.

She started dealing with Burton Parker in 2015 as Guy Finelli's agent and then exclusively when he entered free agency after the 2018 season. Parker loved her red hair and fuller body. She was lanky and well-toned from her workouts. Things were always cordial between them and they became friendlier after Guy's retirement. She worked with Burton to invest in their movie production company and foundation, and then became a great support for him during and after his wife's illness and death.

"My dear friends and family," Charlotte spoke out loudly as she joined the crowd. She was best friends with Sally and Patty and hugged them closely.

Alex and Guy kissed and hugged her together. Their partnership had made them millions. Charlotte was the current CEO of their production company. Patty was CEO of the Finelli-Santucci Foundation.

Charlotte, now forty-six, looked like the wife of a Hollywood mogul. Her hair was redder than usual and her skin tanner than ever. She was bordering on too thin from her constant 'iron woman' workouts. Her breasts, always a C cup, had been augmented to a D cup, standing at attention on her lanky frame. Her personality had not changed a bit as a very loving woman. She missed not having a child but took care of her stepchildren with a passion. "We are so lucky to have all of you here tonight. Burton has some surprises for you."

After her announcement, two horses appeared in the end zone entrance impressively striding on to the field with their handlers. The kids clapped and shouted out with excitement. Then, in the next minute, a motorized air-balloon, small enough to descend through the roof, landed at midfield. The kids spent the next two hours riding horses and taking the air-balloon over the stadium. The adults relished with excitement, seeing the joy exuding from the kids as they sat on the sidelines drinking wine and eating appetizers.

Burton Parker stood up and declared, "This has been a dream of mine to spend New Year's Eve with our families together. And I think with the unfortunate incident that happened, we hope this heals any bad feeling between the kids. I want to personally apologize for Junior's behavior to my dear friends Guy and Patty as well as Alex and Sally."

"Thank you, Burton," Alex responded. "Sally and I would like to apologize for Hill's behavior. All of this seemed way out of character for both Hill and Junior."

"Agreed, my dear friends Alex and Sally. No apology necessary. I believe Junior bears responsibility for all of this. And I want to thank my new friend Russell for his counsel with Junior. He really looks up to you, Russell." Burton reached out awkwardly with a hug that turned into a handshake. "Thank you for reaching out to him and your problem-solving skills that night. You saved a great embarrassment for my family. And I am in trememdous debt to you, my friend." Burton's face was full of tears as he spoke, always odd in his presentation, but real in his emotional response.

Russell stood, took control, and offered a toast, "To the great men here tonight, who have given DC so much excitement and joy. To Parker, Guy, and Alex… here, here."

Sandy stood and stepped forward, looking lovely in a newly purchased dress for the occasion, "Let's not forget the great women here tonight, who have had wonderful achievements; Sally, Patty, Charlotte. It is an honor to be in your company tonight." All the glasses had been re-filled. "Drink up!"

It seemed like paradise to have such an amazing structure as their backyard for the evening. So many toys for their children to enjoy as the decade was about to come to an end. As the wine flowed easily, Guy looked at the grass of the stadium, and it stirred a memory. He sat at a table on the sidelines with the other three couples and took one of the footballs in his giant hands. The texture was soothing to touch and even better to smell. His head filled with thoughts of his last game ever, a furious comeback with a decimated team, playing both quarterback and safety. And then with no field goal kicker on the thirty-yard line, down by two, with no timeouts, and the clock counted down the seconds, to three, two, one…he did the unthinkable! He took the snap, looked downfield, stepped up, and dropped the ball straight down and kicked it, causing an explosion on the field and throughout the world. A drop-kick sealed his legacy, finished his career, and took down "The Turk." He smiled as he spun the ball into the air and pulled it in tight one last time. It felt like heaven, at least for this moment.

Surprisingly, in the far-off corner of the field away from the other kids, who were riding on the horses or surveying the city in the half-sized hot-air balloons, were Junior and Annie walking cautiously with their eyes down, exchanging small talk about basketball.

"You must be excited about playing with Hill and the boys this season. I guess you never saw that happening," Junior offered nervously.

"It is a bit overwhelming to be honest, but yes, exciting at the same time. I have a lot to learn but playing with Hill is like a dream come true. And Chamberlain is like a center from the NBA 1960's. I think I can really help those two scorers especially, and the team."

"I can't wait to watch your team play Annie… Can I ask you something?" Junior said cautiously, almost sweating in the sixty-degree weather on the field.

"Well, Junior, we are talking, you do not have to ask me to ask a question, that would be redundant." She gave a hint of a smile.

"I want to fully apologize to you for what I did to you. I'm not asking for forgiveness because my actions were truly hideous, but I was hoping you could accept my apology." Junior had his eyes down and looked fully beaten down by his shameful behavior. "I acted like a predator, someone who should be locked up. I am seeing a counselor and a psychiatrist who has put me on medication. And I have sworn off all other drugs and alcohol." He stopped walking and finally looked up at Annie, "I hope someday we can be friends again."

"I appreciate that Junior, and I accept your apology, but has this ever happened before?" Annie eyed Junior like a prosecutor.

Junior looked down, realizing honesty would be the only route to friendship or beyond with Annie, "Yes… three other times I have been forceful with girls trying to feel them up. My counselor has told me that I am obsessed with breasts. She thinks it's because of losing my mother."

"What do you think?" Annie asked forcefully.

"I think it's because I'm a stupid asshole, trying to get what I want. Either way, I'm finished with it."

"Anything else happened with those girls?" Looking for the whole story, Annie persisted.

"Well, the one time my date let me get under her bra while we were kissing, and I… took it out."

"Took it out?" Annie questioned, not sure what he was talking about.

"Yeah…you know!" Junior pleaded, hoping not to describe it any further.

A picture of a boy's member clicked in her head as she tried to keep a straight face, "Okay, I understand. That is pretty stupid Junior… Well, just tell me what happened?"

Junior had both hands in his pants and was politely kicking the grass as he looked down and muttered, "I started beating off, when she wouldn't touch me."

"Does the counselor know that?" Annie was appalled at his stupidity.

"I'm too embarrassed to tell her that Annie!"

"Well, you just told me!" She took both of his shoulders and tried to shake him out of his foolishness.

"But I don't want to lie to you, I trust you," Junior pleaded.

"And I turn you on, I suppose?" Annie realizing the real problem for Junior.

"Obviously, Annie… You were everything to me, and I attacked you. It's insane!"

"Junior, this is a difficult question, but very important. Are you comfortable masturbating?" Annie decided to get to the point of the problem

"Wow… You are something, Annie… No, I'm not. As you know I'm Catholic and live at a Jesuit school!"

"Well, I am comfortable with it, and you should be, too, if you want to be friends again." She gave him a quick hug and looked at him, "I absolve you of your sins, and 'yes,' I will go to a Prep dance if you want and maybe a movie or two before that. But nothing is going to happen below the belt and that thing of yours is not coming out, agreed?" Annie tried to manage the problem for Junior. She also thought of her need to cover the school year with a boyfriend she could control.

Junior was speechless and just shook his head affirmatively.

"Now, let us see what the kids are doing, or people are going to talk about us."

Junior cracked a big smile and felt a surge in his member for the first time since the dance. *She is right*, he thought, *I need to masturbate and learn to enjoy it.*

The party of twelve reassembled and took the elevator up to the owner's penthouse suite, two-hundred feet up. It had views of the field and East Capitol Street behind it. The Capitol, the Washington Monument; and World War II, Vietnam, and Lincoln Memorials lined up in the brightened darkness of the city. Champagne was on ice for midnight. Anthony and Brandy were too excited to think about sleep. They both wanted to see 2030 arrive in person. The monitors around the suite had on four different views with DC, NYC, Philadelphia, and Boston ready to start the countdown. Around the room, couples found a spot to watch together; Alex and Sally, Guy and Patty, Burton and Charlotte, Russell and Sandy, Hill and Malak, Lil and Chahna. Anthony had a girl on each arm, Brandy and Hannah. Annie stood behind Anthony on the couch with her arms on his shoulders.

Junior stood at the end of the couch, feeling relieved after an extraordinary conversation with Annie. *She must be from another planet*, he thought, *no one could be that brilliant, beautiful, and athletic*. He was even more enchanted with her now than before, and he could not wait to play with himself tonight after midnight. The tingle in his pants spiked every time he looked at her. He made sure he was behind everyone to hide his surging member.

Suddenly, his dad hugged him from behind and asked if he was having a good time. He smiled and said, "This is great Dad."

Charlotte was just under his height and thrust herself into his chest. It felt good to be held by her. He closed his eyes, imagining it was Annie's chest pushing into his. She whispered in his ear, "This will be a great year and a successful decade for you my dear. Enjoy the celebration."

The lights were out; an eerie blackness took over the massive structure as the sky merged into the open roof. A single rocket surged towards the oculus. Burton Parker shouted out, "Here we go folks!" Charlotte hugged him from behind with pure excitement. Three more rockets blasted off, followed by dozens more. Junior was in heat. He was excited in too many ways and wanted closeness. He hugged Charlotte from behind as she was still holding on to Burton. His member felt the grind of her nicely developed behind. He reached for his dad but fell short. Charlotte took his hands and pulled them around her ribs tightly. She was breathing hard with excitement and reacting to Burton's bursts of joy. Junior closed his eyes and grinded hard, as Charlotte barely noticed. The fireworks kept pounding the air with explosions that caused a deafening echo throughout the structure. The group was cheering and shouting with excitement.

Junior knew a surge was about to happen; he held on tightly and moved his hands to feel Charlotte's breasts from the outside of her dress. All he could imagine was Annie's face and body as his member let go with complete ecstasy, coating his underwear with a sticky mess. Charlotte's face was buried into Burton's neck, kissing him, feeling deeply turned on by his outward surges of joy. She was imagining their love-making upstairs in the suite alone. She barely noticed Junior's groping her from behind, but she was happy to be the object of his affection in that moment. It felt nice be surrounded by the two men in her family for once.

As Junior came back to earth, he slowly detangled himself from his stepmother and headed for the bathroom. Once he was alone, he looked in the mirror and noticed the thickness of his member and how well it performed. The grinding was a new experience for him. Now he felt confident he could keep it in his pants or masturbate on his own in private. Annie's permission and encouragement in a strange way made him feel like a real man.

~36~

Valentine's Day weekend was the first big dance of the second semester for those young men at Prep. The senior class had booked the best rock-swing band in the DC area and were expecting a full crowd at the big gymnasium. Junior was riding a six-week high in his life. The basketball team had put Prep in the top five in the area at 15-0, and Junior was the leading scorer in the area at 30.3 points per game. More importantly, he had three dates with Annie that went perfectly, including the latest make-out session that led to his first real feel of her lovely right breast. Annie let him unbutton her blouse a few buttons and slip his hand into her bra for a couple of minutes, then she shut it down, knowing it was taking everything in his power to not pull-out his rock-hard member. After his driver dropped Annie off, Junior put up the privacy screen and smiled from ear to ear as he stroked himself, thinking he was the luckiest guy on the planet. He was getting to like this masturbating thing.

Russell attended the dance with Sandy at his side, surveying the set-up of the scene at the gymnasium. She was officially separated from her husband, who had moved back home to New York and was seeking another job. Russell was spending two nights a week with Sandy, usually on weekends, and having continuous sex-capades each night.

At the same time, his emotions were being tested with Annie dating Junior. At their last piano lesson, she assured him, "It is part of the Plan, and a great cover for the semester until my sixteenth birthday and graduation. Once I am in college, nobody will care or know how old I am." Russell had concerns for her safety, but she assured him, "That is not going to be a problem. He can handle himself now." Then Russell wanted to know all the details of their physical-ness. She rolled her green eyes and then stared at him with distain, "Russell, I have very little skill in lying, unlike you. I will not have intercourse or any below the belt interaction with him, again unlike you with all your women!" She reminded him.

He weakly objected to that accusation, "Well, I'm not seeing Abbey for now."

"But what about Sandy?" she was well-informed about the divorce proceedings from Lil.

"Yes, we are together a lot, but we are close friends that like to have sex. She knows I love you completely."

"I guess that is better than your situation with Abbey. I hope that is over, she was very dramatic."

"Me too, but you never know with her."

"What is that supposed to mean? That you are on call for her whenever she needs sex or to just listen to her weeping about her new boyfriend?"

"Something like that… Hey, we are still friends you know," as he avoided her playful hit on his arm. Annie showed uncharacteristic upset at his joke, "and I'm good at listening, sometimes."

"At least you are honest about it, but such a dog in heat at times. Have fun watching me at the Prep dance."

"I hope it turns out better than the last one." She smiled back at him this time impressed by his retort.

The basketball season for Hill and Annie was on course for great success. Coach DeBone had taken the advice of Coach Melendez and worked Annie into the line-up – slowly. She was having mixed success. At times, she flew around the court like a magician making passes and layups, but she was not aggressive at all on defense. She stayed away from most of the players and seemed lost on what she should be doing.

After several discussions with Coach Melendez, Annie suggested the coaches craft a version of the 1-3-1 zone based on her watching Cloud footage of "Pistol Pete" at *LSU*, Gail Goodrich at *UCLA*, and every point guard with *UNC* in 1960s and 1970s that would allow her to float from side to side near the top of the key. It would take advantage of her quickness, protect her physically from too many sweaty boys, and give her an edge on fast breaks. Hill and Chamberlain would be in the middle with the two starting forwards, Lance Ball and Howard Dennis on the wings. The coaches agreed and installed the intricate zone in the last practice. The team was not excited about the slow choreography of the zone in practice, but it allowed Annie's exceptional memory to recall every nuanced position wherever the ball was on the court. It would take some time for Annie and the whole team to get comfortable with it.

With starting point guard Ronnie Dominic on the court, they played strictly man-to-man defense. He was everything Annie was not, built like a linebacker at six feet, two-hundred thirty-two pounds, he played in-your-face defense, but was a bricklayer on offense. His best move on offense was passing to Hill and setting a ferocious screen to free him for an open jumper. His ball handling was adequate but not flashy. Being so wide, guards could not get around him as he dribbled the ball behind him when covered. At times, he loved to back his defender into the lane and had some touch on a jump hook shot close to the basket. For three years, he played on the team to keep in shape for football and already had a Division I scholarship at Rutgers. Coach DeBone begged him to play his senior year, even though his college coaches objected. Being a part of the starting line-up was a brilliant coaching decision and done partly out of necessity—Ronnie was having the time of his life. Being half-Italian, he immediately became close with Hill and Annie. He was a leader, an enforcer, and was looking forward in getting Annie into the starting line-up. His role, eventually, would be the first player off the bench at either forward or center position and point guard.

WJ was 13-2, and with six games left in the regular season, they were assured a playoff spot in the county and state playoffs. They had three weeks to get Annie in the line-up and the new defense installed. She was working with her Grandpa Phillip, on a hypnotic trance to see all the open space on the court and not all the smelly bodies of growing boys. Coach Melendez was sharing her Cloud images of playing the '1' at the top of a 1-3-1 defense. Neither "Pistol Pete" or Gail Goodrich would be called a talented defensive player, but on a great team like *UCLA*, Coach John Wooten wanted his '1' to be sneaky and pester, poke, prod, push, pull, and ploy opponents into mistakes. Then position themselves for the steal from behind or stay on the wings for the outlet pass. The 1-3-1 took the other four players, who needed to be exceptionally quick and lanky, to act like eight players on the court. The idea was to double team everything and stick to the ball like glue as soon as the opponent came across mid-court.

As Annie learned her necessary movements on the court and watched Cloud footage for hours, she noticed a 1969 game of *UNC's* Charlie Scott playing the bottom '1' in the 1-3-1 defense. At six feet, six inches, Scott was a freak of nature at that time, a precursor to Michael Jordan. He was a quick guard who was bigger than most forwards at the time, who could jump higher than any Center in College Basketball with a sweet jumper. Before David Thompson at *NC State*, he jumped the center-tip for *UNC*. Annie saw him patrol the baseline like a panther hiding in the brush of the wild. Thin and long, he disappeared at times behind his center in the lane and then darted or jumped to cover the flank of the defense, sometimes swatting shots off the backboard from behind. Players with clear lay-ups would look behind themselves and see the ball flying down the court with a Carolina-Blue clad player.

Annie realized the switch that the coaches needed to make defensively. Initially, they practiced with Chamberlain as the bottom '1' and Hill patrolling the foul lane in the '3'. She could see that a quicker athlete who could jump, like Hill, needed to play the bottom '1' in the zone. Chamberlain would be a more natural talent to clog up the lane in the middle and slide down to the baseline when necessary. Coach Melendez realized she was right and made the adjustment in practice. It was an immediate success. They performed at an up-tempo pace and barely gave up a shot to the second team players in thirty minutes of playing defense.

It had been a crazy six weeks since the New Year's Eve party for Annie and Russell. As they tried to survive the brutally cold winter that brought on the new decade, their relationship was going through a dormant stage like a bear sleeping for the winter. Other than ninety minutes together during their piano lessons, they had not seen each other. As life became busy and full of activities, their hearts felt vacant and ignored. They relied on eventful calendars to distract themselves from the yearning to be together. They were not depressed, just distracted from love for now.

No one at the dance would be outside tonight. The headmaster had extra security around the gymnasium to make sure there were no incidences like the holiday dance. Junior had invited both Hill and Lil and their steady dates, sister and brother, Malak and Chahna to the dance. After the New Year's Eve party, Junior asked through Annie, if he could personally apologize to Hill after watching one of his practices. Hill accepted the offer and cautiously listened to the apology. Hill admitted that he was wrong to punch Junior, but Junior interrupted and said he deserved it. They laughed and eventually hugged. Hill still was concerned about Annie dating Junior. He felt like there was a reason missing for why she would give him another chance. He was right.

The dance was looking like a success without incident. Annie and Junior danced most of the night and held hands. After a break in the music, Annie made a point of meeting with Russell and Sandy, hiding away from the crowd in the back corner of the hall. Annie seemed to enjoy the awkwardness of the interaction. She played with Sandy's hair, while giving her compliments and pointed out Russell's cufflinks looking impressive. When Junior finally joined her, she made a point of kissing him on the cheek and hugging him, bragging that he was the leading basketball scorer in the DC area.

Sandy asked if they were going to play each other at some point. Junior answered that if WJ won the state, they would be invited to the new DCMV tournament at the end of March that his father was sponsoring. "But honestly Sandy, they have no chance of winning the state tournament much less the county playoffs."

Annie glanced up at Junior with a look that was seriously evil, she stepped back and kindly berated him, "Junior, beware of predictions, remember what got you into trouble in the first place. You could not beat me in one on one, and Hill would have you for lunch if we ever played each other."

"Isn't she the funniest, Russell!" Junior said, looking for some support.

"I wouldn't make her mad Junior, that's a big mistake," Russell answered.

"I would not worry about it my dear Junior. I do not think you will beat the Catholic school champion Good Counsel or DeMatha. That will save you the embarrassment," Annie continued without raising her voice while managing to smile at the end.

"Boy she can talk some trash, can't she? That's what I love about her!" Junior announced, trying to save face.

Russell stepped forward and rescued him by taking Annie on the dance floor. "How about a quick twirl, Annie?"

"With pleasure, Russell."

Sandy took Junior by the arm and headed in the other direction and held him close on the dance floor as the music began. Her breasts were deep in his chest as she whispered in his ear, "She's a wild card, that Annie. I wouldn't challenge her about anything, Junior."

"Oh…thank you Ms. O'Malley, that's probably good advice."

Sandy moved her thigh into his groin trying to distract him. "You smell nice tonight Junior and such a good dancer."

Luckily for Junior, the song was not a long one because his hard-on was a full rocket ready for blast-off. "Thank you for the dance, Ms. O'Malley, excuse me I have to go to the bathroom." He headed away quickly feeling very confused.

Annie whispered into Russell's ear, "I miss you so much, my heart feels numb." As the music finished, Russell separated quickly and looked away from Annie as he clapped for the band. She headed off to join Lil and Chahna, Hill and Malak for some distraction.

Sandy came to Russell's side showing more public display of affection than in the past. She did not really care what people thought of her or the rumors of her divorce. She enjoyed Russell as much as she could, knowing it was temporary.

"What did you do to that poor young man?" Russell smirked suspecting some foul play by Sandy.

"He was going to the bathroom because I think something was cooking in his pants." Sandy said playfully.

"You are joining the pervert club, I see…"

"Just giving him some advice about Annie; the poor boy has no idea what he's up against!"

"It looks like he was up against you for a little too long, my dear."

"I can't help that, Russell, you boys just can't control that thing between your legs apparently when you get a hint of my chest against your body."

"It is a force of nature! You remember Hurricane Sandy when we were kids?" Russell loved his own metaphor.

"I think that's when they really started to grow after that storm hit the coast!" Sandy laughed while arching her back.

"Thank God for mother nature!" Russell eyed her chest as he took her towards the hallway. "I think we can split from this place."

"Sounds good." Sandy sounded relieved.

Russell whirled her away towards Boland Hall and his elevator. He was on a mission of diversion from thinking about Annie. More precisely, Annie and that spoiled kid, Junior. It made his stomach turn and Sandy was the right antidote. They were hopping down the hallway like Dorothy and the Lion on the yellow brick road.

Quietly, from behind he heard his name, "Russell, are you leaving?" he turned to see his girl, standing stoically in the latest fashion dress that fit her perfectly. Her hair was curled for the first time that he could remember, and her eyes had extra eyeliner and shadow. She was trying to look older, it seemed. He felt frozen as he caught her eyes. "Are you not going to say goodbye?" she uttered in a tone that he did not need to hear because Russell could read those lips. They were so precious and pleasing when they moved. Never a motion of panic even when she was challenging him or joking.

"We were taking a walk for a minute… I was coming back. Sandy needs some air." Russell let go of Sandy and took some steps towards Annie.

"Oh… I see, pardon me for interrupting, please take care of Ms. O'Malley."

Russell kept walking and was now only 10 feet away, hoping to talk quieter.

"I can call you later, we just needed to get away for a bit." Steps came loudly from down the hall; Junior was done in the bathroom. He was looking relieved and all put together when he noticed Annie.

"Hi Annie, I was wondering where you were." He uttered finally noticing Russell. "Hey, Mr. Santucci…" Then within a few seconds, Sandy had walked down to join them. "Oh, Ms. O'Malley. Wow, a little party out here."

"No, Junior, they were just leaving without saying goodbye, very bad manners, I suppose."

Annie grabbed his arm and twirled towards the gym. "Have a good night you two!"

Russell felt a dagger pierce his heart that was magnified by the vision of the two of them walking arm in arm. Luckily, Sandy rescued him and turned him away. "We need a drink, Russell, let's get out of here."

They walked quickly through the deepening cold between the buildings to get to his elevator. As the door closed, Sandy kissed him passionately on the ride up. He fumbled for his keys to open his suite. The coast was clear. She grabbed the scotch as they made it to the bedroom. They each gulped a swig, several times as they erased their clothing. The kissing and the alcohol were not distracting him from the image of Annie whisking away with Junior and knowing he would be touching her. He looked down at his limpness. Sandy pushed him down and got on her knees. There was not a penis she couldn't get hard with her mouth. It was a specialty from years of Catholic school. Her husband was addicted to it and could not get hard without it. She felt used by him because there was nothing else between them now. She wanted her friend, Russell, to be happy and that was her present job. It gave her hope in the world, for she loved Russell, *even though he was a crazy pervert*, she chuckled to herself.

After a few minutes, there was life in his member. Russell lifted her head up and pulled her on to him. He nestled in her breasts, as she climbed on him. For the next few minutes, he was free of his obsession, unchained from the power of Annie. Sandy took authority over him, making new noises of passion. She became lost from the sensuality of the stroking between them. It took a long time, but she reached her apex, not aware of the world around, and even who was below her. A floating in the clouds was her present form, feeling above it all without weight. It may have been another minute or an hour, but she finally could hear a grunting from below. She opened her eyes as Russell was in despair as he came inside her. She collapsed on top of him as they both felt tears flow down their faces. They kissed slowly and deeply for minutes before they tumbled together to the side holding each other as life supports floating on a slow and winding river. They became comatose in minutes without a dream but woke up together in an hour sensing a nightmare.

~37~

On the floor sat Russell's pants pocket with his phone buzzing in it. He turned away from Sandy and swung his legs down to reach for it. At the same time, Sandy turned over to the other side of the bed as she heard her phone play, *I Heard It through the Grapevine*. After listening to their messages, Russell uttered, "what a shitstorm!" They quickly put on their clothes and bolted for the elevator. As they stepped outside without coats, they were smacked by the coldest temperature in years and immediately started shaking as they ran to the gymnasium.

"This is going to really suck," said Sandy between chattering teeth. A crowd of kids were in the lounge off the entrance hall to the right surrounding the television in the corner, watching the announcement. They bypassed it and ran through the gym hall toward the coaches lounge. The lights were still low as the band was putting equipment away. Russell held his breath as he opened the door, Sandy followed close behind putting her hand on his lower back. All of them were in there.

"This is so terrible..." Lil ran to Sandy and embraced her with Chahna behind her. Hill and Malak were holding hands with their eyes looking down.

Russell finally saw her and felt relieved; she stood up and nodded to him to come over, "Maybe you could talk to him," Annie stated matter-of-factly, "I am not sure what to say to him."

Russell sat next to Junior, who was bent over with his hands covering his face. "Hey Junior, it's Russell... I'm here for you buddy. What happened?"

"I told him to stop...to stop working all...all the time!"

"His father is dead… Burton Parker is dead, Russell!" Annie stated and then whispered to Russell, "His heart just exploded. He refused to listen to his doctor's orders to stop working all day and all night."

"He thought he had to be invincible… He thought he wasn't successful enough; worried people didn't like him…nothing…nothing was enough! Now he's dead… Oh my God!" Junior sobbed into his hands and bent over on his lap. He was rocking himself like a baby.

Russell and Sandy surrounded him on the couch, Russell with his arm on his lower back, and Sandy playing with his hair and rubbing his arm. After ten minutes, he fell into her arms and eventually on her lap and then asleep. At 1 a.m., a black limousine pulled up in the back parking lot in front of the gymnasium. The temperature was zero degrees Fahrenheit with the wind totally still; and the cloudless, moonless night as dark as a black hole. The driver scurried around the car and opened the door with his breath steaming into the air, she stuck her five-inch heels into the asphalt and stood to survey a structure soon to be re-named Parker Field House.

Charlotte Roberts Parker was now full owner of the wealthiest professional franchise in the world, the Washington Potomacs. There was no pre-nuptial agreement. Burton's Will would stipulate that a fifty percent stake and control of the team would transfer to Junior Parker at the age of thirty if he completed college, law school, and five years of work with the team by that young age. Each child would receive a one hundred-million-dollar trust fund by the age of twenty-five and completion of college. Their living expenses would be taken care of until then. Immediately three billion of his assets would be liquidated and given to the Finelli & Santucci Foundation, specifically for work in the DC area, and would become the Parker Foundation. Then, fifty million would go to Georgetown Prep. That would leave approximately ten billion for Charlotte in assets. She was now the wealthiest woman in the DC area.

Her black dress extended to her mid thighs, showing off her tight, athletic legs. She wore a headdress with a veil that extended over her cleavage. It was a sexy, though dark outfit, for a woman in mourning with attitude. Charlotte was meticulous in her planning, and in her short number of years in marriage to Burton Parker, it became clear that this day would come sooner than later. The bitter cold seemed not to bother her as she reached the entrance. Once inside, her heels echoed as a group of kids stood quietly in front of the gym door watching her go by. The television was silent, the clean-up crew stood motionless as the headmaster met her and said his condolences receiving a head nod from Charlotte. He led the way to the coaches lounge door. She became animated as she saw Hill, Lil, and Annie standing halfway to the couch. They each hugged her as she opened her veil to speak to them. "Thank you so much for staying here with Junior, I miss you so much. Can you call Alex, Sally, Guy, and Patty for me while I'm here, so I can speak to them? I want to be with all of you at the house in the morning."

They re-introduced Chahna and Malak to her, "I hope your parents know you're out so late. You're so sweet to be here with Hill and Lil. Please come in the morning to the house, I want to spend some time with you two. I have heard so much about you. I'm kinda like an aunt to them, it's complicated... So I have to check out girlfriends and boyfriends in the family!" She smiled with intensity.

Annie stood quietly behind her cousins and waited for Charlotte, "My sweetheart, Annie, I want to hear everything about your basketball and catch up on some rumors! I miss you so much."

Charlotte hugged her intently and whispered in her ear, "Is it true about Russell? We need to discuss your future. Don't worry, I'm great with secrets!" Annie could barely muster a word, paralyzed by Charlotte's support in the middle of her grief, she stood motionless.

Finally, she made it to the couch and hugged Russell, "I am deeply sorry, Aunt Charlotte... It's so sad!"

"Yes, but we're all together now, which is all that matters. You have been a great support for Junior. Burton loved you for that and gave you credit for Junior's great success this year." She kissed him on the lips and told him to come to the house with Sandy in the morning, then knelt down in front of Sandy and slowly kissed Junior still asleep. "Charlotte is here, my dear, everything is going to be alright. We're going to go to the house for now and let you sleep. Then everyone will be there in the morning. We'll all be together. That's what your dad would have wanted."

He slowly opened his eyes as she kissed his cheeks, "Mom, I'm so sad right now!"

"It's okay, sweetie, we're all here. Your sisters are home sleeping, they will need you in the morning. Everyone will be there. Nothing is going to change. This is what your dad wanted. This is why he worked himself to death."

He rose to a sitting position and let Sandy go. Charlotte rose from her knees to hug Sandy, "You are such a doll and now a good friend, Sandy. I hope you can be with us tomorrow."

"Of course, Charlotte. I'm so sorry for your loss. Mr. Parker was a hero to our family and to all of DC. He was a character that will be sorely missed!"

"That says it perfectly Sandy!"

• • •

Burton Parker had turned off his computer to end his work week on Friday night, February 15, 2030 at 9:47 p.m. after finishing a phone call to the head of his advertising empire in NYC.

Mr. Parker had made his money on Madison Avenue in the early eighties with the onslaught of the personal computer era of advertising. He built offices in the top twenty cities in America by the end of the decade to secure his first billion and parlayed that into the purchase of a football team in the late nineties. His shrewd investing after the dot-com crash in 2000 made him another fortune in technology businesses in the new century. He was awkward socially, but a brilliant futurist. He changed football to a less violent global game, built the greatest stadium in history, and brought championship events to DC. In his sixties, he hiked the Himalayas and studied Buddhism after his first love and wife died of cancer. He came back a new man and found a new love in Charlotte, who became his partner in everything he did.

He had promised a night together with Charlotte, after Brandy and Hannah were asleep. He was a man of his word. They had dinner together under candlelight and looked outside at the view of the Potomac River that he created almost three decades before. He had illegally cut down dozens of trees on National Park Service property to improve his view from his mansion on twenty-three acres of precious land in western Montgomery County in Maryland. He paid a million dollar fine and promised to replace the trees. He found trees that would only reach twenty feet high on the descending property before the river.

He was on six blood pressure and heart medications but would not take his beta-blocker medication for days at a time if he was spending time with Charlotte. He wanted to be good and hard to satisfy her. He planned on taking the medication after midnight when their romantic time was finished. At times, he could not get enough of Charlotte. It was not just sex, but her brilliance and that they could argue without anger. He had learned so much from her, especially about parenting. His relationships with his three kids had drastically improved in the past five years.

After dinner, they braved the cold and dipped in the hot tub for twenty minutes. They started foreplay in the water and finished lovemaking in the cabana house near the pool. Charlotte retrieved her robe, kissed her husband, and went back inside. Her last words to him, "Burton, don't fall asleep out here, come in soon, take your medication and get some sleep. I love you, dear."

He nodded as he nestled his head in the pillow, "I love you too, Charlotte... Thank you for everything." After a few minutes, he turned over and felt his member still throbbing and slightly hard. He loved his increased heart rate without the medication as he stroked himself for a few seconds, it made him feel like a young man to be free of the medication and to make love with Charlotte. *Life was great*, he thought.

Finally getting up, he grabbed his robe and thought about the great feeling of one more dip in the hot tub before opening the door. He took a deep breath and braved the cold naked, reaching the hot tub in ten seconds. He laid down his robe on the freezing concrete decking and stepped in. Each step felt like the difference between absolute zero in the universe and the fire of life invading his body. The invigoration dashed his memory of chills in an instant, as he kept his head just above the water line against the side of the spa. Breathing the frozen air equaled the extreme heat of the tub. It was riding the edge of life that kept him excited and interested in tackling his next project. He looked up at the blackest of clear skies on the coldest of nights. By the end of this new decade, the thirties, his dream of handing off the Potomacs to his son, with Charlotte's guidance, would be in progress. Brandy and Hannah would be almost finished with college, and he would become a humanitarian to his hometown.

Even his member felt hard again as he thought of the future, which included making love with Charlotte again tonight. That thought pushed him to leave the perfection of the hot tub and find his love Charlotte. His hot body started to feel the numbness of the zero-degree temperature as he stepped out of the tub. It felt initially like football weather in the Fall as he took steps towards the door to the house, but he was almost frozen without his robe on as he opened the door to the inside. Death had entered through his bare feet, up his legs, and then into his chest like a muscle spasm caused by electrocution. He managed a step inside, and with his last bit of air called out, "Charlotte." He was dead of a heart explosion before he hit the floor...a stroke before midnight.

~38~

Junior insisted on returning to school and attend class on Monday. His father was laid out on the fifty yard line at World Space Stadium with the roof open as Burton Parker had commanded. Almost a half a million fans and friends passed by his open coffin to pay their respects to the man that had brought a record three consecutive World Championships to DC. On Wednesday, a funeral service was held at the Prep Chapel. The school was shut down and all students attended with his family and close friends.

Alex Santucci spoke at the funeral and told a story about Burton Parker, "On a hot July morning in 2012, Burton Parker, a football owner, tracked me down in Kensington because my phone was off to tell me that I had been selected to replace an injured player for the All-Star Baseball Game. Then, he flew my family and I to Kansas City to play in front of my home team at that time. It was that day, Burton became part of our family, so it was only fitting when he married a Santucci, my stepsister Charlotte, in 2025." Alex laughed with tears in his eyes as he proceeded to introduce his brother to speak.

Guy Finelli slowly stepped up to the dais to give the eulogy. He called Burton, "The greatest man that nobody really knew, because that was the way he wanted it. He didn't care if he looked good, as long as his city and team did. In his death, he left a three billion dollar donation for our foundation to help DC, I will call it the Parker Foundation. In his life, he planned and funded the World Space Stadium and Hotel project, helped bring the Olympics, the World Cup, football and basketball championships, all to DC. Now his billions will make him the greatest contributor for DC in the twenty-first century, and it wouldn't bother him if no one remembered." He paused before ending, "When I retired, he congratulated me instead of complaining and fulfilled my contract. When I wanted to make movies, he invested a hundred million dollars without a concern. When I wanted to invest in West Baltimore, he matched my three hundred million dollars in private because he did not want to upset the people of DC. In the past decade, he matched that amount in donations to different DC foundations, anonymously, to make up for it in his mind. But the best thing about Burton Parker was not his unending generosity, but his friendship, a never-ending bond of unquestionable trust and undying support. And I, for one, will miss him immensely."

The following two weeks, Russell took over as Junior's caretaker at Prep. Junior moved into Russell's suite and spent the nights on his couch. At the same time, Annie wanted none of Junior. She had a ton on her plate and could not tend to his needs. Besides learning to play an intricate defense against sweaty boys, she was overwhelmed with the extra English work to graduate in May. And she did not want to think about losing a parent. Thoughts of her mother dying had been popping up more in past six months since she fell in love with Russell. *This love thing is complicated*, she thought.

On the basketball court, Junior was free of emotional pain. His concentration while bouncing a ball was simply – nothing else in the world mattered. He barely noticed that Annie was not around or had not called; and he loved to spend time around Sandy and Russell. They were his companions for dinner and after homework. They talked, watched TV, and sang at the piano. Every day was getting a little better for Junior, though he was not ready to return to being just a high school student.

The headmaster had given Russell permission to open the gym when Junior would wake up around midnight with nightmares. Russell would take him to the gym and rebound shots for thirty minutes to would wear him out. Then, they would then play one-on-one to eleven. Russell would always lose, but was improving his offensive skills, especially his jump hook. On defense, if he gave Junior any room outside, he would drill the jumper. If he played him too tight, Junior would fly by him, but Russell loved to recover and fly above the basket to sometimes block it off the backboard. Overall, Junior was becoming an unstoppable scoring machine.

Prep finished the regular season 21-0 to take the IAC crown. They were now qualified for the private school side of the DC city crown. They would participate in the DC Public/Private School tournament.

Annie was looking forward to her first piano lesson since Burton Parker's death with Russell. Being busy had helped her forget her longing for him, but it still felt like centuries since they had touched and talked. WJ's regular season had ended with an upset win over Springbrook to tie them for the regular season county Championship at 19-2. She had played fifteen minutes in that game and started to feel like a real contributor. Their 1-3-1 zone was still a work in progress, but it was not a matador defense either. She was starting to see her role on defense, which was helping her play on offense. Besides getting beat up quite a bit, she was learning to use her jumping ability on offense. She was floating one-handers in the lane consistently and not getting her lay-ups blocked because she was getting closer to the basket. Being comfortable on the court was becoming her best asset.

Hill was playing like the best player in the county. Besides eighteen points per game (ppg.), he was getting over ten rebounds and two assists a game. All the attention he was getting defensively was allowing Chamberlain to be the team leading scorer with twenty-two ppg. Defensively, Hill was loving playing the bottom '1' in the 1-3-1 zone. With Chamberlain guarding the lane, he would seemingly be in three places at one time on the baseline.

He was praying for a showdown with Junior in the State vs DC Championship in late March. The rumor was that it would take place in the World Space Stadium on the Friday and Sunday, at the end of March, of the *Final Four* tournament in DC. With the Stadium set up for basketball, it could hold 110,000 fans and be the largest crowd to ever witness high school basketball. It would be free for all students and all proceeds would go to the Parker Foundation. The four teams would include the winner of State of Maryland 4A, State of Virginia 6A, Catholic School, DC School/Private School tournaments. To be one of the four, a school would have to win four games in their state or league playoffs. It would be an amazing competition. If Prep could make it through the DC School/Private School tournament, they could meet WJ in the semi-finals of the DCMV tournament. It was an unlikely scenario because WJ would have to win the 4A State Playoffs. Annie was focused on winning the State Championship, since she had lost the volleyball state crown, but Hill wanted the match-up with Prep so bad he could taste it. For almost a month, he could think of nothing else.

Russell came to the Finelli house afterschool on a Wednesday. Annie's grandparents were in Florida, and the house was theirs. Her father, uncle, stepmother, and aunt were spending every moment setting up the Parker Foundation with an organization to handle a three billion dollar payout within a year or so. The Enclave was silent except for the security team on patrol around the property. Annie used all of her discipline to keep her hands off of Russell. He looked distracted and talked for the first half-hour, unloading his feelings about taking care of Junior.

"He needs to go back to his room on Friday; the tournament starts this weekend."

"You and Sandy have done a great job. I am sure Charlotte is very thankful for your time and effort."

"He is really traumatized. Thank goodness, he has basketball. I'm not sure what he will do when that is over. I can't babysit him forever."

"It is weird that you have taken over that role."

"You know it is unusual that I have grown fond of him. I hated him after the incident, but that time he apologized to me in his room really started a bond between us. I think he'll make a better adult than a Junior in high school." Russell laughed at his own joke.

"I hope that is true about all of us, Russell." Annie said trying to keep a straight face. She put her hand on his forearm and lifted it to the keys of the piano. "Let us start playing something. This morbid talk is distressing."

"You're right but let me say one thing... You're an exception to that rule."

"What rule is that?"

"You're a better adult as a high school person than most people are as older adults."

She wanted so much to kiss him, but just laid her head on his shoulder for a few seconds. "Thank you, Russell... Now teach me something new!"

~39~

Annie was depending on her best friend, her memory, to map out her assignments in the 1-3-1 defensive scheme. She had the basics down but needed more practice time before the playoffs to become the pest necessary to make her an asset on defense. On offense, since coming off the bench in the late first quarter of games, she would match up against tired point guards and back-up guards in the early second quarter, and dazzle them with amazing ball-handling skills and wizardry to advance into the front court, surprising passes for assists and lightning moves into the lane to score.

Every opponent would try to full court press her, as she took the ball inbounds, or off a rebound, but they quickly would be trailing her in the front court. Finally, in the second half of games, the opponent's coach would drop back into a zone and force her to shoot or pass off quickly. Even though she was bypassing three-point shooting, she could penetrate zones with the help of screens by her teammates. Sometimes, it would look like secret service agents setting up an opening for the president to get through a crowd.

Coach DeBone was a master of screening. He grew up in Indiana, where Bobby Knight was still adored and studied for his multiple screens on offense in winning three *NCAA* championships in the twentieth century. Because of his chair-throwing antics, abuse of players as a taskmaster, and his methodical play on offense involving countless screens, his teachings in general had fallen on deaf ears during the three-point era of basketball in the twenty-first century. But to Coach DeBone and now Coach Melendez, his style was perfect to keep Annie free of the sweaty boys.

After hours of viewing the Cloud over the past months, Dennis and Janet found the key to the screen game, the opposite setting of the secondary screens. They knew this would help Annie weave into the middle of the court, and more precisely the lane, if the zone was set up to clog the middle. They practiced it for weeks and then implemented it in the last four games. As Annie crossed midcourt, usually Hill would come from the wing to set up the first screen at the top of the key or above, and then Chamberlain would come from the other side near the lane to set a pick facing away from Hill just below the foul line. These perfectly timed screens would allow Annie to zigzag and then sneak into the key and finally the lane, using a variety of dribbles, behind her back, between her legs, or thrown in front of her and sometimes through a defender's legs. Once in the lane, she could shoot a runner or pass to Chamberlain on a pick-and-roll or to either forward Lance Ball or Howard Dennis on the baseline for an easy lay-up or short jumper. The most spectacular option was a jump in the air and a one-hundred-eighty degree twirl to pass to a wide-open Hill behind the three-point line and watch him drill a jumper. After about four of those, the opponents would go back to man-to-man or wipe their brows when she returned to the bench.

During a practice in the first week of March, Annie came early with her teammates to run through the zone defense like a choreographed dance for a Broadway show. Before the coaches showed, the twelve members of the team were there to support her in rehearsing the defense. After an initial concern about her joining the team, she had become a favorite for every team member. They knew they were in the playoffs because of her and Hill, but her potential could gain them a state championship. She worked so much harder than any of them that it was embarrassing. Finally, at midseason, the whole team picked up the pace in practice. Since then, it was all business.

Beverly Broomfield, a teammate and star player from the volleyball team, was there at practice waiting for Annie to finish. She played and trained for volleyball year-round and was going to be on a scholarship to Penn State in the fall 2030.

"Hey Annie, what can I say, you're a real trail blazer. We've been to all the games. All the girls are psyched about watching the playoffs."

Annie was surprised to see Beverly because she was not her closest buddy on the volleyball team but was still happy to talk with her.

"Should be fun. You look great. Anything new?" As usual, Annie got to the point.

"Actually, there is. I wanted to get your opinion on something."

"Sure."

"I ran into Junior Parker at a future leader's meeting a couple of weeks ago and then again at an orientation with Penn State, apparently they are recruiting him."

"That is interesting. Do you know him?"

"Not really, but he knew all about me. He asked me out after both events…seems kind of lost with his dad passing."

"Did you go out with him?"

"I had conflicts both times, but we've texted and face-timed during the two weeks since. I wanted to talk to you first before I decided to date him."

"We have moved on from each other since his dad's death. I saw him the day after, and I told him that the situation was too close to home for me. And I wanted to put everything I have into basketball right now. I suggested to him to do the same thing."

"You are to the point, Annie, I wish I could do that."

"That makes two of us. I wish I could be more like you, especially your height!"

Beverly laughed and gave Annie a hug. It felt good to be close again to her teammate.

Annie felt her warmth and looked up at her, "So you guys are going out?"

"More like hanging out at first, I think you could call it. Like you, I don't have a lot of time, but I like watching him play, and we talk pretty easily with each other… I sort-of like him."

"That is nice to hear, he is pretty handsome, but he can become aggressive, you have to set ground rules with him. Otherwise, he is fun and intense at other times."

"Thanks for the advice. You know Junior and I are exactly the same height?"

"I guess you will see eye-to-eye on things then."

"Very funny, Annie, now you're a comedian… Good luck with the playoffs. The girls will be cheering you on."

~40~

The babysitting of Junior was over for Russell, and his life seemed to be returning to some sense of normal again. The fourth-floor hall had a normal quiet at night as Junior acted like the rest of the boys, in his room studying when he was not busy with basketball and class. And now, a new girlfriend possibly was on the horizon, according to news from Annie. They seemed both relieved at the news, knowing that Junior had served his purpose as a part of the Plan. Annie was free of him, and Russell could escape his jealousy that had been creeping closer to his emotional core.

There were loose ends for him to clear up. He needed to see Abbey to make sure that relationship would not backfire on him and become a big problem. They had not seen each other since Christmas but had talked several times. She had been in South America, Brazil mainly, for six weeks, as an opportunity from work came up, and she thought, *I could use the change of scenery.* Russell agreed, but now she was back and wanted to see him.

The part-time job on the weekends had been abandoned, and Russell was curious as to the state of affairs with the boss and Abbey. *I'm sure she would tell me the truth, if I asked*, Russell thought. She had offered a dinner in Georgetown, but he wanted to meet at a piano bar off H street where he worked while in college. It was familiar to him and quiet before ten p.m., where he could minimize the embarrassment if it got out of hand.

She was waiting for him at a small table in the corner at eight p.m., with just a few patrons at the bar as the piano man was playing softly in the background. Abbey looked professionally dressed, with her hair cut shorter, just touching her neck above her shoulders. It was a new look with a suit jacket and matching skirt just above her knees. Fortunately, Russell thought, *she has really toned back her sexuality for the night.* They chatted for a while, mostly about her being in Rio and enjoying the warm weather since January.

"Maybe I could have stayed a couple more weeks. It's too chilly here." She laughed at her complaining. "But Russell…how are you doing, you know how much I miss you. Have you moved on from me, yet?" she asked cautiously.

Russell was not versed in breaking a girl's heart. "I've been busy with Junior Parker at Prep. I will admit that Sandy and I have been hanging out some. She's needed a friend since her husband left before Christmas."

"Wow…and I was worried about that teenager! You have always been a sucker for big tits, Russell. Mine haven't been big enough for you?" She eyed him sheepishly.

"Yours are perfect, Abbey, and you know that," Russell winked at her, "though they're hard to see with that jacket on."

Abbey grinned from ear to ear at the compliment, glad to hear that Russell might still be interested. "I'm not seeing the weekend boss anymore, that was pretty stupid of me," she admitted. "I'm not sure what I was doing with that group. But now I'm feeling more focused with this opportunity at work. They want me to rep all of Latin America."

"Good for you, Abbey, you will be great at it and make lots of money I hope," Russell thought about her constant struggles with money.

"Could be a jackpot in a couple of years…lots of travel though! Can we stay in touch and see each other, if it works for you and me?" Her eyes had a pleading look that melted Russell's defensive front quickly, like a blitz up the middle.

Without hesitation, Russell answered, "That would be perfect Abbey." Russell thought about explaining further, but he realized it was a minefield, and it was better to be succinct at the moment. He was happy that it would fit the Plan perfectly. As he sat back and finished his drink, he visually digested Abbey from head to toe and thought, *she was still a fox, no doubt about it*, as he felt a stirring in his pants. He quickly ordered another scotch.

Abbey had an *Embassy Row Suite* in the downtown west end for a week. Her lease was done on her apartment, and the company was paying for her to be in DC for a week every month until her travel was done in the Fall for a year, then she could get a new place. After a quick dinner and several drinks, they caught a cab to 22nd and N Streets. There was no talking on the ride over as they held hands and looked out opposite windows wondering if they were ready for what was about to happen. The ride and the thinking were done quickly, as they scampered into the hotel and on to the open-glass elevator, riding up ten floors. They kissed passionately on the elevator, as Russell felt her ribs from front to back under her jacket, then pulled her in close. The doors opened, they stayed connected and scurried down the hall to her suite, pausing twice to kiss each other while looking for her room number. They laughed as it seemed to take an eternity.

Russell followed Abbey inside and closed the door behind him as she flipped off her heels. Russell approached her from behind as she took off her jacket and slid his hands under her blouse as she unbuttoned the front. Her bra was quickly disposed of as he took hold of her perfect breasts, noting they were a quarter the size of Sandy's. But it mattered not to him, as he fondled then amused, *because women's breasts have their own perfect character and I have loved any pair I have ever had the privilege to feel.*

She turned around and quickly disposed of his pants and shirt. His member grew perfectly hard in her hands, as she felt overwhelmingly wet inside since the cab ride, imagining him on top of her pounding away. She had thought of it for months, *but I never knew if it would ever happen again.* Tears flew out of her eyes as he finally entered her and thrusted several times. "Oh, my dear Russell…you feel so good. Please don't stop." She kissed him through her tears and then laid back to enter heaven on earth.

Russell let go inside of her within minutes and felt immediate trepidation as he rolled off Abbey and made it to the bathroom. He knew that she was happy and satisfied as she ducked under the sheets and curled up with several pillows, emotionally returning to the third dimension after such an out-of-this-world experience with Russell.

The mirror in the bathroom looked back at him with concern. Would he be able to be with her to make it work until the Fall or longer, while he waited for Annie to get older? Or should he do the right thing and get out of the relationship now? Should he put all his chips in with Sandy? *She would understand and be supportive*, he thought, *or maybe she would get too serious about him.* He realized that he had to hedge his relationship with Sandy by being with Abbey until at least the Fall. Five or six meetings at the most with sexual encounters likely. He knew he could do it, but would he want to hunt a fox?

~41~

The DC Public/Private School Playoffs involved the top eight public high schools in DC and the top eight private schools in and around DC. Prep accepted an invitation as winner of the Interstate Athletic Conference. The first eight games were played on the second Friday in March in four locations throughout DC at six p.m. and eight p.m. followed by four quarterfinal games on Saturday at the DC Armory at two, four, six and eight p.m. The two semi-final games were on the following Friday evening at the same location with the championship game the following evening. The new DCMV (DC, MD, and VA) tournament would be two weeks later on a Friday and Sunday.

Excitement was growing in the DCMV area with all four tournaments (State of MD, State of VA, Catholic Schools, and DC Public/Private Schools) happening during the same two weekends. Burton Parker's death had given rise to the DCMV tournament and a strong interest in high school basketball. It helped that his son, the leading scorer in the DCMV area, and the son and daughter of two local sports heroes, could be involved in the finals weekend event at the World Space Stadium. This along with College *March Madness* being played on these weekends and the *Final Four* coming to DC contributed to a convergence of events that made for a perfect basketball whirlwind of excitement.

The DC area had always been an unheralded basketball mecca since 1946, when the great Red Auerbach coached the Washington Capitols and almost won the BAA crown (precursor to the NBA) in 1949. They played their games at the Washington Coliseum or then known as the U-Line Arena still located in the now exciting NoMass (north of Massachusetts avenue) area of DC. It also hosted *The Beatles* first American concert in February 1964 and the ABA Washington Capitals in 1969 with the great *Rick Barry*. Auerbach, a native Washingtonian, moved on to coach the *Boston Celtics* but still lived in DC during the off-season. Players like Elgin Baylor, Aubrey Nash, George Leftwich, John Thompson, Dave Bing, Sid Catlett, Austin Carr, James Brown, Adrian Dantley, Len Bias, Danny Ferry, Johnny Dawkins, Grant Hill, and Dennis Scott, to name a few, came from the DCMV area, and most became college and NBA stars. Some also became great coaches, general managers, or broadcasters in college or professional basketball.

Cole Field House hosted two *NCAA Basketball Final Four* tournaments. One in 1966, when the first all-African American starting five from *Texas Western* beat the all-white *Kentucky Wildcats* and the second was in 1970 when *UCLA* led by coach John Wooden won their sixth out of seventh *NCAA* National Championship

Maryland and Georgetown captured the city starting in the 1970s with great college basketball, both winning NCAA crowns. The NBA Washington Bullets won a championship in 1978 and went to the NBA finals four times in the 1970s. Burton Parker had tried to bring a DCMV high school basketball championship to DC for years; only his death made it possible.

Junior Parker and Prep would play at Anacostia in the first round of the playoffs. Their newly refurbished field house was packed with two-thousand fans and tons of media following the son of the fallen owner. There was a moment of silence before each game of the tournament for the new hero to DC, Burton Parker.

Junior did not waste any time in taking over the game early with a blistering shooting display of twenty-eight first half points, including seven for seven from the three-point line. Anacostia cut the lead in the third quarter to a dozen points, but it was the closest they could get in the second half as Prep pulled away in a 99-81 win. Junior ended up with thirty-seven points.

Coach Jeffries cleared the bench with five minutes remaining and a thirty point lead, and specifically told his subs not to exceed one hundred points under any circumstances. They certainly made it close for Father Jeffries, a Jesuit English teacher at the school and a young basketball coach at twenty-eight, who grew up watching the *Golden State Warriors* win crowns in '15 and '17 in Northern California. He coached with the same philosophy with Junior Parker as his Stephen Currey.

Father Jeffries came east to study at Georgetown and entered the priesthood after graduation. He loved being at Georgetown Prep and wanted to someday be the headmaster and then father in charge.

After losing an elite player in Hill Santucci just before the season opened, Father Jeffries did not panic and visited one of the best athletes at Prep on Monday working out at the Field House gym. Dirk Nielson was the starting QB on the football team and the best athlete at Prep. He grew up in Germany and was named after Dirk Nowitzki, the great NBA player from Germany. Dirk Nielson was six feet, six inches and a bull in a China shop on the basketball court. His father had encouraged him to focus on one sport, football, and put his first love, basketball, on the back burner, because his future was as a quarterback in college and maybe professionally as well.

Father Jeffries had a whole speech ready to convince Dirk to come play on his team, but he did not need it. As soon as Dirk saw him, he knew what he wanted; before Father Jeffries even spoke, he said, "Coach, I hear Hill is transferring, I would love to play if you need me. I'm in great shape and been working on my jumper."

Coach Jeffries was stunned and did not know what to say. So, he just shook his hand and finally said, "Do I need to call your parents?"

"No, Father, my Dad has always left it up to me to decide. I didn't think you needed me before with Hill and Junior, but now I have the whole paint to myself!" He laughed with a boyish confidence.

"Yes, you will, my son; and God, I believe, is looking down upon us with the Holy Spirit." In the first playoff game against Anacostia, Dirk Nielson had fifteen points, nineteen rebounds, and seven blocks. *Not bad for a quarterback*, Father Jeffries thought.

Beverly Broomfield met Junior after the game. The two of them were taken by limousine to watch WJ take on Wise High School, a school in Upper Marlboro Maryland and defending state champion, in their first-round game at the famous Cole Field House on the Maryland campus. It was now a football practice facility but was used for the first round of the state basketball tournament for the great history in the building. Five thousand fans packed the limited stands along with many media outlets for the six p.m. game.

Russell sat along with Alex, Sally and Lil; Guy, Patty and little Anthony; Phillip, Carol and big Cousin Joe; who were sitting next to the volleyball squad behind the bench when Beverly and Junior joined them. Coach DeBone knew if they could survive the first four minutes of the game, they would be in it, but Wise was blazing fast and jumped like no other team in Montgomery County.

In the locker room before the game, Ronnie Dominic was walking back and forth as the coaches were espousing their game plan to combat Wise. He was mumbling as he pulled on both sides of the towel behind his head. Finally, Coach Melendez stood and interrupted Coach DeBone, "Ronnie, what is going on with you, can you tell us?"

Coach DeBone looked up, not noticing the nervous energy of his tough as nails, starting point guard. He took a couple of steps towards his senior player, whom he adored, "Ronnie, can you join us or share with us what you think?"

Ronnie slowed down his shuffling and finally turned to Coach DeBone, who waved for him to come up front. With his head down, he took the invitation. He reached the front and half turned to the coaches and half to his teammates, "I'm sorry, Coach, but I want to win this thing so bad. This is the best team in the state, and it sucks that we have to play them in the first round. No one has any respect for us."

Everyone stood in silence, waiting for the clincher.

Ronnie used the towel to wipe off his sweaty face and push back his hair. He looked up at his teammates, especially at Annie. Then, he turned to Coach DeBone, "Coach, we have to start Annie and trap these guys from the first whistle to the end. Then, if the starting five falls over, I'll go in, but not until then."

Coach Melendez was the first to smile; then, his teammates in the front, let out a yell of support. Chamberlain messed up Annie's hair and hugged her with support and yelled, "Yea, Coach, yea!"

Coach DeBone stepped forward and put his hand up, the sign for the circle, the team leaped forward to crowd-in together, full of energy, from their heads to their toes with arms around each other for support. "Okay, let's go out with the 1-3-1 trap from the first second and keep up pressure until you drop. Annie, you're the man," he smiled and then continued, "I want clear outs for Hill on every possession until the first time-out, otherwise dance in the lane Annie. Chamberlain stay focused on defense, don't shoot it for now unless it's a dunk. Let's put on a show folks!" They raised their arms with a one, two, three, Big Train!

Annie had practiced and thought through this moment with Hill for months. She could see in her mind the tip going to Hill and back to her and then a clear out for Hill. She understood it all in her mind. Coach DeBone was protecting her on the court, initially letting Hill get established because no one could cover him, and they always played man to man. She envisioned a first quarter time-out and then Wise would switch to zone defense. Then coach would switch to the screens-up-the-middle offense.

To her left, twenty feet away in the stands, stood a trilogy of important men in her life together, Russell with Guy and Phillip on either side of him. They all meant so much to her in different ways. Guy made her feel secure, Phillip helped her see clearly, and Russell opened up her heart.

She closed her eyes to focus on the clear pathways on the court and not the clusters of sweaty boys around her. Phillip had spent hours with her on her concerns that could cause her great anxiety. Her choreography was clear on defense, her majestic flow on offense would be instinctual.

She thought of her mother for a moment and felt a tingler whirl down her spine. They were together now for this moment. She would slay the dragons of sweaty boys for her tonight. As she opened her eyes and heard the sold-out crowd raising the roof with their cheers, it had been pleasing to block out the obstacles. She was in the Cloud now with "Pistol Pete", seeing him flow with the ball as an extension of his arm and get to the spots of the court that he had taken a million shots from in practice. Annie would not take a shot unless she could make ninety percent of them in practice. Her three-point shot was hovering around sixty percent in practice, not good enough for a game, she believed. Ten years of practice and watching the Cloud. She was ready to run like a Spartan leading the Big Train into battle.

The tip went as planned. Her hands felt numb sliding over the ball as she prepared a dribble. She saw her route through an unforeseen double team, a slide step to the right, then behind the back with the dribble, a cut back left, now through the legs, a spin move at the key, then a crossover dribble into the lane, a floater from the lane for two points. Hill patted her butt, "Great play, keep doin' it if it's there, girl." She backpedaled into defense. The feeling in her hands came back, her breath was slowed, she could see nothing but the ball. Then, she did something she had never done before in front of other humans.

Her feet felt light, her legs were loose, in the lay-up line she was laying it in the basket with ease. No one on her team noticed. She remembered during the summer last year, she was playing by herself after a track practice. Her high jump practice was off the charts. She thought she would try it after laying the ball in the basket five times. She felt ready. The women's ball she used was an inch smaller in diameter than the men's ball. She usually practiced with the men's, but for this she grabbed the women's ball. She started at half court and with a normal layup route, she took off and clanged the ball off the back rim. As she went back to half court, she adjusted her steps to take off just a little closer. She was buzzing from head to toe, as she looked around the inside of the bubble to make sure no one had come in. She remembered her footwork and headed to the basket, three dribbles, two steps, but the ball slipped out of her hand. It was very hot, and she was dripping sweat from head to toe. She got a cold pack as she took off her jersey and shorts and left on just her sports bra and panties. The cold pack dried up her hands as she pulled her hair back tighter. She laid the cold pack on her neck for a moment as she tightened her shoelaces. She settled in at half court and shimmed her butt to stay loose. As she closed her eyes, she remembered the David Thompson story of soaring in the air against Maryland as told by her Grandpa. *Could I be lighter than air? Yes*, she asked and answered. Her perfectly toned body stood nearly naked, pounding the ball at mid-court, as she executed her approach like a high-jump attempt, bolting into the take-off and soaring up to the rim. Her arm rose above the rim higher than ever. The ball felt secure in her hand and then it happened: The Slammer prevailed!

In front of her was the best player on Wise, Abeni Marjani. He was simply too big for her to cover, but until they went to their zone, she had to make the best of it. As he dribbled down the court, he barely noticed her as he called out a play. She spread out with her feet wide and her head barely three feet from the ground as she waited like a predator for the cross-over dribble. As Abeni looked over her, surveying an opening to the left as he dribbled with his right. Annie timed it perfectly, diving at his feet as he attempted a quick cross-over dribble, she knocked the ball behind him and tumbled by without contact. Abeni tripped over himself, looted of the ball as he rolled on the floor. He stood quickly, bitching to the referee, as Annie corralled the ball at mid-court. Wide open, she approached the basket like a high-jump attempt. The ball felt secure in her hand as she soared with her two final strides and rose to get her elbow above the rim. Her right hand spread like never before and captured the ball. Five-thousand people, already standing, held their breath with anticipation for the impossible. A cavernous scream filled the hallowed arch roof of Cole Field House at full volume. The Slammer finished with authority and left no doubt of her accomplishment in an instant, as she landed on the ground. She let her hair flop around her face, hiding a proud smile to her mom, as she headed back to defense. The hysteria in the crowd mythically morphed to a hundred thousand basketball fans through the Cloud that would maintain they saw it in person.

Annie's heart was pumping with a fury as her foe carefully met her at half court, looking at her like she was an animal he had never seen before. Hill quickly came for the double-team and knocked the ball away. Annie bumped it forward and in "Pistol Pete" style, punched it down court to Hill, who pulled up for a three-pointer, and swished it through. The next possession quickly turned into another turnover and a Hill three-pointer, causing a Wise time-out. WJ had flown ahead to a 10-0 lead that they never let go of all game.

Coach DeBone made sure there was no celebration as he calmed down the troops, saying only, "Let's act like we're starting the game. Nothing different until the first time-out I call. Let's go." The troops came together for a one, two, three, Go Big Train!

The crowd had stayed standing the whole timeout; Russell was trying to stay calm as he watched Annie intently in the excitement. Both Guy and Phillip were screaming encouragement as they stepped up on the bench seats. Russell stayed silent but felt so stimulated by her performance that he checked himself to make sure he was not growing in his pants. There was no action down there, just frenzy in his heart. Sally caught his eye and ran into his arms for a hug and asked him, "Can you hold me up on the bench?" as she found a spot into between Guy and Phillip. She smelled so delicious as he held her hips in front of him, hoping it could be Annie some day at an event with him sharing the excitement.

The game carried on without an ebb to the exhilaration in the crowd. Annie's family and Russell drew closer together. Soon, Charlotte and Sandy found their way to their spot in the bench and joined the party. Sandy had a flask of scotch that Russell took a healthy swig. With Sandy at his side and Sally falling into him after each of Hill's baskets, he was getting plenty of body contact to keep his heart pounding. Another swig of scotch helped keep him calm.

Hill took over in the first half, as he had his way with every Wise defender that tried to guard him. Every time he scored, he pointed to Junior as he headed down court, like a warning that he was coming for him. Junior kept calm and nodded back to him as Beverly took advantage of the excitement to physically molest him.

At halftime with a healthy lead, Coach Melendez took Annie to the side and asked her specifically about her three-point shot. Annie was zoned out with her mind only thinking about seeking direction from her memory of the Cloud. The Slam was not in her consciousness, just her role on defense and offense for the second half, "I have only one question Annie…" She nodded, "What were the odds of shooting from the three-point line in your last practice?"

She gave a hint of a smile at the question, a wave of love flowed through her as she looked deeply into Janet's eyes and realized that her mother would know her as well as Janet did. She enjoyed the recognition and answered, "Sixty-eight percent…thirty-four of fifty."

"That's outstanding, you know, they will be double teaming Hill from now on and maybe Chamberlain, too. You will need to shoot when you're open."

"But in a game, the percentage could drop drastically. It is more efficient for Hill to continue to dish off to Lance and Howard from the baseline."

"Coach DeBone and I agree on this. It does not matter if you miss, Hill and Chamberlain will rebound. Stay beyond the key and shoot. Then drop back on defense. We need shooting from an angle on the floor that frees up the middle for Hill and Chamberlain inside. Just do it, okay?"

Annie's smile was fully exposed now as Janet's logic seeped into her thinking. The coaches knew more about basketball strategy than she did. It was reassuring to her that her hard work on her three-point shooting could help the team. Suddenly, her mind slowed down a bit. *Now I can have some fun in the second half,* she thought.

The party in the stands barely slowed down as the Cloud was full of replays of The Slammer making history. Russell felt like an outsider as the women chuckled about Charlotte's storytelling in front of him and the men replayed Hill's one-on-one moves to his side. Russell found some relief as he watched Annie return to the floor for warm-ups. It was surreal to see her at five feet, eight inches with her floppy hair and playing with the boys. Just her physical movements made him happy as she stood at the three-point line draining jumpers. It was hard for him to imagine how much stronger she looked from her last volleyball game in the Fall. Her transformation into a young lady was exciting for him to watch. Besides being in love with her, he was her biggest fan.

Charlotte shouted out to him, but he couldn't hear. She leaned forward to him and kissed him on the lips, "Thanks for all your help, Russell. Junior is doing so well and has a new girlfriend. I hope these teams get to play each other." Russell could see she had probably finished Sandy's flask or her own, as she nestled in close to him. "I don't know who I would cheer for, you know?" she offered playfully.

Russell felt her chest heaving into him and lied, "That would be a tough one!"

Sandy saved him as she pulled Charlotte back into women's group and winked at him.

Nursing a twenty-two point, third quarter lead, Coach DeBone had not had to call on the 1-3-1 defense yet nor had Annie launched a three-pointer yet. Wise's Abeni Marjani started to take over as he intently kept his ball handling from causing a turnover. He worked methodically into the lane for a series of short jumpers and layups as he cut the lead back to ten points. At the break before the fourth quarter, Coach DeBone called for the 1-3-1 and made it clear that taking the open jumper was imperative for the offense to get into a flow again without looking directly at Annie.

She was ready to perform, because she was getting worn out by Abeni's big body sweating on her, something she tried to ignore. Hill called for the ball quickly as she passed half court. He dribbled to the wing almost trying to secure a double team and flung it back to Annie who was dead center at the three-point line. She drilled the first one.

The 1-3-1 set up and trapped Abeni immediately. He managed to knock over Annie for an offensive foul call. The next four minutes looked like a clinic in trapping the ball on defense and beating the double team on offense. Annie hit six consecutive three-pointers. Both her and Hill were over thirty points and ten assists for the game.

In the stands, Russell felt a great relief as the lead soared to thirty points over the defending state champions. Sally was mauling him after every three-pointer as Sandy had returned to his side. Sally's petite body felt closer to Annie's than Sandy's or the lankier Charlotte. It reminded him of wanting to be with Princess Kate when he was a kid as he watched her on television. It was all so exciting at the moment to feel her body so much and to hold on a bit too long. The more Annie sank three-pointers, the chummier he felt with Sally. It was a great distraction that kept him from wanting to be with Annie.

The crowd sang out with joy as Coach DeBone was able to clear his bench with four-minutes to go and a thirty point lead. Abeni tried to keep Wise in the game but was finally pulled at the two-minute mark, having scored thirty-five points in a losing effort. He would be wearing a Kentucky blue next year for a national audience, most still remembering that a young woman stole the ball from him and dunked while he sat at mid-court.

As the buzzer sounded, Abeni Marjini was the first player to hug Annie and lifted her in the air as he shouted to the cameras that she was something special. For that few seconds, she did not mind being held by a sweaty boy!

~42~

The excitement at both Prep and WJ, ten days later, on the Monday morning after each won the DC and Maryland tournaments was something that could only be produced by teenagers in love with the world until the next Friday when they faced each other in the semi-final match-up. Both squads survived four games over two weekends, playing like finely tuned orchestras through Mozart, Beethoven, Puccini, and Tchaikovsky symphonies. Each performance needed abilities they were not sure they had but were able to dig down deep and hit all the right notes. Their conductors, Coaches DeBone, Melendez and Jeffries, relied heavily on their starting five in each contest. These players were now stars in the halls of their school where they roamed.

At each school, the principal had cancelled morning classes on Monday for a mandatory assembly, which no student would have missed. A week of partying leading up to the match-up between WJ and Prep in the semi-finals at World Space Stadium at nine p.m. on Friday night was the only thing on anybody's mind in those schools.

On metro and national levels, the sports media were pre-empting discussion about the College *Final Four* to talk about this match-up between the children of DC sports royalty: Hill Santucci and Annie Finelli versus the future King of the Washington Potomacs, Junior Parker and his high school all-American football QB turned basketball teammate from Germany, Dirk Nielson. Even German television was covering this week of basketball heaven. The tickets for the Friday night game, all one hundred ten thousand, had been taken by ten a.m. The other two semi-finalists were perennial high school basketball powerhouses that would square off at seven p.m., DeMatha, the undefeated Catholic School league champions and W. T. Woodson, the Virginia State champion.

The Friday school day was shortened to noon at the four schools for the concert and parties being set up in the parking lots at the stadium. Any student in the area could attend with a downloaded free ticket. A perfect storm of popularity had come together to create this fever. Not since the 2020 Global American Football (GAF) Championship that opened World Space Stadium, had DC been so a-buzzed about an event. And this would be in perfect spring weather with the cherry blossoms at full bloom. The city was already packed with normal mobs of sightseers and fans of the *Final Four* College Basketball teams for which people had already taken off work to enjoy for at least the weekend if not the whole week.

By Wednesday, Russell and Annie were in desperate need of their piano lesson hour at four p.m. Russell arrived through an entrance on Oldfield Drive to avoid the press and extra security set up around the Enclave during the week. As he walked around and then down the steps from the Santucci Estate to the grandparents' house and through the backdoor entrance, he felt butterflies in his stomach wondering how he would feel when alone with Annie.

His experience over the last two weekends of watching her compete against the sweaty boys, and feeding off the affection of Sandy, Sally, and Charlotte, were experiences he discussed with Deacon Robey in his last two sessions. Somehow, seeing Annie play in front of thousands with great success made him feel somewhat insecure. The closeness he received from the women was like getting refuge from his vulnerable feelings. Everything seemed to revolve around his member when he felt uncertain about himself. He was easily drawn to the physical attention of the females he trusted and admired both sexually and personally. When Sally celebrated in his arms and Charlotte thrust her chest in his face, it turned him on and helped neutralized his insecurity. His sexual encounters with Sandy after the games were incredibly intense as well. His heightened sexual reaction to Annie, going back to their first meeting three years ago, was only quenched with intense fantasy or sex with Abbey or Sandy.

His time alone with Annie, now that they had expressed their love for each other, was not full of sexual anxiety for him. The slight touches on the arm or shoulder, the few intense hugs, the volleyball celebration kiss were nice, but when they talked in the car or during their piano lessons, it lifted the pain of insecurity and the burden of uncontrollable sexuality for that day and a few more afterwards. It was why he was convinced she was the one for him.

She opened the door for him and stood back, knowing that her grandparents were in the family room. He was greeted like a dear family friend by Phillip and Carol. They never hinted that they knew of his love for their granddaughter, but he got the sense they would be thrilled to have him in their family, officially. They put on their walking shoes and shouted out their intentions for a long walk in the park, leaving the house to them.

As they walked towards the front of the house and the piano, they held hands as soon as the door was closed. They sat together on the piano bench and talked, "What's it like to be such a star, Annie? You seemed to be floating on air out there on the court."

"Thank you for asking," she said as she looked at him with her wide-opened green eyes. "It is the hardest thing I have ever done, but I am doing something grand. My dream is to be great!"

"Are you getting enough rest?"

"Enough… I have a lot to process for Friday night's game. So many variables and I have to work on my three-point shot and defense."

Russell was well aware of Annie's statistics for the four games to win the state tournament: eighteen points, twelve assists, three rebounds, four steals, and one turnover averaged per game. She was twenty-five for thirty-four from the field, an astounding seventy-three percent shooting percentage, which included thirteen for twenty from three-point land and all eleven from the foul line. Only Hill's outstanding thirty-three points and twelve rebounds per game performance got him the MVP award for the state tournament. He paused as he took in her smell and the heat of her body. She was in a bright orange top that almost matched her hair. Her top came short of her pants revealing her amazing stomach muscles when she lifted up. "Annie you shot sixty-five percent on three-pointers. That was amazing! And seventy-three percent altogether, and perfect from the foul line. How about you just get enough rest and food this week."

She put her hand on his back softly and smiled, feeling happy that he had memorized her statistics. She had not looked at the score sheet, but she knew her numbers exactly. "I was only seven for fourteen from three in the last three games, that will not be enough if Junior is on fire. And the other shots should be ninety percent or higher, not eighty-five percent and the foul shots are pretty automatic at this point, so…"

"So…so… so, yes, yes, yes…you could be better, but you performed in the state tournament like a star. How about only four turnovers in the whole tournament."

"Yes, thank you for noticing that was great." She leaned into him a little as she rubbed his back. "What if you had a concert and you only hit seventy-three percent of your notes? Would you be happy?"

"Speaking of piano playing, let's get to the lesson!" Russell laughed as Annie moved to a piano ready stance with a huge smile. They played together for thirty minutes. Most of the time, he would play a part and then she would copy it with her amazing recall. Finally, she stood up and asked that he play for her. He acquiesced.

As he played, she laid her hands lightly on his shoulders, watching his hands fly through a new piece she had never heard. He had no sheet music in front of him. She closed her eyes and felt the sound pierce her chest and through her lungs, feeling the refreshing oxygen fill her body in a way she had never experienced before. Her thoughts went into the future, seeing themselves as a couple frolicking down a hill carrying a picnic basket towards a creek. It was a spot with no one around for acres. They put down a huge blanket and sat in the shade eating and holding each other while laughing in the middle of conversation. Suddenly, the sound of an expected door opening made her step away from Russell and sit in a chair, where she waited for her grandparents to enter the room. Russell continued playing his new material. Once again, she closed her eyes for a moment to see her heaven.

As he finished, Phillip and Carol stayed back in the hallway not wanting to interrupt the moment. Annie opened her eyes as tears rushed out as she took in the beauty of the just finished music. It moved her like never before.

Russell asked, "Are you okay Annie?"

"Just perfect Russell… Perfectly happy, Russell, thank you for the lesson."

~43~

The last time they walked out on the stadium floor, it was covered by a football field before the New Year's Eve party. Both Junior and Annie felt strange as they had shoot-arounds in an empty stadium with their teams at different times. The echoes of the basketballs bouncing was endless, as they tried to imagine one hundred ten thousand fans cheering while they played. There would be no echoes during the game, just decibel levels of noise that doubled the biggest concert they had ever attended. And they would be the target of that noise, their play modulating the level while giving them a surreal sense of performance possibilities. Would a missed shot quiet the crowd or rustle up boos? Would the constant buzz of sound lift their play off the floor like a magic trick or leaden their legs twice the normal gravity?

Annie was not looking forward to covering Junior in a man-to-women defense. She suggested to Coach Melendez that Ronnie Dominic should start and take some fouls early covering Junior in the first quarter. She knew they could not let Junior get into a rhythm in the building that Burton Parker built. *He could play out of his mind and not miss a shot all game*, she feared.

"Annie, you won't be left on an island covering Junior. We may put Hill on him or switch to the 1-3-1 early in the game or possibly a diamond and one on him."

"That makes sense, but we only practiced that once during the week."

"That's true, but just think of it as an extension of the 1-3-1 with Hill in the middle instead."

"We should double team him from the beginning, get him frustrated and out of rhythm." Annie was animated with authority.

"I'll talk to Coach DeBone about that idea as well, but don't worry. Offense is going to win this game, and nobody can stop you and Hill if you're thinking clearly."

"That is a good point coach."

The weather was a magnificent spring day full of sun and warmth after a brutal winter. The grounds around the stadium were set up for a beautiful afternoon of tailgating or what they called picnicking in the twentieth century. A man-made meandering arm of the Anacostia River was turned into a creek that surrounded the stadium and allowed for blankets to be thrown down on the grassy banks of the perfectly clean water of the futuristic looking stadium. The whole area had gone through a tremendous transformation that attracted thousands of families to use for exercising, meals, reflection or just plain talking on a daily basis. An event like this one would make the entire area a party scene. Peace officers added a sense of security to the area but were relatively ignored by most people. Alcohol and pot smoking were legal activities, but leaving trash was grounds for arrest and huge fines. Single unisex bathroom units were plentiful.

With the temperature hovering around sixty degrees and no wind to speak of, the roof stayed open for the first game at seven p.m. DeMatha and Woodson took the court to a half-full arena. The rest of the crowd was enjoying the extra hour of daylight until the mandatory eight p.m. entrance time.

In the first half, DeMatha had struggled to keep up with Woodson's star backcourt and was losing by a surprising ten points at half-time. As the crowd settled at full capacity during the fifteen-minute break, the Staggs regrouped and planned to come out with their patented full-court press. In the first three minutes, the defensive intensity seemed to backfire as the Woodson guards quickly found their way through the double teams for some easy baskets. When the lead grew to sixteen points, Coach Wooten called his last timeout and told his group, "this is the last time you will hear from me, no more substitutions, no more plays called from the sidelines, no more yelling of directions. I will be sitting on the bench, watching you decide to play like the undefeated team that you are or throw this whole season away. Either you will die on this court as losers or come out as survivors and winners." With that, the grandson of the greatest coach in high school history Morgan Wootten, who won 1,274 games in forty-six years at DeMatha, sat down and folded his arms.

The speech apparently shook up the talented five senior teenagers, all with college scholarships in their future, because they went on a 24-0 run the rest of the quarter. They refused to sit down for the break as Coach Wootten sat quietly in his seat enjoying the raucous crowd and an eight point lead. With the noise level continuing from the partying crowd in the fourth, the lead grew to sixteen points. With less than four minutes, Coach Wootten called another timeout. The surprised and tired DeMatha five gladly took the open chairs on the bench. "I lied to you. I had a timeout left." Coach still refused to smile as he substituted his second team to finish the game for an 82-72 victory and a spot in the finals Sunday night against the Prep vs WJ winner.

The number one high school team in the country had done what everyone expected them to do: get into the finals. It was not pretty, but Coach Wootten would not let the undefeated Staggs lose to a Virginia or a Maryland Public or Private School on his watch.

At 8:50 p.m., the ocular roof on the World Space Stadium started to close as a series of fireworks sprung out from the roof to coat the sky with bright white explosions of light. The crowd rose to their feet in excitement as both teams entered the court and their bands played competing fight songs. Annie and Hill did their practiced dribble and passing routine that led to a dunk by Hill to start their lay-up line. On the other end, Junior and Dirk did a similar dance to start the Prep warm-up line.

Annie felt an intense spring in her legs as she easily finger-rolled the ball over the rim. Most of the fans behind the basket stood during the lay-up line wondering if Annie might dunk during warm-ups, cheering excessively every time she touched the ball. Chamberlain, Hill, Ball, and Dennis all slammed the ball easily during every turn. During one drill, Annie took center stage inside the foul circle, receiving the rebound pass with a spin, turn, and dribble and a no-look pass to the next lay-up contestant. After a dozen of these, one to every teammate and again to Hill, she headed to the basket as Hill faked a lay-up, went under the basket, then alley-ooped a pass to Annie, who softly dunked it over the rim. Half the stadium fans were watching the show and exploded in a loud reaction to the theatrics. Some complained that it was not really a dunk, but most fans were impressed and were now looking forward for a show during the game.

Poor Junior Parker had a sinking feeling. He was sweating up a storm and felt uncomfortable with his shot as he sat on the sidelines before the game. Coach Jeffries tried to console Junior as he sat on the bench with a cold towel around his head. "That little bitch is trying to show me up again, I can feel it coming. Her and Hill have it out for me. They want to embarrass me."

Coach Jeffries was dismayed, "Junior, they're supposed to have it out for you. It's a championship tournament. They're trying to derail you, son." He looked around and saw Beverly Broomfield looking concerned. He waved her over, "Beverly, see if you can talk some sense into him."

"Junior… Hey Junior, this is no time to have your feelings hurt. She's got game. You know that, so do you."

Junior looked up with scared eyes and was about to say something when Charlotte showed up with several pills in her hand. "Jesus, Junior you forgot your medication this morning. Here, take these." Beverly got a cup of Gatorade and forced Junior to take the pills. Charlotte and Beverly found spots next to him on the bench, both rubbing his back. "Hopefully that will take effect quickly. He's a manic-depressive, just like his dad, Beverly. He has to take his medication or bad things will happen. Like this!"

Coach Jeffries called his players around Junior, hoping to normalize the situation. The starting line-ups announcements were coming soon. Charlotte and Beverly melted back into the seats behind the bench, as Coach Jeffries hoped his best player would take control of the situation. Dirk Nielson stepped forward like the quarterback that he was and gave directions to each of his fellow starters. Eventually, Junior uncovered his head and finally stood up to join the circle of teammates. His eyes progressed to make him at least look awake, as his medication started to take him from the edge of despair, but would it take him to the top of a mountain of victory?

Guy Finelli sought out his daughter as she came into the meeting room after team warm-ups. In a few minutes, Coaches DeBone and Melendez would meet with the team with some final words. Coach DeBone asked Guy Finelli to say a few words before they headed back out for the announcements of the starting line-ups.

As a father, Guy had matured since he had Anthony over nine years ago. He slowly had become an important person in Annie's life. He tried to do a lot of listening and storytelling with her, but not lecturing. Tonight, he felt different and wanted to tell her directly what he thought. Regret was not something he wanted to feel after the game. He knew he had something important to say to her. Now he had to figure how to say it.

He found a cubby hole in the hallway as he escorted her with his brawny arm around her. He knelt in front of her and held her shoulders as he met her eyes. He was almost level with her even on his knees. "Annie, I have to tell you this, please forgive me if I'm intruding, but this is your night, you need to take over and score, like "Pistol Pete" did. All the eyes will be on Hill and Chamberlain. Get 44, and you'll win. The assists will be there, but not until you stun them with a barrage of scoring like they have never seen before. I feel this in my heart and by watching them closely. There are times when you are a great athlete that you have to take over, and this is one of them. Go for it, Annie!"

Annie's smile was the biggest of her life as she took in the truth from the great Guy Finelli, but tonight he was her dad and was thinking of the best for her. She agreed and felt it all week as she watched film. Now she was sure. They headed together to the meeting room.

Coach DeBone said only a few words and let Coach Melendez speak and introduce Guy Finelli, "Gentlemen, yes, gentlemen I am speaking to you first. Tonight, is a special night because Coach DeBone and I believe it is Annie's night to take over. We think it is the best way to win and time for everyone to watch it. She will lead us to victory anyway she decides. We will all be here to support her. Am I right?" Her teammates jumped off their feet and roared with approval. "Now here the greatest athlete you will ever meet…Guy Finelli!"

Guy Finelli stepped forward, "I will be brief: Enjoy tonight boys… Yes boys, I'm talking to you; don't think of anything but victory, no worry about your stats tonight, especially scoring. Don't worry about missed shots if you get a perfect pass, turnovers, fouls; just rebound and play defense. This will be the formula for victory, tonight. You have a Jackie Robinson, a Jessie Owens, a Serena Williams type player as a teammate. She is a pioneer and a special athlete, and this is a monumental night for all females that have ever competed with males, and you're going to be part of it!"

He paused for a moment, looking at the eyes of the teenage sweaty boys, starstruck by his appearance and old enough to have experienced his greatness in this very stadium. And in this very room, he organized his deleted team, from food-poisoning; a squad of players to play both offense and defense and comeback from a 39-0 deficit to win his third football championship in a row. Then, within twelve hours, he secured the evidence to take down the most ruthless gangster who controlled West Baltimore for decades. They watched him on the Silver Screen as a movie star for the last decade and now they were teammates with his daughter. Both of them, plain people that went to their public school and became champions, just like them. And now they would be on a national stage. They all thought, *where do I sign*!

"One more thing, if I may Coach?" Dennis and Janet both beamed with their smiles with excitement at the chance to extend the intense moment of motivation, "Annie's mom would be so proud you, not just Annie, but all of you as teammates because she was a great teammate and a hero to all women and her country."

~44~

Victory in a great basketball game is often captured or surrendered on one last perfect play or heartbreak. A shot is made, missed, or blocked; a ball is stolen, passed, or thrown away. But sometimes, a player performs a play so special that it sends a sonic boom of sound that shakes society for a spell or a stretch of time. This happened on March 29, 2030 at 11:11 p.m. at the World Space Stadium in front of 111,111 rapid fans. With the roof open, the propulsion of liveliness went into a complete hush of silence for .111 seconds, then to an epic roar for 111 seconds, demanding to be heard throughout DC and the world.

The game opened as a stage for the mediocrity of basketball with both teams looking like the scared teenagers that they were. The basketball seemed to have been coated in oil as it slipped out of hands on many occasions before the first timeout in the opening quarter. The score seemed irrelevant, as the game waited for one of the teams to show up and play beyond averageness.

Junior Parker was the first to appear with some competency, as his medication seemed to kick in some energy. He hit three three-pointers in a row to extend the Prep lead to 13-5. More importantly, Annie Finelli picked up her second foul on the next possession. She locked eyes with Coach DeBone daring him to take her out. As the score rose to 18-5, Ronnie Dominic entered the game for Howard Dennis and brought the ball up-court. Coach Melendez called the first of several double screens to free Annie or Hill off the ball. Chamberlain and Lance Ball were the enforcers as Annie flew around the baseline, losing her sweaty boy and catching the ball from Ronnie behind the three-point line, *swish!*

The 1-3-1 zone locked down on defense with Ronnie on a wing of the three, causing a turnover. Ronnie fired the ball over half court to Annie for another pull up three, *swish!* Hill corralled a rebound away from Dirk Nilsen on the next Prep possession and before his legs hit the ground, he flipped to Lance Ball who passed to Ronnie to Annie in the front court for another wide open three-pointer, *swish!*

A time-out was in order, but Coach Jeffries refused to give in and yelled to his defense to "get on Finelli." Junior Parker looked determined to bring the ball in the front court but was encircled by Ball, Dennis, and Hill. The ball was surrendered and delivered to Annie, unattended in front of a screaming Father Jeffries and behind the three-point line, *swish!*

Finally, a time-out, as the Father reached for his rosary from his pocket before the players made it the sidelines. Defense was discussed, plays were prepared, egos were elevated, but little did it help to hold off the onslaught. Missed shot, rebound, double screen left; thee-point shot by Annie, *swish!* Missed shot, rebound, double screen at the top of the key; three-point shot by Annie, *swish!* Missed shot, rebound, double screen right; three-point shot by Annie, *swish!*

End of quarter, maybe a prayer might work, *Hail Mary full of grace, the Lord is with thee…* It did not help. Two more missed shots and two more turnovers started the second quarter, *swish*, *swish*, *swish*, and *swish!*

A television timeout intervened as a cease-fire for three minutes with five minutes left until halftime and WJ ahead 38-18. Annie had thirty-three points on eleven straight three-pointers. Coach DeBone wanted to take her out with her two fouls, but feared mutiny if he did. In the next minute of play, he regretted his decision. Annie picked up her third foul and sat out the rest of the half. Prep closed the gap to fifteen points at half-time 51-36.

Junior Parker felt finally settled after his medication had an hour or so to kick in. He started the third quarter with confidence. He went right after Annie with a drive and scored, but more importantly, the official called a phantom foul on her. It was her fourth and put her on the bench for the rest of the third quarter. Junior took full advantage and scored on assorted drives to the basket and three-pointers. He tallied twenty-two points in the quarter as Prep took the lead 72-69 going into the fourth quarter.

Annie sat on the bench, sweating, knowing she was just one of them. Watching and learning from the Prep defense, she planned out her fourth quarter. Her dad knelt behind her for a few minutes and whispered in her ear,

"Drink a whole bottle of water, you got this, stay upright on defense with your feet and no reaching in. And remember, avoid the defender if you drive to the basket; they're going to try to draw an offensive foul on you, rise above them all my dear!"

Annie closed her eyes to take it all in. It felt so special to have him whisper knowledge in her ear; but it was more, it was pure love. She felt at peace with nothing to prove, keeping her eyes closed for another moment. Then, another voice spoke to her. *Have fun, Annie, you're a woman now.* She opened her eyes and the female voice was gone.

Her season was a foul call away from ending. No contact with the sweaty boys. Her teammates made sure of that. On defense, she flashed in front of Junior and to the side, then a double team from a teammate would take over. On offense, Ronnie was having the time of his life, bringing the ball up and finding her on the wings. He had fourteen assists and loved backing Junior into the paint for a couple of short jumpers.

Hill was a man possessed, playing defense and rebounding like it was hand-to-hand combat. The referees were letting them play inside the paint, as the experts would say. He had five dunks already along with three three-pointers. Chamberlain was patrolling the lane like a hawk, swatting away shots that came in his territory. He never touched the ball on offense and did not care.

And yet, it was getting down to a war between Junior Parker and Annie Finelli as the last minute of play approached. Junior held the ball with the game tied at ninety-eight. It was already a classic game. Parker had thirty-seven points and had been unstoppable in the second half. Finelli had fifty-one points, including eighteen points in the fourth quarter, playing with four fouls. Nobody could lose, really, because the crowd would remember the game for years. Except for Hill and Annie. As the clock hit ten seconds Hill came to double team Parker. Junior threw the ball inside to Dirk as he ran through Annie and Hill into the lane. Chamberlain stepped up to block his path, but Junior stumbled through and cut back to the wing. Dirk dribbled away from him with seven, six, five seconds. He jumped back for a fall-away jumper but fired instead to Junior on the wing with four seconds. Wide open from three-point land, he fired a jumper… Bulls-eye!

It took a while for the court to clear and readjust the clock. The lead was 101-98 after Junior Parker nailed his thirty-eighth, thirty-ninth, and fortieth points for the evening. Coach DeBone drew up the play in the huddle, "Ronnie, you throw it in to half-court or just in front. Hill and Lance run a crisscross off of Chamberlain's screen at the half-court circle coming towards Ronnie. Make it quick and get out of the way. Ronnie, Chamberlain will be wide open after they go through, fire it to him. Annie get open on either wing and you should have two seconds to shoot it or take a dribble or two. Chamberlain catch and throw to Annie; no hesitation, please."

"Hakuna shida, coach!" No problem, Chamberlain answered in his native tongue.

WJ set up for the inbound as Prep set up their defense. Coach Jeffries thought about an intentional foul but wanted it to play out because he was a basketball purist. This was a classic game that deserved a natural ending. Ronnie took the ball from the referee. At the whistle, he ran left to right on the baseline and found a clear alley to Chamberlain just turning around. He fired the pass, and with one hand, Chamberlain redirected the ball to Annie on the left side of the three point line, but the ball traveled to her left. As she nabbed it, her feet were two feet inside the three-point line! The crowd shuddered with despair.

Instead of stepping back, she threw a dribble to the foul line and ran behind it with two large approach steps. She corralled the ball with one hand as she rose into the air, above the sweaty boys, launching to the basket with the clock at :012. Junior leaped up to protect the rim as she flew over him with her knee smacking his mouth at just less than a second :008. With her right hand securely around the ball, she slammed it through the net, shaking the foundation of the athletic world.

The mess of bodies on the ground untangled as whistles blew and meetings started on the sidelines with all the game officials. The teams regrouped into their own huddles under the net. Annie was guarded by Hill with a full hug as Lance, Chamberlain, and Ronnie surrounded them. Junior sat on the floor inside the defensive circle on the floor with a bloody mouth. He was checking for all of his teeth as he realized the foul would be on him. As he got to his feet, relieved his teeth were in order, the referees announced a foul shot for Annie Finelli at :004 on the clock. If Annie, a ninety-seven percent foul-shooter, made the basket to tie the game, it certainly meant overtime. She had only missed three foul shots all year. Her *Rick Barry* underhand-style, foul-shot had been almost perfect since she was ten years old. What nobody knew, except her Grandpa, was that she had also perfected how to miss a foul shot as well.

On the sidelines, Phillip had worked his way down to be with his son, Guy Finelli, behind the bench since halftime, leaving the rest of the Finelli and Santucci clan in a suite twenty rows up off the floor. Annie emerged from the huddle and was escorted by Hill to the foul line. She turned to the sidelines and caught sight of Guy and Phillip behind the bench. Her smile was full of evanescence as she nodded to them. Phillip realized immediately what was going on, he whispered to Guy, "She's going to miss it on purpose, oh my god!"

"What are you talking about Dad? She's almost perfect from the line, no chance she'll miss."

"No Guy, I mean on purpose; she's practiced it for years."

"I believe in her, Dad, she must know what she's doing!"

"And everybody thinks they'll be an overtime, Holy Mary Mother of God!"

Annie stood at the foul line, bouncing the ball. With her fifty-fourth point she would tie the game at 101-101. Everybody was standing watching, but very few could be still. The energy from her viscous leap to the basket was still emanating from the wooden floor to the surrounding fans. Suddenly, she held the ball in front of her, raising it to shoot from above her face instead of holding it between her knees and floating it in like she had perfected for years.

An odd hush hit the crowd watching her release the ball, leading to a silence of confusion as the ball arched toward the basket. Annie took a step back at release and roared forward with two steps and a leap as the ball perfectly hit the back of the rim and rebounded forward. Phillip watched as his heart stopped, feeling a déjà vu from 1973 in Cole Field House, his arm intertwined with his son's. Cameras shot thousands of digital images of the majestic presence of a fifteen-year-old, young woman, flying through space and grabbing the ball with both hands. The Slammer finished the improbable play, as she dropped the ball softly through the net to win the game 102-101. Annie Finelli had scored fifty-five points. And a sonic of sound rocketed into the atmosphere through the open roof.

Annie's body was heading towards a disaster after hitting the bottom of the backboard with her head, causing her to spin awkwardly towards the floor. Junior Parker had been near the baseline as the ball bounded out, he saw her leap and dove towards the floor under the basket. His stretched-out arms softened her fall while cradling her head. A crowd sprung to the scene as Coach Melendez quickly got to her knees to check Annie on the floor. Coach DeBone and her teammates cleared around her. She asked, "Annie are you okay? Annie… Annie?"

Junior got to his knees and whispered to Annie, "You won, Annie, fair and square!"

Suddenly her eyes opened, and a partial smile came to her face until she moved her shoulder, which put her in deep pain. "I think I broke my collarbone, Coach."

"Okay…just stay still… Annie, you might have a concussion as well."

She looked up to see Junior and muttered, "Thanks for saving me. You did not have to do that, Junior." As she surveyed his bloody mouth, "Sorry about the knee as well."

"We even now, I guess. Friends forever, I hope?"

"No doubt, Junior, no doubt."

~45~

Russell stood on the beautiful slate and brick patio at Phillip and Carol's house in the Parkwood Enclave on a beautiful Spring Saturday. It was a graduation and birthday party for Annie on May 26, 2030, who was now sixteen. He surveyed the large crowd with a view of the woods of Rock Creek Park behind them and noticed all the Finelli, the Santucci, many friends of Annie from WJ and known and unknown acquaintances of the two powerful families. Even the Parker family was in full attendance along with Sandy and her father Brooks O'Malley. It was the party to be at on the WJ graduation circuit. Protection was ever present outside the security fence.

This date and this event were significant for Russell in many ways, first of which was the birthday Annie had achieved. It relieved some pressure from legalities that seemed unlikely to happen, but nonetheless they were ever present in his mind.

Just as important, Russell's future would depend on the networking happening at this party. An eighteen month concert tour would start after the new year that was being negotiated between Charlotte and several New York music agents for opening acts during a Europe and Asian tour that involved several big city symphonies. Guy, Alex, and Charlotte had stepped forward with funding for the idea. They wanted to promote Russell and his music. It would be presented to him as a done deal within a couple of days. If he agreed to it, he would have six months to prepare.

Russell wondered how relieved Annie would be now that she was done with high school and the ever-present adoration from the adolescent crowds, especially the boys. She could now be away from multitudes of fans until college in the Fall. Unfortunately, she would be away from him for good parts of the Summer because of a trip to Europe with her Aunt Sally and her cousins; and an internship with NASA at Cape Canaveral starting in July. They would have a two-week time period of maybe just two hours alone together, before a long separation, starting with her at school in August. Little did he realize that he would only see Annie six times in the next two years and would be standing in the exact same spot at her eighteenth birthday party wondering where the last two years had gone.

Russell caught her eye, as she stood in a circle of friends from her volleyball team, sitting on the ledge of the waterfall with the statue of St. Francis spouting water from several animals and birds he was holding. The mist emanating from the flow gave her face a depth of maturity he had not seen before. It was like witnessing her in the future as an older woman. He wondered if that dream could ever really happen for him. Her eyes twinkled as she smiled with an especially wide grin towards him. It made him think of the look he saw from her after the victory over Prep. Her performance was indescribable for most, but for him it was an expression of who she was – a special person. He remembered after the victory visiting her in the emergency room.

Laying in a hospital bed after midnight, with a taped-up shoulder and a grogginess from a concussion and medication, she was motionless trying to minimize the pain shooting from her broken collarbone up her neck and through her shoulder and chest. A cast of family milled about the room, an area behind a curtain, as Russell entered and quickly walked up to her bedside to take her hand. She felt his touch and opened her eyes with that wide grin, he saw today. They spoke silently with their eyes, as they had learned to do in the past year, expressing love and affection to each other. Her pain started to minimize from his touch, and the morphine drip attached to her arm finally surpassing the pain. He wanted to talk about her performance, a herculean effort, that would redefine that Greek myth to include the strength of a woman. *Yes, it was only a game,* he thought, but it was an event witnessed by millions of people to show that greatness has no script, no boundaries. It was achieved by practice, learning and exploring new heights. She was a new pioneer and now more than ever, he wanted to support her in the journey of life.

His concern about Annie's recovery overshadowed the loss by WJ the following Sunday to DeMatha in the finals. The crowd was thinner even though it was sold out, but the game was surprisingly competitive without Annie Finelli. Hill Santucci and Chamberlain Ekesie combined for eighty of the ninety-six points in the five-point loss to the number one team in the country. Hill's fifty-two point performance put him on the map of every college coach in the country. It was unclear if the loss of Annie for the game would have changed the outcome. The sweaty boys from WJ played their hearts out while missing their courageous comrade.

Annie went home without surgery after a couple of days of observation, and with the appropriate pain medication. On Sunday, she was propped up in bed to watch the championship game, cheering for her sweaty boys. Russell came by each day when she returned home for a week and was invited each night to dinner by Phillip and Carol, whose nursing skills came in handy for the week. Annie did not want to go to school wearing a sling for her arm, so her schoolwork was received and finished in the Cloud. Russell helped her with typing assignments and tutoring her if necessary. She waited until after Easter to return to WJ when she felt mostly healed. Annie's eye for fashion did not include casts, slings, or band-aids.

Over the next month, every student that passed her in the hallways smiled and waved as though she was their best friend. She learned to respectfully look at no one in the eye as she moved through the hallways, always walking with a teammate or two from volleyball or basketball. They became her unofficial watch-outs for her around the school. Guy Finelli had a security team around the school that stayed in hiding everywhere she went.

At the final school assembly in May, the State Championship Flag was unfurled and raised next to her father's football and her uncle's baseball championship banners, to be forever hanging from the ceiling. Her team stepped forward one by one to accept their rings, the final two were Hill and Annie. Their family of Finellis and Santuccis was front and center as the overflow crowd stood and cheered for several minutes. A video highlight was then played of the semi-final game that really threw the crowd into a frenzy.

Annie's teammates from the volleyball team re-performed the *Candy-O* sketch in her honor and finally a group of art students along with the art department presented an amazing sculpture of her stretching out at the basket with the ball in hand thrusting through the net and her knee smashing a faceless defender (they all knew it was Junior Parker!). It was named "The Slammer" and Principal Reddick announced it would be forever showcased in the WJ school entrance.

The crowd at the party dwindled down to mostly family as Russell checked in with his Grandmother Laura, "I'm fine my dear. It's a beautiful thing with young people around. I'm going to soak in every moment of this. You go talk to her. She's waiting you know!"

Russell laughed. It seemed like the internal joke was that everyone in the family knew that Russell and Annie loved each other. They were respectfully quiet about it, not wanting to openly encourage it, but were happy about it behind the scenes. Somehow, the adults in the family respected Annie and Russell to be either holding back physically or be incredibly discreet about it. They were hoping for the first but were willing to settle for the second because they were certain of the love between them.

Sandy came up to Russell with her father Brooks, "You know my dad Brooklyn O'Malley."

"Please Russell, it's Brooks...Sandy tells me your playing has reached a new level. I hope they are taking care of you at Prep."

"Yes, thank you, Brooks, it has worked out quite well." He took a quick look at Sandy and smirked a bit. "Your daughter has been a big help this year. I hope things work out for her and John." Sandy was moving for the summer to New York to experiment living with her estranged husband. The divorce was on hold because the long-distance counseling seemed to be working. Russell and Sandy had stopped having sex after Easter – a resurrection for her marriage vows. There was still some holding and fondling and some kissing, but all with their clothes on and for very short periods of time. It was not perfect, but they knew the end was near and that love was somewhere else for both of them, but in a way, they had saved each other to get there.

They said their goodbyes, and Russell walked over to the waterfall and sat on the ledge at the corner next to Annie, who still had a small audience in front of her and on the other side. She backed herself slightly to touch him and stretched out her hand for a moment on his knee. He listened to the conversations and smiled. After fifteen minutes or so, she finally turned her knees around the corner and laid her head on his shoulder for a moment. "I miss you so much, when do I get my sweet-sixteen kiss?" She lifted her head, smiled, and held his hand.

"Well not here my dear," Russell said quietly, "We'll sit at the piano later and play with each other."

She smiled at the double entendre and squeezed his hand as she let go and turned her knees back to her crowd. "Hopefully in an hour or so I can meet you there. Maybe after you drop off your Grandmother." She said quietly with her face turned towards him as she was now facing away from him sitting on her corner of the ledge.

Russell stood up and looked at his watch. He headed inside Phillip and Carol's house to find the piano. He felt some playing in his bones. His Grandmother was sitting in the family room with them and laughing heartily, "Russell my dear, don't worry about me, somebody will scoot me home if I need to go, but I'm having too much fun right now."

Russell stopped for a minute and stared at the stone of the fireplace and felt the love in the family room for almost seventy years. "Please play, Russell. The living room is all yours. We'll stay in here and listen and make sure nobody bothers you." Carol spoke out to him.

"Thank you so much," He felt a great deal of emotion standing there awkwardly. Feeling great acceptance from such gracious people. The past two and a half years had felt like a long journey to reach his real manhood. He had learned so much about himself. The extended love from the Finellis was something he never expected. It helped him find creativity as he learned to become disciplined in his craft and his life. It mirrored the awkwardness of the moment, "I think I will sit down for a while. I hope Annie can join me in a bit. She's the star of the day and will be pretty busy for a while."

"Well don't worry, we'll send her towards the piano when she comes in. I'm sure she is looking forward to it." Carol said with such confidence. The oddness of the certainty crashed through his bones. An unspoken respect of their love was being shown and a protection of their future.

Russell nodded and walked through the den to enter the living room. He headed for the piano and sat down. Tears filled his eyes as he closed them to start playing. Within a minute, he was lost in the music.

After an hour of playing the music in his hands from his head, Russell rested. He put his fingers together, stretched them, and then felt his eyes and the trace of tears that had dried on his face. He felt human again and oddly at home. It was quiet and peaceful even as the soft sound of socks entered the room hoping to surprise him as he played. He rested his fingers on the keys and started a peaceful piece that he liked to play when he enjoyed the quiet. Annie quietly slid on the bench next to him. He continued his playing as she wrapped her left arm around his back and her right arm gently on his strong forearm. She positioned her face on his bicep trying to be a girl that needed a kiss. Her face was full of brightness from being in the sun and a glow from the impending excitement.

Russell tried to ignore her, but her smile grew larger. He finally stopped and dropped his head. Annie took his chin to face his. He cradled her face with both of his large but thin fingers and pulled her close. Their eyes were deeply focused on each other almost discovering their intimacy for the first time. As their lips touched and their eyes closed, they both felt their pulses go haywire. Their tongues met and swirled in immense pleasure. Their bodies felt weightless for a moment. After a minute, they separated their locked lips to take inventory of their existence, but quickly felt comfort with their lips together again. Russell felt all parts of Annie's chest and back, it was like being in heaven. She wrapped her fingers in his hair and felt the skin on his back and chest. It was like exploring a new planet. Finally, they retreated into a long hug and separated into their parts of the bench and both rested their hands away from each other and on to the keys.

Russell played some bouncy chords and invited Annie to follow. Their bodies felt electric as they enjoyed the fun of the piano exercise; and like many lessons before, it was the backbone of their intimacy.

~46~

The next six months went quickly for Annie and Russell. She enjoyed the time in Europe with Hill and Lil in June, especially the ten days in Italy and the week in Ireland. She found her Mom's parents' hometowns and realized how much she needed to find out about her maternal Grandparents in Arizona. She hoped during the semester break to visit them.

In July, she headed south to college at the *Florida Institute of Technology* in Melbourne, a quick thirty minutes from her Grandparents' condo in Cape Canaveral. She spent a month on an internship at the Kennedy Space Flight Center and then started school in mid-August majoring in Aeronautical Engineering. She was hoping to finish in three years and enter NASA's Astronaut program. Her schedule was full and hectic every day as she looked forward to Friday at noon when her classes ended to head up to the condo and spend the afternoon on the beach at Cape Canaveral. She got some much-needed alone time in the evening, biking to the Banana River to watch the sunset, to the Port to eat seafood and listen to music, and then a bike back to the condo. When the sun went down, she loved having her longer hair blow in the wind as she glided on the bike. She felt somewhat reckless not wearing a helmet, but it was Florida, and you did what you wanted, even at sixteen.

Most Friday nights she would Cloud Time with Russell for at least an hour. They mostly talked, and also played their pianos together, but mainly she wanted to hear him perform at least ten minutes at the end of every call.

Then, she would take a long bath in the huge whirlpool tub and find time for herself, thinking about the music, the conversation, and the thought of being with Russell. She would touch her perfectly defined chest and rib muscles, her wonderfully sized breasts and extended nipples and splash with the bubbles of the water with her right hand while exploring her genitals with her left hand. Her fantasies on Friday nights after their Cloud Time had her on top of Russell, lifting herself up and down on his member, feeling it as deep as she wanted in her vagina. She imagined having her breasts hanging over him, feeling fully extended and large, as he captured them in his hands as they swung over him like forbidden fruit in the garden of Eden.

At times, she saw herself plunging down on him to kiss his handsome face. When she came, her body shook as she fully extended her feet with her toes pushing off the end of the tub as she felt the energy rebound up and down her body. At the end, she would collapse into a ball and slowly submerged into the water to feel the weightlessness and the throbbing of her body at the same time. Occasionally she would hold her breath, as long as possible; and stretch out in the tub, fantasizing a cuddle with Russell, and then finally emerging into the air. Sometimes, she would touch herself again because her genitals wanted more contact and more fantasies. When she felt done, she would grab her robe and walk out to the balcony and smell the ocean air as she curled up in a chair. The sound of the ocean waves dampened any remaining pressure or loneliness she might had left in her mind and body. Finally, she would be dry and go inside to crawl under the covers with the door open to the balcony and sleep naked under the covers with pillows between her legs for company.

• • •

The fall of 2030 would be the last teaching semester for Russell for some time. The headmaster was excited but sad to have Russell take a leave of absence to tour, starting in January 2031. He would keep his piano and belongings in the suite. The headmaster was happy to make it available for Russell's return. The notoriety that Prep's music program would receive from the news of their music director's tour and his new music would be worth any expense it took to replace him and keep his room unoccupied.

He spent every idle moment during the Fall practicing and finishing his music for the tour. Initially, he prepared to play for twenty to thirty minutes before a symphony orchestra took the stage. It was hoped in later legs of the tour that some of his music would be played by him with the full orchestra. He was set to record several CDs in December.

Before Thanksgiving, he spent a good deal of time with Charlotte discussing the tour and recording details at her mansion on the Potomac. They were less than twenty years apart and were always fond of each other. He had fantasized about her when she first came on the scene in 2012 when he was ten. Since the untimely death of her husband in February, he had been her shoulder to cry on and ear to listen. She was always supportive of him over the years and available to talk anytime. Many times, she would come to see him play at a bar downtown. When she became involved with Burton, she always kept in touch with him. They were true friends and technically she was his half-aunt. *It was complicated*, he decided.

She was totally committed to his love for Annie, but at the same time she was a lonely rich woman, still trying to find her way in the complicated DC wealthy social scene as a widow. When the kids were asleep, they swam and used the hot tub. Eventually they became affectionate and for a short-time, lovers. It would be the last person Russell would ever be with physically before his love was consummated with Annie in the future.

The first time, wine was the culprit. Charlotte pulled out her favorite Pinot Noir and drank the whole bottle while Russell sipped on his scotch. She decided to dispense with her bathing suit while in the hot tub and eventually made her way into Russell's arms. Her body shuttered when her nudeness first felt his skin. She collapsed emotionally in his arms and stayed there for an hour crying. After they emerged from the spa, she begged him to stay over with her in her bed as he led her inside and dried her off. She snuggled into a ball under the covers as he grabbed a book from hundreds on the shelves and sat up for a while and read. He fell asleep wearing a robe under the covers.

Daylight, like an early alarm to start another adventure, entered through the windows. Charlotte was still in heat, but sober as she woke, and searched under the covers for his member. She put her warm hands on it and got it to respond. Taking away the sheet, she moved over it and took her lips to it, and then her tongue and mouth. It responded like a plant needing water. Consciousness overcame Russell as Charlotte climbed aboard. It became quite a ride for Russell to start the day.

Charlotte had been Guy Finelli's first in 2012, when they met and rendezvoused in Arizona during Alex Santucci's streak in August of that championship year. It was still a family secret, but one that Russell was aware of from his Uncle Alex. Now, he shared a woman with his potential sweetheart's father, and being a relative of some kind on top of that. As Charlotte rode him with enthusiasm, he wondered what Deacon Robey would think of this scene. He looked it over and realized that *I am done with feeling guilty and could not care less what he thinks and I am not a pervert*, as her perfectly enhanced breasts hung in front of him and felt wonderfully real. *I am now into borderline incest apparently*, he pondered.

After he finished, Charlotte stayed on him for a long time, feeling every morsel of the experience. It was like being in an oasis in the desert, and she was not sure of the next watering hole. The line had been crossed with Russell, but she was certain it was best for both of them. She, Guy and Alex were bankrolling his future and believed in him, so *she believed in him a little too much*, she thought, *but they were both adults and could handle it. Besides, I'm not in love with him and he clearly loves Annie.*

They got dressed and laughed about being together over breakfast and coffee. The kids never suspected a thing seeing Cousin Russell in the house. They figured it was all about business and, technically, it was. He was the talent and she was the producer.

Russell spent the Thanksgiving holidays and the week after in the pool house. Charlotte had a piano brought in for his artistic energy. He had created several jams over the years with his trio at times that were up-tempo. As he expanded these jams and made some arrangements to the music, he started naming them: "Twist, Swing & Shout," "Swwwoooshshsh," "Up & In," "Getting Harder," "Jammin' Slammin'," "Hearts Together," "Coming Soon," and "Beach Boogie." The up-tempo blues fell in-between rockabilly, swing, and rock music. He was shocked at his energy about creating a non-classical CD but liked the idea of recording with a bass player and drummer. After finishing his pop masterpiece, written and recorded in seventeen days, he named it *The Slammer*.

Then, he finished arranging the piece he created for Annie with inspiration from her *Candy-O* routine. There were eight pieces to the concerto that lasted forty-two minutes. He was able to record it in six hours without a mistake in playing. He knew he was ready for the tour; the question would be if he could find two musicians in the symphonies that would learn the jams from him, which would give him a chance to play a few tunes from the pop CD in concert as well.

He had good feelings about "Twist, Swing & Shout"; because it was too catchy to ignore, and easy to get up and dance to. Charlotte knew how to find airtime; working with R&B stations first, then public radio and then, god forbid, a pop channel. It was in the 1960s that Henry Mancini, Percy Faith and others would send out an instrumental piano song to the airwaves that would become hits. It seemed improbable now. *But with a catchy tune, played by someone with real talent and money behind it, well… It could happen*, she thought.

A holiday CD was recorded as well that gave him three CDs for sale for his tour. Charlotte spent a million dollars to set up Russell for the tour in 2031, which included money to get music airtime and advertising in the Cloud before the concert started in Europe. The Finelli and Santucci families were followed in Europe like royalty. Sally and Alex would spend two weeks in January introducing the tour to nine cities in Europe. The crowds and the local press would love it, Charlotte was convinced.

By the time Christmas holidays came, Russell was dog tired and barely managed to attend the Christmas Eve party and Christmas Day meal. He saw Annie at both events, and they spent some time kissing and touching when they were alone for a minute or two, but he was petulantly contented to say goodbye for a long year and a half away and get some rest. The next eighteen months would be like the last eighteen months, an arduous journey to another birthday: number Eighteen. Her sixteenth birthday was a life preserver, thrown into the sea by a passing boat, returning in two years to rescue him from just keeping his head above water. Eighteen would make it totally legal to be with Annie anywhere. When they were together for real in the future, he wanted to be an equal partner with his own career and greatness. He owed that to her if they were to be together forever.

~47~

Amazingly, Russell's tour in the winter and spring months was such a success that the summer leg was being reworked to have him play with a trio and then with the entire Symphony in the middle and the end of concerts. His CD, *The Slammer*, had crashed the Pop, R&B, and Dance charts. It was now in the top-40 in all three UK and European charts. Charlotte had spent another million dollars in advertising across Europe, ahead of his tour locations, showing his face on billboards and playing his sound on radio ads. It was working: the media had no choice but to interview the American. And Russell was enchanting, talking in French, German, and Italian when necessary. *Who knew*, Charlotte boasted that her client knew four languages. *Thank goodness for a Catholic education*, she laughed. Also bringing Sally and Alex during the tour was pure genius, the crowd and media could not get enough of them.

The start of the concert would be Russell alone playing his concerto pieces for ten, then twenty and as long as thirty minutes by the end of the summer tour. Then, the symphony would play for fifty, then forty, and as short as thirty minutes. When the trio was added, Russell would start with his highest charting song, "Twist, Swing and Shout" then play "Swwwoooshshsh," "Getting Harder," "Jammin' Slammin'," and "Beach Boogie." As the tour proceeded, he developed an encore of an improvised version of "Head over Heals" and "We Got the Beat" by *The Go-Go's*. The crowds would be dancing the entire time and wanted him to come out at the end with the symphony.

By the fall of 2031, there was a growing list of offers to tour in the Americas. The CDs had purposely not been released in the US, but singles were available from the Cloud. Charlotte wanted to create an excitement in all of the music charts before she brought the unusual music concert stateside.

Charlotte met with Russell at least once a month on the tour. Her private jet made the commute reasonable. They would meet for dinner on an off day in a new city, then walk the streets, listen to music, and return to her hotel to make love all night. Once a month was all either of them wanted.

After twelve months on tour, Russell came home for the holidays. Charlotte agreed that a break was necessary, both in the tour and their intimacy. She was focused on creating a Spring tour in the Americas. They could return to Europe next fall if the interest kept up. Russell was glad to return to his suite at Prep, where he was treated like a huge celebrity, which he was becoming. During the Winter break, he helped with recruiting of students and fund-raising events. But the best thing was a student and family only concert he gave for Prep in the gymnasium at the beginning of the Spring semester.

Because of his notoriety and a Spring tour starting in March up and down the East Coast, the dark side of the media had leaked stories about perversion and incest in the Santucci and Finelli families. Since there was no physical proof or witnesses, the mainstream press passed on it. If anything, it helped with sales of the *The Slammer* CD and tickets for the concerts.

Annie had stayed at school for the short Winter semester for the second straight year. She was now on course to graduate at the age of nineteen in 2033. Guy, Patty, and Anthony spent two weeks in their condo with Annie during the holidays. Phillip and Carol came down as well and stayed afterwards through March. Annie had some interruption to her masturbation schedule, but she was glad to see some of her family for three months.

She was very excited about Russell's success and his touring on the East Coast. After her eighteenth birthday, on May 26, 2032, she followed him from Philly to NYC to Hartford to Providence to Boston to Portland and then a week off in Prince Edward Island in Canada.

Charlotte rented a house there, isolated from the world, just outside of Charlottetown. She had always wanted to go to her namesake town, and by now she had found a boyfriend to replace Russell, Cary Collins, a former teammate of Guy Finelli's from high school to UMD to the Potomacs. It was a great match-up for Charlotte. He was tall, blond hair, athletic, never married, and wealthy.

The four of them had their separate rooms in various parts of the house, which had twelve bedrooms and fifteen baths. Russell had been on tour for

Annie's eighteenth birthday party. He was glad to be with her away from the family for that. He was done pretending. The week of Annie following him on the tour was nice, but they did not sleep together. He could not have the distraction, but now with a week off, away in Canada, they could really be alone.

Charlotte had a chef come in every night to prepare dinner, otherwise they were on their own with a stocked kitchen of food, drink, and fruit. They had an indoor and outdoor heated pool with jacuzzi. And of course, a piano and a basketball court. It was warm enough to wear bikinis outside and sun worship. Charlotte had planted several fake news stories that they were in NYC or on Long Island in East Hampstead. A local friend of Phillip Finelli had set up the rental, the chef, and security for the week.

Annie had started on the pill when she started college. Sally had recommended it even though she was only sixteen at the time. She said to her, "Honey, you're an adult now as far we as we are concerned." She had imagined for years what intercourse would be like with Russell. At first, she expected it to be uncomfortable, except if lubrication was used. She read about all the different kinds and talked to friends at school about it. She also did not want Russell to use a condom. He had not been with a woman for a while (the whirl with Charlotte had never been revealed) and was clean as a whistle according to his last physical in May. She had planned for everything.

The four of them sunned near the pool with the temperature near 80 degrees on one of the first summer weekends in Canada. A high-pressure system had lodged in the northeast area of the United States and brought perfect weather to start the vacation. Annie was in her Florida bikini of orange and green with her hair pinned up. She had a year-round tan with her freckles dominating her face. Charlotte was machine tanned and wore a cowboy style hat to keep her face from getting red. Her body looked strong and tight in a one-piece suit.

Both Cary and Russell looked healthy. Cary was built like the ex-football wide receiver stud that he was, along his with longish blonde hair. Russell was a bit shorter but had worked out religiously on his tour to look trim and healthy. His shorter hair with curls was styled by the music industry. A tan would add to his good looks.

A two-on-two pool volleyball game became competitive after the first few games with the couples facing off. Annie ended up dominating the series and saved Russell from losing his male ego totally to Cary. The games moved to the basketball court after some drinks with cooler temperatures. Annie once again dominated the action, but this time Russell showed his improved skills under the basket and stayed up with Cary. By the time dinner was served, everyone was famished and feeling high from some cookies from the locals. Annie took a bite of one and settled in with a pleasing feeling that led to great laughter during the conversation. She enjoyed Cary telling stories about her dad and mom, when they met, the summer they lived together, and what she looked like pregnant. For the first time, the news about her mom felt invigorating and not sad.

Annie wore a light orange dress that was cut down the middle to her belly button, showing a great deal of both breasts and her beautiful tan, which clearly had some topless time on the beach in Florida. She wore no panties because it was a vacation and only three people could possible see the red of her pubic hair, which grew wild except for trimming to fit in a bikini bottom. Cary would be a gentleman and never look, she assumed, and was comfortable if Charlotte had a curious interest, being a woman. But most of all, Annie wanted to give Russell a feast of looks during the evening, privately of course, before they made love for the first time later under the stars.

The dinner of locally caught salmon and grown vegetables with a wine Charlotte had sent in from Europe for the night. Annie liked wine but sipped one large glass all evening. She wanted all of her faculties to be in good shape tonight. It had been a month since she turned eighteen, the age that Sally had recommended to wait before intercourse. The extra month was worth the wait and seeing Russell for ten days straight was heaven.

By now, the family was well informed of the seriousness of her feelings for Russell. Some had suspected for years but trusted both parties to use their best judgement. People like Charlotte had stepped up to protect the relationship and keep Russell busy during Annie's time finishing school. The side benefits had been helpful as well.

As the night sky descended on the Island, Cary and Charlotte went inside for the evening, leaving the younger couple alone out in nature. They took a long walk around the property, stopping to kiss several times. They ended up in the spa, where Annie asked Russell for some help unzipping the back of her dress. He did so, slowly kissing her open back as he took it down a couple inches at a time. Her heart fluttered at every kiss as she held up the front of her dress. Finally, he finished at the sexy small of her back and slid his hands around to feel her tight abdomen and ribs under her breasts. Annie let go of her dress and wrapped her arms around his neck stretched athletically behind her as he moved his hand over her pristine and pleasing breasts with nipples ready to nourish. She enjoyed being exposed out in nature, as she turned towards Russell and then into his arms. She helped him undress and slowly took his member in her mouth for a luscious thirty seconds of stroking, putting him at the edge of euphoria, before leading him into the waters of the whirlpool.

They held and fondled each other for thirty minutes in the jacuzzi, taking time to stretch out in the cool air descending on the night on Prince Edward Island for a quick moment or two. Finally, they made it to the cabana room with the windows wide open and the skylight above showing an in-between full and three-quarter moon beaming light on their special occasion.

Her Aunt Sally had counseled her to take her first partner while on the bottom to learn about her vagina and how he fit into her. "Discover the good feeling points and feel his strength, then if ready, raise to the top and feel your masturbation point that you know what feels good on the outside while you keep learning what feels good inside. Be strong with your muscles in your pleasure and let your breasts hang down for full feel and oral play on your nipples. Do not worry about orgasm, just enjoy the moment." Sally's vision gave her a playbook to follow.

As she coated his member with lubricant, she held her breath as he finally entered her. Four and half years after they met, three years after she knew she loved him, they were finally together. She exhaled slowly as he settled in nicely and was surprised at the comfort of the feeling. He stayed quiet and began to slowly move himself inside of her. She lost herself in their kissing as he stroked slowly. Every part of herself went from numbness to being alive. The shock waves of feelings were overwhelming. She remembered to turn over and get on top. Russell smiled happily at her leadership and saw a goddess on top of him with her hair flaming red in the moonlight and her breasts looking large and perfect. As she closed her eyes to feel the new experience, her hands on his chest were her only connection to sanity. She could not feel anything else; her body was feeling maximum input. Her orgasm began as a slow spasm and then spread into an overwhelming thrust throughout her body with her breasts feeling on fire as Russell held them like she was floating above him, then suddenly he thrust deeper in her and exploded with bursts of himself. The thumping of ecstasy inside of her finally waned into a soft buzz in the next few minutes. She finally collapsed into his arms and smiled trying never to forget the moment.

~48~

The week together was a pause in a hectic three years of college for Annie, and Russell's ascendency to becoming a successful performer. Rumors about their romance were highlighted in publications everywhere. Luckily, the media left Annie alone at her school, *Florida Institute of Technology*, as she finished her last semester of college in 2033 at the age of nineteen.

Ironically, the only time they saw each other during that year was for the eighty-ninth birthday party and funeral of Uncle Anthony Finelli in mid to late January where they had met five years prior in 2028 for his eighty-fourth birthday. He died in great style at the piano, finishing "Moonlight Sonata," by his favorite composer Beethoven, and playing it perfectly for the first time in years on the next day after his party. It was the eightieth anniversary of his Grandpa Gerardo Finelli's death in 1953.

He had prepared, for his quiet birthday celebration with family including Russell and Annie, to play the Beethoven masterpiece without mistakes at the party but failed. In the next morning with the sun shining through the expansive windows, he woke up and headed to the piano in the bedroom and played with Flo at his side with great adrenaline and energy. She asked the Cloud to record the performance, because he was so excited about playing for her after his performance at the party the night before. For a minute or two, they sat chatting away as he warmed up and then it happened; he became young again, as the energy flowed through his hands like a prodigy. He performed like he was possessed, playing with a flair and panache that was new and creative. It lasted throughout the concerto with great verve and vigor.

After he finished, he closed his eyes and enjoyed the embrace with his wife of almost sixty-seven years. Then, she let go and he lifted his hands to his heart and fell peacefully into Flo's lap. His face became peaceful and his breathing ceased as he finished his greatest performance.

• • •

The graduation and birthday party on May 26, 2033, also served for a special surprise: Russell and Annie announced their engagement. After the party, full of drinking by most and smoking of herb by some, the decision makers in Annie's life met with the couple in the family room at her grandparents' house. Sally Keegan was the first to talk, "We are so happy with your announcement; can we ask if you set a date?"

Annie spoke first, as though she was the lead attorney in the case, "I will be working at NASA in Cape Canaveral for the next year and Russell has plans for a tour overseas for the next year. We thought next summer would be perfect."

"Where would you live?" asked her father, Guy Finelli.

"We would hope in one of the Enclave guest houses, until we know our further plans."

Carol spoke cautiously, "My dear, I was in the same position with my family and your Grandpa, and my family convinced me to wait until I was twenty-one to get married. Something about being able to drink legally at my own wedding!" A bit of laughter cut the nervousness in the air.

"Thanks Grandmom, that is an important issue," she said smiling, "Did you hate waiting the extra year?"

"Well, I was still in school, so it did help a great deal to be there and we were able to see each other quite a bit, and back then we had to worry about paying for it and school."

"Paying for what?"

"School and the wedding, my dear."

Annie smiled nervously, realizing the shelter of her life, never having to worry about money. "I do want to thank all of you for taking care of me. I have never had to worry about money, and I am sorry to say that I have taken that for granted."

"I don't think your Grandmom was trying to make you feel bad Annie," Russell interjected, "it was just the situation for her that is different for you. This is really my fault for wanting to get married so quickly. I guess now that

I am thirty-one, it feels like it's time for me, but it might be better to wait for you." Russell confessed while taking Annie's hand.

Her father stepped forward, "Annie, your mother Anna and I never got the chance to get married because I guess I was too young and playing football, so there is the other side of the spectrum. Sometimes things are just different for different people. I think you should do what you want and not do what some of us think is right." Guy stated emphatically.

"Thank you Dad, but what do you and Patty think?"

Patty seized the opportunity to speak, "Annie, I would tie up Russell as soon as possible and not let him get away, if it was me. That's what I did with your dad when I got the chance."

Guy laughed and squeezed Patty's shoulders, "As your father, I think you should be twenty-one, but as someone who loved your mother, I wished we had been married, and obviously with Patty I'm happy how things turned out, having your brother and all. You have my blessing any which way you choose." He stepped forward and gave her a kiss and hug.

"Thanks again Dad," as Annie teared up for the first time. She squeezed Russell's hand tighter.

"How about you, Uncle Alex?" Russell asked.

He hesitated for a minute trying to organize his thoughts, realizing he had some deep feelings on the subject. "Russell, you have exploded on the music scene. It kind of reminds me of my 2012 summer when I got hot with the bat. Things heated up with Sally too, I could not get enough of her as I kept hitting the ball out of the ballpark," he laughed, "so, I understand, but Annie is young and talented. The extra year will just help both of you get your careers solidified. And let me be clear about something, because of the greatness of the Finelli and Santucci families in generations before us and their hard work: Both of you will never have to worry about money. But you will have to worry about others now, because of who you represent; greatness is part of our legacy and now you will have a responsibility to carry that on and continue to take care of others when we are all too old."

"Thanks Uncle Alex, you and Aunt Sally have been my parents along with my Dad and Patty. I love you guys so much. I understand what you are saying." She was letting tears fall down her cheeks as her voice stayed steady. But Annie had one elder left, she wanted to hear from: her Grandpa Phillip. He was now the pillar of the family with Uncle Anthony gone. "Grandpa, what do you think?"

"I love both of you so much and I'm so proud of you for going after your dreams. People have no idea of the perseverance, trust, and discipline it takes to go after a forbidden love. I should know! What you both have accomplished in your lives is unbelievable." He paused for a moment, took Annie by the hand, and looked at her with his serious deep brown eyes. "But let me talk to you, Annie, because you are my granddaughter. I think you need two years to get yourself set for greatness. Something wonderful will happen in your life when you're older. I can feel it! It will transcend all of us because you have already done things that only your father has done by the time he was nineteen. He did it in the sports world, then in movies, and now fighting evil in the cities. You will do something that is even greater. I'm not sure what it is but I am sure of it. So, take the extra year to get ready for it. The love between the two of you will be there forever. And you do want to be able to drink legally at your own wedding and honeymoon, trust me. Just ask your Grandmom about our wedding night and honeymoon."

"Phillip, you're awful! Annie, we just had fun my dear, don't listen to his nonsense."

"We sure did, Carol, we sure did!"

Annie laughed as a great relief to all the emotion she felt. She hugged Russell and looked at him, realizing they had made their decision. "Waiting for twenty-one it is, and it will be a real party folks!" Annie declared, as she stood up to hug and thank everyone.

The love of family was floating around everybody as Phillip opened champagne to celebrate the decision. Annie leaned over, while holding her glass, and asked Carol, "Grandmom, what date did you get married in June?"

"It was the thirtieth, and by coincidence it was the sixty-fifth anniversary of my grandparents' wedding."

Annie did some math in her head, "That would be perfect, Russell, a Saturday in two years. We could have a party Friday night, right here, like my grandparents did, that would be way cool." Annie turned to her grandparents, "Grandmom and Grandpa, if we wait two years, can we have a party the night before our wedding on the slate and brick backyard, like you did...pretty please!" doing her best six-year old imitation.

Carol whispered into her precious granddaughter's ear as she received a hug from Annie, like she did when she was that six-year old child, "nothing would make us happier, my little Miss Pretty Please."

~49~

Two more years into the mid-2030s and the world grew a little safer as hope and excitement prevailed about human achievement. The sky became more interesting at night to gaze at, as bases on the moon were now permanent, and already sending materials and the first humans to Mars. The first crew of American Astronauts would travel for eight months in the Orion spacecraft and land at the end of June in 2035.

Annie was now working at the NASA Goddard Space Flight Center in Greenbelt, Maryland as an Aeronautical Engineer with an eye on entering the astronaut program as soon as she became eligible. Her star appeal had not gone unnoticed by NASA and some started discussing grooming her to be the face of future travels in Space Exploration.

Russell had ended a successful run of touring the world with his popular and classical music. He returned to Georgetown Prep as their music director but had already moved his Steinway Piano and his other possessions from the suite to the guest house next to Phillip and Carol's house. He wanted to teach and write music, play with his trio locally, and be near his family for a while.

The party on Friday night before the wedding, in the backyard of brick and slate, with the St. Francis fountain flowing of champagne; and music alternating between a piano trio playing and a DJ spinning sounds, with food hovering on trays everywhere you looked, keeping with the crowds until they were empty and then returning automatically for refills. It could not have been more festive and fuller of excitement as the crowd waited for the appearance of the majestic couple.

Phillip Finelli was shooting off champagne corks into the sky, trying to reach his son's houses, acting like he did at his party before his wedding day some forty-nine years earlier. He was keeping up with the consumption for those afraid to take from the fountain. A fleet of drivers had been hired to drive people home, when it came to that, late at night, so that any excuses to not drink, eat cookies, or smoke herb was not acceptable unless they were under doctor's orders (which he was ignoring his own for the evening). As a writer, Phillip adored Francis Scott Key Fitzgerald, and at times would visit his gravesite up the Pike in Rockville for creative ideas. He saw this party as his version of *The Great Gatsby*.

As daylight was about to rest for the day, Annie and Russell came out the front door of the guest house and walked down the steps to the slate and brick to finally appear in the backyard. Every bit an adult at twenty-one, Annie Finelli flashed her rocket red hair, which she had let grow long for the wedding, and pulled down around her neck to the front of her bare left shoulder that contrasted beautifully with her light-yellow dress, cut from the top of her left breast to over her right shoulder. The pleaded dress bottom showed plenty of her toned thighs and curved calf muscles. She looked like a twenty-first century woman of fashion with equal parts of beauty and strength.

Russell projected a tall look with his light-caramel colored, perfectly tailored jacket and white pants with matching caramel, colored Italian shoes. His curly blond locks, still highlighted from his tour, sat atop his handsome head. His broad shoulders had become accented from his cardio-swimming in the last two years to help strengthen his upper body on the tour.

Annie had become older looking and Russell younger looking, to narrow their plus-decade age difference. They fit together nicely as they greeted people with calmness and happiness. Annie had learned a style of social interaction that was similar to playing chess, trying to stay three or four moves ahead of people as she talked with them. Once trust was established or she knew their moves, she could be comfortable and interact more naturally, but like all social interactions for Annie, she had to learn first, then act. Only her physicality came naturally to her, always smooth, balanced, and powerful.

As midnight approached, a small group of classmates, teammates, friends, and family crowded around the piano in the living room of her grandparents as Russell and Annie took on the keys, joking around, and leading some singing, while shots of tequila and sometimes scotch were being refilled religiously. Even the influence of alcohol could not keep her from playing "Moonlight Sonata" on a dare from the crowd. The *oohs* and *aahs* were interrupted quickly by Russell, who followed with a medley of *Chuck Berry* and *Little Richard* chords on the keys that had everyone dancing on the golden hues of the wood floors.

It was the greatest of all nights.

~50~

The Chapel of our Lady of Lourdes at Georgetown Prep was a perfect setting for the wedding of Russell and Annie. It was dedicated in 1933 and built with stone and marble from Europe in an Italian Renaissance architecture style. The elegance inside was matched by the beauty of the bride, groom, and their guests that packed the pews. A full Catholic Mass would be performed with the ceremony along with music provided by Russell's students at Prep.

Annie Finelli was dressed in a Berta Illusion Mermaid gown that featured a plunging neckline, long sleeves, and open back with plenty of see-through netting and gorgeous hand-sewn lace over the important secretive parts of her body. There were only a handful of women in the world who could wear such a beautiful and sexy gown and she was one of them. In a word, she looked stunning. Her red hair was pulled back into a single ponytail and her ears adorned with simple long-hanging pearl earrings. The gasping from the students alone, as she walked down the aisle, added to the drama of the ceremony. Guy Finelli looked his handsomest as he walked her down the aisle to the altar and gave her away to Russell. He trembled as he turned to look at her and give her a final kiss as his unmarried daughter. Her beauty and presence overwhelmed him as he thought of taking her out of her dying mother, twenty-one years ago. He almost cradled her in his chest after giving her a warm kiss on the lips, feeling her energy and joy in her love for Russell. He whispered in her ear, "Your mother will always be with you and I as well, we love you as one, Annie."

As they finished their embrace, Annie said, "Dad, I love you so much and thank you for saving me." She winked at him as she took her spot next to Russell.

Russell was so thrilled to be alive as he dressed for the wedding on Saturday afternoon in his suite in Boland Hall. His piano was gone and most of his clothes, but he was glad to have spent one last night there after the raucous party last evening. He had thirty minutes left before walking over to the Chapel at 4:30 p.m. Figuring out his black bow tie and putting on his suit jacket were the only things left to do. On a trip to NYC, when Annie bought her dress for twenty-thousand dollars, he found a Brooks Brothers Tuxedo, double-breasted jacket that he could not ignore. Fortunately, Annie loved it because it gave him a British look, she told him. And he knew she loved the look of royalty.

He stood staring out over the windows, in almost the same spot where he wondered how he could fall for a fifteen-year-old girl, six years ago. It felt good that his love for her was being vindicated by the wedding. For all of those years in hiding, and all of those jokes about robbing the cradle, along with the looks and stories written during his tours when they became a famous couple, today would make it legal and respectable. Nobody, except a handful of people, accepted his feelings about Annie early on; only Sandy was a real friend that loved him. She gave herself to him to keep his love for Annie. *It sounded crazy*, he thought, *but it was true*. Charlotte did as well, he remembered. She believed in his talent and put herself out there for him. It was true that both women were lonely from losing relationships, and that he gave them intimacy, but it was still quite a gift. Russell realized how lucky he had been that those two women friends had saved his love for Annie. Now both were in love again with men and in relationships that gave him a sense of great joy and satisfaction.

He was thankful to his Grandmother, Laura Santucci, who supported him throughout as well. She was still going strong at ninety-eight and would be at the wedding today. She was so special to him and gave him love that his parents were not capable of giving. Speaking of his parents, they would be there today and hopefully would warm up to the idea of his marriage by the end of the day. They were less than enthusiastic about it, but that was not a surprise to Russell. They were still adjusting to his success as a musician and their notoriety as a couple.

Finally, there was Abbey that came to his mind. He wondered if she was in Brazil, Argentina, or Venezuela. It had been over four years since he saw her in DC for a series of rendezvouses. Then, he went on tour and she left for Latin America, they both returned to the States for short periods and set up a time to meet downtown. She was so excited to see him, and he was ambivalent.

He had told Charlotte that it was over, and he wanted to be only with Annie when she turned eighteen. But Abbey was persistent, calling every night. Finally, he agreed to meet her in his favorite music bar in DC, but he was in love with Annie and did not trust himself. He lost his mind in his indecision and became paralyzed with anxiety. He felt like a coward because he could not call her to break it off. He turned off his phone, played his piano all night, and sipped scotch. It was a total blow-off, something he never expected of himself, but he let it happen. A day later, he listened to the final message, the one at the end of several calls wondering where he was. It was a blistering speech, full of anger and animosity from her high horse of integrity. She sounded wounded, calling him a coward and a pervert, and wishing him a life of pain and agony with that red-headed teenager, "How could you treat me like this?" Were her last words. To this day, Russell wished he had acted like a man and called her to end it.

Overall, the Plan had worked with minimal casualties, he thought, and a great union was about to happen. Russell knew he was far from perfect, but in his mind, *marrying perfection was the next best thing*. Suddenly, there was a knock on the door, and he smiled as he left his daydreaming from the suite's window for the last time and opened the door. It was his best man.

"Wow, you are one handsome nephew if I may say so myself," Uncle Alex heartily hugged his favorite nephew and friend like a proud father.

"Thanks Uncle Alex, are you ready for this?"

"Can't wait to see how gorgeous you two are going to look together. Your Aunt Sally was crying all morning getting ready. She is a bundle of nerves. It's all tears of joy for her dear Annie." Alex reported. Now almost fifty-nine, he still looked like a star ballplayer and idol to baseball fans in the country. He was looking forward to being with Russell for this magnificent day.

"You and Sally have been the best caretakers and friends we could ever have, Uncle Alex." Russell said softly.

"We love you two like our own children...we will always be there for you." Alex spoke proudly.

"How about one drink of scotch before we go?" Russell smiled.

"Now you're talking Russell, bring it on. I think we're going to need it." Alex laughed heartily.

A few hundred fans and well-wishers had circled the entrance to the chapel in an orderly fashion behind the road, to see the beautiful couple emerge from the classic looking church. The bride and groom and their parties entered from side entrances behind the security to avoid notice.

Russell and Alex stood below the altar steps, watching Annie walk down the aisle with her father Guy Finelli. Beside them stood the ushers, his brother Raymond, her brother Anthony, and her cousins Hill, Joe, and Walter (Aunt Grace's ten-year-old son). Opposite them stood the maid of honor Aunt Sally, and the bridesmaids; Aunt Grace and her twelve-year-old daughter Laura, Cousin Lil, Hill's fiancée Malak, and Annie's friend and volleyball teammate Beverly Broomfield. In the middle, stood Deacon Robey, ready to officiate the wedding and Father (Coach) Jeffries excited to perform the Mass.

Hill had finally given up alcohol during his senior year of college. He worked with a trainer to change his eating and drinking habits. It was his best season and ended a four-year career as the fifth leading scorer in UMD basketball history. His partying days were over, and he was ready to get married to Malak. Her parents wanted him to have at least a year of sobriety before planning the marriage. Malak's brother Chahna was having similar trouble getting Lil to agree to an engagement. She was ready to travel for a year and would consider an engagement after that. Annie would soon focus on getting her cousins into marriages with Malak and Chahna and start living in the Enclave guest houses. She thought it would be the right thing to do.

Alex held back the tears watching his brother hold Annie so close and whisper into her ear before turning away to sit with Patty in the front row. He was so proud of the journey his brother had taken to become a parent. Giving up custody to Sally and then learning to become a good father while supporting her decisions all the way. It had become a special relationship and he was a true hero in her life.

Annie spoke loudly with her vows without need for the Deacon to say them first. Russell did the same thing without a stumble, relying on his performing abilities to match Annie's talent. Deacon then proclaimed them as being one and their kiss that followed was slow and solemn. With their eyes closed, they remembered their first real kiss on the piano stool at her sixteenth birthday. Their lips felt so warm and tender together that it was hard to part. As they heard the cheers, it was real to know they would have the rest of their lives together.

After the Mass was finished and blessings given, they clung together as they walked quickly down the aisle towards the sunlight out the door. Faces they would remember forever and hands reaching out to touch them as they went by. A crowd had grown to a thousand cheering for them as they reached the driveway. A car would whisk them away to a quiet spot on the grounds of

Prep for some pictures along with her wedding party. After thirty minutes, they were taken across the Pike to the Academy of the Holy Cross Alumni Hall for the reception. It was quiet and peaceful for a private party.

Annie and Russell went in separate directions at the reception, meeting and chatting with their guests non-stop for an hour before dinner was served. The excitement of spending time with them had the guests on their toes.

Russell first met with Sandy and her husband, now happily together with a newborn baby and another on the way. The awkwardness was extinguished after Sam admitted to Russell, "you were the best thing that ever happen to Sandy." Sam had clearly loaded up on the open bar, "I was such an ass, you were her best friend. Luckily, she gave me a second chance. I love you man."

Sandy rescued Russell with a big hug and kiss, "Don't listen to him Russell, he just missed my big tits." They laughed together as they told some stories about the dances they chaperoned together. "Don't be a stranger, keep in touch. I'll always be there for you."

Annie worked her way to see Junior and Beverly at a table with her other volleyball teammates. Junior wanted pictures with Annie and the whole team and then just with Beverly and then him and Annie. He held her tight with his arm around her waist and took a moment to remember her delicious smell and beauty. He was glad about his life, finishing up at Penn State and preparing for law school. He had given up playing Division I basketball after two years and now enjoyed intramurals and studying. The idea of being an owner of the Potomacs at the age of thirty was his only goal along with marrying Beverly. For that moment, being close with Annie made him think of a love that he lost, but when he saw Annie together with Russell in front of the altar in the chapel, kissing as a married couple, he realized that he never had a chance.

Russell had a few quick meet and greets with guests on the way to see Charlotte and Cary at their table. They were holding court with a host of guests who loved Washington Potomacs football. After saying high to the court of guests, Russell took Charlotte to the side for a big hug and kiss. "You changed my life Charlotte… I can't thank you enough for believing in me and being such a great friend to me and Annie."

"It worked out great Russell for both of us. I needed you, and you needed me. I always loved you Russell, even as a teenager when you were shy but kind and very talented. Not many people can play like you can. It is so much fun to watch and listen to you perform. You don't know how many times I came to see you at those bars you played in college. Even loaded up with scotch and high on pot, you were effortless in your playing. I was kind of a groupie back then, but I never let you know it. The tour seemed like an easy decision and a chance for me to get away and create music with you. Yes, the sex was just as creative." She laughed boisterously.

Russell smiled and said, "I think we're partners in the business of life, Charlotte," he winked as he gave her a kiss on the cheek.

Annie was buzzing from all the love in the air. She felt beautiful and sexy in her dress as she found her coaches Janet Melendez and Dennis DeBone drinking at the bar together. According to the rumors, they had been having an affair for quite a while. Annie buried her face into Janet's shoulder and hugged Dennis forcefully. "What a treat to find the two of you together. Janet, you changed my life so much. How did it all happen?"

"It was easy, Annie. I got to see you run and jump and practice like no other athlete I had ever seen. You did all the work Annie."

Dennis chimed in, "She's right, Annie, you ended up knowing more than we did as coaches and that is saying something, because Janet is the smartest coach I have ever met."

"That she is, Coach. I will never forget either of you. Thank you for making my life so exciting."

Annie left her coaches with tears in her eyes but smiled with joy from her memories with them. She found Russell and wanted to be next to him. They walked hand-in-hand, seeing others along the way, stopping for pictures, and listening to stories. Finally, as dinner was being served, they made it to the wedding party table. It was a circular table like the others with Raymond sitting next to his brother Russell and Anthony next to his sister Annie. Walter and Laura sat next to their mother Grace. Hill was in the middle of Malak, Lil and Chahna while Beverly, Joe, and Alex surrounded the petite Sally.

Russell and Raymond discovered they had lots to catch up on and promised to keep communicating on a regular basis even if they were continents apart. Their parents Kenneth and Jill came by for a group picture and told a story about the two of them as siblings many years apart. Both seemed to be genuinely happy at the outcome of the marriage – finally. Grandmother Laura was escorted to the table and passed her love to everyone. She whispered to Annie, "You are the sexiest and most beautiful bride I have ever seen and that is a good thing… Trust me, my dear."

Grace announced, "I have instructed the DJ to play the *Cars*, *ELO*, and *Bowie* tonight, and I hope the trio will be playing swing music that everyone can dance to." Annie lifted her glass to show her approval. Anthony changed seats to be next to Laura and Walter. They had become best buddies. He was sneaking some champagne to both of them as he did at the party the night before. Annie had her eye on them as the trio put a finger on their lips for her to keep a code of silence. She laughed as she pointed two fingers at them and then her eyes, implying she had eyes on them.

Cousin Joe and Alex joined Hill on the wagon after being lit up last night from champagne and scotch. It had been a rough combination for their brains. Luckily, it was a party and therefore they were the loudest at the table, telling a story about seeing Russell at Uncle Anthony's birthday party almost eight years ago when Annie and Russell first met. It was exaggerated, funny, and embarrassing, but everyone was laughing. "You were making a lot of noise in that bathroom, brother," Joe bellowed, "Was it something you ate or something you played with?"

"My nephew is such a cradle robber or maybe it was the Steinway that you were interested in. You know I had to buy that thing for him, or he would have been depressed. I think it helped your career, Russell."

"Annie, did you know that it was the Steinway he was interested in and you just came along with it?" Hill chimed in, not being able to resist the ribbing of his dear cousin.

"Listen you boys, my cousin knew what she wanted and went for it. I saw them look at each other at her fifteenth birthday party and I knew Russell was toast at that moment. Annie's found her love and reeled him in." Lil stood and toasted to her cousin, "I love you like my sister, Annie, and Russell don't listen to these hooligans, you had no choice!" *Hear, hear* the table chimed in.

Both Malak and Beverly added stories about playing with Annie and being her friend. "Thanks for making me feel normal Annie," Malak said, "I love you honestly."

"Me too," added Beverly, "you gave me great advice about Junior and helped me get a scholarship."

"That was all you Beverly. You made me a volleyball player, being so patient with me. And you Malak are perfect for Hill. Hopefully, we will be neighbors soon!" Annie walked over to hug and kiss them both.

As she walked by her cousin Walter, he asked her, "Are you cold in your dress? It has a lot of openings in it."

"Luckily it is warm out, Walter. Do you like it?" Annie asked as she leaned over to answer him.

"You look pretty delicious for a girl." He giggled.

"Well I could eat you up, too, my dear little cousin. I think the champagne has made you silly!"

"Not really Annie, I just think you're beautiful." He stood on his chair to hug her closely.

Annie waved for her table to come together for a picture as she leaned over to her Aunt Grace, "I think you have a real character here, Aunt Grace."

"He likes girls a lot!" She laughed, "Hopefully, he will get as lucky as Russell did finding you."

"I think we're all pretty lucky." Annie said without thinking but just feeling it.

"Oh, wow…a contraction! I've never heard you use one before?" Grace said with great awareness of the moment.

Annie paused and smiled at her awesomely beautiful Aunt Grace and felt very real, "hey, maybe Walter squeezed it out of me. I guess I'm human now!" Annie laughed heartily, realizing that she *contractioned* some more.

"I never doubted that for a minute, my dear Annie." Grace beamed glowingly.

"Thanks for everything Aunt Grace, your music mentoring really opened up a big world for me." They shared a close hug.

"I think you can thank your Grandpa for that!"

"I guess we all can." Annie pictured the memory of holding her Aunt Grace.

Finally, they stood quietly as a table for the picture and took their seats to eat their dinners as the stories at the table continued and the calls for kisses between the bride and the groom continued from throughout the room.

There was only two speeches everyone wanted to hear at the end of dinner and before the dancing started and that was from her Grandpa and Grandmom, Phillip and Carol Finelli. At eighty-two and seventy, they still looked dynamic and loving. They sat together and told stories about Annie when she was young and learning how to make sounds, and how *Please* became her favorite word. Carol was the first to call her *Miss Pretty Please*, she told the crowd. They all laughed at her nickname. Then Phillip told a story about reading his books to her at an early age. She insisted to hear a chapter every night and would remember every detail about the chapter the next night. That was when he knew she was going to learn quickly in school. They became best buddies after school reading books, playing basketball, and talking about family. He summed up his talk by saying, "I always worried about my kids and how life would treat them, with Annie I was never worried about that, I just wondered how life would keep up with her."

They laid in bed in the penthouse on the thirtieth floor of the World Space *Marriott* Hotel in DC. The views of the city were spectacular as they made love and continued drinking and eating while staying up until almost midnight. It was a special time in human history because on June 30, 2035, the first two humans would set foot on the surface of Mars.

They stretched out naked on their stomachs as they watched the ten-foot-wide screen showing the landing craft door opening. Officially, it took eight minutes of real time for the activity on the Mars surface to be conveyed to Earth. The man and woman astronauts in their white, slimmed down space suits came down the ladder to the red surface of dust together. As they paused on the last step together, they carefully placed their right foot at the same time, jointly saying, "Man and Woman step together on this new world and march forward as one for all of humanity on Earth."

Russell finished his scotch as his member grew hard and reached out to rub Annie's back as she stared intently at the massive screen. She hardly noticed her husband's attention and his excitement as she held her breath while the two humans bounced along taking steps from the spacecraft on the surface of Mars. One of them took out a small hammer and knocked in the flag, they were holding together, into the red surface. The Stars and Stripes stood perfectly.

She finally exhaled and took in a big breath as she turned on her back to receive Russell's rock-hard member. He kissed her passionately as they became one. After the kissing and loving ended, she whispered into his ear, "I want to be there some day."

Russell caught his breath and looked at his beautiful, beaming bride and asked, "Where my dear, Annie?" Wondering what she was thinking about in this world. He was ecstatic that this night had finally happened and would do anything to please her or take her anywhere on this Earth to make her happy.

Annie calmly answered, "Walk on Mars, my dear Russell. I want to walk on Mars!"

~Epilogue~

Annie Finelli walked in her space suit with an earthlier bounce as she kicked up some red dust of the Martian surface. It felt less jumpy than the moon atmosphere where she had been many times. Her stomach felt antsy all morning, waiting for her chance to leave the shuttle after four months of space travel from Earth in the massive Space Cruiser now circling Mars. The Cruiser had cut the travel time by half between Earth and Mars with a new system of Ion-Drive propulsion and provided a hundred times more room than the Orion Space craft that first landed on Mars in 2035. The possibility of human travel to a Jupiter or a Saturn moon had now become a reality by the end of the century.

The light of the Martian morning made for a perfect time of exploration and work on the outpost. At the age of thirty-five in June 2049, she was officially the forty-second human to walk on Mars and the tenth woman. Her project that morning was to start assembling the new barracks deposited near the landing site in the previous month. It was mainly connecting lines for air pressure, water, and energy – kind of like a massive Winnebago at a campsite. The permanent station of buildings was about to be finished in the next year. In the next decade, dozens of humans would live and work in two-year cycles on Mars.

Annie would not be a part of that cycle, because she was four months into a pregnancy. She had been artificially inseminated with Russell's sperm before the mission to become the first pregnant woman in space travel. Her pregnancy during the eight-month mission would be studied for future space travel, perhaps out of the solar system.

After a return to Earth, she would continue to live in her Grandmom Carol's large home with Russell and their new baby. Her Grandmom, who was now eighty-four, was looking forward towards decades of good health and caring for her new great-grandchild.

Alex and Sally, Guy and Patty, Grace and her husband; along with Lil, Hill, Anthony, Walter and Laura and their spouses and young cousins would live in the Parkwood Enclave.

In the decades to come;
it would be full of sprinting into the extended sunlight,
bashing the baseball suddenly in spring,
swimming in the pool throughout the summer,
feasting on football and the falling of leaves,
bouncing the basketball below the bubble,
surviving the winter and sledding in the snow,
enjoying every feast with family and friends,
gathering to converse and spread love with good cheer,
and to search the stars in the moonlight sonata.

Annie was excited to raise her kids in the potential, new rocking fifties and see them become teenagers in another possible rebellious sixties. She adored these decades from the twentieth century, and often wondered if history would repeat itself.

She found a spot off the trail a step or two and near the new living quarters for space workers that would be perfect for a quiet personal ceremony. *The view here with the more distant sun seems pleasant and peaceful for Grandpa and Uncle Anthony*, she thought, as she unzipped a small pocket on the outside of her space suit and pulled out two snack-sized, sealed plastic bags, each labeled. She moved some red dirt with her glove on the surface and ripped open each bag and poured out the gray dust of their remains onto the surface of Mars, mixed them together, and covered them with her glove playfully, swooshing the surface of red dust into the air.

The brothers had been with her for the whole trip, keeping her company, and now their ashes of carbon would be free to mingle with other elements on a new planet. She thought of them, as she stayed knelt on one knee, and the realm of knowledge and emotion that each of them gave to her that produced so much comfort and joy in her young years as a girl. The world as a young woman had been scarier without them, especially without her Grandpa's counsel and storytelling as she traveled space for the last six years, but she had managed to take them everywhere she explored. And now a part of them would be in the farthest outpost she would reach in the solar system.

At home on Earth, she would give birth to several children and nurture them along with Russell with the heritage and values of their families to live into the next century. All would grow to be good souls on Earth, and one would seek the heavens of the Milky Way.

CPSIA information can be obtained
at www.ICGtesting.com
Printed in the USA
LVHW030908061220
673162LV00004B/27

9 781646 106813